THE SUPERNATURAL AGE

A CAUTIONARY TALE

DAVID ALAN SMITH

outskirts
press

Preface

DECEPTION…?

It is as old as the truth.

Everybody knows…it…exists. Everybody knows…it…by name. Everybody knows what…it… does. And.., everybody knows why…it…does it.

Nevertheless…, what everybody doesn't know is when this age-old craft and its invisible authority slithers into one's mind, spirit and soul so as to put them under its mesmerizing spell—tricking them…, manipulating them…, and controlling them like a life-less puppet on a string.

Yes…, everybody knows what *deception is*.

But they do not know when they are being deceived.

PART ONE

'...THE CLEANSING...'

Chapter One

NEW SOCIETY

Carson City, Nevada: 2043

"What time is it?" Joel nervously asked.

"Uh, let's see—time for you to tell me again how great and how awesome of a brother I am." Randy joked.

"Oh, yeah right!" Joel bounced back with a chuckle.

Randy looked at his watch. "It's ten after six. We've got plenty of time."

As they inched their way to the check point, Joel shifted and repositioned himself in Randy's ol' pride-and-joy; his blue '64 Chevy pickup. "You know, I love this old truck, but you gotta do something about these seats, dude. I feel like I'm sitting on a concrete bench."

"Stop complaining! We look cool." Randy playfully insisted.

"Oh yeah, we look real cool, Randy. Give me a break—maybe twenty-five years ago, but being that were both headed for fifty in a couple years I'd hardly say we look cool. Unless of course you mean in a dinosaur sort of way—there're lots of people who think they're cool."

Randy had to laugh. Frustrated though, he went on to remark, "Man, I just hate these things."

"Yeah, I know. Me, too," Joel dreadfully agreed, "me too."

One by one, car by car they'd get closer and closer to the random scan by DSS (Domestic Security and Surveillance). It was slow, but they at least had a beautiful view. Coming out of South Lake Tahoe, Hwy 50, headed for Reno, they were atop the lower mountainside looking down on Carson City peacefully sitting at the bottom of the valley.

Early in the morning, it was sunrise. The sun was just peeking over the top of the mountain with all its glory. Rays of light seemingly piercing holes and glimmering through sporadic portals in the rain clouds made it especially striking. It was beautiful.

Carson City stood out like a gem. Seeing the old and deteriorating historic little town long past its heydays briefly lit up sort of revived it, at least from a distance. Like a long forgotten ageing Broadway actress finding her way back onto a darkened stage, all alone and without even saying a word, a powerful spotlight casting its brilliant theatrical beam directly on her would once again bring her back to life.

Though it would obviously be short-lived, it was calming to see the beams of sunlight hit the little city. It was also in a lot of ways sad. Carson City was one of many communities dying in the wake of modern America's so-called progress and saving the planet. What made it sad is it didn't have to be this way.

Finally, after about twenty minutes of waiting, Randy turned down the radio as they slowly made their way towards eight stone faced police-soldiers in raingear and head-cams. The King's Men; it's what many had sarcastically come to call them. They were the product of America's fundamental transformation. What was once called 'the police', 'the cops', and 'peace officers' in blue; were now called 'Social Justice Enforcers' in vivid green; a far cry from military green or the green of ICE, now abolished. It was closer to an environmental green; a clean sort of green symbolizing peace and closeness to nature.

By design…, under mob-rule and mob-mentality, along with a complicit Congress and President, instead of eradicating the police of whom were fiercely and constantly under assault, demonized, shamed, even imprisoned and killed for so-called police brutality and racism; it was politically decided to alter and restructure 'Law Enforcement'. Policing was now all about enforcing 'social crimes'; things that offended people, things that didn't do enough or even say enough to end discrimination, racism, and inequality, and last but not least…, things that violated the environment, the climate, and the planet.

It was just as well. After the mob won their campaign to criminalize the police, most of the officers of old threw up their hands and chose apathy. After that, it didn't take long for the old school police to ignore or turn a blind eye to real crimes for fear of being arrested themselves; handcuffed and perp-walked for violating the mob-mentality laws of 'social justice'. Most of them, those with half a conscience, retired or resigned shortly thereafter; and who could blame them.

It was a shame, but more so sad really. Old school and traditional policing quickly became a thing of the past. Thus, in time the police of old eventually evolved into the police of new; new blood of whom Randy and Joel are about to face once again.

Getting cushy salaries and premium benefits via taxes and tolls paid by the bulk of society; the C-Class citizens in the private sector; the 'Kings Men' inherited a sense of superiority. It was actually more like..., or closer to a sense of supremacy..., like Nazis soldiers. Some would often go so far as to describe them as a sort of 'New Age Gestapo'.

Needless to say, the Kings Men were content and comfortable. If one couldn't see it in their face, it could always and easily be detected in their demeanor and attitudes. Being well-paid and treated so good; the loyal and rigid roadside regiment would follow protocol to the tee; enforcing the law.

They were young; mid thirties max, a couple of them early twenties or so, maybe even younger; six men and two women, in this case. Their youth however didn't change the fact that they were grim. Being that it was a bit windy and facing them under a blanket of swirling, dark and heavy clouds only made them look that much worse. They came across as menacing and unfriendly.

Still, was it enough to hide how happy they were inside? Not hardly. Like all B-Class Citizens, all those in DSS loved their lucrative upper-class citizenship, their power and position of authority.

Enlisted by America's Fourth Branch; their official name wasn't the 'Kings Men', 'Social Justice Enforcers', or even the 'Enforcers' despite these names frequently used to identify them. No…, this particular new breed of police is officially known as the 'Faction Eight Global Police' there to protect and to serve. As always and by law, they took an oath to protect and to serve.

Of course, the times had changed. Their priorities and orders had change. They were there to — protect and serve — alright, but it was the A-Class Citizens, and themselves, the B-Class Citizens, and the Planet they'd be protecting and serving.

It was the typical double talk so commonly used by the Leftwing demagogues; seasoned liberals, progressives, socialist, communist, democrats, feck-less republicans and turncoat republicans; fill in the blank, they were all the same. In modern America's case; protecting and serving those who were in charge of protecting the Planet, protecting the Environment and protecting Humanity was of course deemed as protecting and serving the People.

How good of them. So much love…, so much con-cern, so wonderful and so caring, so thoughtful; how could anyone think otherwise? Right now, Randy and Joel were on the verge of getting another dose of some of that love and concern there to protect them and serve them for their own good.

"It ticks me off to know our taxes are actually pay-ing these asshole thugs to harass us." Randy quietly grumbled to Joel as they slowly came to a stop. Taking his voice down another notch while rolling down his window he turned to Joel and whispered one more little grievance before having to face the music.

"It just sucks, to know they slap a frickin' toll on us too every time we're forced to go through these stupid things."

Even though it was softly spoken, Joel heard it loud and clear. Needless to say, he had the same sen-timents. It was irritating, even infuriating if one so chose to gnaw on it long enough.

Having already scanned the License Plate, four of

the eight armed police-soldiers would take formation around the truck. Two of them moseyed over to the driver's side window. Two more would spread out on Joel's side of the truck about ten feet out and ten feet apart. Two would remain up ahead guarding the road while two more circled the pickup; one from a distance with a Visual Probe—scanning and searching for weapons, ammunition or contraband hidden in the truck and the other with a trained dog sniffing out what the Visual Probe might have missed.

Of the four that approached the truck, three had their assault rifles in hand but pointed to the ground. The fourth however had a far more powerful weapon in his hand. It would be the CD officer armed with an AP18; a lightweight portable CPU (central processing unit) and database that posed the biggest threat. It gave the Faction Eight Police everything they needed to know when it came to pointing their guns to the ground or targeting in on people. They called the powerful little unit MOM, an acronym—Monocular Observation Module.

Having been through this before, both Randy and Joel already had their ID's out. They knew the routine. Being herded and funneled into a checkpoint like cattle and sheep was only part of the time consuming humiliation. They'd also have to jump through the hoops of questions and balance the pains of interrogation on the tips of their noses to appease and satisfy the latest sector of security added to America's Civilian Army.

Even though the checkpoints were random, they were frequent; too frequent. What was once every couple of months or so was getting to be at least twice a month for most. It wasn't hard for the average C- and D-Class citizens to figure out that it wasn't so much about security as it was collecting tolls to feed the State and its insatiable appetite for lucrative living.

Now stopped and the engine turned off, Randy and Joel sat quietly waiting for the Faction Eight Police to do their job. With a cautious approach—giving the inside of the cab and truck bed a quick once over, the CD officer (check and document) flaunting his AP18 proceeded to Randy's open window.

-Chapter Two-
JESUS FREAK

"Good morning, gentlemen," rolled out of the officers mouth. "Are you chipped?" he asked.

"No sir, we are not." Randy replied as he did his best to ignore the head-cam recording his every move and word. Even though both he and Joel have been through it before, being video recorded still made it very awkward and uncomfortable to say the least.

"ID's and Domestic Passports please." the officer requested. Randy handed them over to be scanned. Within seconds, all was well on the CD officers monitor and earpiece. The ID's and Passports matched the Facial Recognition Scan. Also, no red alerts — just some standard yellow and orange flags.

"Are there any firearms or ammunition with you, on you or in the vehicle?" he asked with authority.

"No Sir!" Randy promptly answered.

The officer paused momentarily. He took a gander at his monitor, looked up and dialed in on Randy.

"Randall Alan Stevenson," he said almost in a tone of interrogating a prisoner. "I see here that you have a Smith and Wesson .38 Special Revolver. Do you still have this weapon?"

"Yes..., yes I do."

Glancing back down to his screen, "How about this uhh—this Remington 12-gauge shotgun? Do you still have this weapon?"

"Yes I do."

"Are there or have there been any more weapons added to your civilian arsenal?"

"No sir!"

"Very good—because you do know that you can only have two firearms in your possession. Is this not correct Mr Stevenson?" the officer asked with his eyes fixated on the monitor.

"Yes sir—only two. I am aware."

"Is your arsenal still located at 2625 Pine Valley, South Lake Tahoe, California?"

"Yes!"

"Are they locked, unloaded, Child Proof, and up to the Safety Standards and Codes?"

"Yes, yes they are."

The officer pondered. "Hmmm..., I see here that you were OK'd on a random home search and compliance inspection last year. Good. I see you've complied with the Semi-Automatic Weapon Relinquishment Laws. Good. How 'bout uhh—let's see here—State issued ammo? Are you still in compliance as to having in your possession sixteen rounds or less for these two weapons?" he asked.

Randy couldn't help but feel like a common criminal having to answer to the Parole Officer. He also couldn't help but feel a bit of resentment. He did well to bite his tongue though. Hiding his anger, he went on to answer once again, respectfully and to the point. "Yes…, yes on both of those questions."

"Twelve .38 caliber bullets and…, says here—four shotgun shells purchased …, gosh—over a year ago on Ammo.Gov. Still have 'em, huh? Haven't gotten anymore…., on the black market?" He probed.

"No sir. That's all I have. At ten bucks a pop…, you know—per cartridge…, can't afford to get anymore or use 'em up for that matter. Never know when you'll need 'em for protection." Randy added to patronize the officer; telling him what he figured he wanted to hear.

"Yep…! That's why we still uphold the Second Amendment." The officer praised like it was a wonderful thing letting people have a gun or two with no more than sixteen bullets. It irked Randy. He sneered inside; mentally gnashing his teeth in anger, yet he didn't show it.

"Second Amendment…, my ass," he thought to himself, Joel too for that matter. The officer was quick to brag about Randy's right to own a gun, but nothing about paying with his life if he'd dare break the iron-fisted guidelines and restrictions that came with it. The 'Second Amendment' was now nothing short of a joke. What became of it was travesty, just like the First Amendment.

After documenting the answer, the CD officer un-expectedly took a casual step back so as to admire Randy's old truck. "Wow! You sure don't see very many of these ol' guys anymore. What is it—a sixty-four? Sixty-five?" the officer politely asked.

"It's a sixty-four. I've had it for awhile, thirty years at least." Randy boasted.

"Yep…!" the officer noted. "It's kind of a shame that this time next year these old vehicles will no lon-ger be street legal outside of parades, exhibitions and Hollywood contracts. But, as you know, it's for the best. It's really too bad that they do so much damage to the environment and disrupt the climate. My grand-dad used to have one." he added. "Oh well—what's the odometer reading?"

Randy looked down through the steering wheel and cited the numbers clearly rolled over. "Uhh, let's see…, 2-2-3-1-1-2."

The officer peered into the window to verify Randy's answer and skimmed over his AP18 monitor. "Well, you're good there too. Out of the 500 miles al-lotted to you this year, you still have another 293 miles left. Good for you—no citation. Better use them miles up though before the ban, huh."

The officer then shifted his attention to Joel silently sitting on the passenger side. Joel was outwardly calm, but inside he was leery and anxious. The officer modestly glanced into the cab past Randy and got a good look at him. He went directly to his touch screen and MOM told him everything there was to know about Joel.

From there the officer knew enough to know he didn't care for him at all. Unlike Randy having to answer to a yellow flag alert stipulating firearms, Joel had to answer to an orange flag—an affiliation alert. It was the kind of alert that turned a standard interrogation into a rude and contentious hate fest.

Grimacing, the smug CD officer looked in at his subject quietly waiting to be questioned. He just stared at Joel as he listened to Communal Intel brief him through his earpiece. It was however only a handful of seconds. Again, likened to an interrogation the officer would follow up.

"So! Who do we have here? Jonathon Joel Stevenson. Stevenson…, Stevenson. Randall Stevenson and Jonathon Stevenson; so—you boys married?" he obnoxiously asked with a smirk and loud enough to get a rise out of his comrades in arms. It worked. The other police-soldiers snickered.

"Funny!" Randy said with a half-hearted go-along laugh. "No, we're brothers," he added so as to answer the question respectfully.

"Yeah—I can see the resemblance, but I wasn't talking to you was I?" the officer rudely asserted. He again fixated on Joel and continued his snide inquiry.

"Well now, Jonathon. I see here that you've been flagged with a big, bright orange icon here on the database—another Christian Fundamentalist. How 'bout that? Well, let's see here—you're not a Catholic, you're not a Mormon—says here that you're uh, a Jef—a Jesus-Freak. Oops!" he promptly blurted. "Oh! I'm so sorry Mr. Stevenson. I meant to say Jesus Fundamentalist. Please forgive me. You know—sometimes I just get this big giant official JF reference on my monitor a little mixed up with the street lingo. You know how it is?" he sarcastically explained knowing darn well it wasn't a mistake.

The CD officer's phony apology and tone resonated loud and clear. Both Joel and Randy knew right away where he stood and what he thought about Christians. The hatred, resentment, the ridicule and mocking; Joel's gone through it many times over. What's one more? Still, he was tense. Already knowing where the CD officer was going, he braced himself and waited for the onslaught of questions he'd have to answer as well as everything else in between.

"So! Is it true, Mr Stevenson? Is MOM here telling the truth? Are you a Jef—one of them Born Agains?"

the officer briskly asked with a sneer.

"Yes sir. Yes I am." Joel nervously answered.

"You know it's laughable to think just how many there are of you who still have the word—sin in your vocabulary. Humph! It doesn't matter I guess. You still have to obey the law.

You know Mr Stevenson…, the Catholics, Mormons, Muslims and Jews, most of them have enough sense to comply and conform to the Truth Neutrality Legislation. I mean hell…, even a bunch of your creepy Christian denominations have enough sense. But you Jesus Fundamentalists—you're a…, well—I don't want to say stupid. I'd say you're a stubborn breed aren't you? And here you are Mr Stevenson. It looks like you're one 'em. Looks like you're a little reluctant to comply. Looks like you're having a little problem with obeying the law."

Keeping his roadside investigation on point he'd take another look at his monitor. "Let's see here—oh brother," he hissed shaking his head, "another Israel lover. Whatever! Well, your phone calls and emails look clean—no guns, no Climate Change Denial citations or anything else to suggest you're violent or hostile. But…!" he announced as he looked up again at Joel. "You're still on the list—under investigation. You've been tagged a domestic agitator Mr Stevenson—a threat to our Unity Laws, Collective Ordinances and our Peace and Security Maintenance Programs. That's not good." He firmly asserted and continued.

"As you well know I'm required by law to ask you a couple of simple little questions here so as to confirm exactly where you stand in our society. You can understand, right Mr Stevenson? We really do need to know who the troublemakers are—you know—the Uniters and the Dividers. We need to know who's with us and who is against us if we're ever gonna evolve, progress, and synchronize."

Even though the officer spoke nicely, he was most intimidating and menacing; especially with an armed unit backing him up. Joel already knew the questions he'd be asked to answer. So did Randy for that matter. They had already briefly discussed it as soon as they unexpectedly found themselves being corralled like cattle into the police-soldiers welcoming arms.

Seconds passed. Joel was ready. So was the officer as he proceeded to ask his questions in the name of the law.

"Well now, let's see if you've had a change of heart since your last inquisition. So, which is it, Mr Stevenson? Is Jesus...A...way to heaven or is Jesus... THE...way to heaven?"

Being the same exact question he's been getting in the Federal Census for the last five years amongst other checkpoints, Joel was well aware of the answer he was supposed to give. But once again he already knew he just couldn't give them that answer. He was well acquainted and quite familiar with America's new laws and ordinances too, but he was firm and wouldn't comply. Having a higher obligation, an obligation to God — to Jesus Christ, he simply refused to submit.

"Well Mr Stevenson — which is it?" the officer prodded.

"The way," Joel affirmed, "Jesus is the way to heaven."

"Humph," the officer muttered as he jeered at Joel with a hateful smirk. Displeased, he slowly shook his head and went on to finish his Check and Document procedures. "Well, that's one down and one to go," he said. "All is not lost though Mr Stevenson. You can still redeem yourself in spite of your — let us say hallelujah answer to the first question. You wanna restore your citizenship? You wanna reestablish yourself in society? You wanna be able to vote again? If so, I suggest you comply with the law and give us the answer we need to hear."

Clearly in no mood for nonsense, the officer looked directly at Joel, locked eyes and glared at him. He'd set the stage with a few spiteful remarks though before he'd shoot Joel with the second question. "You and your kind say Jesus is the one and only way to heaven.

You say if one doesn't receive Jesus as God and Savior they will go to hell. Second question—and oh how I love to ask these questions," he added.

"Is this a belief, Mr Stevenson? Or is it the truth?" he asked with the perfect blend of delight and intimidation.

Joel's heart was pounding and his gut was tied in knots but to his credit, he wasn't about to waver. He didn't have to think about which answer to give simply because he was sure of his answer. It would be the same answer to the same question that he's given to the State again and again over the years in both the Census and these roadside inspections and investigations.

He was however momentarily speechless. It wasn't on purpose though. He was just a little tongue-tied and choked up fighting a lump in his throat. The officer, being extremely impatient wasn't at all impressed with Joel's delay. He quickly followed up—more firmly, more direct, more hostile.

"Well...? Which is it Mr Born Again Christian Man? Is it a belief or is it the truth?" he sternly pressed.

"It's the truth!" Joel asserted.

The answer burned the officer up. Sneering with utter disgust, cross and irritated, he slightly shook his head and hurriedly moved to finish up.

"Ok!" he sharply snapped. "Well that's number

seven — number seven out of ten Mr Stevenson. By law, I'm to tell you that you have three and only three more chances to change your mind, or let us say, change your answer. If you do not comply by or on the tenth inquisition you will be arrested on sight and sent directly to the Camp with the rest of your buddies unwilling to recognize and conform to the Coexist and Climate Change Legislation. No trial, and all property confiscated by Global Affairs. Do you understand, Mr Stevenson?" the officer sternly warned.

"Yes sir! I do." Joel softly replied.

"What was that? I couldn't hear you Mr Born Again Christian Man, you — you little Jef. Do…you… understand…?" he added even louder, like a drill sergeant speaking down to a measly recruit.

"Yes! Yes I do." Joel again answered loud enough to make it clear; very clear.

Randy sat there like a rock, frozen, quiet and still. Almost holding his breath, he just looked on. He was so disenchanted with everything. He found it hard to comprehend that America had fallen to such dismal standards. It was ridiculous, but nevertheless quite the reality. As Randy pondered, the officer would have the last word. He'd moved to wrap it up because the sprinkling had turned into a slight drizzle.

"Where you guys headed anyhow?" he asked.

"Reno," Randy promptly answered, "to the airport."

The officer stepped back from the door window a bit, just enough to take a proud, cocky stance and look Joel in eye without having to slouch down. Feeling the need to scold Joel, wanting to give him a piece of his mind he laid into him.

"You know, this is why we can't stand you guys. Haven't you heard? Nobody owns the truth. The rest of us are open minded, smart enough and willing to say we all simply believe in a belief. Why can't you? But, you just can't bring yourself to do that now can you Mr Born Again Christian Man. You sit there and tell everybody you and you alone believe the truth as if you own the truth and everybody else is beneath you believing in lies and empty, meaningless beliefs."

Joel and Randy could feel the vitriol and hatred in the officer's voice. It was thick. They could feel he wanted to yank Joel out of the truck right then and there and haul him off to the Camp. If it had been Joel's tenth inquisition, he would have gladly done so. Randy was starting to worry that the officer was ready to go out of his way to find something, anything to arrest them or give them a citation. He so hated to be at their mercy, but there was nothing they could do. So, like Joel, he just waited and hoped it to be over so they could be on there way. The officer however wasn't quite finished reprimanding Joel. He had a few more things to tell him.

"Well, it's the law now isn't it Mr Stevenson? Nobody can stake a claim to the truth and that includes you. The Truth Neutrality Laws was the best thing that ever happened to America. It's so nice to see all of you Christian Fundamentalists having to lower yourselves and admit that you believe in a belief like the rest of us. Watching you hardcore Jesus Freaks having to squirm and confess that what you believe isn't the truth is just flat out good." The irritated officer would finish his bitter rebuke with a threat.

"You don't believe the truth Mr Born Again Christian Man, you believe in a belief like the rest of us and that's that. You and your kind, all you Jef's don't own the truth, never have owned the truth and never will. Don't forget it. You got three more chances to tell us you believe in a belief. You got three more chances to renounce your claim on the truth or else? And another thing, you might want to rethink your support for those stinkin' little troublemakers over in Israel too. Like you, there's nothing good about Zionists."

Clearly the CD officer was extremely perturbed. Joel's whole body was trembling. Even so, feeling compelled and even a bit courageous, Joel was just about ready to respond, but wisely stopped at the last second. In more ways than one, thankfully he thought it best to hold his tongue. The officer quickly glanced up at the sky assessing the rainfall getting heavier and then took one more jeering look at Randy and Joel. He stepped up to the window and handed Randy their ID's, stepped back and waved them on.

-Chapter Three-
TWO KINDS OF LOVE

Randy gladly started the truck, put it in gear and like a dog with its tail between its legs speedily crept on out of the tense gauntlet of questions and answers. He too was a little shaky. It was nerve racking. It again made him angry to think he, with his tax dollars was the one paying these guys to interrogate and badger them and treat them like lower life forms and criminals.

There was just something so wrong about it. Paying people to make your life miserable was something that America was never supposed to do, but that's what the Left side of the fence kept voting for in the name of love, sensitivity, fairness, tolerance, political correctness, security, social justice, controlling the climate, and saving the planet. Liberal Love gone Socialist gone Communist pretty much summed it up: Progressivism. Randy couldn't help but reflect on it.

Liberal Love, even with the best of intentions, was somewhat laughable and silly in many ways. Then it became annoying, then infuriating and disgusting. It wasn't until it was too late that the bulk of America found out just how dangerous it was from the very beginning...; that it was actually a political cult in the making.

After driving a few hundred yards away from their little nightmare, getting away as fast as he could and catching his breath, Randy had to speak up. As if the officer wasn't enough, being also a bit agitated at Joel, Randy took up where the officer left off.

"Man, I thought for sure he was going to pull something out of his hat to impound the truck, or give us a citation or even arrest us. Dude..., give it up," he hammered. "Can you just give it up? Why do you have to keep on insisting your Gospel crap is the truth when you know darn well it's just a belief?"

"It's because it isn't just a belief, Randy. It is the truth," Joel gently argued.

"So, what...? Maybe it is. Who cares? Jeez Louise, all's you gotta do is say it's a belief and you can get on with your life. Just tell 'em it's a belief and they'll leave you alone. You're still free to believe whatever you want to believe. You can still believe it's the truth. They don't care. You just can't say it's the truth. It's like the Christmas thing." Randy reminded, "We can believe it's the birth of Christ all we want—so what if we can't put up the Nativity Scenes. So what if we have to say 'Happy Holidays' instead of 'Merry Christmas' in public. It's no big deal. Give me a break. Just tell 'em it's a belief, Joel, and be done with it."

"You know what...?" Joel fired back. "I just can't do that. You know what it's all about Randy. You know the little game they're playing. They do the same thing to you. And you know darn well it goes a heck of a lot further than this 'Happy Holidays' shit. When you had to get rid of the America Flag sticker on your truck so they'd stop vandalizing it—keying it and flattening your tires..., what about that?" Joel charged.

"Yeah, but it's not all of 'em on the Left that get that vicious."

"Humph! You're right about that, but there's enough of 'em to make us think twice about going against the grain—enough of 'em to make our lives miserable. Besides, the ones on the Left that don't get violent and destructive..., those smug-assess just go around saying we deserve the abuse. Not only that; wasn't it you, not that long ago, having to lie on your resume and job application to get your job at the Casino? You knew if you didn't check Democrat or Liberal for your 'political affiliation' they wouldn't have hired you—or even consider you. It's like Stalin's Soviet Russia—frickin' Liberals. You would have never gotten the job. It's what they do. They force you to comply, and if you don't, you're screwed. That's what pisses me off." Joel griped. "Now they're getting us Born Agains to renounce Jesus Christ by forcing us to say God's Truth is nothing more than a man's belief. It sucks. It's evil; it comes from the depths of hell, from Satan."

"Satan...! Oh brother, here we go," Randy mocked.

"Believe me, I get it," Joel affirmed. "I know what the New Age Liberal Love bandwagon is all about. If I confess to you, and confess to that little twerp CD Officer back there, and the rest of America that Jesus Christ is just another way to heaven or..., or the Gospel isn't the truth..., that it's just a frickin' belief, oh yeah—it'll suit all of you just fine. God, I hate those questions." Joel raged.

He took in a breath and let out a hefty sight. He tried to calm down but it didn't work. He was still upset; so much so that it compelled him finished his thoughts on the matter.

"Man..., do I ever get it. No truth; means no authority. No truth, means nobody's right and nobody's wrong. No truth means; nothing to impose on others. No truth, no harm no foul; it's happy...happy...happy! Its group hugs and everybody skipping through the frickin' tulips in loin cloths and sandals throwing rose pedals in the air. Everybody renouncing their claim on the truth means no more strife, no more war, no more bickering and fighting. It's all equal; it's all neutral— its peace and love forever. Yeah..., I get it!" Joel rambled off nearly shouting as he ran out of breath.

"Well, what's wrong with that? It's good. It makes

sense. And yeah..., it is love," Randy argued. "It is pathway to peace and harmony if you really think about it and look at it,"

"Oh man, don't you get it Randy? There are two kinds of love. Getting along is one kind of love. The other is the love of someone saving another's life. That's the love of Jesus and what he did on the cross and it's the love we pursue. It's perfect love. There's not one iota of hate in the love and passion of someone moved to save another's life. What we call love, reaching out to save people from the ledge of eternal hell, even Jesus dying on the cross with that message is what you guys are calling hate. As for this love of everybody getting along—oh yeah—there's plenty of love and perfection there. I could just feel all the love, peace and perfection just oozing out of the barrels of those guns back there. C'mon— that's love, that's godly, right and good? I'm supposed to bow down to that?" Joel asked in frustration. "Look—I know the good intentions, Randy..., but trust me, all of this stuff, what we're seeing, all of these Coexist and Truth Neutrality Laws; it's all evil. It's called the...*falling away*...; it's in the Bible. It means time is getting short and there's nothing good or godly about it."

"Oh my God, time is getting short, it's the end of the world," Randy mocked while pretending to be in a panic.

"You just don't understand, Randy. If I give them the answer they want to hear, it's like — like selling my soul. If you knew the scriptures, the Gospel, if you knew the Bible, or the heart of Jesus, what he was all about and the thing's he'd say and told us..., you'd know what I'm talking about. You'd see the proof" Joel insisted and continued.

"You'd know the tons of things in there that put the fear of God in you. You'd know just how dangerous it is to think the Bible and the Gospel of Jesus Christ is beneath you or something to ignore, and heckle, or half believe or play around with. It's serious stuff. But, you don't know. That's why you don't understand, can't understand and will never understand why so many Born Agains are flat out refusing to bow down and submit to America's new laws and demands. Some are, the Mormon Church has, the Catholics and the Pope have conformed and sold into this believing in a belief crap for the sake of getting along and galvanizing their Ecumenical Movement. But as you can see, many aren't. I'm not." Joel declared.

"Yeah, I can see that and it about got us arrested," Randy griped.

"Yeah — I know..., and that's why it sucks. Still..., we just can't give in to the 'Woke Liberal Supremacists' or these..., these 'Cancel Culture Puritans'. We just can't. Striving to be accepted by people and society, like giving the DSS, and now you and the rest of America the answers you guys want to hear is your way of getting us, even forcing us to bow down to you instead of God. We're not going to bow down to the collective because the collective isn't God.

I mean seriously, they actually think we as people have the power to change and control the climate and the weather. Am I missing something?" Joel beseeched. "Talk about being God. That's…, I don't know, it's one of two things. They're either incredibly stupid or incredibly arrogant to think we have that much power. Either way, this frickin' idea that humanity actually has the power to change and control the climate and neutralizing the truth is nobody I want to bow down to."

Randy would think and had to somewhat agree. "Yeah…, well you're half right. Climate control…? Jeez – what a joke. It's gotta be the Liberals crown jewel of sanctimonious stupidity. It's right up there with mandatory helmets for toddlers taking baths."

Caught of guard by the snide remark, Joel had to chuckle. Randy always had a way to make people laugh in spite of serious dialogue. "It's so stupid that they have to use a barrel of a gun to get us to accept it. You know I've said it before and I'll say it again. The day they started to penalize and arrest people for criticizing Manmade Climate Change was the day

America gave into communism." Randy declared.

"I mean it's weird — they're using a barrel of a gun to force us to say manmade climate change is the truth and not a belief, but on the same token they're forcing you to say the Gospel of Jesus is a belief and not the truth." He rationalized. "Nothing's changed, huh. When it comes to the Left and the Liberal Pharisees, it's always been double standards. Isn't that what you call 'em…, Liberal Pharisee's…?" Randy asked in passing.

"Yeah…, that amongst some other things," Joel said.

"Well…, I call 'em frickin' ass holes or…, Liberal idiots. How's that for love?" Randy sarcastically said with disgust, "I don't know…, they just so piss me off."

After his short huff, he'd quickly go right back to scolding Joel though. He was still angry despite the slight twist in their argument. He went right back to the beginning as to why he was so bothered by Joel's standoff.

"Still, Joel, seriously…, you gotta stop with this holier-than-thou Jesus stuff yourself. It's like you're a Pharisee really. Talk about crap!" Randy snapped. "I mean, really, a belief's a belief and that's that. Just roll with it. Get it over with. It's getting you and even me in too much trouble. All's you gotta do is say your Gospel thing and your Jesus-is-God thing is a belief and not the truth, and manmade climate change is the truth and not a belief and we all live happily ever after. It's so simple." Randy reasoned.

Joel looked down, slowly shook his head and said, "It's simple for you, but not for me. I'll go along with the climate crap because that's not going to cost me my soul. But, Jesus? I'm not gonna take that chance and I'm not gonna compromise. He is the way, the truth and the life and no one comes to the Father but by Him. I'm not going to give Him up for the sake of being accepted and approved by society. I'm just not gonna go there. I don't care how simple it is. I don't care how popular it is. I don't care how reasonable and respectful and harmonious and godly it supposedly is. I'm not going to put Jesus second and turn around and bow down to society and all of your Unity Laws, and your Peace and Security Maintenance Programs, and your..., your — whatever they're called — Coexist Ordinances. And from the looks of how fast these Sensitivity Camps are filling up this last year — I'm not alone. We're not going to renounce our claim on the truth. Jesus said he is the light of the world. He is God the Son, his resurrection proves it. And God doesn't go around telling people his beliefs. I'm not gonna go around telling people that I believe what Jesus believed. It's just flat out stupid and pointless. He told us the truth and I believe him."

"See…, gotcha, right there!" Randy blurted. "You just said you believe him, that's a belief."

"Yeah…, but it's also the truth." Joel said.

Still scowling, Randy once again as usual just rolled his eyes. Seconds passed after that. It got uncomfortably silent as they crept on into Carson City. But, the conversation wasn't quite over; nor was the day. And the day, this particular day? It would be the day that changed the world.

Joel, feeling the contempt in his brother's demeanor knew he had to go a little further with his thoughts if there was to be any closure. He really didn't want to just drop the subject, because it was important. Joel really wanted Randy to understand. Besides, he really didn't want to end his short visit on a sour note. Even if they skipped it and dropped the subject at this point, both of them knew they'd be parting ways with bitterness and pretending all was well between them. Acting as if nothing was wrong would only leave them unsettled and even guilty.

It would be touchy. Of the two, Joel was always a little more composed and rational. There was no way Randy would take the initiative to calm things down. So, once again it would be Joel moving to smooth things over.

He'd soften his tone, and slow his pace though so as to be more diplomatic. Taking it down a notch, taking it down to a discussion, a conversation instead of an argument was imperative. Through it all, he needed to let Randy know that giving America's militant Coexist Society a couple of little words and renouncing his claim on the truth wasn't as simple as his older brother so seemed to think. He needed to pour out his heart, his thoughts and his soul into it.

"What they're doing is wrong," he carefully said. "It's pretty much just like the Roman Empire. When they were brutally killing all the Christians—it wasn't because the Christians said Jesus is God. The Romans didn't have a problem with that. It's when they'd say Jesus is the one and only God that they were butchered. What do you think is happening now?"

Randy remained quiet and kept his eyes on the road. He was still wound up. He was still steaming, but he was listening. He was taking in what Joel had to say. Knowing it, and thankful for it, Joel went on to finish.

"They're doing the same exact thing. These ultimatums; asking us is Jesus…a…way to heaven or…the…way to heaven. Is it a belief or is it the truth? There isn't really any difference. They're persecuting and prosecuting us just like they did the Christians back then."

"Yeah, but they're not killing you. They're not throwing into a pit of hungry lions." Randy snapped back, still in argument mode.

"Maybe not, but you see how they're treating us though. You can see what they're doing. You know darn well it's gonna end up like Europe. It's getting bad. Right now, this Coexist crap is forcing us to go underground. They're forcing us to close the doors to our churches if we don't give them what they want. They're censoring scriptures, turning our Pastors into common criminals if they dare utter anything out of the Bible that offends people. The Child Protective Services (CPS) is even taking our children away. Child Abuse—can you believe that? Child abuse! If they find out or even suspect any of us telling our children the Bible is the truth or the Word of God—we lose our kids. Just look at what they did to Sean. What is he now—in second grade? The school's giving them tests, and interrogated them, and even bribing them so as to see what it is that their parents are teaching them. Oh yeah—no big deal! They're breaking up our families, hauling parents to sensitivity camps, confiscating our belongings, taking our children from us because the CPS don't you know is all about love and protecting our poor little children from being brainwashed and abused by us evil and wicked Bible Thumpers who dare to tell their children the Gospel of Jesus Christ is the truth. But hey! At least they're not killing us." Joel said sarcastically.

He wasn't finished though. He was riled up. He

did it to himself. He went on to vent even more frustrations that he apparently needed to get out of his system.

"And look what's happened to the people. All of these informants, neighborhood spies, concerned teachers and coworkers; they're coming out of the woodwork, making our lives miserable. Even families are ratting out their own flesh and blood to the State to get the perks and reward money. And this latest thing—forcing all the Christian based churches put these stupid disclosures on all of their Church fronts, signs, brochures and tracts—A Pathway to Heaven. What's up with that? And why is it just the Christian churches? How come the Muslims don't have to put the same disclosure in front of their Mosques and stamp it all over their literature? I guess we already know why for that matter." Joel elaborated without even realizing that he was now rambling on instead of explaining.

"If we can just get rid of these Christian and Zionist Fundamentalist, then these Islamic Terrorists will stop terrorizing us. Blame the Christians and Zionist for all the Islamic Terrorist attacks on America, accuse us of agitating them, stamp us out to appease them and hey, liberal America will finally be able to rehabilitate these evil bastards chopping everybody's head off; great plan. Now that's love!" Joel bitterly said. "I guess I should be thankful it's just the Camp and not the Coliseum that we're being rounded up and taken to—at least for now."

Joel had lost track. What started out as a lighthearted mission to explain and defend his faith was now an angry rant. Clearly, Joel was really bothered deep down. Even though there was calmness about him for the most part, it was quite apparent that he had been keeping a lot of his frustrations bottled up. Without even realizing it, the cork was popped and Joel was letting it all out. Randy still remained silent and continued staring at the road ahead. Without even trying he had somehow become more of a therapist listening to Joel's troubles than somebody needing to hear the Gospel.

Getting no response from Randy, Joel too stopped, turned his head, replanted himself in the seat and stared at the road as well. He knew he had blown it. It wasn't like him to go off, but maybe it was good to get some of this stuff off his chest. It would be about a minute before another word was spoken. It would be Joel who'd again speak. This time however it wasn't really so much about getting Randy to feel his faith or understand his trust in Jesus as it was him simply thinking out loud. It was somber.

"America screwed us over." he went on to say as he gazed out the window. "Israel's 'bout the only place left in the world for Bible believers to enjoy what we used to call freedom. It's the only place left where we're still free to say it's the truth. Thank God for Israel. Ever since they squashed Russia and the Islamic Alliance like bugs in the Coalition War — Israel's the place to be. And Manning? And America," Joel said with a tone of disgust, "What a joke. Opting out and unwilling to lift a finger to help Israel defend itself from that huge-ass frickin' invasion was evil as far as I'm concerned. Whatever..., Israel didn't need our help anyhow — they had God on their side. They wiped those dudes out fast, big time. You know the Coalition War was another —"

"Yeah, yeah, yeah — I know!" Randy interrupted. "Another Biblical Prophecy that came to pass. Gog, or the Magog, or Gog McGog — whatever the hell it was — you've only told me about a thousand times. Geez...!"

By this time Randy was feeling empathy for Joel despite his grumbling. He could hear the passion in his brother's voice and feel his sadness. He could see that Joel was really upset, probably even more than himself; not only at what had happened to them back at the checkpoint but everything going on in America. After Randy absorbed Joel's little history lesson about the Romans; its comparison to America and his up-date on current affairs, after having calmed down a bit himself, he delved back into the conversation. It would be without angst.

"You know, Joel, I do see your point." Randy said. "I always have. I see all this discrimination going on against you guys and Zionist too for that matter. And you are right—I don't understand. Christians? A lot of people don't. Sheesh…! Why anyone would choose to die like those Christians back then and even now you guys being so willing to walk away from your lives, your belongings, even handing your children over to the State for something so seemingly unimportant doesn't make any sense. You guys are choosing to go to these stupid Sensitivity Camps and for what? You can't say a couple words? You can't say you believe in a belief—it's gotta be the truth. You know I hate to say this, but I can halfway relate to that jerk back there giving you a hard time in a lot of ways." Randy admitted.

"I mean—yeah! It's unbelievable to see the Liberal fruitcakes have taken things this far, I'll grant you that. But, what's even more unbelievable is your reluctance to comply with such an easy law; even to the point of losing your own children for Pete's Sake. Yeah…, you're right—I don't get it Joel. It's weird—just flat out weird. You guys are fruitcakes too." he added half-jokingly. "Why do you guys do it? I just don't get it. It's beyond me." Randy said as he shook his head.

"It's called faith." Joel proudly insisted. He was

stoked that Randy broke his silence. He was even happier to see he went back into conversation mode despite the negativity and insults. Joel was happy to see that his little rant didn't chase Randy off. If anything it brought him back in. "Praise God." he whispered to himself. As for Randy, he went on to criticize. It was at least honest, and Joel always appreciated his honesty.

"Faith, schmaith, it still doesn't make any sense. People dying and giving up everything they have because they just can't bring themselves to say a couple of words—words that can actually bring peace and harmony instead of strife and war. It's a mystery alright." He took a moment and pondered. He contemplated on the whole conversation and plucked out of it something that Joel had mentioned.

"I wonder how many Christians renounced their claim on the truth to save their skins from the lions or to stay with their children." Randy pondered.

"I'm sure there were plenty of them. A lot of them I'd say. But, it's the ones who didn't renounce their faith that got all the recognition. I'd say that's some pretty brave stuff."

"You call it brave, I call it stupid." Randy said. Joel had to lightly chuckle once again. He was delighted to see Randy was back to his old self. He was relieved to see that he himself too was somewhat back to his old self. Through it all, he also knew there'd be no changing Randy's mind anytime soon. He would however as usual leave his older brother with something to think about. Half-jokingly and really far from being offended, Joel would give Randy something to chew on in regards to his remark about the difference between brave and stupid.

"So, are you calling me stupid?" Joel joked, looking at Randy with a jovial smile. Randy looked at Joel and saw his humor. He had to laugh.

"No, I'm not calling you stupid. Come to think of it, I'd say you were pretty brave back there. Man...! That was intense. I know I wouldn't have gone as far as you did." Randy assured. He was in a sense sort of proud of his brother for that matter. He had to hand it to Joel for sticking to his guns the way he did.

"Oh, I don't know." Joel replied as he turned to stare out his passenger window again. "I think you would have done the same thing. In fact, one of these days, I'm pretty sure you gonna have to go through it whether you like it or not."

"What do you mean? You think I'm gonna fall for the Jesus crap? Sorry pal—I don't think so. I mean don't get me wrong. Jesus was great, he still is. Everybody loves Jesus—everybody that's not an idiot that is. He was good, a good man. I can even honestly say that Jesus is the Son of God, but God the Son? Eh...!" Randy jeered. "I don't think so. You know I believe in God and I believe God sent Jesus as—I don't know—a representative, but God dying on the cross to keep people from going to hell just doesn't jive. I just don't think I'm ever gonna go there, Joel. It'll never happen." Randy boasted.

Joel didn't press it. Even though he had plenty to say about Randy's Quasi-Christian assessment, that there were several holes in his foundation, he just rolled with it, with a bit of optimism even. "You know what they say Randy—never-say-never."

Randy just smiled back. From there he went on to apologize to Joel. "Hey, I'm sorry I got so angry with you back there. Like you, I guess I'm just upset that things have gotten so far out of hand. I mean things were getting pretty bad over the years, but as soon as we put Manning into the White House, everything went down the toilet. America went to hell in hand basket real fast—too fast. I mean this is really incredible, and bad, and sad too. It's like all those dismal futuristic sci-fi movies. An iron-fisted police state, a database, checkpoints, facial identification scans—I hate those stupid head-cams too. Harassing us, intimidating us, censuring us, treating us like criminals, Sensitivity Camps—and we actually pay them for all of this crap. It's jacked up."

"Yep, it sure is. It su...rrre is." Joel slowly concurred.

Randy really didn't know what to say after Joel's bleak confirmation. The both of them knew things were bad. Both of them also knew they could keep on complaining but it was useless. In fact, if they weren't careful it would get them in serious trouble.

It was time to drop the subject. They could just feel it. So, they did without any qualms. Thankfully, the rift between the two was mended. With the tension vanquished, and both calmed down, they were now able to finish their ride together in peace.

-Chapter Four-
ANTAEUS THE GREAT

They still had a good amount of time left before they'd get to Reno. Randy took in a big breath and let out a heavy sigh. He'd be the first to make a move to get past their deeper conversation.

"What time is your flight again?" he asked so as to lighten it up.

Joel going along with their mutual decision to escape the tension reached into his shirt pocket and pulled out his itinerary. Even though both of them knew exactly what time Joel's flight was, they went through the motions so as to tone things down.

"Let's see." Joel said. "Southwest Airlines, Flight 759 Departure from Reno, NV 10:05 AM, Arrival Tucson, AZ 1:15 PM." he confirmed.

Randy went ahead and turned the radio back on as they were making their way through Carson City. There used to be a freeway that bypassed going through town, but the Zephyr Cove Earthquake three years back put a couple of the overpasses out of commission. Sadly, there were a lot of things out of commission for that matter.

A good part of America's entire infrastructure lay

in near ruins, waiting to be repaired. Everybody knew the repairs weren't going to happen anytime soon, if even at all. Money was seemingly nowhere to be found to address the nation seriously in decline. Randy was spot on right. America crumbled to pieces when they put the America-hating leftwing Marxist in the White House.

President Lowell Manning…? A lot could be said about a so-called world leader who daintily bounces down a staircase limp wristed and their hands flopping up and down like a couple of dead fish. To watch him swagger to a podium, cocky and proud, with his chin up and nose in the air; clearly self-absorbed — his body language spoke volumes. He didn't even have to say a word to read him.

Joel couldn't help but remember watching him strut out to the mound in New York Stadium to throw the ceremonial first pitch so as to start the World Series several years back. It was just flat out embarrassing. To sit there and watch America's almighty, all-powerful new President on International Television awkwardly and clumsily windup and toss the baseball like a toddler developing their motor skills only to have the baseball land halfway to home plate left a very unsettling image of America's new leadership.

The pathetic feat, even though it was hardly anything to be concerned about, it left a burning impression. Like Joel, it left many with doubts, uncomfortable and far from feeling safe and secure. And from the way things are, there was good reason to worry.

Of course, it wasn't Manning's uncoordinated motor skills or his wimpy physique that made him the most destructive President of all time. Nor was it his stereotypical spoiled-brat, man-child king image or the fact that everything in his life had been handed up to him on a silver platter that did it. It wasn't that his wife wore the pants of the family either. It was his ideologies that gave him the destructive crown.

In all truth, it wasn't so much about him as it was about the larger part of America allowing him to destroy the country. It was indeed the larger part of America; a certain side of America that would elect Lowell Manning to be their fearless Commander in Chief. He was fearless alright; not because he was a man of stature, courage, grit and integrity though. He was fearless because there was a delusional side of America who would feverishly surround him, shelter him and protect him from anything and anyone that could point out his flaws and expose his dark, sinister behavior.

It was mostly the Liberal Media and the Leftwing Activists; ass-kissing sycophants who'd circle the wagons around him and protect their prize possession.

They along with low-information voters who literally worshipped the Liberal Media as much as they worshipped the liberal politicians they'd protect with propaganda and cover-ups.

It was a side of America that pampered Lowell Manning, who babied him like doting parents obsessed with this idea that their ugly, evil and deranged child is the most perfect, most awesome, most talented gifted child in the world; a spoiled brat that could never ever do anything wrong in spite of the facts that proved otherwise. It was nothing short of pitiful and sickening. It was a syrupy love affair, an unholy relationship, but a dangerous one; one that carried America over the cliff.

The lying, the scandals, the corruption, the lawlessness, the barrage of Executive Orders, the extravagant lifestyle, the excessive and extended vacations, the imperialism, the neglect, the incompetence, the narcissism, the excuses, all of it, all these blatant and in our face things this man was allowed to get away with because his minions were plagued with the demented-doting-parent-syndrome was nothing short of criminal. The ones who idolized him, likened to the underdeveloped minds of children idolizing a Purple Dinosaur was another nice addition to his list of delusional voters.

All of them, both groups, the demented-doting-parent-syndrome people and the people plagued by the Purple Dinosaur idol worship mentality; they'd excuse or rationalize or cover up Manning's anti-American endeavors, tactics and less-than-honorable leadership. And criticism…, any criticism of their special little 'rightwing-hating god who could do no wrong; it was met with mean-spirited, even vicious and hostile retaliation. Yes…, this is why Lowell Manning was fearless.

Vowing to fix America, vowing to heal America, avenge America, and right the wrongs of America, vowing to fundamentally change America, and do away with tradition and buck the status quo; a nation consumed by vindictive special-interest-groups with axes to grind, socialism recipients, and godless vision-aries chasing a religion-free Utopia found their new cult-of-personality in the White House and his sugary vows most refreshing. A new face, a new agenda, a new image, and a new beginning sat well with a self-exalting nation full of liberal sages and environmental militants seizing the moral high ground.

It sat well with learned intellects madly in love with their fabricated intelligence; an intelligence that was above and beyond the time-tested virtues of com-mon sense. It sat well with a country swarming with full-blooded malcontents and Labor Unions obsessed with unwarranted entitlements and near childish de-mands. It sat well with ethnic and gender tribes led to believe that Equality and Fairness was all about revenge, retribution and getting even with America's historical upbringing.

Electing Lowell Manning also sat well with millions upon millions of people addicted to living off of other people's money. From the Welfare State to Government Employment, Lowell Manning was the high-flying Santa Claus President of love and fairness promising them more and more and more. It was a sordid and sinister bond likened to obedient dope-addicts madly in love with their dope-dealer dishing out the dope, the goods, the welfare, the food stamps, the paychecks, the pensions, the benefits and everything else that stemmed from other people's money.

Like ticks and fleas on a once mighty and beautiful prize-winning Golden Retriever, the Government Welfare State and Bureaucracy in collusion sucked the blood out of it until it was nothing but a bag of bones taking its last gasping breaths was America's story. It was convenient as was methodical. Each and every tick and flea could look in a mirror and honestly say that they alone didn't kill the once vibrant and healthy prize-winning Golden Retriever and it would of course be the truth. But it was only a half-truth.

They themselves and by themselves didn't, nor could they have ever sucked all the blood out of America. It was the collective; an army at that who'd fight to the end and protect each other like family to get their financial fix from the State. It was sad and quite frankly a shame.

Nobody, no one group or one person could be blamed for draining all the financial blood out of America and turning it into an anemic bag of bones gasping for air. Most just couldn't see what was happening. For a lack of better words, the ticks and fleas in the ears couldn't see the ticks and fleas on the stomach. And the fleas and ticks on the back couldn't see the fleas and ticks on the neck; and so on and so on. By design, the blood finally ran out.

The Santa Claus Politicians, the dope-dealers living large on the racket, if you will, knew exactly what was going on. After hijacking the social issues as well, their power in numbers was inevitable as was unstoppable. They worked it and worked it and worked it until they seized all power over all people. In short, mob-mentality Democracy murdered the Republic.

In turn, the A and B Class Elitists would rule the C and D Class Serfs. Worse however, the death nail was how the D Class would keep on voting for the A and B Class because they'd be the ones who'd confiscate the goods from the C Class to fund the D Class greedy appetite for welfare. The saying that spawned out of it..., 'there's really no difference between greedy welfare recipients and greedy bankers' was quite revealing.

Greed is greed. They were one in the same when it came to breaking America's kneecaps.

The fundamental transition in progress over the last hundred years finally came to fruition with President Manning at the helm. Sadly, modern America's misguided and coddled generation wasn't savvy enough to know what their ill-omened leader in the White House knew. They weren't savvy enough to realize that America's liberty and freedom went hand in hand with America's tradition and status quo.

Sadly, they were led to believe that they could actually do away with tradition and the status quo and still be able to keep the fruits of traditional liberty and freedom. Sadly, they were wrong. We were wrong.

A campaign geared around fixing America and repairing America was nothing but a ploy to dismantle and unravel America, so as to remake America, change America into Lowell Manning's America; a new America with a new and improved soul. Stirred by asinine ideologies, moved by concocted hope, driven by a pointless need for change, and ultimately allowing a lawless President to execute his communistic schemes under the guise of love, fairness, sensitivity, civil rights, social justice, and saving and perfecting the planet; little by little, America found itself forfeiting and swapping more and more of its more sacred liberties and freedoms. The freedom to go from South

Lake Tahoe to Reno without being stopped and harassed by the Peace and Security Gestapo would be one of these freedoms obliterated by Manning.

So, through the heart of Carson City they'd go. Joel would set his sights on the decrepit community falling just short of being a ghost town. Strolling down the main drag, hitting the various streetlights, he quietly gazed at the ragged sections full of empty graffiti ridden homes and burnt out buildings. Broken windows and trash strewn about in the drizzling rain made it very ominous.

He liked to think the rain was there to cleanse the once nostalgic little town from all the Marxist Engineering that Lowell Manning and his leftwing ilk had imposed on it; on all America for that matter. Like the intimidating check point, it was yet another dark reminder of how America voluntarily voted to carry itself over the threshold into the makings of another third world country. It had come to be just another 'banana republic'.

It was discouraging. It was disappointing. It was angering. The worst of it however as Joel sorted through his mixed emotions was found in the fact that it was all true. It was all true and there was nothing…, nothing at all that he could do about it except keep on praying like so many others.

Time had rolled around. It was the top of the hour;

7:05 AM. Randy reached down and turned his radio a little louder to catch the morning show. Liberal talk shows and State propaganda was about the only thing left for serious radio listeners.

The once popular conservative talk shows that helped hold America together for so long has long since been banned from the airwaves and internet— 'hate speech'. After a couple of conservative radio talk show host assassinations and attempts; it became clear as to how serious and dangerous Liberal Love and its visions of Utopia had become. And listening to sugar-coated monologues from liberal talk show hosts didn't help in the very least. It in fact made things worse.

"Good Morning..., Good Morning..., Good Morning..., America...! And how good America is this fine day." would be the boisterous and chipper announcers inspiring words shouted out to millions of listeners. "I have three words, America; Beau—Ti—Ful...!

Hey, not only in the nation but right here in beautiful down town Reno, the friendliest city, with the friendliest radio station, KLIF featuring none other than America's friendliest radio talk show host. It's yours truly, me—Sal Salli at your service and to share the love folks—to share the love."

"How sappy is that?" Joel said.

It was only because he found Sal Salli's vibrant

assessment of America just a little disingenuous. Randy turned to Joel with a countenance that totally agreed with his sarcastic remark without even saying a word. In silence, he went right back to watching the road. Sal Salli however went on with his perky upbeat spiel.

"Well ladies, gentlemen, and the gender-select, he's at it again. The news of the morning is big..., B...I...G...G...big! If you haven't heard already, Gaia's Giant—'Antaeus the Great'—Mother Earth's Champion obviously just can't get enough.

Oh how I love this man! We all love him! The man is unstoppable, not only in the ring, not only in Hollywood, not only in California, as if being governor isn't enough; Ezekiel 'Bronze' Solomon is now shooting for, what else...., the Presidency. That's right folks..., you heard right. It's official. Our very own Governor Bronze Solomon has set his sights on being President Manning's successor." Sal bragged.

"Geez...! What next?" Randy moaned.

"Well, it looks like we're on our way to another duly selected president. Humph..., from a wimpy, little wet rag, mommy's boy to a creepy 7 1/2 plus foot giant—a pro wrestler..., with twelve fingers; geez—only in America." Joel hissed in amazement.

"Antaeus the Great...," Randy scoffed shaking his head with a smile, entertaining the thought. "Well at least he's got some balls. Manning..., the little woosie is just flat out embarrassing. The guy sucks big time."

"Woosie or not — his 'useful idiots' adore him — it's sickening. Oh well..., they got what they wanted — they got their dark and dingy, pathetic little liberal-communist paradise." Joel grumbled.

Less than interested in Sal Salli carry on, Joel drifted off as the radio became more and more fleeting and faint. Sal's three words depicting America this morning; 'Beau — Ti — Ful...' stuck in his mind. Far be it as far as Joel was concerned; Randy too for that matter.

It was enough to send Joel into his own personal synopsis of America. He pondered on the country; where it's at in this day and age, its recent history, where it's been, and where it was going. It was far from cheerful. It was actually sad, and depressing, even hopeless if not for Jesus Christ and the Gospel — *'the light of the world'*, the only hope to speak of in his opinion. Still, hope or not..., the State of America was bleak.

-Chapter Five-
STATE OF AMERICA

Taking in the slums of Carson City as they drove through would sink into Joel's thoughts and melt into a depressing story. Almost like reading a book, a narrative if you will, he'd recite his own silent account as to what he now sees in America, and what he's seen. Sal Salli was wrong…, or paid to lie like all the Media.

'Beau—ti—ful'…? The country had already grown dark and was getting darker by the day, so some believed; Randy and Joel being two of them. As usual, each day seemed to be just another day to those who were unfamiliar with the divinely inspired freedom handed down by the Founding Fathers and their Bibles. The sun would rise and the sun would set, and the post-modern norm of incremental leftwing tyranny would faithfully persist as if it was always supposed to be this way.

The nation; now controlled by political mobsters, a nation now financially broke and plagued with class warfare, social upheaval, crime, corruption, illiteracy, censorship, terrorism, viral diseases and an influx of natural disasters was beaten. Still, in the face of all the calamitous headwinds and brokenness, American in-genuity remained quite prevalent. In the midst of its crumbling empire, America managed to keep itself exceedingly busy, wasting no time or opportunity. Within a couple of years, weathering crisis after crisis; the 'Land of the Free' had sewn a new flag. It fash-ioned a new name. It birthed a new spirit, and gave rise to a new agenda to harmonize what else but a new surrogate National Anthem.

The departure of what some had called — God's Grace on Thee — was typical in the eyes and ears of modern America's impressionable children who were of course now brainwashed to think and believe they were no longer Americans, but Global Citizens reared to resent and accuse America of being evil. For them, the hours would come and go, seemingly moving fast-er and faster in light of hyper-technology and a culture glamorizing adolescent sex and promiscuity hurrying them along. And with each passing season rendering another remnant of liberty and freedom burned at the stake, there came another boastful promise from an-other sanctimonious liberal elitist justifying its neces-sity as moving America and the rest of the world that much closer to heaven on earth.

How the larger part of modern America became so stricken with the inability to figure out why they were finding themselves further and further down in the bowels of societal stench and darkness with each and every heavenly promise is perhaps the biggest mystery shrouding its demise. The closer America would supposedly be to their so-called "heaven on earth", the more bias, divided, hateful and combative it would be. The harder it would drive itself to their dreamy politically correct ambitions of global love and peace, social justice, environmental perfection, freedom from religion, fairness and equality the more greedy, seedy and needy, impoverished and enslaved it would become.

One by one, step by step, further and further down the staircase of America's decline, a spoiled, delusional and preoccupied generation bent on pushing the extremities of sexuality, secularism, materialism, tribalism, entertainment, evolutionary godhood and a global utopia was oddly enough conditioned to commemorate, even celebrate the greatest nation's downward spiral into the pit of ugliness and depravity. The quote unquote "greatest nation" that had once been commendably and honorably coined, 'America is great because America is good' was shamefully now laughable in the global community.

Quite frankly, America was no longer worthy of the admirable praise it had once inherited, even merited. It goes without saying that it was also hauntingly emphasized that 'America would seize to be great if it seized to be good'. In short, America was no longer great, but it wasn't because America had seized to be good. It was because America had redefined its definition of good.

Redefining good, redefining God, redefining morality, virtues and ethics, redefining religion, marriage, terrorism, liberty and freedom had redefined America. Redefining genders, redefining racism, redefining smart, excellence and exceptional had redefined America. Redefining compassion, redefining education, and redefining independence had redefined America. Redefining justice, redefining civil rights, fairness, equality, love and hate, redefining what is right and what is wrong had redefined America.

Redefining history, redefining the Constitution, as well as the sanctity of life, redefining unborn babies, redefining family, the police, patriotism, and priorities; all of it, every bit of it had not only redefined America with warped and distorted ideas of what is good and great, but it forged each and every step down into the dank, dark and filthy liberal hellhole it had become. Oddly, the masses heatedly refuse to accept the fact that America was in decline because... truth... itself was also redefined.

After a certain point, the craze was pervasive enough to reflect on the sporadic rise of homeless and destitute street preachers ramping up Biblical significance, Gospel invitations, calls for repentance, prophecy, and of course dire warnings. *"Woe to those who call evil good and good evil..., who put darkness for light, and light for darkness"* ...was one of the standards in a handful of scriptures they would often recite before being arrested for hate-speech, or run off, or beat down, sometimes even killed.

People would marvel, mockingly of course, but marvel just the same at the street preacher's determination, but more so at their courage to voice things that mainstream America had bitterly grown to loathe and despise. The curiously brave preacher's boisterous, yet passionate appeal to anyone who would listen certainly tapped the conscience imprisoned in the back of people's minds, but it was seldom ever enough to squelch their desire and devotion to ignore and laugh off the fanatical ramblings.

Strange, that so many would be so quick to laugh though. Strange, they'd be so quick to snicker and jeer in light of the plague of wretched conditions surrounding them, their families, and their children. Strange that so many would be so quick to roll their eyes and scoff at the fanatical ramblings in light of trying to make ends meet with each and every collective decision and political promise taking their standards of living lower and lower.

All of the descending steps, though they were

decorated and laced with all kinds of new hedonistic freedoms, lewd liberties, outlandish civil rights and eccentric entitlements; the core of the declining staircase was generating more and more complications, more hardships, and more hostility for everyday America. It was only a matter of time before the 'curse of the vicious cycle' had put its noose around the neck of this once wide-eyed and vibrant child of a nation. The worse conditions would get in and amongst its self, the more America's "Fourth Branch" would tighten the noose on society. And the more they'd tighten the noose; what had already gotten worse would faithfully worsen.

After a while, it was crystal clear. The political establishment tending to society had become a gateway to power rather than an obligation to uphold the Constitution on behalf of the people who put them in office. It became a Political Syndicate that was now, at the moment, controlled by President Manning who saw himself as being closer to a mafia kingpin than an American President. Under him it was the Administration, the White House Administration that had come to be known as the "Fourth Branch" turning America into a communist enterprise.

The entire Government, from politicians to the lowest of employees, had tipped the scales and became nothing short of self-serving. Shortening the chain and yanking its leash on the social order was proving to be quite profitable and rewarding for all those directly or indirectly connected to the State. Under President Manning and his Fourth Branch in these latter days, it was now all about the government using society, exploiting society, abusing society, nudging and shoving society and manipulating society to feed the government's insatiable appetite for control.

All those with their eyes open, which were few, could see that the days of politicians, civil servants, and the countless sectors of government serving "We the People" were over. Clearly, it was now the other way around. "We the People" were serving them. The Constitution, America's "babysitter" thoroughly vetted and mentored by America's parents, the Bible and Christendom, though it was extremely resilient it was far from being invincible. Like a lock on a lockbox keeping honest people honest; the Constitution designed to keep an honest government honest had finally been dismantled. After that, the nation quickly fell apart.

America was paying the price. They truly were getting what they deserved. They were getting exactly what they kept voting for; a new America, a modern America, a liberal America, a sensitive and politically correct America, a diverse America, a freethinking America, a more loving and fair America, a smarter and better America that no longer needed to heed the parental components that came with America's founding. In fact, to make it official, they didn't just refuse to no longer heed the parental components that came with Americas founding…, they murdered them in cold blood.

For lack of better words, the larger part of America merged into what could only be described as spoiled-rotten brats; but it was more than that. It was a psychological issue; some say demonic in nature, others say a mental disorder. There is and has always been a cure for it…, it's called 'grow up', but for whatever reasons, this particular group of people purposely refused the cure. These are adults that somehow managed to inherit, or perhaps retain, the same identical mentality to that of the grumbling, disgruntled teenage malcontents and ingrates madly in love with their fabricated intelligence.

It's the typical teenage intelligence, fabricated intelligence that magically pops into their heads one day and magically makes them all-wise, all-intelligent, and all-knowing. The magical intelligence leads them to believe they are victims of parental oppression. Rise up and resist quickly becomes the mantra and battle cry. Thus, in turn, they wage war because their fabricated intelligence magically gives them the intellect, the right, the authority and justification to spitefully attack the parental oppression, which was at one time simply called parental guidance and discretion.

In America's case, they didn't just attack the nation's parental guidance…, after a century of hate and resentment—they ended up murdering the parents. They had a name; and it wasn't…'The Hateful, Grumbling, Disgruntled Teenage-Minded Malcontents, Ingrates, and Victims of America'. No…, they're called Liberals. Regardless of the name, it is they who had finally murdered the parents and the babysitter. They killed the parental components that made America, protected America, and preserved America.

With their pitchforks and torches, the angry mob of disgruntled malcontents hunted down Capitalism and Conservatism. They smothered Capitalism to death and went on to bludgeon and club the life out of Conservatism like clubbing baby seals. They hunted down, captured and burned Fundamental Christianity at the stake. And lastly, the armies of liberalism surrounded and cornered America's 'babysitter', the Constitution, and proceeded to butcher and dismember it—and were happy and glad for it.

Sadly, they'd gloat over their murderous rampage and victory; and for what? What a prize, some victory. The 'Liberal Love-gone Socialist-gone Communist' revolution that cut the mean ol' evil America Empire of European Colonialist down to size and turning it into another third world country in the making; yes indeed — some victory. Electing and putting Marxists, Socialists, and Communists in the White House and Congress; yes — what a prize.

Thanks to Hollywood, Public Education from Daycare to the Universities, complicit parents, and probably the most evil and diabolical of them all; the... Media..., America's last generation was totally oblivious to what they were murdering and what was lost in their 'rise up and resist' revolution to stamp out their evil parental oppressors. In the end, the only thing the liberal minions and supremacists would be told and taught is to be proud of the war they waged; that they were justified, and to salute its victory despite the rotten and rancid fruit it produced.

Joel knew the liberal wrecking ball was bashing up America long before he was even born. But to be in the generation of having to witness the last few bastions of 'old school' America fall, fold and crumble; only to watch the Liberals gloat, boast, and celebrate like ritualistic savages manically chanting, singing and dancing around the bonfire burning their kill was particularly sickening to him. He went on to lament how it all came down and where it landed. Pretending to be free was about all that was left. Finding solace in entertainment helped, but it was a cheap and temporal fix; likened to illicit drugs purchased on street corners.

America...? 2043...? What could be said...? It was no longer the United States of America. It was now the 'United STATE of America'. It was a new America. Some even referred to as such; calling it 'New America', like New Mexico if you will. Putting a leash on society so as to regulate the climate, so as to preserve the environment, and save the planet as well as sustain and uphold the rules of 'social justice' would turn One Nation under God into One Nation under Surveillance.

A new honorary 'Independence Day', now June 13th, was quite fitting as well in view of America's fundamental transformation. Scratching the 4th of July off the list of American holidays, along with Washington and Lincolns birthdays went well with the demolition of Mt Rushmore. Deleting other holidays off the list and tearing down statues and memorials by which to note and commemorate America's history was oddly enough pleasing and joyful to the liberal mobs.

As for the...New Independence Day...; it was still all about winning independence; winning a war. It was winning the 'cultural war'; the war Liberalism waged on all things America — its founding, its Founding Fathers, its Judeo-Christian roots, its battles, its history, its success with capitalism, and it's stature on the world stage. New America's new independence was being liberated from such so-called atrocities and oppression despite the fact that the so-called atrocities and oppressors, America's parental components, gave them the 'liberty and freedom' to rise up and wage such a war.

It remains a mystery as to why and how it could possibly be so; nearly impossible to rationalize, let alone understand Liberalism's war on America. The Liberals had their reason's, there was no doubt about that; plenty of reasons, hundreds of reasons, thousands of reasons to justify their crusade and war on all things America. At the end of the day, however, there was really only one reason to attack America...; it was out of 'sheer hatred'; or in their terms 'sheer love'. It' s amazing; the power people have, and the things they can do with 'fabricated intelligence' — things like fabricating new definitions of words to light up the darkness in their souls. If only the fabrications were honest; then maybe they'd have a sound argument, or at least an excuse for their war and behavior.

Joel, many times over, talked to friends and family about the State of America. At the moment, he couldn't help but reflect on what he'd often say of the Liberals. "They'd hold their cup in the air; a golden chalice with 'love' written on it," he'd say, "with justice, equality, fairness, sensitivity, compassion, diversity, peace, reprisal, and empathy written all over it as well. Yes..., they'd raise their godly cup high in the air to propose a toast, and honor and commemorate everything they stand for. The only problem is…, it was filled to the brim with 'hatred'. It wasn't the cup in their hand they'd consume; it's what was inside the cup."

There were many theories along with both; plenty of accolades, as well as plenty of insults to explain and identify the nonsensical behavior of those who declared a 'cultural war' on America. Still, the fact remains — it happened. Liberalism had finally won, and that's all there is to it.

With new independence came the new flag to commemorate 'New America'. It wasn't anything fancy. It was in fact, if anything, simple, but it spoke volumes. The new flag was still wrapped around symbolism by way of 'colors', but the colors were now revering… 'tribal identity'…; where 'hyphenated-Americans' and 'identity politics' ruled the day. Seven vertical stripes; red, black, brown, yellow, pink, rainbow, and green would now symbolize…race, gender, sexual orientation, and creed. The red, black, brown, and yellow stripes represented race and ethnicity. The pink stripe represented gender diversity and feminism. The rainbow-tinted stripe represented 'sexual orientation'. And the green stripe represented the national creed of environmentalism. These are the tribes of America that converted the 'Supreme Court' to a 'Tribal Council'. These are the tribes that won their so-called independence by winning the 'cultural war'.

By design…, 'white' and 'blue' didn't deserve a place on New America's new flag. Why should they? Why would they? It was, in their minds, the two evil and unjust tribes Liberalism fiercely fought against to gain their independence. It was these two oppressive tribes, white and blue, they were liberated from. Why would they be on the flag?

As for the old flag…, 'Stars and Stripes, the ol' red, white and blue'? It would still be waved and displayed in some circles, a house here and a house there, a store here and a store there. 'Red, white and blue' commodities were still available, and apparel — it would still be sold and worn under certain circumstances, but with great risk, and only if one so dared to do so. Extensive and intense persecution and prosecution, both ravenous and rabid in nature, came with any public display of 'red, white and blue'.

If not shamed into removing it, it would be met with retaliation, hostility, fury, intimidation, badgering and threats that ultimately led to terrorism, riots, vandalism, even violence; all in the name of 'liberal love' and 'social justice'. After the Liberals got away with fabricating another virtue; criminalizing conservatism — those who'd confront, or even attack the Conservatives and Jef's were never really seriously prosecuted; even the hostile and violent ones. In fact, they were more apt to be praised, put on pedestals, turned into heroes, and even deemed as 'patriots'; of which did nothing but give them the incentive to persist, and teach their children to follow suit.

Making things worse; those who dared to publicly display 'red, white and blue' were not only bullied by the New Americans, they were also subject to legal prosecution. Citations, fines, arrests, reparations, and even imprisonment would have the last word on anyone who'd defend or flaunt the 'red, white and blue' in any form or fashion. The crime...; inciting violence, offending people, purposely picking a fight, inviting a brawl, needlessly provoking peaceful citizens, causing trouble, violating political correctness — fill in the blank.

Of course, enforcement couldn't happen without an eager newfangled police force that'd be more than happy to do the honors of policing the evil conservatives and Jef's. 'Domestic Security and Surveillance' (DSS), the 'liberal police', the 'Kings Men', the Civilian Army', the 'Fourth Branch', the 'Police Soldiers', the 'Social Justice Enforcers', the 'Faction Eight Global Police', the 'New Age Gestapo'..., many names, no doubt, but no less one and the same. Young liberal-communist, social justice activists, and 'save-the-planet' do-gooders were the honorable ones who filled the void left by the 'old school police force', who too were shamed, prosecuted, terrorized, demonized, and eventually forced into retirement for upholding the traditions of the 'old school police force'; of which the New Americas redefined as being nothing but 'racists practicing police brutality'.

As for the resistance, those who'd rise up and combat the Liberal Totalitarians mimicking Nazis Totalitarians, whose threatening mantra 'You're either a Nazis or else' was no different than 'You're either a Liberal or else'; it took a while, but they finally made their move to stop the Nazis-like totalitarians. The long anticipated and so-called 'new civil war'; it did indeed happen—'War of the Flags' is what it was called. It was however short lived and never very potent.

Conservative Militias, called the RWB Militias (red, white and blue) were formed when the gun-round-ups ensued; they'd fight and hold their ground, mostly just homes, small businesses, a small handful of neighborhoods and communities, even a few towns here and there, but they never really stood a chance against the power and weaponry of the Faction Eight Global Police. Homes, estates, mansions, and various hideouts in the hills and mountains were like shacks, shanties, and barriers of twigs in the face of the Global War Machine. Strongholds, even ones in the wilderness were easily found and obliterated, most of them in less than a day's work—blast them out, clean it up, and move on to the next one.

Eventually, the RWB Militias peppered across

America dwindled in numbers and strength, and finally surrendered to apathy for the sake of their children—most of them, that is. There were some though who fought to the death—God Bless them. Still, if they weren't demonized by the media; portrayed as evil-doers, then they'd conveniently be exploited for entertainment value, or just flat out never reported on to symbolize they died in vain or were of no importance—like vermin.

It was just as well, Joel thought, because America was no longer sovereign. It was now global in nature; just another neighborhood in the World City. Its borders were opened up and the rest was history. Like a safe and secure family home opening its doors and letting everyone in the neighborhood, and then everyone in the city come in and run it to the ground, this was New America—The United STATE of America. Again; all in the name of 'liberal love' and 'social justice' that such a thing was allowed.

And yet…, still to this day, the Liberal Supremacists and the liberal lemmings blame the Conservatives for the impoverished, decrepit and dilapidated State of America. There are plenty of labels and names to brand and call people who believe such idiocy, but Joel would once again do his best to steer clear from thinking these names, let alone utter them. But, who knows, he may have a change of heart tomorrow and let loose. But that's tomorrow; today is today.

As it sits…, New America this day is one of ten factions in league with the Global Union tending Global Affairs. It is called the Eighth Faction. President Manning isn't really a President in its original sense, he's a Curator. The Eighth Faction is his, as are "We the People" are his; enslaved.

The random checkpoint that he and Randy were forced to endure, but minutes ago; by DSS—it was more than just a checkpoint. It was a reminder as to who owned who. It was a reminder that New America isn't America at all—it's the evil twin that murdered the parents; the parental components of America—Conservatism, Capitalism, and fundamental Christianity, but only after they had the pleasure of raping, molesting and dismembering the nations babysitter—the Constitution.

What makes it so mysterious and impossible to understand, Joel pondered. The fall of America; the disgruntled and bitter teenage-minded liberal malcontents murdering the parents, and dismembering the babysitter—they're happy for it. Yet, they blame and continually blame the parental-minded Conservatives and Jef's for the ugly consequences that stem from their senseless crimes.

As he wrapped up his mental documentary, Joel just closed his eyes and shook his head ever so slightly in disappointment; not anger, just disappointment. "Fabricated intelligence...," he silently surmised. Intelligence built and maintained by fabricated facts, pseudo-definitions, emotions and feelings? It's really what destroyed America. It too took a while, but the devil, he who comes to 'steal, kill, and destroy, finally had his way.

-*Chapter Six*-

TIME TO GO

"So—are you gonna get chipped?" Randy asked.

The question popped out of nowhere and snapped Joel right out of his somber trance. Half alert and absorbing the question, Joel had to take a few seconds to gather his thoughts. As soon as he did he had a quick enough answer.

"No way, dude. There's no way I'm gonna get chipped. What about you? Are you gonna do it?" Joel asked.

"Nope—not me," Randy assured. "These frickin' National ID Cards are bad enough. Rebecca and Jake went ahead and had Sean and Skye chipped though. They bought into the GPS stuff, you know, tracking them in case they get lost or kidnapped. So—are they going to go to hell for taking the—what do you call it—the mark of the beast?" Randy jokingly asked with a short chuckle.

Joel smiled. He couldn't help but go along with the joke. "Oh yeah..., they're going straight to hell. We gotta save 'em. We need to go back and surgically remove those things. Now...!"

"So what is the deal again about the Mark?" Randy

asked. "Cuz I have a feeling all of us are going to have to take that chip sooner or later. If we take it does that mean—you know…?"

"No. Taking the chip by itself doesn't seal anyone's fate. A chip, or an embellishment of the chip or even something else—maybe a tattoo—whatever it is—you have to swear by it and pledge your allegiance to the antichrist when you willfully accept it. When that day comes you'll have a choice. You either pledge your allegiance and take the mark or get executed—beheaded is what the Bible says. It's the pledge that's gonna seal the fate of people in the end.

"What brings this on?" Joel asked.

"I don't know. I was just thinking." Randy answered.

He quickly changed the subject though. He went on to dig into Joel's life a little bit. It wasn't that he was so interested; he was pretty much just passing the time as they cruised along. "So…? How's the lady friend? What's her name…, Leah? Do I hear wedding bells?" he teased.

"No…, no wedding bells. We're just close, like sister and brother sort of close. But, she's fine…, doin' ok. Leah's a great gal. She's witty, funny, smart…, like you Randy," Joel said with a chuckle. Randy rolled into a proud smile accepting the jovial comment like an award.

Joel continued. "Maybe that's why I like her like

a sister, being she reminds me of my brother. As for us, as an item…, nah! But—," Joel added, "if you must know, I have been spending a little time with another girl that might…, well maybe tip over to a more romantic side of things."

"Yeah…, what's her name? Is she a Jesus Freak like you and that Leah chick?" Randy asked poking fun.

"Oh…, brother," Joel chuckled, "No…, I don't think she's a freak, at least not yet, but I'm workin' on it." He joked. She's new to the faith…, new in church."

"Well…, her name—does she have a name?" Randy prodded.

"Julie…, Julie Montez, she's cool—became good friends with Leah too. She wanted to go with Leah to pick me up at the airport, but she had to work."

"Leah…, sounds like she's a pretty nice gal—gotta be the Christian in her…, huh?"

"Yeah…, she's great. We're definitely on the same page. She knows her Bible well, and man…, we get into some deep Bible talk. You ought to join us some time; we'll chat live on line."

"Oh yeah, right…, and put me in coma? I don't think so, fool." Not me…, you can keep your Jesus stuff to yourself. Besides I've heard enough Bible and Jesus crap over the last thirty minutes to last me a life time." Randy joked.

Joel just continued to smirk and chuckle.

"So…, are you gonna tell your gal-pals about our wild and crazy party and how much fun we had?" Randy asked.

"What party?"

"You know. The party we had with DSS. Are ya gonna tell 'em about that Enforcer, how you had to do a table dance for him, and…, and how he was all over you, smothering you with all those hugs and kisses, and sticking dollar bills in your pants."

"Your funny," Joel remark. You're just full of jokes today, aren't you? But, yeah…, I'll tell them. Leah's actually going through the same thing I am. The Coexist Gestapo is after her too. She's not gonna comply with the new ordinances either. It's so unreal. Our Church closed its doors and it's only a matter of time before we're taken to the Camp. I don't know. I just don't want to think about it right now. Right now, I'm thinkin' it'll be good to get back home and settle in—get back into the swing of things."

By this time they were out of Carson City and well on their way up Hwy 50 towards Reno. The clouds had started to break up and it was looking like it was going to be a pretty nice day after all. They were quite sure they wouldn't be hitting any more checkpoints. And Sal Salli rambled on with his liberal Left-wing propaganda. Traffic was light and things seemed to be back to normal. It was peaceful, but not for long. In a second, it all changed. In a second, it all ended.

BAM...., BOOM...! Out of nowhere a shot of lightening cracked across the sky. It startled Randy and Joel, fiercely jolting them, they jumped. If the seatbelts weren't on they probably would have went through the roof. It was loud, deafening, and powerful; so powerful that they not only saw it and heard it, they felt it—a sonic-boom. It went dark within seconds, like an eclipse, like something placed in front of the sun. It wasn't clouds, or smoke..., it was more like a huge blanket..., a sort veil.

In the same moment, the truck came to stand still, so did the oncoming traffic. They all just stopped, but it wasn't on impact. It wasn't like they crashed into something. It was as if they were grabbed by something; grabbed from behind by a giant and held in place. The motor kept running, even straining to move the truck, but the truck wouldn't budge.

Randy too was pinned to the seat, he couldn't move. He yelled and tried to look over at Joel but couldn't turn his head. He was like frozen in place. Looking straight ahead, he could see the oncoming traffic and was able to look in his rearview mirror. He could see that all the other cars had stopped as well, in front of him and behind him. Nothing was moving. He could see the people in the cars closest to him. He could see that they too were pinned in place like he was. He could see them trying to squirm and move. He could even see their eyes, filled with fear, straining to look at their surroundings only to see a mirror image of him doing the same.

Joel was however in a different state. He was free. He was shaking and trembling, but he was free to move about. Things were going down, things he never expected, but nevertheless going down. He looked over at Randy, frozen in place, pinned, and panicking. He leaned over the seat, touched him, and grabbed his arm and tugged on him. He tried to pull and shake him loose, but nothing budged.

It became real clear, real fast; there was nothing he could do. He knew it, he just knew it. Joel heard the voices. As soon as he heard them he knew. Having already pulled back in defeat, he again reached over and put his hand on top of Randy's right hand white-knuckling the steering wheel.

"This is it, Randy. It's time. I've gotta go." Joel explained. Randy again started yelling, not knowing what was happening. He wasn't in pain, he just couldn't move.

"Randy…, Randy…!" Joel yelled so as to overpower Randy's panic. "Listen to me…, I'm going now. I've gotta go. I love you. Tell Rebecca I love her too. Listen, my Bible, get my Bible. It's in my suitcase. Get it. I put something in there for you," he clamored.

He took a quick glance around at everything going on. He was in awe and excited. The feeling that consumed him was beyond imagination, unfathomable. He'd turn back to Randy and bid him farewell one last time. It wasn't slow and sentimental, far from sappy. It was fast and short…, pressing and hasty.

"I'll see you, Randy. I'll see you. Take heed, cling to Jesus and…, well…, just 'believe God'." He pleaded loudly and firm. "You gotta believe Him, Randy." He took one last glance at his brother in silence, a mere second and blurted, "Man…, I gotta go—I gotta go…, Godspeed!"

Randy, out of the corner of his eye, was able to see Joel turn and slide out the door and walk off towards something. A light, a vision, he couldn't quite tell. Grunting and straining, he struggled to wiggle free or at least turn his head, but it was no use. As for Joel, it wasn't but seconds before Randy could see that his brother was gone.

Suddenly, as quickly as it came, the hold, the restraints, whatever it was broke loose. The truck and the oncoming traffic snapped back into motion like a stubborn bolt rusted on an engine cracked by a wrench. Randy and the other drivers nearly collided as they quickly found themselves managing their vehicles instantly moving again at full speed. Jerking and pulling, they swerved past each other. The cars in back of him weren't so lucky. It wasn't a head on collision, but a collision no less. Right away, car's pulled over as they regained control of not only their cars but themselves. By this time, the instant darkness that fell upon them was already gone as if it never went dark in the first place.

After he slammed his truck to stop, Randy ran back to where Joel disappeared or where he thought he saw that light thing just out of his sight. He yelled and yelled for him. There was nothing, so it seemed. It would be on the ground, everything that was left of Joel. His clothes; pants, shirt and shoes, everything he was wearing lying still, quiet, empty and bodiless. Randy buckled to his knees, frantically looking down and around, and sifting through Joel's clothes he panicked even more.

He'd run his hand over his head in bewilderment and confusion; wondering what was going on. There was really nothing to go on. He didn't know what to do. He heard some hollering and a ruckus within earshot of where he planted himself. It was coming from the other drivers, coming from where the crash was. "Where's my baby? My little girl, Sarah…, SARAH…," came screeching out of the small panic-stricken collage of people. He jumped up and ran over to them, not only to help them but to find out about Joel. Maybe he was over there. He didn't know.

Running into the heart of the small gathering, he'd be stopped short. Grabbing Randy's arm, "Did you see it," one of them asked all wound up. It was a middle-aged woman about his age.

"What," Randy asked. "See what?"

"The stairs…, the light…, that guy…, that guy in your truck. He just walked in and he was gone," she hysterically ranted.

"Walked into what?"

"I don't know, but I saw it. I saw something like…, like a door, stairs…, I don't know, something weird. That guy in your truck, he just got out like he was holding someone's hand and walked into it and…, and he was gone. All of it, it all disappeared. Everything ended. It was right in front of me, I saw it. It was about all I could see," she nervously blurted

Randy just looked at her. He didn't know how to answer her let alone what to ask. He was dumbfounded, mixed up, even delirious. He was quickly drawn back to the commotion, the crowd and the woman desperately carrying on about her missing daughter. He hustled in to see if he could assist in any way, but clearly there wasn't anything there for him to do.

Everybody was in shock squabbling as to what had just happened and tending to the injured and the raving woman. Three people were injured, but not seriously. The front of their SUV clipped the back side of a car that swerved across the lane in front of them. It sat upside down about forty feet away. It was a little Toyota Corolla, an older model twisted and mangled up from the collision and rolling over several times.

"There isn't any driver. The driver's gone," was the standout words coming out of the other handful of people tending to the Corolla. The buzz was all over, going back and forth about the missing girl and the bizarre standstill. People were searching the premises to see if maybe the driver was tossed out but there was nobody there to be found. In the mix was a young man, early twenties or so; a kid from Randy's perspective who kept on insisting that the woman driving the Corolla was gone because she disappeared. Randy heard him telling others that she just got out of her car when everything was frozen and stopped, walked over into this light thing and disappeared with the light, insisting she was abducted by aliens. It was the same exact thing that the woman who pulled Randy aside said about Joel.

Randy quickly went up to him, "Where...?" he asked. "Where did she disappear?"

He pointed, "Back there."

"Please, please show me" Randy pleaded.

They hurriedly took a walk, even halfway jogging back up the road, away from the ruckus to where the guy thought he saw the woman get out of her car and disappeared in the beam or light or whatever it was he saw on the side of the road.

"There…, right there," the kid said as they neared the end of their short destination.

"Oh no…," Randy uttered and started running ahead. The kid just looked at him and followed. He really didn't see what Randy had already spotted. The clothes, the women's clothes like Joel's, lay alone whisking and strewn about from the wind.

"Oh, God…, oh no," Randy spoke out loud. "I don't believe it…, no way."

"What…?" the kid asked.

"It was the Rapture." Flustered and nervous, "The Rapture, it was the Rapture…, the Bible, you know, the Bible, the Christians…," Randy tried to convey, but it was useless. The kid didn't know what he was talking about. He did however know all about the prize laying there in the midst of the ladies belongings. He quickly bent down and picked up a beautiful gold diamond ring. He shuffled the clothes a little more and found a gold necklace as well.

"Whatta doing," Randy snapped at the kid.

Defensive, cocky and shrugging, "I don't know…, she's gone. I may as well have 'em. There's no sense in leaving 'em here." the kid justified as he slipped the treasures into his pocket. "I mean…, if she comes back or we find her, I'll give them back," the kid assured.

Thinking it wrong, shaking his head, half surprised and half disappointed, "Jeez...," Randy questioned. For a second, it bothered him to see how the kid was so easily lured away from everything going on with a couple pieces of jewelry.

"What....?" the kid barked to confront Randy's scrutiny.

"Never mind," Randy said as he turned to scamper back to get Joel's things left on the ground. He took a couple of steps and abruptly stopped. He was stopped dead in his tracks. Caught of guard, both he and the kid were met with a very unwelcoming sight.

"What the hell...?" the kid snapped.

About fifty feet or so, pacing back and forth was a small pack of coyotes; six, seven, nine or ten. It was hard to tell and counting them was the last thing on their mind. They were off to the side a bit but sneaked in far enough to cut them off from heading back to the scene of the accident. Randy and the kid froze. Leery and unsure; they just stared at the unpredictable gang of wild canines. The coyotes didn't appear to be scared, hesitant maybe but not scared. They didn't even look curious. They looked dangerous and they were dangerously close.

"Whatta we do," the kid nervously whispered.

"Don't move," was about all Randy could think of saying without really knowing what to do.

Twitching, yelping and snarling like hyenas, they seemed to be anticipating as to whether or not to attack. One would dart in a couple of feet, but stop short, then another, and another, then two as if they were taking turns, taunting each other, daring each other to be the first to go in for the kill. Randy could see a couple of them were foaming at the mouth. He was scared, really scared. It was enough to even draw him away from what had just happened with Joel and everything else going on. It all vanished for the moment. Right now it was him and his young guide facing off with these rabid coyotes that mattered, nothing else.

Suddenly, hearing a car come up the road from behind them, the kid just quickly turned around and took off running towards it away from the threat. It was enough to trigger the coyotes, they immediately charged. With the kid high-tailing it, leaving Randy there to confront the coyotes on his own, Randy didn't hesitate. He reacted and reacted fast. He took off running as well, but off to the side going across the road. Thankfully the car had already slowed down trying to figure out what was up with the kid. The coyotes split as they neared them. Of the bunch, only one went after Randy, the rest raced towards the kid banging on the windows of the car.

Randy could hear him yell. "Let me in, let me in," he screamed. "Please…!" The people in the car wouldn't be so kind. It wasn't but seconds before the raving coyotes would catch up and attack each of them. As for the car, it sped off. Randy already on the other side of the road turned on the lone coyote as it grabbed him by the heel. He'd fall to the ground, turn and start kicking for dear life. Kicking, and kicking, yelling and using his fist to fight off his attacker was the only thing he could do. It worked. After a handful of seconds, thirty seconds maybe, the coyote dashed off to join his gang of killers.

By this time, the kid's blood-curdling screams were over. They didn't last long once the larger part of the pack caught up to him and ripped him apart. He tried to run and even made it over an embankment into a ditch, but that was it. It was a horrible sound. It bothered Randy. Even though it was over quickly and already running back to the crowd as fast as he could, he could still hear the screams echoing in his head. The crowd had also heard it off in the distance, but couldn't really make out what was going on.

Looking on, they saw Randy running towards them. As he came up, he paused and cautiously looked back to see if there was any more danger in pursuit of him. Gasping, out of breath, hunched over with his hands clinching his knees he'd address the curious on-lookers now wondering what else could possibly be going on.

"There's a…, a pack of…, a pack rabid coyotes back there," he'd get passed his lips in between catching his breath. "They attacked us. They attacked us and that kid…, that kid that was with me," he said. "They killed him. You gotta get outta here," Randy warned. "Be careful". He looked around for the car that abandoned the kid, but it was nowhere in sight. It kept on going, even past the scene of the accident. He then straightened up, took in a big sigh and another deep breath. Seeing no reason to stay, he simply rushed off without another word.

Running back to his truck, he was already deeply thinking about what happened to Joel. He needed to make one more stop. On the side of the road, where his brother disappeared, Randy took a moment and gathered up everything that was left of him. From there, it was off to the truck just up ahead. Getting there, he hurriedly tossed Joel's stuff into the cab as he slipped into the driver's seat. He grabbed his phone sitting on the dash. He was so fixated on the weird account that he didn't even think about grabbing it as he rushed back to find Joel.

It was now however back in the palm of his hands. Even though he was sure people had already called 911 to report things, he couldn't help but do the same. It was mainly to report the horrible fate of the young kid. 911 he dialed. It would be nothing but a humming buzz that would answer. He tried it again, the annoying buzz. A third time, slower, making sure he was hitting the right numbers…, again nothing but static. He hit his speed dial, calling Jake and Rebecca. It was futile. Annoyed, "Forget it," he snapped. Wasting no time, he just tossed the phone down on the seat and started the truck.

He'd make a speedy U-turn so as to head home, back to South Lake Tahoe, but quickly stopped. He was torn. There was a part of him that felt he needed to stay there and look or even wait for Joel. Again, he just didn't know what to do.

He screamed as if he was in pain. "What do I do? What to do," he yelled. The radio was still on, but buzzing with static. Sal Salli was gone. He turned the dial to see if anything would come through. Maybe there'd be some answers, but like his phone it was useless. Harshly, he turned it off. He took a few moments to make a decision. It didn't take long. It was time to move.

He'd make his way past the scene of the accident as safely, but as fast as he could. By this time, a larger crowd had gathered. The ones who barely saw the coyote attack or believed Randy's warning were already back in their cars or gone. The rest were oblivious.

Driving through, he carefully scoured the premises in search of the crazed coyotes or more lurking about.

He didn't see any. There was something else he didn't see. No police, no paramedics or an ambulance, none of them were there tending to the fiasco. He thought it odd. As he observed the people busily moving about, back and forth, and in and out of the area, he was sure that they too were being challenged. He was sure that the more and more they were finding out, the more and more frantic and confused they were becoming; just like him.

Randy managed to get passed the main commotion, but only to be taken back to where the kid was killed. His stomach went sour and cramped up as he approached the spot where it all happened. He'd slow down, way down. He thought about the woman who disappeared like Joel. He even took a second to think about the little girl that the one lady was screaming about. Fighting off the coyote quickly crossed his mind. He thought about how he was able to kick it off without getting bit. Deciding to wear his thick work boots this particular morning paid off.

The thoughts only amounted to a handful of seconds. A few seconds more would put him at the very spot where he briefly saw the kid desperately running over the embankment only to be devoured. Randy was glad that he couldn't see over the embankment and into the ditch. He didn't even want to imagine the grisly mess left at the scene of the beast's crime. It wouldn't however be enough to squelch the haunting screams now planted in his memory. He felt bad, really bad for the kid. So much so that he was tempted to stop and tend to him. But logic won. He knew there was nothing he could do and the coyotes were still out there. Besides, there was already too much to do. He had other things, more important things to consider and worry about.

He'd step on the gas and go. His thoughts, racing as fast as his truck, would race through his head. So many questions, so many scenarios, everything; it was just so much to think about. The only thing he knew was he just didn't know. He didn't know what to expect, what was ahead of him, or even if he'd make it back. Where's Joel? Was it over? Those coyotes, how weird? Was there more to come? Was it the Rapture? Was it something else? It was so overwhelming, everything. Everything that had just happened, all within thirty minutes would take Randy nearly over the edge. But he wasn't the only one. Far be it.

In a modest two bedroom upstairs apartment, it would be on the outskirts of Tucson, Arizona where Leah would find herself on her knees sobbing to no end. In the middle of her living room floor, on her knees one minute, and the next she'd be laying facedown clawing the carpet in a desperate attempt to grasp it in utter despair. Leah would find no comfort. There would be no comfort, no comfort at all. The minutes would pass, and like a wounded and dying animal, she'd once again scrounge up just enough strength to drag her self across the floor in search of something..., anything.

She really didn't know where she was going, let alone where to go. Inching her way, weeping and crawling without any direction, without a compass, it would be her bedside where she'd finally end up this time around. Using the sheets, blankets and spread, anything she could cling to, she lifted herself up to her knees once again. Proving to be as repetitive as a broken record, Leah would again scream in agony. Boiling with rage she'd yell in anger and shoot her rattled thoughts off in every direction. She wanted Him to hear. She wanted Him to know just how furious and broken she was. And as the broken record of emotion moved around, she would find herself right back where she started, exhausted and hoarse. She'd cower and collapse, she'd bury her face in the sheets, only to whimper, sob and plead one more time.

"Oh Lord..., LORD...please. Why...? Why, Lord...? Why...? Oh, GOD...., please don't leave me," she'd softly beg.

"Please come back. Jesus. Please..., please, don't

leave me here. Come back. Come back...," over and over again. It would however be to no avail.

Mildly impaired with marijuana and the residue of an all-night drinking binge, her daughter, Nicki Dawn, being now just short of seventeen years old would step out of her hateful and unruly character long enough to actually console her mother for the first time in her young adult life. Being nothing but trouble and a painful heartache for Leah over the last six years, Nicki was suddenly taken in with compassion and sympathy towards her mother. It would be the first time since she was a child. Hardly remembered; a precious, young, naïve, but sensitive and insightful little child holding her mother, softly and gently rocking back and forth, it would be Nicki as early as four years old who'd comfort her hurting mom over the years.

Unstable, living from room to room and back to the car again, round and round they went. It was rough. Leah was quite successful when it came to losing jobs and establishing abusive relationships. Being formally introduced to every insecurity, every snare, every trial and hardship that comes with a young and reckless single mother's legacy, it would be Nicki Dawn helping her face and endure the onslaught of all her mistakes. Leah would eventually clean up and get her life somewhat together, but Nicki had fallen away; drugs, alcohol, promiscuity, defiant, heartless, Godless..., the works.

The warm and sentimental relationship in their early years, being an essential part of their survival had disappeared with Nicki's loss of innocence. Leah's concerted efforts to mend and smooth out their indifferences were futile. Nicki would shun her mom's conciliatory gestures over the years. She had a new life, a life that Leah knew well. The old adage, "the apple doesn't fall far from the tree" would once again prove to be true. It's been a harsh and abrasive relationship that worsened by the day. Nicki kept it cold and distant. She glamorized her defiance and more often than not, she'd fan the flames.

Still, Nicki would set it all aside when she saw her mom howling in despair after the Rapture. She'd kneel by her grieving mother. She'd silently caress her back and stroke her long dark hair now horribly disarrayed. She would attempt to wipe Leah's swollen and tear stricken face with a cool damp washcloth every chance she'd get. She'd hold her, she'd softly and gently rock with her like she used to when she was that precious little child. She'd cry with her.

Yes, Nicki too would be crying. She was again, naïve and really unable to fully understand her mother's anguish as she was so many times before as a child dealing with her mother's grief. But, like then, she knew something was horribly wrong. She knew her brokenhearted mom of seventeen long years needed her more now than ever before.

This time however would be different. It was much more than just being there. As tough, strong willed and independent and even invincible as Nicki made herself out to be with all of her godless friends and Chad, her likeminded boyfriend, she found out quickly just how vulnerable and frail she truly is. In the past it was always all about being there for her mom, but this time she found herself needing her mom just as much as her mom needed her.

What happened to Nicki during the Rapture was quite sobering to say the least. Like many, it slapped the stupid, and the defiance and the arrogance right out of her. Nicki was scared. She too was frightened and burning with anxiety, uncertainty, and now guilt. She too was frazzled, disturbed and shaking. Even so, it was really nothing compared to Leah. It wasn't even close.

Unlike her beloved, but unruly daughter, Leah was a believer. She was a Born Again Christian, a Jesus Fundamentalist like Joel. And like him, she too was fairly well-versed and devout. She wasn't a half-hearted believer; she was a true, hardcore believer.

Even though it had become extremely unpopular, offensive and even dangerous in public, she believed God. She believed the Bible, she believed the Gospel of Jesus Christ with all her heart, mind and soul. She believed and she knew the Rapture was imminent and sure. Like Joel and with Joel, she looked forward to it along with every other Rapture-believing Christian.

She would even faithfully and politely encourage and invite her cherished daughter to join her every chance she'd get. She so wanted Nicki to have what she had found, being an inner peace like no other. The Holy Spirit; it was an inner peace that somehow defies and thwarts all doubts, worries and circumstances that comes with life. It was comforting, convicting and relieving.

Leah was living proof that there was an abundance of hope and joy in Christ, joy in believing, and even joy in hardships and trials as the Apostle Paul shared. Like many, she would however be put to the test as of now. Hope and joy? For Leah, it had seemingly come and gone in light of what had just happened a few hours ago.

Finding comfort in a promise made by Jesus himself would now mean more than anything. Leah would need it more than ever. She would have to put her faith in it more than ever. She would have to trust it more than ever.

"....*and lo, I am with you always, even to the end of the age.*" was the promise. It would however take time to rekindle hope and joy in such a beautiful promise. Like any serious wound, the cut in Leah's heart was not only fresh, but deep. It would not heal over night; if it was to even heal at all. Right now, as comforting and beautiful as the promise is and has always been, it wasn't even on the radar. Leah, like so many other Christians, was just too distraught, too numb, dumbfounded and confused, and even too angry to pluck out encouraging scriptures to soften the hammering blows of anguish and brokenness.

Here she was a true believer; a Born Again stuck, locked in and still lumped with the unbelievers. Here she was, defeated and left to contend with the Tribulation looming over the horizon. Here she was traumatized, broken and lost. In essence or for a lack of better words, Leah, as a believer, a true believer had missed the boat.

-Chapter Seven-

TEN MAIDENS

It would be Leah who would truly know the meaning of being "left behind". It would be Leah who had to find out the hard way that being "left behind" wasn't anything like all the books she had read or movies she had seen. Being "left behind" wasn't supposed to be for believers. According to all the books and movies and seemingly every other Christian, believers, all believers, all Born Again Christians were supposed to be instantly and automatically whisked away, right out of their socks in the "twinkling of an eye" without warning.

Sadly, for Leah and so many others, it wasn't quite that simple. Sadly, for Leah and so many others, they paid a heavy price for thinking and believing the Rapture was actually going to be as simple and easy as the movies and books made it seem. Sadly, for Leah and so many others, they had put their trust in a fabrication that left them totally unprepared.

In short, Leah was misled. She was tricked. She was in a sense indoctrinated with a false impression. She was led to believe she was ready for the Rapture of the Church when in truth..., she wasn't; as so many other

Born Agains had to find out. They saw a movie and they assumed. They read a book and they assumed. They jumped on a bandwagon and they assumed. They entertained a popular notion that was most convenient, outwardly plausible, and showy; and they assumed.

Led to believe it was all about…"poof"…and the Born Again Christians were gone, Christians instantly disappearing, without warning, in the "twinkling of an eye" proved to be not only a gross misinterpretation of the scriptures, but a crucial, devastating and irreversible mistake for many, too many believers. It would be a mistake that would leave them more vulnerable now than ever before. It would be a mistake that could easily end up costing them their very souls in the long run if they weren't careful.

Leah would be one of these Born Again Christians who had to live with this unfortunate mistake. It is why she was reacting so…, so lost…, so alone…, and forsaken. It would compete with the thought of Noah's wife being unable to make it inside the Ark as the hatch was closed. This is what had Leah and so many other Born Agains pacing the floor and in fetal positions weeping, squirming, crawling and howling in agony. This is what had her stomach in knots, her head in a vice and her heart on the ground. This is what was horribly tormenting her as Nicki Dawn did everything she could to lessen her misery.

Unlike the larger part of the world grieving in like-manner, Leah didn't lose a child or a pregnancy or loved one. Leah lost something else. Leah lost her chance to be raptured.

The door was open, it was right there within a matter of steps, and she lost it. The door slammed shut. The hatch was closed. It was time to go, but the time came and went. She missed the boat that would have carried her away from this ill-fated island in the center of the universe being plunged into the Supernatural Age.

Leah lost her chance in a way she never expected. She wasn't prepared. It was as simple as that. She was ready, but she wasn't prepared. Like soldiers in arms ready for battle without ammunition, like football players and spectators ready for the Super Bowl without a football, or a patron in New York City waiting for a cab with no money in his pocket, like a NASCAR driver raring to race with no gas in his car; too many Born Again Christians were ready for the event, but unprepared to address it.

Jesus had told the believers how it would be. In one of his passages he told of ten maidens eagerly waiting for the bridegroom's arrival. Like the Rapture, his arrival was imminent and sure, but the exact time was hidden from them. So the maidens waited, knowing he would come whilst knowing he could come at anytime, even unexpectedly. All ten maidens believed he was coming. All ten knew he was coming. It could even be said that all ten maidens were ready. It would however be only five of them who would go. Five were taken and five were left because of the ten, only five were truly prepared.

It was really quite simple and quite clear. Merely believing and anticipation is not being ready. Being prepared, on the other hand, is. This is and has always been the whole point behind Jesus' short, but insightful parable. It would be a parable that too many Christians were swayed to overlook and quite frankly forget.

All the Born Again Christians that were indoctrinated to think and believe the Rapture was to happen just like the books they had read and the movies they had seen were in for a rude awakening. Even those who had written the books and promoted the books, along with all those who had their part in glamorizing and popularizing the movies that captivated mainstream Christianity were shaken.

In short, the…"zap rapture"…was a lie. The only thing it did was prepare the Believers to be unprepared. Because of it, too many believers were caught off guard instead of caught up in the clouds. Leah would be one of the sheep led astray. Leah would be one of many sheep prepared to be unprepared.

Too many believers assumed the Rapture was judgment; the righteous go up and the unrighteous don't. The believers go, the unbelievers don't. They were wrong. The Rapture wasn't judgment, it was just an opportunity. It wasn't so much about Jesus saving His own from the Tribulation to come as it was Jesus giving His own an opportunity to escape it.

Leah assumed her anticipation and belief in the Rapture was the ticket to automatically ride the Rapture Train, as if she was already on the train. When in truth; anticipation and belief in the rapture was nothing more than the ticket that opened the door to the train. The train arrived as promised, as anticipated. The door would be opened to Leah as it was Joel. The opportunity would be given to them.

Stepping onto the train however required a lot more than anticipation and belief. It required faith, real faith and unwavering trust. It was something that the books, the movies and mainstream Christianity miserably failed to mention to the believers.

Though the barrage of books and popularized movies were saturated with extremely good intentions, sincerity, and presented as a service to God, it was risky business. Even though they were in effect faithful and true to God's Word, and loyal to the Bible, and a mighty plug for the Gospel of Jesus

Christ; misinterpreting, and shortchanging and second guessing the Scriptures in regards to something so powerful, so critical, important and life changing as the Rapture of the Church was something that needed to be carefully, very, very carefully thought out before tossing it out into the mainstream spotlight for all to see, for all to digest, consume and ultimately believe.

Getting the entire world familiar with the Bible's Rapture was a wonderful thing; noble and praiseworthy. Going so far as to encourage the entire world to believe it or at least consider it was even better. Letting the entire world know that it was imminent; that it could happen at any moment was also a wonderful and mighty thing. But getting them to think and believe it was going to be…"zap"…and all the believers would instantly disappear proved to be quite damaging. POOF…, out of nowhere and you're gone turned out to be a terrible and insufficient telling of the truth.

One could only speculate about all those who had their part in originating, shaping, promoting, teaching, preaching, glamorizing and popularizing the "zap rapture". In all honesty, the wrong and disservice really wasn't so much about theorizing the "zap rapture" as it was flooding the entire world with it and popularizing it and glamorizing it to the point of indoctrinating too many for too long with it. The movies, the books, the preaching and the teachings, even with the very best of intentions, fervent prayer, and Jesus on their hearts weren't very well thought out when it came to the Rapture.

Prematurely, even hastily flooding the world with nothing short of another half-truth methodically orchestrated and implemented by none other than Satan, the "*Father of Lies*" did its harm to many Born Again Christians. Satan had once again done what he has been known to do best; tweak the truth just enough *"to steal, and to kill, and to destroy"*, as Jesus puts it. And that it did. His methodical ruse to condition the Rapture Believing Christians with a false impression, false security, a false idea and false doctrine served him well.

Getting the believers to believe in the "zap rapture" instead of the "freewill rapture" had indirectly managed to...'*steal*'...many believers one and only chance to escape. '...*to kill*..., it had already managed to take fragile and unstable believers down the avenue of suicide. There was no telling as to how many more souls would be lost in the Tribulation; souls that would have otherwise been saved had they been prepared with the truth instead of misled with a glamorous and popular assumption. As for...'*and to destroy*'...in Satan's bag of tricks; it has certainly destroyed Leah now struggling with how the Rapture really went down.

It wasn't secret. It wasn't quiet. And it wasn't

visually selective. The entire world witnessed it in its entirety. The entire world saw what the believers saw. The entire world heard everything the believers heard. The only difference was the unbelievers were held in place, completely restrained. They were conscious, awake; privy and able to see it all go down. They could yell and scream, but they couldn't move.

Time wasn't stopped, seconds passed as normal. It wasn't that they were frozen. It was more along the lines of being held by unseen forces and heavily weighted down; held to the point of barely being able to clinch their fingers and turn their heads, let alone lift their arms and move their legs. Outside of these details hidden and omitted from the Scriptures for whatever reasons, everything went down exactly as the Bible described it and promised; exactly how the Apostle Paul foretold.

'For the Lord Himself will descend from heaven with a shout, with the voice of an archangel, and with the trumpet of God. And the dead in Christ will rise first. Then we who are alive and remain shall be caught up together with them in the clouds to meet the Lord in the air. And thus we shall always be with the Lord. Therefore comfort one another with these words.'

As promised, the Rapture did indeed come without

warning. It ended up taking all those who died in Christ from past generations first as promised. The believers who were still alive were indeed whisked away and caught up in the clouds with Jesus as promised.

'In a moment, in the twinkling of an eye', at the last trump...' they were even changed into incorruptible bodies as promised. But, the Rapture also came with something else; something that all the movies, and all the books, and the bulk of Christians for whatever reasons, by whatever powers somehow managed to overlook. The Rapture came with an option. It came with God's eternal gift of freewill.

The Rapture came with a certain amount of time allotted between its arrival and its departure. It wasn't a certain amount of time allotted for the whole world including the Born Agains to sit there in awe. It wasn't a certain amount of time allotted for people to let out all of their ooooh's and aaaah's or to scream for dear life. No, this would not be the case.

The very short and limited time allotted during the Rapture was for the believers and the believers only. It was a certain time allotted for them to make a decision; to use their gift of freewill and make a decision. Should I go or should I stay?

It would be a decision that all believers were forewarned about. It would be a decision that they were emphatically told many times over that they would one day have to make. Yes..., the children, the precious little children, toddlers and the unborn babies and the mentally innocent would be gathered by the Angels and whisked away without having to make a decision, but for the believers, it would be different. The believers would have to decide.

For some, it was a very simple and easy decision. It was easy for Joel. Yet, for as many there were who had found it to be so simple and easy, there'd be just as many who would find the decision to be extremely difficult. Leah unexpectedly found out she was one.

Too many believers didn't think they would actually have to think when the Rapture came. "Zap..., you're gone"; what's there to think about? This is what sabotaged their better judgment.

Like Leah, most of the Believers were flat out petrified when the Rapture came. They found themselves in a stupor, confused, and unsure, suspicious, reluctant, fearful and yes..., unprepared, just like '*the ten maidens*' Jesus spoke of in His parable. Spending all their believing days expecting to be instantly whisked away in the "*twinkling of an eye*", without warning, without thinking just like the books and movies made it real easy to be overconfident and complacent. Their confidence however wasn't set on the Scriptures per se; their confidence was set on what many pulpits, books and movies had taught them.

Born Agains found it easy to believe, but having to choose left most of them in shock. Most of them really didn't know what to do; it was so sudden, but far from instant. The believers, all the believers knew what it was. They knew exactly what it was. They knew it was the Rapture. They could feel the indescribable glory, the warmth, the gentle tug, even the touch of Jesus himself. It was friendly, powerful and inviting. And the Voice upon voices..., voices high and low..., so soothing, gentle, kind and welcoming.

"Do not fear."

"Do not be afraid."

"Come. Come." would be Jesus, and Angels beckoning, whispering, inviting, encouraging and calling. It was beautiful, so peaceful and unimaginable. There wasn't any doubt about it. The believers knew exactly what it was, yet many, too many would balk and hesitate. They just weren't prepared. They were so conditioned and dead-set on being "zap, you're gone", that they just could not fathom let alone register the impact of having to make a decision.

Too many would over think. Too many would analyze. They'd step back examine, and weigh it out. Over the course of a couple of minutes they'd attempt to assess everything that they would be leaving behind. Did they miss something? Did they need to do something first, turn off the stove, leave a note? Did they need to hide something or get rid of something, something embarrassing; something that would leave loved ones with a bad image of them? Did they need to get something, get their kids from school, or inform their spouse, say goodbye to their parents or quickly feed their dog or grab their cat?

Like the ten maidens eagerly anticipating their bridegroom, the Born Agains were as ready as anyone could ever be for the Rapture, but prepared they were not. It would cost them dearly. Stricken with their unseen love and attachment to the world would end up leaving many believers in the wake of finding out just how prone and unready they really were.

It truly was heartbreaking as Leah would have to find out. So many Christians, brave, so courageous and confident to think themselves as being one who would be willing to die for Jesus found out that they weren't even able to take His hand and peacefully walk away with Him. Oh, did they ever have to find out the hard way, and find out quick.

Like the maidens waiting for their bridegroom; believing would not be enough. Knowing would not be enough. And waiting and anticipating would not be enough. The Born Agains were allotted just enough time to choose one way or the other. They would ultimately have to decide. They would have to make a choice. Like Joel, Leah too had to decide.

Would it be Jesus...or...the world? Should they stay or should they go? Should they leave their life or hold on to their life? After it was all said and done, it could not be said that they were not told.

"In that day, he who is on the housetop, and his goods are in the house, let him not come down to take them away. And likewise the one, who is in the field, let him not turn back. Remember Lot's wife. Whoever seeks to save his life will lose it, and whoever loses his life will preserve it. I tell you, in that night there will be two men in one bed: the one will be taken and the other will be left. Two women will be grinding together: the one will be taken and the other left. Two men will be in the field: the one will be taken and the other left."

It was Jesus himself who had made it so very clear. The passage wasn't about...believers...and...unbelievers...being taken and left as the books and movies and mainstream Christianity made it seem and led so many to believe. Like the maidens, it was for the believers; some will be taken and others will be left. Whether it was some believers would be taken by Jesus and the others will be left in the world, or some believers would be taken by the world and others would be left in the hands of Jesus, it was the same.

In light of the scriptures pointing out that all Born

Agains are given over into the hands of Jesus; one taken by the world and the other left in the hands of Jesus was fitting when it came to the Rapture of the Church. Regardless, no matter how one would want to interpret it, it was what it was...; many, too many believers were not taken in the Rapture. Of the maidens, five taken five left, in light of two in a bed, one taken one left, in light of two woman grinding grain together, one taken one left, in light of two men in a field one taken one left; it was as much as necessary to imply that half of the Born Again Christians lost their chance.

It of course was impossible to know; only God knew how many were taken and how many were left. The exact number was really beside the point. The point was Leah wasn't alone. There would be hundreds of thousands, if not millions of other Born Again Christians dealing with the same personal tragedy.

As for Leah, she wasn't on a housetop. Nor was she in a field or grinding grain with another woman. She was right there in her living room. And it would be Nicki who'd she'd go back for. It was Nicki, screaming and yelling for help that Leah chose to run back to in spite of the love filled touch of Jesus and the Angels beckoning and calling her.

The Rapture came and it went. It would be Nicki instead of Jesus that Leah would decide to cling to.

Losing her life to preserve her life fell through. And it would be the world instead of the clouds where Leah would end up. The pain was unbearable. The agony, the despair and regret was overwhelming.

Losing her chance was taking its toll on Leah. It was killing her from the inside out. And there would be no hiding it. She was angry, even furious that she was forced to make such an impossible decision..., Jesus or Nicki.

-Chapter Eight-
'AMELIA, AMELIA'

"IT...ISN'T...FAIR!" she screamed as loud as she could. Straightening her posture, rigid and clinching her fist, Leah again found herself looking straight up at the ceiling, yelling at the top of her lungs with everything she had. Sharp, loud, and to the point. She so wanted to blame God..., blame Jesus for her own lack of better judgment. But then again, was it bad judgment to stay? Like vocal cannonballs, she'd fire them off one by one; scolding God, scolding Jesus. She had to let them know that it was their fault, not hers as to why she lost her chance.

"Why...? Why...?" she blasted. "You know I wanted to go. You know I would have gone. You should have waited, if you had only waited? I believed you! I trusted you!"

She gasped and took in another big breath and shouted again, even louder.

"Why couldn't you have waited? Is this how you treat those who love you? Is this how you repay all those who have given their life to you? And trusted you? You leave us here to...DIE! Or expect us to just take off and leave our children behind to DIE!

This isn't the way it was supposed to be, DAMN IT!!!"

It would be anger again sneaking into the heart of Leah as she desperately tried to cope and deal with her anguish. Nicki would have to step back every time Leah would be moved to vent her rage. Wisely, she dared not speak a word to Leah at the height of her fury. No words of comfort, no words of encouragement or agreement…, nothing. She remained silent and still.

Nicki wasn't about to leave her though. She would patiently wait it out. She'd go back to peeking out the windows, checking the TV, attempt to make some calls, but she'd be more than ready to approach her mother after each and every fit of outrage.

After the fury would subside, again and again Nicki would not hesitate to tenderly slide in next to her and absorb as much tension and pain as she possibly could. It would be then and only then, after Leah had simmered down that Nicki dared to speak a word to her mother. Even then, there wasn't much to say. Still, though the words were short and few, they were meaningful and to the point.

"I'm sorry, mom. I'm so sorry" was about all that Nicki could say. She couldn't help but feel guilty. After listening to her mother's raving rants and prayers come and go she pretty much got it. Nicki understood why her mom was so upset in a way that totally differed from the reason why she was upset. Nicki was flat out frightened and scared; Leah on the other hand was suffering a broken heart.

Nicki knew the whole concept of the Rapture of the Church, being that her mom and Joel shared it with her over the years. Scoffing and rolling her eyes this time however was no longer an option. Even though Nicki really couldn't bring herself to say for sure that it was the Rapture and her mom actually missed it, whether it was or wasn't, her mom thought it so. So, Nicki rolled with it, which went on to suggest, even tell her that Leah actually missed her chance to be raptured because of her, Nicki thought. This is why Nicki was touched with a sense of guilt. This is why she was more inclined to say sorry to her mournful mother more than anything else.

Nicki's gentle apology and soothing words spoken so soft and calm was a sharp contrast to the words she was saying and how she was saying them immediately before and after the Rapture; or during the Rapture for that matter. During the Rapture, being so intense, so terrifying and overpowering, understandably there was an entirely different vocabulary rolling out of Nicki's mouth. The power of the Rapture took on a whole different meaning when it came to her.

Unlike her mother's experience, there was nothing

friendly, inviting or beautiful about the Rapture. Like Randy's experience, it was ominous and foreboding, and that's without even knowing the half of it. At this point, both Leah and Nicki were unaware of the children, and unborn being taken as well. To the unbelievers, it was earth shattering, maddening and most revealing as to just how little people are in the hands and power of the Living God. And His mighty, even unfathomable power was on full display.

Lightening bolting across the sky from horizon to horizon, east to west, instant darkness, anything and everything mobile held in place by unseen hands, weights and forces, glowing orbs and lights, translucent figures, doorways and what looked like stairs going up, the heavenly voices, only to end with a loud booming thud, flash and earthquake...; there was plenty enough there to give Nicki good reason to scream and yell and carry on like no one's business.

Fortunate for her, she didn't lose a child or a loved one through it all. Still, children or no children, when it came, when it tarried, and when it left, there was nothing small or trivial about this huge and mighty miracle out of the sky. Nicki freaking out and going crazy was only to be expected and for good reason.

It all happened right after one of their usual, knockdown, dragged out arguments bordering just short of actually going to blows. Leah, smartly would always back off before it would go that far. Still, the fights were vicious and unnerving. Nicki was just impossible.

Not only was she impossible, Leah was finding her once precious little girl getting more and more hostile and unpredictable, even violent. Bullying, threatening and intimidating were becoming standard procedures and tactics for Nicki Dawn every time they'd butt heads. Quite frankly, Leah was scared of her own daughter. It wasn't a good feeling, but her undying love for her was so much stronger than her fear of her.

There was really nothing new about disobedient and uncontrollable teenagers. Leah being one them back in the day knew the defiance and knew it well. These latter days however, when it came to unruly offspring, the indifferences were taken to a whole new level. Nor were the indifferences limited to merely teenagers. Ten, eleven, twelve years old, even on up to their early twenties, thirties and forties; the brood would have many parents on edge and cautious.

Too many parents were no longer dealing with what used to be ordinary insubordinate behavior. They were finding themselves dealing with dangerous, brutal and explosive sons and daughters. This is exactly what Leah was facing this morning prior to the Raptures unexpected visit.

It would be the 'once again' syndrome. Once again,

Nicki had come staggering into the apartment half lit and half asleep. It was again in the middle of the week. It was again right on schedule. Like clockwork, it would be Nicki addressing her mother in the morning right before her mother would have to shuffle off to work. It was the same ol' approach driven by the same ol' need.

Nicki would politely ask her mother for more money; money so she could do it all again. Leah would once again be reluctant. Leah would once again point out how wrong it was for Nicki to be doing what she was doing. And once again, Nicki would erupt and the war would start.

Back and forth they went; five minutes or so. Getting louder and louder and more and more toxic and fierce, Leah would have to back down. She'd grab Nicki's Transfer Card, reach into her purse and take out her PDT (Portable Debit Transfer) and swipe another fifty bucks on to it. Just like before, and the time before that, and the time before that; it was more about shutting Nicki up with appeasement than an act of kindness on Leah's part.

Nicki took the beefed up card in a huff and shuffled off to her room so as to gather some things. Leah on the other hand would sit down and catch her breath. Strangely enough, Leah had learned to calm down rather quickly after her confrontations with Nicki and her raucous behavior. It would be the inner peace and joy she had come to know so well. Forgiving; both forgiving and forgetting would be a huge part of the inner peace she found in Christ.

Seeing so much of herself in Nicki, the feisty, independent fireball she once was, she couldn't help but modestly shake her head and let out a halfhearted chuckle. It was enough to shrug off the heated argument, and even smile. She loved Nicki so much...; so very, very much.

As any loving mother would, she worried about her too. In turn, she prayed for her. Without ceasing, she prayed fervently in light of how wicked, unstable, and dark the world had become; more especially over the last decade. And Nicki, her precious little girl was dancing right smack dab in the middle of it.

After packing a few things to see her through another unsavory adventure, Nicki came storming out of her bedroom. Cold as steel, unapologetic, and without remorse she made a beeline to the kitchen totally ignoring Leah pleasantly sitting there on the couch finishing her coffee. Rigid, fast and brisk she stuffed her backpack with some drinks and snacks, zipped it up and headed for the door. And then it happened. Right out of the blue, out of nowhere; it happened as it did with Randy and Joel hundreds of miles away.

It was a loud boom. Even from inside the apartment,

in broad daylight it was quite easy to assume a blast of lightening had speedily shot out across the sky. Instantly it was dark. Instantly a loud rumbling voice, shouts and trumpets in the near distance and instantly Nicki was stopped dead in her tracks halfway to the front door.

"Mom..., Mom...!" she frantically yelled within a couple of seconds. She yelled as loud as she could.

"I..., I can't move! I can't move...! Mom...! MOOOOOMM!" she screamed in utter fright as she tried to squirm and break away from whatever was holding her. She could feel the hands. She could feel the weight, so much weight. Oh, how she struggled to lift her feet and move her arms. It was all she could do to just turn her head; just like Randy in his truck.

Leah, on the other hand, like Joel was as free as a bird. Nothing would be restraining her and holding her down. After rapidly sitting up and regaining her composure, coffee all over her and shaking from the blast, she quickly stood up in shock. The first thing she focused on was Nicki, but between her thought and her natural instinct to instantly rush over to help her, it would be that quick that Leah would suddenly be hit by the revelation; it was the Rapture.

She knew, just like Joel, she knew it. She just knew it; simple as that. The darkness was already lit up with shimmering lights when a sensation, a tingling magnificent feeling hit her and consumed her. Her senses were magnified and her instincts were heightened. Undone and overwhelmed by its Glory and Power she'd fall face down in undefiled reverence and fear.

Out of the darkness, immediately and simultaneously, the voices, the visions, and the illuminations and orbs whisking, frolicking and dancing about had entered the dimension. Leah was still prone, face down on the floor, but Nicki could clearly see. There was a door, a translucent doorway not more than six or seven feet away from Leah.

It was stunning, glowing, and brilliant like shining gold, silver and glimmering diamonds. It was so bright, but blinding it was not. There would be a foyer just inside the doorway and a radiant stairway clearly leading up. It wouldn't be until Leah heard the heavenly voices that she would slowly look up and see everything Nicki was seeing.

"Amelia, Amelia…, don't be afraid. Do not fear. Come." was the beautiful Voice upon voices beckoning her, calling her. It wasn't her name, but for some reason Leah recognized it. She knew it was her they were calling. It was so wonderful and so alluring. The fear in Leah did indeed dissipate, in fact almost instantly. It vanished and it would be replaced with utter ecstasy, elation and bliss.

She felt a warm hand tenderly grab hers. It was so soft, so kind, graceful and sensational. A translucent figure gradually stemmed from the hand; materialized into a body. No details, just a radiant and glowing body of light. Leah could sense it was clearly an angel. It gently lifted her arm so as to raise her to her knees and onto her feet. Not wanting to tarry, the graceful and saving angel by the hand would gently tug her so as to lead her to and through the golden doorway, into the foyer and up the stairs.

"Come, Amelia! Come…, it is time. Come with me. Do not be afraid," would peacefully yet persistently invite her.

Leah was so taken in by the Glory; so much so that Nicki's maniacal screams had become faint, even distant, but not gone by any means. Star struck, awestricken and mesmerized, but far from hypnotized, Leah being encouraged; being led by the angelic figure and by her own freewill and wanting more than anything to go would begin to mosey towards the doorway. Closer and closer with each and every step, she'd feel more and more at ease.

"MOOOOOMM…!" would screech across the room. Nicki, persistent with her cries for dear life wasn't letting up. It was just enough, and loud enough to turn Leah's head ever so slightly. Unmoved though, Leah would slowly keep moving towards the doorway, the foyer and the stairs.

"HELP…! MOOOOOMM…! MOOOOOMM…! HELP ME...! PLEEEEASE…, MOM! HELP MEEEEE," Nicki cried with everything she had.

Hysterical, gasping and unable to move Nicki feverishly continued. Finally, all at once, Nicki's panic-stricken calls for help pierced the air and landed on Leah's ears. This time it would be enough to get Leah to hesitate. She stopped. She was already through door, in the foyer, with one foot on the stairs, when she would modestly turn around. She'd take a double take at the stairs; twice even. As inviting as it was, it would however not be enough to carry her through for the moment.

She looked back inside the apartment. She'd see her daughter calling to her, so she made the decision. Leah let go of the angelic hand and hurriedly rushed right out of the translucent foyer straight back into the living room, back to Nicki. She'd grab her; she'd pull her, and push her. She was doing everything she could and as fast as she could to break her lose from her invisible bindings and weight.

Nicki was frantically bawling in fear. She'd grunt and groan trying ever so hard to twist and turn so as to assist her mom anyway she could to break free. It was the Powers of Heaven that they were trying to loose, and it was clearly useless. Nicki wasn't budging. Still, the both of them tried with all their might.

The voices would keep beckoning Leah…, "Amelia, come, come, it is time. Amelia…, Amelia."

It would be the last of the voices. Leah hearing the voices would of course not know it was the last call. She just needed a couple more seconds, that's all; just a few more seconds.

By this time she had fixed herself under the backpack strapped over Nicki's shoulders. She firmly planted her feet and with vigor and oomph, Leah pushed and strained as hard as she could to bust Nicki out of her standstill. And with a blast of a trumpet, a flash of light and a deafening thud, the Rapture was over—just like that.

As fast as a light switch turning off a light, Nicki's binding too instantly ended with a snap. In the same way Randy, and Randy's truck, and the cars, trains, planes, jets, rockets, missiles, bullets, birds, animals, fish, submarines, drones, everything in the entire world in transit and temporarily held in place was cut loose in an instant. Breaking loose, Leah and Nick shot across the room like a rubber band only to slam into the front door; the same front door that Nicki was so eagerly heading for as she contemplated her grandiose exit of slamming it shut on her way out.

Of course, the Rapture changed everything. Not only did it change Nicki's adolescent and petty plans of storming out of the house in a huff, it changed the entire world. Things were never to be the same.

After crashing headfirst into the door, it wasn't but a second or two when a rumbling earthquake, mild but very distinct would rattle the windows and shuffle them about. Just as quick, the darkness was gone and all was still. Two...? Three or four minutes...? It was really hard to say at this point as to how long the miracle lasted.

In its coming and going, it was however enough time for the Angels of Light to gather the children, the unborn and the mentally innocent. It was enough time for the believers, being all the Born Again Christians to choose as to whether or not to go...; or stay or go back. Lastly, and more importantly, it was enough time for the entire world to absorb a most powerful message noted in the Scriptures.

"So that you may know that I Am God," would not only seize the world and capture their undivided attention, it would cast them into utter fear. *"So that you may know that I Am God...,"* would not only seize the world and capture their undivided attention, it would cast them into utter fear. And...fear...it would be.

Right away, both Leah and Nicki hysterically screaming and by instinct would try to jump to their feet after they crashed into the front door. They were however both so weak. They had zero strength, zero energy and their stamina was completely drained.

Their knees instantly buckled from beneath them when they tried to get up. They just didn't realize how much was taken out of them during the whole fiasco. Out of breath, whimpering and emphatically crying in between weighted sighs and yells of exhaustion, both Leah and Nicki were spent. It took a handful of minutes before they'd somewhat catch their breath and crawl to a chair, a table and the couch to pull themselves up to their feet.

Once they gathered a little strength and still in panic mode they quickly pounded on what had just went down. Nicki Dawn simply wanted to know what was going on. She wanted to know what happened. She wanted answers; like everyone else in the world. Leah on the other hand knew what happened. Yes…, she too was screaming and carrying on, but it was despair, not a demand for answers that had ignited her chaotic screaming, bellowing and hollering. Nicki went one way. Leah went the other; both were off and running, yelling, panting, and screaming in their own ways to address their own concerns.

"What the hell…? What the hell was that? Mom…, MOM…!" she screamed. "What just happened…? Oh my God, my God…! Mom…? Mom…?" was about all Nicki could utter for the first few minutes of the Raptures aftermath. Heavily breathing, yet short on breath, ranting and raving, walking back and forth trying to shake it off and gather her thoughts would take the little seventeen year old teenager on a head spinning journey into madness right there in her own living room.

All in a matter of five or ten minutes, shaking and quivering, carefully peeking out the windows, crazed and nervously searching for her phone…; her help-lessness and littleness was quite telling. Turning on the TV, getting on the Internet, and using her phone once she found it, anything to get some details as to what was going on was futile. Like most everywhere else, all power was off or disrupted with static. All Satellites had gone haywire. It was nerve-racking.

She could see and hear people outside of her apart-ment going crazy, as crazy as she was but she wasn't brave enough to get in the mix. All sorts of thoughts zipped in and out of Nicki's mind. Radiation, conta-gion, disease, alien attack, people gone crazy; she just didn't know. And being that she didn't know, she played it safe. She immediately locked the doors, shut the shades and chose to stay inside. She decided to hide, at least for the time being.

Leah had also gone off into her own little world of madness. It was where her emotional rollercoaster began. For the first twenty minutes or so right after the Rapture, both Leah and Nicki were lost in hysteria.

Their adrenaline was boiling over. But, Leah's raving madness would eventually take a dive.

When she truly had to accept what she had just lost, what she had actually missed…; it hit her hard. It hit her…, really, really hard. In mid pace, she dropped to the floor, right there in the middle of the living room. On her knees, she keeled over into the fetal position and cried. She'd cry like many, at par with mothers who had just lost their children, their babies or a child. Missing the Rapture, especially when it was right there at her fingertips was just so over-the-top devastating.

It wasn't until Nicki saw her mom collapse and break down the way she did that she would change her tone. Though she had managed to turn into an arrogant and obnoxious hellion over the years, she was still quite insightful. And to her credit, there was still a heart of gold buried deep beneath her rebellious veneer in spite of her unsavory friends and boyfriend.

It was a sweet and compassionate heart of gold feeling and knowing it best to kneel down by her mom and console her. It took a few moments to sink in; a few moments to really truly digest her mom's devastation and why she was devastated, but it eventually became quite clear. Going from complete and utter hysterics, yelling out questions and screaming for answers to words of comfort happened rather quickly. It was good of Nicki, most loving.

Though she'd draw her attention to her mother's anguish and despair, it didn't keep her from looking over her shoulder. Still rattled and scared out of her mind, she couldn't help but wonder and fear something else was on the verge of happening. It kept her on edge, wide-eyed and uneasy.

Leah on the other hand knew better. She just knew it was over; that is to say the Rapture. This isn't to say nothing else was on the verge of happening because there was. It would be something seven years in the making, but no less on the verge; that would be the Tribulation.

Right now, though far from calm, Leah just didn't have even the slightest inkling to keep looking over her shoulder. It wasn't that she belittled the thought or would have reason to tell Nicki that there was no need to do so; it was because it was just so far from her mind. Thinking about the coming age, the Tribulation; a seven year stint in time or even the next few hours quite honestly just wasn't registering at the moment.

It's what had just happened that had Leah in knots. It was the thought of missing the boat that was consuming her. In all truth, there was actually a part of Leah wishing that something else would happen right now, right this minute, a second chance or even death of all things. She also knew it was in vain. She just knew the miracle was over. At this point she just needed some time to heal like so many other Born Again Christians who lost their chance.

Two and half hours would roll by. It would be a long two and half hours though. Leah's emotional rollercoaster ride along with Nicki's anxiety, fear and speculation has been brutal on both of them. They didn't know what was in store. Neither one of them knew what was going to happen. Nobody knew for that matter. Like Leah though, there were plenty who knew what had just happened. They also knew where they were at in time.

As promised, the Rapture had come and gone. And it would be the Rapture; its coming and its going that would flip the hour glass. It was time. It was time to let time run out.

How long…? Nobody knew. The seven years of Tribulation was a given; seven years sure to come after the Rapture, but when it would start remained in the dark. The Book of Revelation made that clear enough. The prelude to Tribulation after the Rapture was not given in the Scriptures.

It is and has always been a mystery. And now, even after the Rapture of the Church, it would remain a mystery. The only thing that was for sure at this point was the mystery was now here to run its course. Not only was the mystery here to run its course but all that would be in it, all that would be destined to happen before the Tribulation and the Great Tribulation was here. Some of it was already happening. The rest was just waiting to happen. Still, what was waiting to happen was here just the same.

Wasting no time, without a second to lose, the Supernatural Age would seize the world. It would thrust itself into the heart of all life; all people and all animals. Left to accept it, receive it and build on it was the one and only option the world had. It wouldn't boil down to whether the world wanted it or not; they were stuck with it. They were stuck with all that what was in the Supernatural Age. There were stuck with all that was in store. And lastly, they were stuck with what little time was left in the hourglass now flipped.

-Chapter Nine-
DEMONS UNLEASHED

There would be no place to hide, no place to run, and no rock left unturned. The Supernatural Age was for everyone and everywhere. It would not be selective. It would have no prejudice, no bias, exceptions or exemptions.

No place was safe and no one was secure. There would be no place too small, too sacred, or too unimportant. In like manner, there was no person too small, no person too sacred, or too unimportant for the powers of darkness lurking about.

'Be sober; be vigilant; because your adversary the devil walks about like a roaring lion, seeking whom he may devour.'

'...whom'..., is everybody and means everybody. No person and no place too small or too unimportant for the powers of darkness to ravage would include Leah and Nicki, right there in their own little quaint apartment. Yes..., the Supernatural Age; it begins.

Ever so subtle, but ever so quick, the powers of darkness would start to maneuver and manipulate its prey. It would start right after another one of Leah's raging episodes that Nicki would be targeted. Nicki had once again slid in close to her grieving mom. Feeling really quite helpless, she would simply fall back on the only thing she could think of to ease her mother's pain. Again, feeling guilty she would again apologize to her mom.

"Mom, oh mom…, I'm…, I'm so sorry," she sorrowfully shared. From there she'd go on to thank her mother; thank her for coming back for her.

"Thank you…mom. Thank you for coming back for me. Thank you so much. I love you so much." It was deep. Flippant and casual it was not. It was genuine and heart felt. It wasn't "thanks" that Nicki would say to her mother. No, it was "Thank You" from the bottom of her heart.

Rocking back and forth, Leah's face buried on the side of her caring daughters' neck, she'd weep uncontrollably. It truly was breaking Nicki's heart to see her mom so broken. It took her right back to her childhood. She remembered how it broke her heart back then. And like then, she would cry with her mother.

"Mom…, mom please…," she whispered. But, it wasn't the only whisper in the room.

"Dmitri…," slithered into Nicki's ear.

It startled her. She heard it. She heard it quite clearly and instantly recoiled with a quick turn of her head.

Still holding her mother, she tensed up. She cocked her neck to look at her mother, so as to see if she had heard it too, but Leah didn't hear it. She was still quite occupied with her sorrow. Nicki had to ask herself if she really heard it. She was sure it wasn't a voice in her head. It was a voice by her head, it whispered right into her ear; a low raspy whisper.

"Dmitri...," she uttered aloud so as to confirm what she thought she heard.

"What the hell...," she murmured so as to question it.

It took a few minutes to adjust and halfway pretend she didn't actually hear the voice or anything at all for that matter. She went ahead and took a deep breath and melted back into comforting her mom. She didn't know Dmitri was in the room. How could she? Dmitri was a demon, a dark angel; an Influencer unseen but very present.

He'd be just one of uncountable others liberated and free to do what they hadn't been able to do up unto the Rapture, of which the demons refer to as the 'Nazarene's Harvest'. 'The Hand' was lifted with the Raptures' coming and going. The Holy Spirit removed. In turn, as promised and foretold, the fallen angels devious desires that had been faithfully kept in check and down to a bare minimal were now unleashed—free to do what they've longed to do.

Likened to "special forces" in military, Dmitri was a Celestial Messenger in the ranks of the demonic army. Needless to say he was delighted. It would be the first time he would actually hear one of them; one of the created children refer to him by name. Even though Dmitri found it to be so delightful to hear his name spoken aloud, he knew it wasn't time for fun and games. The specialized demon had a job to do.

As always patience, stealth, and timing would lead to perfection. Dmitri would wait. He'd wait for Nicki to unknowingly open a window into her mind so as to let him slither in and do what he's been ordered to do; deceive and manipulate.

It would be fifteen minutes or so that would pass since Nicki muttered Dmitri's name. Leah being so exhausted, both physically and mentally as well as emotionally drained had thankfully cried herself to sleep. Sitting on the floor, her back against the kitchen wall, her mother in her arms asleep in her lap gave Nicki a chance to gather her thoughts and talk to herself. Even though she could hear the unrelenting chaos going about its business out in streets, she would move to drift away from it all.

With all the yelling and bellowing set aside she found a moment of peace. She found a moment of time to sit there and quietly dissect, analyze and reflect on everything that went down and what her mom and Joel had told her about the Rapture, Jesus and God and the Gospel and all that other Bible stuff that she always referred to as crap and nonsense to put it lightly

Leah jolted ever so slightly, as if she was dodging something in a dream, but it wasn't enough to wake her. She was still fast asleep. Nicki could hear her mom's heavy breathing and wheezing in and out and out and in. She could feel her neck and shirt drenched in tears and drool. She again focused on how her mom fell to such heart wrenching depths and why.

In turn, she'd only find herself once again laden with guilt. If it really was the Rapture, the whole idea of being taken into heaven or wherever it was the Born Agains were so longing to go; her mom leaving it all for her, her mean-spirited, unruly and miserable daughter, it weighed heavy on Nicki's thoughts. She'd take in a deep, deep breath and let out another loaded sigh.

Even though she knew her mom was out of it, she felt compelled to speak to her yet again. Being half way in tears she'd let it out. She'd let her mother know her sentiments.

"Ah…, mom, I'm so sorry mom. I'm sorry, I'm sorry…, I'm sorry," she stressed. Within a couple of seconds something else would unexpectedly roll out of Nicki's mouth. "Oh, God…, God I'm so sorry."

Involuntarily setting her sights on God, even for just a moment, there would be hope for what was once a godless Nicki. Her mention of God was ever so quick, but it was a start. She went right back to speaking to her mother coiled up in her arms. Taking her tone down a notch; down to moderately whispering she would continue to apologize, but this time it would be followed with a request.

Reaching down, down deep into the deepest parts of her soul, Nicki pulled out something more than just mere words. It would be her heart. She would pour it out.

"Mom, I'm sorry mom. Please forgive me…, forgive me," would spill out and send her crashing into an emotional breakdown. Eye's tightly clinched shut, dropping her head into her chest, taking it all in for a few seconds, only to erupt with a burst of tears is what came out of Nicki's soul this time when she apologized. It would however be the open window Dmitri would be looking for. And he didn't hesitate to sneak in.

As much as he wanted to whisper loud enough as he did when he spoke his name into Nicki's ear, or slap her around for that matter, he wouldn't. There'd be plenty enough time for that in due course. As of now, patience, stealth and timing mattered most.

He did not want to scare the fish away. Even though

all the heavenly bars have been removed and he was now able to do whatever he wanted to do to the created children, he still had to follow orders. Lucifer had plans, big plans and there would be no room for personal agendas or insubordination. So as to please his superiors and follow orders, Dmitri would go back to the basics; tactics used to lure the fish, not scare them away. He'd take is powers of communicating back down and whisper just loud enough into Nicki's ear to deliver…thoughts…, not words. That's what the Celestial Messengers do; these particular demons — the Influencers.

"Why are you saying sorry," he planted right smack dab in the middle of her mind. "She was ready to leave you, high and dry, even to die and…you're… saying sorry…to her?"

It was beautifully set in place. Nicki took it in, hook, line and sinker. Dmitri however was far from finished.

"Oh yeah, yeah…, she came back for you, but it wasn't because she loved you. She did it only because she felt sorry for you. She didn't really want to come back for you. She really wanted to go. Why do think your dear sweet mother is so upset? She's here, stuck with you and hating every second of it. And you know it…," Dmitri declared.

Prodding and kneading Nicki's mind into

drumming up thoughts, stirring up emotions and doubts; Dmitri, now on a roll, wasn't about to stop. He'd continue to work Nicki, poke her with piercing thoughts, sticking them into her mind like pinpoints and tacks.

"She's here stuck with you instead of being where she really wanted to be; as far away from you as possible. You call that love? And you're saying sorry to someone who is angry and sad because they are stuck with you? You're saying sorry to someone who would much rather be somewhere else? Are you really? Are you really saying sorry to someone who wants to be with someone else instead of you? C'mon Nicki…, are you really saying sorry to that…, to her…," he'd ask in the tone likened to a suave and sophisticated lawyer deliberating final thoughts to a jury; insinuating how wrong and even stupid it would be to disagree with him.

Dmitri vocally pouring and planting the thoughts was quickly taking root. Nicki was carefully entertaining each and every one them; one by one. It was enough for her to loosen her embrace of her sleeping mother. She readjusted her position and opened herself to receive some more thoughts about her dear sweet mother.

"She doesn't want to be stuck here with you, Nicki." The demon whispered. "She'd rather be with someone else, with something else..., what was it anyhow? Space aliens, reincarnation into some other life? Whatever it is or wherever it was she wanted to go, your dear sweet mother seemed to think it was a damn sight better than being here with you.

She hates dealing with you," he persisted. "And right now your dear sweet mother hates the fact that she's still here with you. Think about it, look at her, she's in anguish and she's angry not because she missed whatever it was she thinks she missed. She's pissed because she's trapped here with you. And you're saying sorry to her? Paa...lease, Nicki. Don't be so naïve. And look at you, coddling her, and comforting her after she's already admitted how angry she is she didn't leave when she had the chance. She doesn't love you? If she did she'd be happy that she stayed with you."

Patience, stealth and timing, perfection indeed; the dark messenger did well. His Master would be exceptionally pleased. No one too small, no one too sacred, and no one too unimportant; Satan wanted them all. If at all possible, he wanted the Born Agains who remained as well, probably more so than the rest. As it were though, the Influencers would be too hard pressed to go after the Nazarenes chosen; those like Leah.

They were already being temporarily guarded by

Guardian Angels of who were posted immediately after the Rapture's end. They were temporarily being guarded by their 'angels' only because the hand of the Holy Spirit was removed as prophesied and promised in the Scriptures. Due to return though, in due time for their sake, the Holy Spirit will again tend to them, but on a one to one basis.

Dmitri would have loved to whisper thoughts into Leah's head, she was right there, within inches of the demons breath, but he would have had to combat her Guardian Angel, of who was assigned only to Leah, to protect her…, not Nicki Dawn. As for Nicki…, she too was chosen to warrant 'special attention', but not like the Born Agains specially assigned to Guardian Angels; quite the opposite. Those like Nicki, still within Satan's grasp, were specially assigned to demons; sophisticated, well trained, clever and extremely intelligent demons — the Influencers.

Why her, and those like her, if one may ask. It was simple. They were in close relationship to the Nazarenes chosen. If Leah wasn't a Born Again, there'd be no Guardian Angel to protect her. Likewise, if Leah wasn't a Born Again, there'd be no need for a specially assigned demon to tend to Nicki. At this point, Dmitri, like all the Influencers are called to promptly and aggressively sabotage and thwart any influence the Born Agains may have on those closest to them. Nip it at the bud, quickly and decisively, if you will.

The ones closet to the Nazarenes chosen was indeed a different story from the rest of the world. Satan wanted them and wanted them bad; those like Nicki Dawn. He'd pay special attention to them. Assigning the Celestial Messengers to them, messengers like Dmitri to cut them off from the Nazarenes chosen and everything they knew about the truth was not only imperative, but rewarding and gratifying. No, Dmitri had no access to Leah, but Nicki…, not yet chosen or guarded by the Nazarenes Angels was open season.

Nicki digested Dmitri's sinister thoughts like spoon fed applesauce. It went down smooth. She weighed them out. It convinced her to remove herself from her mother resting upon her shoulder. She didn't jerk out of it. She was careful and kind about it. She slowly slid out and reached for a cushion and pillow off the couch, set it down beside her mother and gently laid her down to rest. She really didn't want to wake her.

After all that was said and done, Nicki took the bait. She contemplated the dark message, the lies planted by her Influencer. It would not however be enough to get Nicki to hate her mother, or even dislike her; at least not yet. At the moment, hating her wasn't even close to registering on her mind. She loved her still. She loved her mom probably more now than she has ever before.

Still, it was mission accomplished. The seeds were planted. It would confuse Nicki. Doubt had set in. She wondered. Is it true? Is her mom angry and upset that she's still here with her? It was looking that way.

"Is that love? Is that really love," she asked herself. Nicki was going to have to learn a lot and quickly if she was to get out of this spiritual gauntlet alive. Trust would be the key; who to trust, what to trust would mean everything. Right now she was trusting Dmitri; the voice in her thoughts. Right now, most of the entire world would be listening and trusting the Influencers sent by Satan.

As for Dmitri and the rest of Lucifer's minions, though much work is to be done, it will be, let us say…fun, amusing and quite enjoyable for them. It was sheer pleasure being now able to approach the created children with no opposition. The Hand of God, the Holy Spirit of God, along with the Nazarenes Church removed from the battlefield, leaving only a battalion of Guardian Angels and some Archangels to protect the Born Agains has turned the world into a playground for the Powers of Darkness.

Play they shall, yes work and play. Pleasurable work would best describe it. This would be the dark side of The Supernatural Age. But, there would also be the Light, Christ Jesus, the Nazarene, and the Most High doing His part in the Supernatural Age as well.

And the battle begins.

Bam, bam, bam…echoed through the apartment. It was a frantic knock, someone pounding on the front door. It woke Leah up and Nicki instantly tensed up. With all the sirens and commotion going on, she didn't know what to expect. Police, the DSS, neighbors, Joel, friends, she just didn't know.

Bam…, bam, "Nicki…, Nicki…, are you in there?"

Nicki quickly, but cautiously made her way across the living room. She didn't go straight for the door though. She would instead maneuver off to the side. Bent down, she slowly crept over to the near window, barely tweaked the two bottom blinds and carefully squeaked a peak outside.

She was pretty sure she already knew who it was. The voice, a voice she knew well pretty much gave it away. Still, she wasn't going to take any chances. Bang…, bang, bang, bang…again came blasting and echoing through the room.

"Nicki…? Nicki…?" the voice outside the door shouted, impatiently and now a bit irritated.

Just as Nicki thought, peeking through the blinds, it was Chad, her boyfriend. He was alone. She hurried to the door, unlocked it to let him in. Chad just barged in even before the door was completely open. Nicki quickly locked the door behind him after scolding him to get the heck out of the way. In a panic, like every one else he too would start his rant.

"Nicki…," he panted, "are you ok? God…, I'm so glad you're here. People…, a lot of people and children have been snatched by aliens or something. There gone, flat out gone. My neighbors kids gone and other people, I…I can't even keep track…, and…, and-"

"Chad, Chad, Chad…, take it easy. Calm down," Nicki ordered. "Just take it easy, slow down."

"They weren't taken by aliens," Leah interrupted with a somber and defeated tone.

"What," Chad barked as he curled up his lip and jeered at her.

"Never mind her right now," Nicki asserted. "What do you know? What's happening out there? I mean our TV, the radio and the internet, our cell phones…, nothings working."

Gulping and panting…, "Yeah, I know. I tried to call you right away, but couldn't get through," he said. "I couldn't move, Nicki. Nobody could move. Jerry and Dee…, we couldn't move. Everybody, the cars, and the people everything just stopped."

"I know, I know," Nicki shared, "I couldn't move either. But cars…, and stuff — what do mean?"

"Yeah…, cars, buses, everything froze, dogs, birds in the air — everything!" he clamored. "And all of these little lights, like flashlights the size of basketballs, bright beams, I don't know what they were.

They were like swimming around and whisking past people and… and in and out of cars and buildings, going right through the walls. They were taking the kids, the little kids…," he shouted, and out of breath.

"The kids were just disappearing. I saw a couple of kids lifted up off the ground by those lights and…, and the next thing you know they were gone. They…, they…, I don't know…, Nicki! They just disappeared…, into thin air. Their moms, the children's' moms…, they were…, God—just screaming out of their minds. Cuz they couldn't move; either could I. Nobody could move or…or do anything, we couldn't run, we couldn't fight them, or chase after them, we just had to sit there and watch. It was crazy, Nicki. I'm scared out of my mind."

He took in a deep long breath and moved to finish off his raving testimony. "God…, I'm so glad you're ok though." He insisted.

As he said it he'd sneak in close to Nicki to hug her, but she shunned him and pushed him away. She was a tough girl when it came to him. She wasn't the needy, hold me tight type. In fact, she was never that into Chad. Their relationship, at least from her perspective was more out of convenience than sentimental; image perhaps. There was no love, at least coming from her side of the fence.

Oh Jeez…," Nicki would say as she flopped and

sunk down into the couch. She'd run her hands over her face and plant them in front of her mouth, held together like praying. "Mom…, what do we do?" she asked.

Still sitting on the floor with her back against the wall, Leah just gazed at Nicki and slowly shook her head. She was still half delirious, but sober enough to know there was really nothing they could do. She heard everything that Chad had to say. It was incredible to say the least. Still, she couldn't help but wish she wasn't there to hear about it. Her decision to jump out of the glory and light of the Raptures presence was still killing her. Yet, she'd see Nicki Dawn sitting there on the couch fretting and reflect on how much she loved her.

"Wait," she'd say. "We just have to wait, Nicki. The TV, the radio…, things will be working again soon. I'm sure of that. We'll know soon enough what to do or…," she said and paused, "or what not to do."

Just then, a sound, a good sound slipped into the room. It was sweet. "Meow…," it was Sheefoo. It was their cat, a little yellow and orange tabby. Nicki brought her home as a tiny little four week old kitten years ago promising to take care of her. Of course, it would end up being Leah being the care taker. Still, it was their precious little kitty, their little friend barely peeking past the bedroom door, frightened and leery.

She's been hiding under the bed this whole time. Her sweet innocent little high-pitched meow, even though it was a scared meow was enough to remind Leah and Nicki all was not lost. It was a joy, even a blessing to hear Sheefoo. The tension in the room instantly went down a tiny notch.

"C'mon baby," Nicki would say as she beckoned her with her hand. "C'mon, baby – it's ok."

Sheefoo was too scared. Everything going on, Chad there didn't help. The little kitty was always timid and cautious around other people, especially males. Leah and Nicki were the only two she felt comfortable with. She wasn't a total recluse though. She'd eventually warm up to others but it was always slow and careful. Joel even had a hard time getting close to the precious little feline.

"Come here…, Sheefoo…, its ok girl. C'mon…" would again come from Nicki being soft and gentle. Knowing she wasn't going to come, clearly too scared, Nicki got up and went to her. She tenderly picked her little baby up into her arms and went back to the couch. "Its ok…, don't worry…, mommy's here."

Chad, still nerve-stricken, but not enough to keep him from getting a little jealous would slightly sneer at the cat clearly getting more attention than him. He wanted the attention, or at least some attention. He again tried to slide in close to Nicki so as to get into the mix with all the affection. He'd reach over to pet Sheefoo sitting on Nicki's lap, but Sheefoo too would shun him. She hissed and took a swipe at him. Chad quickly jerked away.

"Frickin' little….," he snapped.

Nicki was shocked, not at Chad, but at Sheefoo. She's never ever done that, to anyone ever. Nicki didn't know what to think. She moved to coddle, caress and pet Sheefoo, giving her the benefit of the doubt.

"She's probably scared with everything going on. I mean look at us? Look how freaked out we are," she reasoned.

Leah just looked on. She felt something. Something was wrong. And she was right. Dmitri, the dark angel was still there. He never left. He's been there all along, watching and listening to them go back and forth with everything that was happening and going on this glorious day of reckoning. He was enjoying it. He hated them. He hated all of them, Nicki, Chad, but mostly Leah, she was of Christ. She was one of Jesus' children, one of the Nazarenes chosen; a child of God — a Born Again.

Dmitri was already in line and back on track. He knew his orders. He knew of all the things he was to do and how to do it and when, and where and as often as he could. He was to take advantage of every opportunity, without being obvious or too overbearing. He was already informed and knew the animals would be used extensively as part of the master plan.

Signs and wonders; they were to be used to set the stage. Dmitri had already summoned one of his subordinate angels from the ranks of *'legion'*, lower end demons — the expendable ones. Sticking to the plan, following orders, Dmitri would take action. He ordered his lesser to enter the cat, possess it, and control it to do their bidding. The demon of *'legion'* was prompt. Without a fuss, without question, and with the greatest of ease; into the cat he'd go.

"What's wrong, sweetie," Nicki wooed to comfort her precious little kitty. "It's alright, its ok." She bent down so as to draw Sheefoo close and give her a hug and snuggle but it would not be a sweet little hug and snuggle she would get. Sheefoo hissed again, viciously. Nicki jerked back along with an attempt to push the cat off her lap, but just as quick the cat would dart. Sheefoo, no longer being Sheefoo lunged at Chad. It was straight for his face.

Chad screamed as he rolled over the back of the couch. The cat tore into Chad as ferociously as it could. As fast as Chad would grab the cat to toss it aside it would attack just as fast. His eyes, being immediately injured by the cats' claws were clinched shut and bleeding. He couldn't see.

Screaming bloody murder, he'd crawl, roll and

struggle to get back on his feet only to trip and bump into things and fall back down. The cat scratching and biting as fast and as much as it could was merciless. Leah and Nicki didn't linger they were on top of it just as quick as it happened. Yelling as well, they were there helping Chad, trying to push, grab and even kick the cat off of him.

On the other side of the dimension, Dmitri was laughing. It was entertaining. He was getting quite the show. He loved it. His demonic subordinate was tearing it up but was eventually hit and pounded on enough to be chased away. It took a run around the living room and secured itself under a little end table. With its claws dug into the carpet, hissing, and glaring, the cat or the demon-possessed cat clearly wasn't finished with its attack. Its eyes..., the eyes weren't the eyes of Sheefoo. They were but they weren't. They were reddish. It was eerie.

Chad, by this time was squirming and crying in pain. He was torn up. His face, his eyes, his neck, arms, his back, even his legs were ripped up, scratched up and bleeding. The cat's claws and teeth slashed right through his clothes. Cussing and bawling, Chad was now getting plenty of attention.

Both Leah and Nicki were tending to him and his wounds the best they could. They would however do so without taking their eyes off Sheefoo. Nicki would quickly grab her cell phone and call 911. She figured she wouldn't get any response but she thought she'd try. Getting zero response, she tossed it down as fast as she picked it up.

"I'm going to get some towels and bandages," Leah said as she scampered off to the bathroom.

It wasn't but a minute before round two would ensue. While Leah was down the hall, Dmitri would ring the bell if you will. He'd sound off another order summoning his underling to attack again. Unhesitant, the cat, in stalking mode would slink and slither a couple of steps before it would jet across the floor and catapult itself off of the couch. It flew right across the room. Nicki, catching the flying leap in the corner of her at eye, by impulse turned and ducked. Chad would not be so fortunate.

The cat was back on him trying to kill him if it could. This time survival instincts kicked in. Within seconds, Chad grabbed the cat already tearing into his shoulder. With everything he had, with his hands wrapped around little beast's neck he rolled over on top of it and snap. He snapped Sheefoo's neck and threw her across the room.

"F…," he yelled, "F…ing thing…!"

Dimitri was still laughing uncontrollably. His subordinate was gone, lost to the imprisonment of outer darkness, but it was worth it. It's what the subordinates in *'legion'* are called to do. The subordinates strategically sacrificed and used to serve the Master and the agenda was already determined long ago. They were devoted, they would faithfully serve the Rebellion, they were extremely useful, they were plentiful, but most of all they were expendable; because their numbers were uncountable.

After the tense battle and seeing her precious Sheefoo lifeless on the floor, Nicki started to bawl. By this time, Leah was back with the towels and first-aid. She heard the short-lived commotion and was out in seconds. She too saw Sheefoo lying dead on the floor. She'd break as well.

"Oh, no…, oh God…, Lord no…," she moaned in anguish. Chad was miserably groaning and whimpering. Nicki was split, she was torn. She wanted to care for Sheefoo, but Chad was the one clearly in need of attention. She was hysterically sobbing.

Handing Nicki one of the towels she had brought out, "Go, see if she's ok," Leah said as she started to address Chad's wounds. Crying, Nicki crawled over to her precious baby. She was still afraid of her.

Shaking and trembling, she'd slowly reach down to wrap the towel over and around her lifeless little kitty. For no reason other than caution, she'd pull back a bit, but go at it again. It wasn't but moments before she had her baby wrapped up and holding her close to her bosom. Nicki would burst with tears like a dam giving way as she held Sheefoo as close to her as she possibly could. She cradled and rocked with sorrow…, so much sorrow.

Sorrow…? Sorrow, pain, worry, anxiety, fear…, it was everywhere. It was rampant. It had imprisoned the entire planet. It was in every household, in every country. The animals, the attacks amongst other things were everywhere stirring everyone. It was all part of the plan, all part of the unholy agenda. '…*signs and wonders*', signs and wonders.

Worst of all, it was only the beginning.

-*Chapter Ten*-

TRIP FROM HELL

It was day one. It was only a couple of hours in to the Supernatural Age and the world was upside down. Would it get better? Would it get worse before it gets better? At this point, nobody knew.

The Born Agains that were left, Leah…; they had a good idea of what was ahead. They weren't however privy to the details of what was to come or how it was all going to go down. They were already rudely introduced to the animals turning into vicious killers and not to be trusted. What was next was beyond them.

Truly, the road ahead was indeed going to be a rollercoaster ride; for everybody, for every single soul. It was going to be a season like no other known to man. The Heavens know, as does the powers of darkness. For some, it was sure to be most dreadful, dangerous, continually unnerving and heart wrenching. For others it would be a time of a great awakening, enlightenment, and elevation; a time to evolve and move forward in the phases of evolution.

For some, it'll be a time to run, to hide, and seek refuge. Still, for many it'll be a time to rejoice, to celebrate, and worship like never before. It would be time to understand, a time to embrace and revere a new revelation, a new age, and a new world. It would be a time to receive glory. It would be a time to receive powers. It would be a time to receive Godhood.

But first…, they would need a light. They would need hope. They would need answers. They would need the Christ, their Christ; the universal Christ. And the dark and fallen angels now with free reign, having already set its course long ago, would begin to deliver with pleasure.

For those who were left, the windmills of thought were going a thousand miles per hour in a world that had come to a complete stand still. Time seemed to be going so slow, yet everything else seemed to be moving so fast. The twist of fate was now just over twelve hours old but it was lingering more like an eternity. People being forced as to what exactly it is they are to believe is now the daunting task that has set the world on fire.

Randy had made it to Jake and Rebecca's house but it wasn't easy. His trip was harrowing. His mad dash back to South Lake Tahoe was anything but a speedy return. It ended up being a long, grueling journey – a trip from hell. A drive that would have been an hour at most any other day took him well over nine hours.

Confined to the seat of his truck, hours on in, unable to do anything else but inch along tested his sanity. He already knew he was plunged into a living nightmare, but he couldn't help but feel he was driving further and further into the heart of the nightmare with each passing mile. Everything he'd see, and learned, and even dodged on his way back only made things worse.

The more he'd come to know the less he'd know. One thing, one mystery only led to other things; things even more mysterious and mind-boggling. And his mind, running at the speed of thought with nowhere to go for answers, running around in circles it seemed didn't help matters. The whole time he was haunted as to whether or not to go back where Joel disappeared. He kept wondering if it was a mistake to leave that spot.

Not even thirty minutes into his time consuming journey, he found out rather quickly as to why there weren't any paramedics or police addressing the scene of the wreck fifteen miles back. There was just too much going on right there in the city. Emergency dispatch attending accidents and whatnot on the outskirts of the city limits just wasn't going to happen. The First Responders hands were full.

Clearly, whatever it was that happened to him and the others back at the scene of the accident wasn't an isolated incident. It was everywhere. On his way back, he'd come across dozens of accidents, cars pulled over, people screaming, fires, and even a plane crash. He'd see what looked like the beginnings of looting. Seeing a handful of store fronts broken open, people running in and out of them with their arms full of stuff so early in the morning spoke volumes.

The peculiar chaos was enough for Randy to double check his door to make sure it was shut and locked. He'd reach over and lock the passenger door as well. Things were sketchy. The wrecks and fires, some serious, some not so serious, were really countless. He'd go back and forth with himself, asking himself; is this really the Rapture? Or is it something else? He just wasn't sure. Nobody was sure; that was about the only thing he was sure of.

He wondered if it was the same all over. From what he knew of the Rapture, it was to be a worldwide event. Looking around at the local mayhem and runaway activity in this little corner of the world only made him wonder that much more. If it was this bad here, he could only imagine how terrible things would be in places like New York City, Los Angeles and Chicago.

Carson City was a mad house in itself and getting through it was even more maddening. The whole time Randy couldn't help but notice that emergency personnel, the Police, the Fire Dept., Paramedics and ambulances seemed skimpy, really skimpy. He knew there was a lot on their table, nothing short of over-whelming. But, it didn't explain why there was so few of them out there addressing the fiasco. There were plenty of alarms and plenty of sirens going off, up and down and back and forth but still it seemed thin. Only a small handful of the calamities were being assisted and the looting was seemingly going unnoticed.

He thought it strange. He couldn't understand why. In retrospect, in light of everything going on, there was really very little to understand; very little. What was there to understand? Out of nowhere, light-ening and darkness, voices and visions, being super-naturally pinned in place, cars coming to standstills, people disappearing; how could anyone understand any of it? And that loud trumpet blast at the end..., what was that all about? What did that even mean?

At one point, he saw a couple of mountain li-ons trot across the street, right in front of him, right there in the middle of town. It was a sight to behold. They were so majestic looking. He slowed down only to watch them gracefully leap up and over a nearby fence of someone's' backyard. All's he could do was hope nobody was back there.

Like the coyotes they didn't seem to be scared; seemingly fearless. They looked determined, like they were on a mission. It wasn't long after that that he saw a dog, a German Shepard chasing a couple of people into a house. Knowing the feeling, he tensed up. Sighing with relief when he saw the couple make it safe inside only reminded him of the unfortunate fate of the kid that was with him at the accident. The blood-curdling screams were still echoing in his head. That too bothered him so.

It was one thing after another. Each and every thing he'd notice or see was just one more thing he'd find hard to understand, let alone get a grip. Questions, it would be questions, more questions, nothing but questions hijacking all of Randy's thoughts as he'd make his way through the city. Thankfully Randy knew Carson City well enough to take some back roads to beat a good amount of the hubbub and road-blocks. It was however only a small consolation. He'd eventually get stuck in traffic and detours peppered with rude, panic-stricken drivers. It was very aggressive, even hostile.

With very little police, a skeleton crew at most, nothing was being tackled in an orderly fashion. Politeness and courtesy was nowhere to be found, let alone law abiding. Cutting each other off, countless fights, arguments and road-rage were everywhere. Randy was so glad when he made it out of the city and back to the mountain, Hwy 50 — or 'The Pass' to locals. He did however get a sour thought as he passed back where the DSS harassed him and especially Joel on the way up.

Their random set up and search station was long gone, but their presence overall was still quite prevalent. There was no escaping them. Their All-Point 24/7 Surveillance Program would see to that. He wondered where they were at. He wondered what they and the man-child President, Lowell Manning and his Fourth Branch were doing right now. He wondered what they were seeing, watching and recording and how were they handling this crazy supernatural ordeal.

He figured Marshall Law was inevitable. Still, keeping order was one thing, battling whatever it is that's causing all the chaos is another. What was going on; bombs, nuclear fallout, or a natural disaster it was not. This is beyond us, he thought—science fiction type stuff. It was just more questions, more food for thought.

On the Pass, outside of Carson City, the chaos wasn't quite so in your face. The storm however was back. The dark swirling clouds, spurts of lightning and thunder and sporadic rain was for whatever reasons more foreboding than natural. The flow of traffic was ok for a bit but it didn't last long. It would get more and more congested and backing up the further he'd go.

It wasn't long before the cars and Randy were inching along due to more wrecks, but more so because there were no detours. It was a pass, limited to one way over and one way back. There wasn't much room for cutting off, squeezing by or breaking through barricades. The only thing Randy could do at this point was crawl along; crawl along and think.

As the minutes passed, creeping past accidents, trying to get through to someone, anyone on his phone and flipping the radio dial was the only thing Randy could do to occupy his time. It was clearly the biggest testing of his patience in his entire life. Never has he been in such a helpless and seemingly endless predicament. Being extremely antsy didn't help matters. But what else could he do? What else was there to do?

Think, think…, and wonder and think again. Think and wonder about Joel, and his disappearance. Wonder and think about how everything went down and everything goin on. It was nerve-racking. It was overwhelming, disturbing, and puzzling to say the least. Being a bit traumatized by the coyote attack, he'd catch himself peering into the thicket of trees and the side of the road every now and then to see if he'd catch a glimpse of some more. That helped to kill a little time, but it wasn't much.

He contemplated a couple of times as to whether or not to assist people at some of the accidents he'd pass along the way. But they were all pretty well packed with small crowds doing this and that. Charging into the mix this far into the mayhem, charging in like a mighty roadside hero there to save the day was bordering on stupid. He was seeing some pretty serious stuff though. It was so surreal. By the time he'd come across each accident, being already hours on in, he figured most of the injured and even the dead were already being escorted back to medical facilities in other vehicles.

Again, there were no Police, or Ambulances, Paramedics anywhere this far out. And having gone through Carson City, he knew why. Although, he still couldn't figure out why there were so few to be seen even in the thick of things, in the city.

His thoughts would again take him around full circle. It wasn't long before he'd be taken right back to square one; right back to the bolt of lightning and the darkness. Recapturing and visualizing each and every event thereafter like a movie projector running inside his head played like a horror film. It was hard to fathom it. It was also unnerving simply because of the reality of it all. There wasn't any imagination or virtual reality going on at all. What was happening was very, very real. And coping with it made it that much more real.

Joel disappearing, the woman disappearing, the clothes, the coyotes, that poor kid, the lady's little girl missing, the whole thing, it would have him going out of his mind. And being stuck, trudging along inch by inch without any knowledge outside of Rapture stuff that he learned from Joel was driving him insane. It was torment.

Over and over, back and forth, going to the radio, no radio, back to the cell phone, no cell phone, both of them spewing out nothing but static was taking him over the edge. He was about to lose it. He was about ready to stop and jump out of his ol' pride and joy and scream or run; anything to break up the grueling monotony.

It was just about there when finally..., finally the radio kicked in. Words, a voice cutting in and out, but a voice nonetheless was enlivening. It was enough to revive Randy's sanity.

"Oh, my God," he sighed with great relief. "Thank God, finally, finally. It's about time."

Randy turned it up right away. He'd punch his old vintage radio presets and turn the dial to get something more solid, a stronger signal. Anything would work anything at all, even a song.

"Aha," he blurted with great satisfaction.

He found something. He found something he desperately needed, some words, a voice, some news to shed some light. He dialed in right smack dab in the middle of a report. A perky and upbeat Sal Salli report it was not. The voice, it was a woman's voice. She sounded nervous, but it was a keeping-it-together kind of nervous. She was clear, strong and very direct.

"...regions to establish order. Above all, remain calm. Panic as of now is our worst enemy. Please remain calm. This is the Emergency Broadcasting Network.

To repeat, the entire world is in a state of emergency. We are now getting confirmed reports that the mysterious attack is apparently worldwide. Europe, China, Russia, the Middle East, Africa..., all continents are experiencing and reporting the same as is the United State of America. In like manner, the temporary but inexplicable holding and restraints on all aspects of life, people and transportation were simultaneous and global in nature. The vanishings as well is an international affair. An undisclosed number of people have vanished, but it is being reported that the children, particularly younger children and infants were targeted. Ages, common factors, common threads have not yet been determined.

Also, the sudden surge of animal attacks, both wild and domestic animals continues to spread and worsen. Injuries and fatalities resulting from the attacks increasingly persist. People are to take extra precautions to avoid and avert any and all contact with all animals and their pets.

Pet owners need to isolate or quarantine their pets until further notice. It has not yet been determined as to whether or not the animals are rabid, infected, suffering from dementia or contagious. As to how and why the animals are affected by the international assault is still under investigation.

All Hospitals, Clinics, Emergency Rooms, Medical Facilities and Police Departments are inundated, understaffed and operating beyond sustainable capacity. Citizens, if at all possible are strongly advised not to burden their operating procedures outside of extreme and/or life threatening situations and injuries until further notice. All citizens are strongly advised to seek refuge and remain indoors until further developments.

President Manning through Vice President Hill has declared Martial Law. Military Units are being dispatched and deployed in various regions to establish order. Above all…, remain calm. Panic as of now is our worst enemy. Please remain calm. This is the Emergency Broadcasting Network. To repeat, the entire world is in a state of emergency. We are now….," would go around again.

The newscast wasn't live, it was a loop. Still it was something. Randy would continue to attentively listen to it over and over despite the repetitiveness. It was extremely informative. It was a darn sight more than what he had been stuck with over the last five, six hours. He went to other stations but it was all the same. The loop was all he'd get. But he was more than thankful. It was bound to update itself sooner or later. Still, what he had was enough to sustain him.

In utter disbelief, "This is too much. This is just too much. My God…, what's happening here?" he'd ask aloud.

Hearing of the animal attacks on the radio took him straight back to the coyotes, those mountain lions and that German Shepard. He now knew the attack on him and the kid wasn't a random confrontation. It had everything to do with whatever happened with the lightening, the disappearing and everything else.

Randy couldn't help but wonder if everything going on was really truly Joel's Rapture stuff or somehow connected to the Bible or Jesus, his second coming. He'd shake his head, but wonder just the same. Whatever it was or is, it's breathtaking, and dreamlike. It's like it really couldn't be happening, yet it was. And the animals he thought. What of the animals? Where do they fit in?

He'd go off into wondering about all the pets of people he knew. He wondered about them by their names, all the dogs and cats along with their own little personalities. He wondered how they were affected or if they were even affected at all. It was just one more thing for Randy to think about as he'd kill the time. Dissecting his newest list of questions and absorbing the newscast, it wasn't but ten minutes or so before

Randy would get another welcoming surprise.

The radio, even listening to the same report over and over, was a huge blessing when it kicked on. But this time it was his phone that kicked on out of the blue. As soon as it rang, he had it in sight, in hand, and transmitting to his earpiece in a split second.

"Hello, hello…, Becky? Jake…?" he'd shoot off like a semi-automatic pistol. He knew who was calling by the caller ID.

"Randy, Randy." fired back, hysterically. It was Rebecca. "Randy, they're gone…, they're gone," she screamed.

"Whoa, whoa, whoa…, who…? Rebecca…? Who's gone? I know Joel is, he, he…disappeared," Randy rattled off.

"Oh God, Randy it's….," was all that Rebecca would be able to get out before the phone would die again.

"Damn…, hello…, Becky…, REBECCA," he'd yell. "Are you still there?" Static, nothing but static was once again there to haunt Randy. It would haunt Rebecca, his sister as well.

After a handful of redials, and texting, getting no response and frustrated he tossed the phone down on the seat with a couple of cuss words to boot. He found himself even more antsy and nervous. His adrenaline was back up. It'd go up a notch however when he pulled over to relieve himself.

Standing by his door, daring not to venture out into cover for fear of the animals, he'd let lose. Screw the people in the cars, he thought to himself. He knew he wasn't the first, he'd seen many people, men and woman, who did the same thing. Finishing and zipping up, he took a quick gander at his surroundings. The line of cars, bumper to bumper made him grumble and jeer because he knew he'd have squeeze back in, only to probably piss somebody off.

Off guard, he looked around towards the woods to see if any animals were prowling about when, 'WHOOSH', an owl of all things, huge…, it came swooping down and plunged its talons in the back of his neck. The large wings flapping were powerful and majestic. He frantically yelled and cursed, ducked down and fiercely fought it off in mere seconds. It scared the heck out of him, drew blood, but it wasn't that critical. Still, it was nerve-racking.

"Shit…! What the f…," he cursed, and cursed again as he jumped back into the cab at the speed of light. Like Chad dealing with Nicki's hostile cat, Sheefoo, he too had a few colorful words and thoughts about the unprovoked attack. It was just one more thing for Randy to think about, and it wasn't good. It was terrifying, and it was making him mad more than anything else.

Thankfully however, on a good note, he was close to home. He was on the verge of getting past the snail-on-a-turtles-back traffic. He'd break away from the jamb at the very first opportunity. Off and running, taking back roads and side routes he was able to get to Jake and Rebecca's house within the hour of his hysterical phone call. He made it just before dusk—finally.

The trip from hell came to an end, but the end is nowhere in sight.

-Chapter Eleven-
PICTURE OF DESPAIR

Several hours would pass. It was now dark. Inside the three bedroom house quietly planted in a carpet of pine trees just outside of South Lake Tahoe were three terrified and unnerved people.

Randy, Rebecca and Jake found themselves helplessly harnessed and corralled in with the rest of the world on a quest. Rebecca was by far the most unraveled. She was broken, completely broken. Pursuit of the truth, for them and the rest of the world, even hours on in was just beginning. Sitting in a dark house with no electricity didn't help. Why the electricity was still off at Jake and Rebecca's home was yet another question but it paled to the bigger questions screaming for answers.

Being lit with candles and flashlights, the living room was dim. In it, Rebecca's hands nervously trembled as she clumsily raced and thumbed through the pages of her brothers Bible. Frantic, with her eye's swollen red and crying, she just had to find the scripture that Joel was talking about in the letter they had just found in the bindings of his Bible. Jake, her husband of thirteen years and Randy being just as nerve stricken and frazzled as she was, anxiously loomed and peered over her shoulder as she sat at the desk recklessly flipping through the pages of the Bible in search of 2 Thessalonians.

In their minds, there was absolutely no time to waste. Every moment seemed to count. Understandably, time seemed to be of the essence in light of what was going on and what happened just past daybreak.

"Here, Becky…., give it to me", Randy softly ordered and gently slid the Bible from Rebecca's shaking hands. He could see that she was totally disoriented, lost and unable to focus.

Leaving Rebecca at the desk and maneuvering to the nearby kitchen table as he peered through the pages more rationally, he sat down and within seconds, thumbed his way through the pages and found 2 Thessalonians neatly tucked away in the same exact place as it had been for centuries. Jake closely followed Randy as if he was tied to him, holding and shining a flashlight over Randy's shoulders so he would be better able to see and read.

"Second Thessalonians, chapter two, verse… uh…," Randy stuttered.

Quickly interrupting…, "Verse three to twelve"…, Jake blurted out as he again glanced at the letter to reaffirm himself.

It was a letter written by Joel. It was a letter

addressed to his loved ones and stashed in his Bible. Randy had totally forgotten about what Joel emphatically told him before he disappeared. Joel rambling on about his suitcase, in it his Bible and that there was something there for him faded from his memory with everything going on.

It took a while for Randy to reflect on it but it eventually came back to him. It was a letter, this letter, the letter that they were now dissecting and picking apart. Desperate for answers they did not waste any time.

"Read it", Rebecca anxiously demanded.

"Ok, ok…, let's see"! Randy instantly responded.

He quickly slid his finger down the page to the second chapter and the particular scriptures that seemed to be nothing short of treasure. Zeroing in on the scriptures that Joel referred to in his letter, Randy methodically and clearly read them out loud so as to share them with Rebecca and Jake.

"Ok…, this is what it says.

Let no one deceive you by any means; for that Day will not come unless the falling away comes first, and the man of sin is revealed, the son of perdition, who opposes and exalts himself that he is God. Do you not remember that when I was still with you I told you these things? And now you know what is restraining, that he may be revealed in his own time."

Randy continued…, as both his sister and

brother-in-law intently listened. *"For the mystery of lawlessness is already at work; only...HE...who now restrains will do so until...HE...is taken out of the way. And then the lawless one will be revealed whom the Lord will consume with the breath of His mouth and destroy with the brightness of His coming. The coming of the lawless one is according to the working of Satan"*.

Randy paused a moment, and slowly repeated the last sentence with a questioning tone, like that of a bewildered and inquisitive detective emphasizing an important piece to a riddled crime; a mysterious clue.

"The coming of the lawless one is according to the working of Satan?" He uttered.

Gazing at the scripture attentively, Randy again repeated the Biblical quote to reaffirm his self as to what he had just read. "The working of Satan"..., he staunchly repeated. Rebecca and Jake had also momentarily pondered as they absorbed the particular scripture and its haunting persona.

Irritable and flirting with hysteria, "What does Satan have to do with all this shit?" Rebecca screamed as if the scripture was stupid and meaningless. Patience was nowhere to be found in her and for good reason. After a short pause and a quick gaze at each other through the dancing light of the candles and a jittery flashlight, Randy went on to finish the scriptures that their lost brother had referred to in his letter.

"Ok..., second Thessalonians, chapter two, verse..., uh, verse..., well verse nine, there's more." Randy asserted.

"The coming of the lawless one is according to the working of Satan, with all power, signs, and lying wonders and with all unrighteous deception among those who perish, because they did not receive the love of the truth, that they might be saved".

Slowing the pace, he went on to finish the scriptures off. *"And for this reason God will send them...strong delusion...that they should...believe...the...lie; that they all may be condemned who did not believe the truth but had... pleasure...in...unrighteousness."*

"Pleasure in unrighteousness"..., Jake bewilderingly responded.

"What was the last part again," he insistently inquired.

Randy slowly read it again with more emphasis, amplifying the more concerning words of the scripture.

"GOD...will send them...STRONG DELUSION... that they should...BELIEVE...the lie; that they all may be...CONDEMNED...who did not...BELIEVE...the truth...but had...PLEASURE...in unrighteousness".

Rebecca, still at a loss of any composure and in tears, continued to snivel and stress her less than satisfied reaction to the scriptures that were just read to her. Finding absolutely no comfort in the spoken word, being even more irritated she wasted no time to voice her outrage, anger and disappointment in the so-called treasure in the Bible.

Sobbing and shaking, "What the heck is he talking about...? Believe what lie?" she blurted out loudly with panic and utter frustration. With tears streaming down her swollen face, "Does all this..., does this look like a lie," she hysterically screamed. "Where's my baby? I want my babies back. Where are they," she screamed even louder. "I want them back," she demanded.

She immediately broke down and again wailed uncontrollably. Rebecca, no doubt was desperate. Like a strung out heroin addict crying out in desperate need of a fix, she needed fast and easy answers. She needed some insight and a sense of direction and she needed it now..., right now — like everyone else.

Having lost their children, like so many other parents, Rebecca and Jake too were stricken with insoluble grief; drowning in unbearable torment and sorrow. They had also lost their brother Joel, of which Randy too would be grief stricken. Losing Joel along with having to witness the unhinged anguish and pain his sister and brother-in-law were forced to endure at the disappearance of their children was no small matter for Randy. Trying to cope with it all, trying to understand it all, and make sense of it all, frantically searching for quick easy answers in a matter of hours and limited resources was just too much for anyone to handle. It was traumatic to even try.

Even though the Bible that lay in the palm of her hands not more than fifteen minutes ago had its share of answers; it wasn't what Becky wanted, let alone what she needed. She needed something else. She needed more than scriptural riddles. She needed her children back in her bosom — to heck with the Bible, the Scriptures, or the truth.

And the truth is..., the Rapture had changed the world, but at the same time nothing's changed. Like most, Rebecca was still consumed with what she wanted, not with what she needed. The Scriptures had more than enough of the answers she needed, but they are worthless and useless in a world that feeds on what the people want; not on what they need. It's the way of the world. The way it's been since the beginning of time; since the Garden of Eden.

Right now, Rebecca's appetite, along with the rest of the world, has gone way, way beyond the simplicity and desire of what they want. It's now a craving; a feverish yen. They are salivating for some quick answers — all of them. But the answers they seek are not so easily found, because they don't exist outside of the Bible — but then again, maybe they do.

In a world where lies, half-truths, and fibs serve as answers…, then yes…, eventually the answers Rebecca, Jake, Randy, and the rest of the world are clamoring for will once again thrive. They will not only thrive, but they will be easily found. Most of all, even more importantly, the answers they crave and will ultimately embrace are sure to be quite gratifying. Satan plans on it.

They may not yet know it, but they can count on it. The devil knows the humankind well; in some ways, nearly as well as GOD, the Most High—HIMSELF. With their God-given gift of 'freewill', Satan and his vast, uncountable army of demons know what the human kind is capable of; in most cases, what they are… faithfully…capable of.

As humans, they are predictable in the eyes of angels and demons, as well as in the eyes of God and Satan. It is only with God however, the 'Holy Spirit' that the sons and daughters of 'flesh and blood' can break the chains of predictableness, enough to thwart the powers of darkness that count on it. But, sadly it is few who do. Even in the midst of the greatest calamity in the history of the world, all but the few remain the same.

Yes indeed…, the Rapture changed the world, but not the hearts of the humankind. Satan knows nothing's changed. No different than a dog returning to its vomit, Rebecca and the rest of the world were primed to go right back to fiddling around with what they've always fiddled with; beliefs, imagination, guesswork, theories, wishful thinking, presumptions, doubts, and half-truths.

Quoting the Apostle Paul…, "*Always learning but never able to come to the knowledge of the truth…,*" is how he so eloquently put it. It's amazing how simple it is, yet so powerful, and oh so, so true. Tricked once again, getting lines crossed between what she needed and what she wanted, Rebecca, the grieving mother was in unfathomable torment as was the rest of the world.

Everything going on, the Rapture and its aftermath was nothing short of a lingering and horrifying nightmare that had come to life. Not knowing where it was going, with no end in sight only made it that much worse. It would be a nightmare that would shove a menacing uncertainty down the throats of every one left to fear and wonder as to what had just happened, but more importantly what was next.

Emotionally torn and ripped apart from the inside out, Rebecca would speak for most of the world. She would speak for her husband Jake as well. Sorrow, suffering, misery and despair laced with unrelenting fear of the unknown were, for the last twelve hours, the only things they were familiar with. Nobody could blame her, or anyone else for that matter for wanting and demanding immediate answers on the spot. Nor could she or Jake be blamed for finding Joel's specially selected scripture near useless and worthless at the moment; where hysteria, panic, and chaos was ruling the day.

Desperation was the only thing they knew at the moment. Their babies were kidnapped is the way they saw it; not saved. Their seven year old son Sean and Skye, their precious little daughter of only four years old were stolen. Pain was in control. She, Jake and the rest of the world's parents, grandparents, and anyone and everyone who were connected in one way or another to children now gone are dealing with pure insurmountable agony.

Innocent, blameless souls, underdeveloped minds that hadn't reached the "*age of accountability*", Sean and Skye had simply vanished along with Joel. If that weren't miraculous enough, for Rebecca and Jake, losing Sean and Skye was only part of the dreadful misery that had stabbed them in the heart like a dagger. For not only were their two precious children taken, but her baby, six months into her pregnancy was also suddenly gone. Like a vapor, another boy, who they had already come to name Michael Ray, simply seized to exist. Jake and Rebecca were shattered.

The whole thing was heart stopping. It was staggering. For the unbelievers, it had always been simple enough to laugh and snicker at the very thought of the Rapture. Born Agains preaching and warning about the supernatural slap in the face was always chalked up to idiocy. But, to experience it firsthand put the world in a tormenting tizzy. It put Becky, Jake and Randy in a stupor; a horrifying stupor at that, to which there'd be nothing to laugh and snicker at. Even worse, it left them helpless. And the demons capital- ized on it.

The world throughout, the demons, more specifi- cally the Influencers; whispering thoughts and urg- es of suicide would easily creep into the vulnerable minds of grieving hearts. The powers of darkness al- ready had their list of unstable people in the world, a list of those who'd be easy enough to persuade unto suicide.

They also had their list of all those who were close to the Born Agains, like Nicki Dawn, those more susceptible to the Biblical truth. Needless to say, the Influencers also raced to them as well. There was much to be done now that Satan and his demons have been set loose.

Sadly, under Vy-Dénzyl's watchful eye — the Angel of Death; the escort to Hades, suicide had prevailed in some. Longing to be with their children and babies, listening to the dark, demonic Celestial Messengers, listening to their lies of heavenly reunions in some glorious afterlife; suicide would serve as the quickest and most practical answer. Craving quick and immediate answers opened a lot of doors and windows for the demons to sneak in.

They were easy to fleece. It was fairly easy to sway and persuade them; being they were so vulnerable. It didn't take much to take advantage of their anguish and grief. It's one of the more evil and wicked things the demons do. Of course, when their love and passion is set on their hatred for the humankind, to despise them beyond measure; why wouldn't they find pleasure in the more evil and wicked things they do to the one's God loves.

Sadly…, the wishful thinking of heavenly reunions with their missing children and grandchildren didn't pay off; as the demons well know. There would be no reunion and no longer any chance of one as well. It was distressing to find out that the truth had no part in their sorrow and grief. The power of wishful thinking spawned by the devil himself would once again prevail over God's glory of the truth.

Though suicidal tendencies were at times up front and center, in most cases it was not an option. For most, the thought of getting the children back or a reunion on this side of death was stronger. It was strong enough to give them a sense of endurance; enough so to repel the dark angels feverishly trying to steal their souls on the avenues of suicide. Rebecca, Jake and a world of other parents who had lost their children and pregnancies, suicide would not be the answer.

Instead, even though it was distant, it would be hope, a thought and a vision of getting their children back that would keep them from jumping off cliffs, swallowing pills, putting bullets in their heads, or nooses around their necks, etc., etc. It would protect them from making lethal choices. Still, agony and despair raged on. There was no getting around it.

There wasn't a living soul left on earth that wasn't left fearfully shaken by the Raptures heart wrenching impact. The astonishing taking of the born again Christians was in itself, awkward enough. There's no doubt the world would have wrestled and struggled with the Raptures extraordinary manifestation with mesmerizing awe and bewilderment if it had been only the Born Agains who were taken. But, being the younger children, the mentally innocent and blameless from all creeds, cultures and religions worldwide also taken, including babies still in the womb, bewilderment and awe was a far cry from the world's real emotional outbreak.

Across the world, from the strutting, self-adoring Hollywood elitist and political demagogues who loved to bejewel their sense of invincibility to the humblest minuscule tribes of Africa, the people were in awe.

From the wealthiest international moguls to the poorest of neighborhoods, people were struck with utter fear. From the devout Atheists, who were proved to be nothing short of intellectual idiots worshipping stupidity all along, to the most dedicated religious practitioners, people were bewildered and dumbfounded.

All of the bewilderment, awe and fear were however overshadowed, engulfed and swallowed up by the dark ominous cloud of emotional torment, grief and sorrow. And there would be no amount of money, and no amount of power, or fame on the face of the entire earth to buy off, or compensate, let alone cure the worldwide devastation. Everybody was touched and affected. The picture of despair was worldwide. And the picture of despair is the very thing that was going on inside the darkened three bedroom home quietly tucked away in the carpet of pine trees just outside of South Lake Tahoe.

Jake, Becky, Randy, and the rest of the world, the trauma was mutual. The anguish and anxiety was mutual. The thoughts were mutual. The options were mutual. And yes…, the questions — they too were mutual. As for the answers, it would once again depend on the heart, mind and soul of each and every individual.

"Always learning but never able to come to the knowledge of the truth…," was once again the clear and present danger. As to how many would be moved to

increase their *'knowledge of the truth'* and how many would go back to fiddling around with beliefs, imagination, guesswork, theories, wishful thinking, doubts, presumptions, and half-truths would be left to fate.

Regardless, the entire world knew they were in it together. They were in the same boat; in this case, the Titanic perhaps. All of them left drifting on an ominous, cold and dreary ocean of uncertainty; in the darkness no less—void of answers. Yet, the answers were there at their fingertips; answers as clear as the explanation surrounding the iceberg that gouged the unsinkable ocean liner.

Be that as it may, truth is the truth; as is reality is reality. And the reality is; nobody was fretting over the iceberg that came and went; the iceberg that hammered the deathblow on the Titanic. It was the folly that followed that consumed them. The Raptures coming and going wasn't any different.

Right now, even though people are in need to know what happened, it plays second fiddle to the hellish predicament they are now forced to endure. They're more concerned about their immediate fate, not to mention their children's fate. It was understandable considering the circumstances; the supernatural circumstances no less.

This explained Rebecca's behavior and emotions to the tee. It was a picture of despair. And the despair forced the broken and grieving mother, and the help-less father, and Randy, as well as the rest of the world to fearfully ponder and nervously wonder.

What next...?

What next...?

-Chapter Twelve-
DEVIL IN THE DETAILS

In the tongue of Angels and Demons:

"Let them panic. Let them scream and squirm; these little cockroaches, dogs, and bitches of the Most High." Vy-Apheélion voiced with elation and pleasure.

In the heart of Los Angeles, the powerful high-ranking demon and his underling in flight over the massive city, hovering here and there, bouncing from rooftop to rooftop watched the slurry of horrors beneath them with glee. It was sheer terror for the people, but for the demons; it was pure entertainment. At the moment; atop the Hollywood Memorial Hospital, peering over the edges looking down on the mayhem and a world gone mad, Vy-Apheélion, in his hubris continued to comment.

"I never dreamed the Nazarene's Harvest would be delightful and fun. It is good. It is very good—is it not Jur-Phalli?" he cheered with a menacing snicker.

"Delightful." Phalli said as the two of them savored the sight.

Without taking his eyes off what he was finding

to be so amusing and agreeable, Vy-Apheélion continued to gloat and revel at the sight below. "Look at
them." He said. "Look at them cringe. Look at them
run—they're so pathetic. They don't even know what
they're running from. Ah yes, to watch them suffer. I
never tire."

"How long, Master? How long are we to let them
run in this season of torment?" Phalli asked out of
curiosity.

"We are to let them quiver, let them cry, and curse
a little longer, Jur-Phalli. Yes…, I'm told a little longer—orders from Lord-Lucifer. They need to suffer
longer. The more they agonize, the more they are tor-
mented and tortured the better. It will work to our
advantage. Timing is everything." Apheélion stressed
and repeated. "Timing is everything!"

Jur-Phalli, in good standing with his superior, listened with great interest. He was absorbed and extremely attracted to Vy-Apheélion's rank and wisdom;
wisdom handed down from the top. He was learning.
He was climbing the ranks himself.

In light of the latest developments, he was getting familiar with Lucifer's masterful tactics, his latest arrangements, plans and schemes so as to flaunt
his authority, reclaim his dominion, and ultimately
prove the Most High God wrong. Vy-Apheélion (Vy-,
a surname of highest command / Jur- a surname of a

lower rank) without reservation, continued to brief his loyal and inquisitive underling. He'd let Jur-Phalli in on what Satan told him directly.

"Like us…, we need to let the other *principalities* of the highest order persist, to each their own dominion. Lord-Lucifer will have me press on — to have our underlings keep torturing these creatures of the flesh with power shortages; teasing them with little spurts of electricity here or little spurt there, flickering and dimming lights, playing with medical and security equipment, street lights, cell phones, computers; anything to make them go crazy as they plummet into despair. Yet, as ordered, we don't touch the 'image capturing apparatus'; video surveillance cameras and such. Those we do not disrupt." Apheélion stressed.

"Why…, my Lord?" Phalli respectfully quizzed.

"Lord-Lucifer has plans. He will use the footage to his gain in due time, shortly I might add. That is our orders…, persist, persist, and persist." He pressed. "Vy-Pécula, Vy-Fonteé, Vy-Gréthos, and Vy-Deélia…, they too must finish their attacks. Vy-Pécula stirring the tempests, the winds, and earthquakes is to be unrelenting, as is Vy-Fonteé's Influencers, and the 'crossovers' under Vy-Gréthos. Our damage needs to be thorough, long lasting, and scarring." Vy-Apheélion explained.

"And Vy-Deélia…?" Jur-Phalli asked.

"Yes…, Vy-Deélia, he's not only ordered to persist, but to ratchet his dominion up a notch. He's been ordered to disperse the second round of '*legion*' — to ramp up the possessions; more animal attacks and…, even more delightful, the flesh turning on their own will commence."

"It'll serve these dogs well, will it not, Master — giving them a taste of their own?" Phalli asserted to please his superior.

Apheélion chuckled. "Yes…, a taste of their own; just a bit mind you — just a little taste. After that, my good servant, when Vy-Deélia's '*legion*' and the other dominions have run its course, then we'll be summoned to unblock their measly little morsels of what they deem as great power — their electricity and technology. Stupid ones…," Apheélion jeered and laughed. "For them to think they have the means and ability to fix and restore the power grid is laughable, yet we'll lead them to believe what they love to believe, Jur-Phalli. And yes…, my good servant…, they do indeed believe they have such power."

"Like the climate…?" Jur-Phalli said astutely.

"Ahh…, nicely said, Jur-Phalli…, yes — just like the Climate. Just look at these fools." Apheélion averred. "I'm sure Vy-Pécula is having a good laugh. I can see him now, taunting them…, 'how's your power and control over the weather and climate working for you today'."

Jur-Phalli had to laugh at the thought, as did Vy-Apheélion, who went on to say, "Ahh…, the things we've gotten these arrogant idiots to believe, Jur-Phalli…, and so easily."

"Only to do it again, Master—make them think and believe it is they themselves who fix and restore the power-grid and energy?" Jur-Phalli asserted.

"Yes…, yes indeed…, and is it not laughable, yet— it's so infuriating, as you well know Jur-Phalli…, that we're called to make them believe such nonsense. Do they not know it is now I and my dominion that opens the faucet and closes the faucet—to give them the firewire or deprive them of it? Do they not know that it is now I who controls their firewire, power, and energy?" He clamored, almost angry that the human-kind knows nothing of the kind. "Keeping these pathetic creatures in the dark and clueless as to who we are and the power we possess is grating, Jur-Phalli."

"Yet…, we know why—do we not?" Jur-Phalli reminded.

"Yes…, yes we do—Hail Lucifer." Apheélion acknowledged, knowing quite well why they remain in the shadows of darkness. "In due time though," he added as he calmed down. "They'll find out soon enough that is we who own their power, energy, and technology. For now, although sickening—we'll patronize them as Lord Lucifer ordered. We'll flick on their portals, restore the fire-wires to their full capacity, open their channels of communication, and replenish the air waves. We shall give these feeble 'children of flesh' the impression they've restored all energy, and they'll feverishly watch the very things we've given them to enslave them. Thus, all these worthless, mangy dogs and bitches will get what they want—some answers. Yet, they'll know not, the answers they get will be as it's always been…, what is *falsely called knowledge*'."

"How long…," Jur-Phalli asked, "how long before we open their lines of communication and disperse the information and give them visuals on their portals?"

"Soon…, soon enough, for now though, let us enjoy first the other *principalities* taunt and tease the prey. Vy-Deélia's '*legion*' is most amusing. Henceforth, communication will begin on a moment's notice as Lord-Lucifer commands. Then we shall feed them. We feed them what we want them to know. But now, for the time being Phalli, my good servant—we wait. Yes…, we wait indeed." Vy-Apheélion pressed.

Everything went as planned; capitalizing on the Nazarene's Harvest—the Rapture. Satan in all of his celestial genius was, as always, extremely strategic, methodical and meticulous. His timing was impeccable. He not only knew exactly when, but exactly how much and where to unleash his power.

Brilliance on display; on his command, Vy-Deélia's second round of *Legion* was deployed. The demon possessions increased; in turn the animal attacks doubled down on humanity. The flesh on flesh would too take a turn from bad to worse.

The 'expendable ones', the demons of *'legion'* already swarming the face of the planet like locusts didn't hesitate to move in and possess all those already susceptible to them; those of whom the demons refer to as the 'opened vessels'. It took nothing at all to enter them, and of course control them. From that point, it wasn't only animals the people needed to beware and fear; it was now other people as well.

Compelled by the powers of darkness, led by... *spiritual hosts of wickedness in the Heavenly places...*, *'unclean spirits'* as the Bible puts it, the demon possessed persons would align with the crazed blood-thirsty possessed animals and boost the number of fatalities across the globe. Unusually enlarged pupils, making their eye's look black, frothing at the mouth, adrenaline peaked, carrying on like wild beasts, fierce, vicious, and aggressive, the souls controlled by *'legion'* fearlessly attacked onlookers.

It was right out of the movies, only it wasn't a movie this time. It was real; as it was in the Gospels.

It was the same *'unclean spirits'*..., the same demonic possession of people and animals; just a different time.

'And when He (Jesus) had come out of the boat, immediately there met Him out of the tombs a man with an unclean spirit, who had his dwelling among the tombs; and no one could bind him, not even with chains, because he had often been bound with shackles and chains. And the chains had been pulled apart by him, and the shackles broken in pieces; neither could anyone tame him. And always, night and day, he was in the mountains and in the tombs, crying out and cutting himself with stones.

When he saw Jesus from afar, he ran and fell down before Him. And he cried out with a loud voice and said, "What have I to do with You, Jesus, Son of the Most High God? I beg You, do not torment me!" For He said to him, "Come out of the man, unclean spirit!" Then He asked him, "What is your name?"

And he answered, saying, "My name is Legion; for we are many." Also he begged Him earnestly that He would not send them out of the country.

Now a large herd of swine was feeding there near the mountains. So, all the demons begged Him, saying, "Send us to the swine, that we may enter them." And at once Jesus gave them permission. Then the unclean spirits went out and entered the swine (there were about two thousand); and the herd ran violently down the steep place into the sea, and drowned in the sea.'

No…, it wasn't the movies. The *unclean spirits* and demon-possession terrorizing every niche, cranny and corner of the world was as real as the day is long. They were relentless. They were ferocious. Also, there was nothing slow about them; they were fast, instantaneous, and unhesitant.

In a matter of hours, they were already being killed by the thousands as they themselves killed thousands more with their brutal attacks. In the streets, in the gatherings and shelters, in churches, even in the households and homes, within families; for all those having to contend with the possessed monsters ravaging civilization, it was kill-or-be-killed. Killing them was seemingly the only thing to do, even the right thing to do.

They really didn't have much of a choice. Any attempt to subdue them or overpower them; to pin them down, tie them up, lock them up, to restrain them so as to take them alive was near impossible. Being the police force was already depleted and Martial Law not yet fully implemented, it was mostly citizens and family members taking down the deranged and vicious zombie-like savages who would charge and attack on a moment's notice.

Emboldened with pure hatred and rage, empowered with superhuman strength, sadistic and violent, they'd attack anyone and everyone on sight. With knives, baseball bats, clubs, shovels, pitchforks, pokers, cleavers, axes, pens, pencils, guns in some cases, whatever the demon-possessed souls could get their hands on they'd use to butcher, bludgeon, and kill all those they'd set their eyes on, even their own family. If no weapon was readily available, it'd be biting, scratching and clawing, and gouging and punching uncontrollably. Many people; people who were already in shock with the supernatural worldwide standstill and the children vanishing; were finding themselves having to fight for their lives on top of it all—all the madness.

It was only the open vessels that '*legion*' and the '*unclean spirits*' were able to possess. This however doesn't go on to say it was too few to count, for there were many open vessels. It would be all those who had already plunged into the deeper and darker pools of the Occult and Witchcraft. It would be those who had already given their souls over to the powers of darkness; to Satan—the Dark Angel and other demons summoned by name. Yes, in the grand scheme of things, there was only a small swath of Sons and Daughters of the humankind willfully worshipping Satan in the world, but plenty enough to forge a small army strewn about the globe.

Having already given their souls over to the forces of Satan, he who owns them; from the most famous of rock stars and movie stars to the least of covens and loyal loners, they'd be the ones the *'legion'* of Vy-Deélia's dominion harnessed and controlled like puppets. Up to now, to the devil's good pleasure; Satan's earthly minions and followers assumed it well to do his bidding over the years. Hate God..., hate Jesus...; to spurn, loath and resent the Holy Trinity—their authority, their presence, their ways. That and despise all those who worship all that is God and Jesus was never a small matter.

It pleased the Dark Angel to see them willfully, fervently and aggressively attack, mock and harass Judaism and Christianity to no end. The Satanists and Devil Worshippers did well promoting and recruiting a loyal God-hating, and Christian-hating, and Jesus-hating, and Bible-hating militia. They were good little soldiers and were used extensively to revere, augment and embellish Satan's presence on earth and his desires. But this is a new era; a new war.

The Rapture changed everything. The Supernatural Age has spawned a new agenda in the already blackened heart of Satan. As odd as it sounds, Satan's revitalized war on all things that are God and Jesus would have no place for the Satan Worshippers of old. They would be conflicting and troublesome. They would be more of a hindrance than a service in the devils invigorating new plans, conquest, and schemes. They just wouldn't fit in with Satan's newest breed of worshippers; for he doesn't want—nor has he ever wanted a near insignificant little sect of people to worship him as the devil—a mere angel. This is insulting. What he wants is a world to worship him as 'God'. This is the desire, and this is his chance. Thus certain things need to be done.

With the dawning of the New Age, getting rid of the devout Satanists was clearly Satan's best option. Devil Worshippers fawning over the existence of Lucifer—the Light Bearer along with their Pentagrams, and their shrines of Alester Crowley, and "Do What Thy Wilt" dogma just wouldn't fit into his newly enhanced and fashionable kingdom already percolating. Standard everyday Satan Worshippers of old would only poison and disrupt his up and coming wiles, trickery and deception.

Satan knew good and well that his up and coming breed of New Worshippers and god-seekers would find it repulsive to know they were somehow connected to devil worshippers. With that, it was time to remove them. It was time to rid them like infected rats. Satan of course had one more job for his God-haters to do. Being at the end of their reign, being now expendable, he'd use his useful little subservient pawns one last time to accelerate his quest to be like the Most High God.

Like Dmitri turning Leah and Nicki's cat into a crazed and murderous demon possessed vessel to do his will, watching it viscously attack Nicki's unsuspecting boyfriend Chad, Satan too found his faithful followers most delightful in their new crazed and murderous state. Watching them mindlessly attack other people, anyone, even loved ones pleased the Dark Angel. In his eyes, watching his foolish little army of loyal followers on the warpath and getting wiped out at the same time was a nice little touch of pleasure and quite gratifying.

There was no love lost; not a single ounce as far as Satan was concerned. How could there be when there was no love for them in the first place. When it came to the Fallen Angel and his sentiments toward the Sons and Daughters of God's Creation; it was the purest of pure hatred for them, all of them, even those who were foolish enough to worship him. Knowing their spirit and precious souls were sure to be cast into the Imprisonment of Outer Darkness upon their death didn't bother Satan in the least. He in fact cherished it and laughed at their dismal fate. Losing his faithful worshippers of old, getting rid of them under such hateful and callous circumstances, it was not only worth it, it was not only imperative; it was most pleasing to the Fallen Angel.

Getting rid of them was all part of a very detailed

plan. It was all about resetting the stage. It was all about conditioning the people to see and observe things in a different shadow; preparing them to receive their Messiah with open arms. It was all about getting the people of the world hungry, even starving for the New Born King; his new born king. In turn, they shall bow down and submit to the 'Light-Bearer'; to Lucifer by name. It is he who'll have all the answers to all their questions. From there his deceitful Kingdom shall rise, by which to prove the Most High God and the Nazarene wrong; and ultimately dismiss, even eradicate the truth.

At this point, it was only the beginning of the dastardly quest; a most methodical one at that. Thus, the horror continued for hours on in. Vy-Deélia's power and control over *'legion'* was strong and impressive. The demonic possession over the animals and Satan's earthly worshippers was clearly taking the worldwide madness to new heights. Vy-Gréthos, the high-demon principality who lords over the 'crossover demons' and manifestations, eventually jumped in and sprinkled the skies with countless UFO sightings so as to tease and taunt the already panic-stricken people and feed their imagination.

The raging winds, tempests, and mild earthquakes under Vy-Pécula's command continued; only to heighten the fear and jamb the blades of intimidation down the throats of every living soul left on earth to wonder. From China to Europe, from Africa to America, from Russia to Australia, from the smallest and remote villages and communes to the largest metropolitan areas and suburbs; there was no escape, for anyone anywhere.

Satan, feeling more and more like the Most High God, would relish the peaking hours. With the Holy Hand that had restrained him for centuries now removed from the four corners of the earth, Satan, now with free reign and wasting no time was anxious to take his power to the hilt. He had only just begun.

He would have loved to take the horrors he's been relentlessly inflicting on humanity over the passing hours further but it would go against his better judgment. It would topple his bigger motive; hinder is newborn agenda. Hence, after a pounding day and half of unidentified torment and darkness, it was time to show the entire world the magnitude and extent of his power. Gleaming with pride, he'd open the portals for all to see, and for all to revere his mighty authority.

-Chapter Thirteen-
FEED THE DOGS

The hours passed. People anguished. People murdered and killed. People fought for their lives. People ran for their lives. People frantically searched for their missing children and loved ones. People trembled, cowered, recoiled, and hid. People grew numb and shut down. People committed suicide. People gave into exhaustion, they buckled and fell. But the demons…; that never tire or sleep…, they rejoiced.

Now perched in the lower tiers of the Eiffel Tower; still being entertained at the havoc in the streets below, Vy-Apheélion abruptly jumped to attention.

"It's time…!" he vigorously said to Phalli at his side.

Out of the blue, in an instant, Apheélion took in a command directly from Lucifer via their celestial telepathy. With undivided attention, carefully listening to everything he was to promptly do; Apheélion would waste no time to carry out his orders.

"It's time. It's time to start opening the grid." He announced. "It's time to feed the dogs, Phalli; time to feed these bitches and cockroaches what they want. The hour has come to give these stupid, pathetic creatures some answers…, some visuals. Go…!" he ordered. "Gather your regiments, scour the realm and align the orders. Remove the barriers and blockage. Get as many portals opened up as fast as you can, but listen…, listen carefully. Keep the larger part of their telecommunications at bay. We're not ready for massive interaction amongst the flesh at this point; not yet—not at this time." He firmly asserted.

Phalli respectfully looked puzzled, yet anxious to carry out his superiors orders. Seeing his servant's silent inquiry, Apheélion quickly enlightened him.

"We need a season of their undivided attention, Phalli." He explained. "They need to sit there, stand there, lay there and watch and take in what Lucifer wants them to see. It is most important, my good servant. They need a season to be still, a season to observe and feel before they start flapping their tongues and running off their foolish mouths via the air channels. They need to fixate, stay focused and receive the message before they start talking about it, and exchanging their thoughts about it, and sorting it out worldwide. This is why we are ordered to open all the visual portals only and keep mass communication at bay. Do you understand?' He sternly asked, bordering on intimidation.

Phalli would get it. He would not only get it, he liked it. Now on the same page and eager to do his part, "The portals, Master...., the entire sphere...?" Phalli asked.

"Yes..., open it up..., all of it. Unleash their mind-controlling boxes. Unclog and revamp their fire-wires and airwaves. We need to show them how much they need a Savior; a God to tickle their desires."

Once again, aroused and impressed with Lucifer's masterful tactics; Jur-Phalli would move to carry out the command. The network, the grid, satellites, everything that had to do with Vy-Apheélion's dominion over electricity, airwaves and signals and the world's addiction to it would be loosened. Phalli would send the word to the minions under Apheélion's command. The dark powers residing over the global crisis of technical difficulties would stand aside. It would open up the information highway worldwide and feed the unassuming masses salivating for answers.

It was well into the next day, some thirty-three odd hours or so after the Rapture that Apheélion opened up the grid. Television, Satellite, News Outlets, Internet Connections, all sources serving the avenues of reporting were slowly getting up and running. News commentators, reporters and video footage would begin to pour in and feed a broken and desperate world.

It would begin to address a world without the Holy Spirit of God and void of the Born Again Christians. It would begin to address a world without the innocence of younger children, toddlers and babies. Lastly, it would address a world left without a single women pregnant. Conception, let alone the birth of a child were at ground zero. All this embellished with the raging winds and the demonic carnage; yes…, the pain…, the fear was indescribable. Mere words couldn't even come close to how terrible things were. And the grid, now opened would reveal it all, for all to see.

Personal communications would however be suppressed down to seeping levels as commanded. Too much interaction in and amongst the masses would only dilute, diminish and distract from the bigger picture. Moving past the limited radio broadcasts, like that of Randy's trip from hell, when the radio kicked on; though they served well as tantalizing appetizers, it was time for the main course. The horrific events over the past day and half would be put on the table, like a feast, to be served to all souls left and still alive on earth; to gobble up.

The portals finally being opened up so as to give the world some visuals beyond what they'd seen firsthand was of course received as a huge blessing, even though God, the Most High wasn't pulling the strings. It was the devil that opened them up. For most, being that it was far too dangerous to be wandering about outside with all the raging storms, demonic attacks and Martial Law in affect shooting first and asking questions second; most people were cooped up and going crazy inside of their homes, churches and shelters; thinking it much safer. When televisions and the internet kicked on after so many hours of pure hell and end-of-the-world madness, yes…, opening up the portals was a blessing as far as they were concerned.

All eyes were gathered and glued to the screens and monitors worldwide. Randy, Jake and Rebecca would glue themselves to the TV as would Leah and Nicki. The whole world would be glued in one fashion or another as Vy-Apheélion unblocked the electrical and magnetic disruptions. Things, details, updates…, it was all being laid on the table; as mention—so as to give the global community something to eat and digest.

Right off the top, the lack of people and faces covering the story and the small number of media networks up and running explained a lot. It answered Randy's question as to why there were so few First Responders, Police, Fireman and Paramedics tending to all the calamities, mayhem and carnage. It explained why the hospitals and emergency facilities are so completely overwhelmed, understaffed and incapacitated. And it was now explaining why there were so few media networks up and running and so few people covering the global catastrophe. People were frantically tending to their own affairs, their own losses, needs, homes and families.

They still are for that matter. Most of them abandoned their civic responsibilities and jobs to deal with their own personal issues, families and loved ones. Even people in the military and Government Agencies were compelled to abandon their posts and go against their vows to serve the public so as to tend their own.

Even now, most of the reporters and anchormen and women were distraught and holding back tears.

For most, it was all they could do to report and update because they too in most cases were directly and indirectly dealing with missing children, terminated pregnancies, lost loved ones, carnage, unrelenting storms, earthquakes and death like everyone else. It was the same behind the scenes, from cameramen to satellite technicians, reluctance to work or tend to their duties was everywhere. Be that as it may, things would however move ahead; slowly, but still forge ahead. In spite of all the personal hardships, pain and fear there were some tightening up the ol' bootlaces and gettin' out there to address all the pandemonium head on. They were getting out there to inform, assist the injured, maintain order, and get some answers.

People were hungry for all of it. They needed it. They badly needed it. They needed answers. Though it be only a small handful of answers to hundreds of questions they'd get at this time, it was welcomed wholeheartedly. In light of thirty plus hours of being in the dark of unrelenting grief, helplessness, torment, death, carnage, fear and despair, yes…, getting details of the ominous miracle and its fallout was embraced with great appreciation despite it all being horrific. At the mercy of circumstance, the people would take whatever they could and Satan knew it.

Details would now be shared. Details of the miraculous event and its impact would be shared. Details of when it happened, where it happened, and the aftermath was all the people would get as of now. As for the bigger answers to the bigger, more important questions; the how, what and the why behind a world turned upside down; the battle raged on. One lone single truth on one side of the fence would once again face off against millions of lies, half-truths and deceit on the other side. With the visual portals back on, people watched, people listened, and people absorbed every detail.

"We do not know, nor have we confirmed anyone who does know what is behind the catastrophic events," would stream out of some unknown anchorman brandishing a British accent. "What we do know is the bizarre attacks, vanishings, sightings, earthquakes and unusual weather patterns are global in nature."

Barry Bona; direct, clear and proper would speak with great concern but with very little emotional attachment. His countenance wasn't really so much about being untouched or detached from everything that was going on, he just looked like he wasn't directly affected. Clearly, he wasn't one who had lost a child or dealing with the death of someone close or even attacked by some crazed animal or a knife-wielding maniac. It was just the impression Randy would get as he, Rebecca and Jake watched attentively. Nicki and Leah, everybody would be watching someone somewhere sharing the details and grateful for it.

Barry Bona went on. All newscasters and reporters went on. In one form or another from one source or another, details came pouring out of every available portal. Finally, at long last, after thirty some odd hours, people across the globe were getting some insight. They were getting more familiar with the impact the Rapture had on the world. They were getting more acquainted with the supernatural event that changed the world in a matter of minutes. Slowly but surely, a picture would be painted for all to see. For the history books, the details would emerge.

Late winter..., 2043; it was Tuesday morning, February 29th, 7:26 a.m. Pacific Standard Time that the world would be instantly thrust into the Supernatural Age. The Rapture, now being coined as the Mass

Vanishing by secular standards happened simulta-neously. Spanning across the globe, the event was synchronized to the very second. It was 5:26 a.m. in Honolulu and 10:26 a.m. in New York City. It was 3:26 p.m. in London and 5:26 p.m. in Jerusalem. Simultaneously it was 6:26 p.m. in Moscow, 8:26 p.m. in New Delhi and 11:26 p.m. in Hong Kong. As for Sidney, Australia..., it was March 1st, 1:26 a.m., a new day. It was however more than the dawning of a new day. It was the dawning of a new age.

An unprecedented amount of surveillance and video footage abroad spoke volumes. It showed ev-erything; that is to say everything outside of what's be-ing called the "lost 2 ½ minutes". None of the Rapture was caught on tape. Footage showing all things held in place was not recorded. In essence, for whatever reasons, the Rapture itself was limited to eyewitness accounts and eyewitness accounts only.

All video footage showed the worldwide strike of lightening, and as if edited, the next available frame would be the 'instant release'; the release of all the people, animals, sea life, and transportation inexpli-cably held in place by unseen hands and forces. It was as if the whole world was put on pause, yet it wasn't; things happened. The billions of video record-ing sources, equipment and cameras across the world weren't scrambled for 2 ½ minutes, they just stopped recording. Like the people, like all facets of transportation from Airliners, planes, helicopters and drones to bicycles, escalators, elevators and cars; all video recording was paused until the prophetic Rapture fulfilled its calling. It was 2 minutes 33 seconds to be exact.

Immediately after the lost 2 ½ minutes, from that point on everything would be documented and confirmed. The surveillance and video footage would cover the aftermath in great detail. Vy-Apheélion had seen to that; he choked the electricity, but kept the cameras rolling. Its haunting footage showed everything. Nothing could be denied. People and children had simply vanished, leaving nothing but a pile of whatever attire they had on at the time of their departure.

Clothes, shoes, under garments and jewelry, wigs and hairpieces, fake fingernails, everything; even down to the unseen remnants of ink from tattoos all lay as they would be dropped to the ground where they departed. Anything that wasn't of their natural body lay discarded. Prosthetics, hearing aids, identification microchips, braces, fillings, stitches, contact lens, bandages and medical appendages from pacemakers to metal plates and pliable tubing, even organ transplants as well as their digesting food all lay where they may, lifeless and valueless to all those who were gloriously taken in the Rapture.

For some, however, the belongings may have laid dormant and lifeless, but definitely not valueless. For it didn't take long for a certain mentality to take advantage of the alluring and vulnerable treasures left at their fingertips. Randy saw it first hand when the kid didn't hesitate to pick up the diamond ring and necklace and put it in his pocket.

Sadly, within minutes it seemed, as frightening and peculiar as it was, amidst all the screams and cries and the chaotic madness that had instantly seized control of the air, there were those who just couldn't resist. Though a little hesitant and awkward at first, but not restrained, those who had lost nothing and had nothing to lose did not waste any time to rummage through the defenseless belongings full of riches laying at their disposal in the public streets and facilities.

Having only to keep a watchful eye out for the crazed animals and possessed people, the opportunists had a field day. Taking anything and everything of value served their unsavory and fearless conscience well. Crazed themselves, unconcerned and totally aloof to their surroundings and the higher meaning and impact behind the miraculous disappearance of so many people...; pillaging lifeless piles of clothes for treasure seemed to be more important. As long as the lifeless piles laid unattended and publicly visible, and the longer they would lie, the more they would be ransacked. It didn't take long before all of the inert piles of what had once been someone's personal belongings were plundered, scattered and discarded all over the place.

Ransacking piles of lifeless clothes wasn't the only thing that was taking the world by storm. Like a raging fire, the looting soon turned the corner and started to fan into higher end stores and malls; even homes. Setting their sights on costly merchandise, the people simply started to rush into the stores and break storefront windows to get their hands on TV's, stereos, cameras, computers, fashionable clothing, jewelry, shoes, I-phones and appliances; even cars, motorcycles, trucks, motor homes. Anything that had a lucrative price tag flaunting dollars and cents was up for grabs; and in the eyes of the hunters, the higher the tag, the better.

Self-indulgence however was only part of the tornado of people sweeping the streets on a crazed and wide-eyed scavenger hunt. Unlike the looters compelled by the spirit of greed, the spirit of survival was even stronger. It was "end of the world" lunacy.

Thousands upon thousands of people spontaneously clicked into survival mode and in droves, they raced and forced their way into grocery stores, and convenient stores, and department stores, and drug stores; any store or facility that carried food and water so as to round up as much and as many provisions as they possibly could and as fast as they could. Had there been any gun or ammunition stores available, which there wasn't, they would have been the first to be ransacked. Within a matter of hours, if not minutes, the countless shelves across the world that had neatly assembled goods for sale were picked clean and torn apart.

The frenzied harvest for merchandise, food, water and other survival provisions didn't go without its share of violence and casualties. People just went nuts. The fighting and scrapping, often to the point of brutality and even death were endless. Fueled by selfish ambition, almost trance-like, likened to the demon-possessed, the people hungrily snatched and grabbed anything and everything they could possibly carry, either off the shelves or from each other.

There were some noble and respectful enough so as to make concerted and half-hearted efforts to discipline or discourage the crazed robbers, but it was to no avail. It had in fact become dangerous; and then stupid and foolish to even try. It wasn't long before the curtains of apathy closed on their concern, even for the local authorities and law enforcement. There was just too much going on, too much going too fast to attend.

The noise was intense. Immediately after the

Rapture, alarms, sirens, horns and screams pierced the air and instantly conquered every single domain harboring serenity and silence. Everywhere, people were panic-stricken and recklessly running around yelling and wailing at the top of their lungs. Even on the most remote of islands and desolate of habitats, the screams alone of people dealing with missing children, lost loved ones and animal attacks were deafening. In the more congested areas, sporadic explosions and municipal utility and power grid failures were unrelenting.

Fires had broken out all over the place. Emergency units were depleted, hospitals and clinics were overrun, and law enforcement was flat out overwhelmed. There were casualties and fatalities on every corner. Dead bodies from all the accidents, demonic attacks and fighting were uncountable. As for the difference between the dead bodies that lay strewn about and the bodies that disappeared, it left everyone to wonder.

Traffic in metropolitan areas was piled up beyond measure. A good part of the people who found themselves hopelessly frozen and wedged in the traffic had set their sights on getting out of Dodge, if you will. For them, it was proving to be a miserable mistake. The streets and highways came to dead halts.

There were others caught in the stagnant mess. There were countless others who had set their sights

on something much more valuable than simply getting out of Dodge. It was something far more important that they didn't think twice about abandoning
their vehicles right where they stood in traffic.

Impatiently getting out of their cars, leaving them
to the fate of thievery, vandals and impounds, these
particular people weren't just hurried; they were desperate. Feverishly racing, meandering and pounding
their way through the onslaught of bumper to bumper
traffic, they were determined and for good reason. It
wasn't running away from the rampant bedlam, these
people were fixated on something else. It was their
homes, their families and loved ones that they were
feverishly trying to get to. It was all that mattered and
all they cared about. It was understandable.

The news got out quick about the missing children.
The missing adults were one thing, but the children…?
When it got out that the children were targeted, that
was it. Hysteria went through the roof. When the Mass
Vanishing concerned their own, panic instantly set in
and consumed them. Even people in the rural areas
who could have easily headed out into the hills for
safety, many of them having it already pre-planned
and prepared for a time such as this, a world in crisis;
even they were compelled to stay for the sake of their
missing children.

The children; it was the children miraculously

harvested off the face of the planet that had set the world on fire. Most of the people in the world did not have a personal stake, let alone an interest in Born Agains. The children, however was a different story. They, the children were the common thread that stitched the whole world together. They were the common denominator of all humanity in all nations. This is what united the world as one; equally ill-fated, equally pained, and equally panicked. Needless to say, the world as one equally worsened at the hands of Satan and his Demonic Minions of Lieutenants, Loyalist and Legion.

Now unleashed and taking advantage of the Living God's mighty miracle; Satan was strategically and methodically amplifying the terror. He is capitalizing on the fear and devastation already initiated by the Nazarenes Harvest. He's taking all the madness and mayhem to a whole new level on purpose and by design.

The abnormal storms, raging winds and hail scouring the entire face of the planet were extremely foreboding and a fury to contend with, yet it wasn't an act of God this time. Earthquakes abroad, mostly mild but quite noticeable were constantly shaking things up. The Dark Angel adding nature's fury to the havoc and bedlam already in motion was in his eyes a nice theatrical touch. It pleased him as did the surge of animal attacks carried out by Legion on his command. It all started slow but it snowballed into phenomenon's that rivaled the Rapture.

Once Apheélion opened the portals for all to see; conditions kept getting worse and worse. From around the world, the video footage just kept streaming in showing more and more people running for the lives. It would show people desperately seeking shelter or being swallowed up by nature's fury. There was footage showing people fighting off, if not being killed by both wild and domestic animals.

If that wasn't enough, adding fuel to the fire, Deélia's second deployment of *Legion* possessing people would enter the video streams. Footage showing fearless crazed blood-thirsty maniacs attacking people like mindless zombies. Like the animals, nobody knew what was going on with them; a viral outbreak, contagion…? Nobody knew and how could have they have known the maniacal and murderous assailants were all Satan worshippers.

As for the rash of apparitions and fleeting UFO sightings in the skies abroad, by Vy-Gréthos; they were strategically being planted as diversions, a detour if you will. They're meant to steer people away from the Truth, the Most High God, Jesus Christ and the Holy Bible. UFO sightings would immediately undermine the theory of the Rapture. Being a masterful tactic, the string of sightings would easily convolute the people's minds. It would serve to confuse them, raise doubts, and feed their imagination. It would open them up and make it easier for them to "*believe the lie*" patiently waiting for them just over the horizon.

Being that it was the Dark Angels season of preparation, there would be more, lots more information for people to take in. The news and reporting would continue to pound nonstop. Flooding the visual portals for all to see, keeping people on the edge of their seats, feeding their cravings for knowledge would persist. More videos, more footage, more reports and updates continued to pound into the horrified hearts and minds of all those watching in terror.

There were plenty of surprises. President Manning was unavailable to address the Nation in regards to the worldwide crisis. It would be Vice President Michele Hills doing the honors. She'd speak the standard, 'be calm, remain inside, Marshal Law' kind of stuff. Being no different than Lowell Manning; her speech, presence and leadership at this point was about as important and inspiring as a wet, filthy rag or the worship of science. It was near worthless. There were very few, if any at all, who'd tend to take comfort in the political spectrum. In light of what was happening, it showed just how small and insignificant politicians really are in comparison to the powers in the Heavenly realm.

As for President Manning unavailable to address the Nation, he was hospitalized and reported to be in critical condition. The Secret Service was apparently caught off guard. Deedee..., the First Family's once friendly and playful sheepdog viciously attacking and mauling the President..., they never saw it coming.

There were other unexpected surprises. Drug Cartels would shut down business. Even a worldwide ceasefire was in effect. Wars and global indifferences; both, small and great, isolated and abroad would for the most part come to a halt. Islam Jihadists would even put a halt to their carnage and terrorism once they found out that their children too were swiped from their arms and bosoms as well.

Oddly enough, the only comfort at all was everybody knowing they weren't alone in all this madness. It seemed to help. To think the entire planet from continent to continent was consumed and cast into the same incomprehensible whirlwind of emotional trauma, chaos, despair, anxiety, frustration and fear forged a sense of unity and togetherness. Countries, factions, sects, religions and cultures were more inclined to bond more than anything. The feelings were mutual across the globe. Fighting, or continuing to fight along with even the incentive to fight would be shelved; at least for now. The only thing unsettling was the influx of domestic crimes, not wars..., crimes against each other.

As it sits…, although the world this hour is somewhat unified by circumstance; they were not unified as to what is behind the circumstance. The world was at one, dealing with what has happened and what was happening, but they were far from being at one when it came to the source, or the forces that initiated the global attack. The truth is still alive and well, eternal by all accounts, but it doesn't go on to say the truth is believed by all. It'd be, in fact, very few who'd be so fortunate.

The 'believers', all those who believed God — whether they left like Joel or remained like Leah, they knew it was the Rapture that came to town. As promised; the truth came to pick them up and take them away. Those who were truly prepared left with the truth. As for the rest, they were left to deal with the truth. It went down exactly how the Word of God said it would.

Once again, the choice would be in the palm of everybody's hands. The fence is still there; still in place to divide the two. They could embrace the truth or combat the truth. At this point, only time will tell as to who and how many will go with the truth and who and how many will continue to chase after beliefs. Only time will tell as to who will cling to God's one and only truth and who will chase after…*the lie*…Satan has in store just over the horizon.

At the end of the day…, this day…, another Biblical Prophecy has come to pass; giving this world just one more reason to believe God, to believe Jesus…, to believe the truth. Being that some 2000 of approximately 2500 prophecies in the Bible have already been fulfilled to the letter, to perfection…; what's one more?

One would think it enough to believe Him; the Most High God, the Bible, yet, for most, it would do no such thing—sadly. But it's only the beginning of the Supernatural Age. If the Raptures coming and going isn't enough to make unbelievers believe; perhaps the Tribulation, Great Tribulation and Armageddon will. And like the Rapture…, they will come, and they will come on strong. It's a promise from God, from Jesus Christ and the Holy Spirit, a prophecy from a book of prophecies that is still, to this day, batting a thousand; a book that has yet to be disproven.

Even so, be that as it may, in a world filled to the brim with lies and half-truths lurking in the shadows, in a world where…*'the god of this age'*…rules; where the…*'prince of the air'*…dominates and controls the hearts, minds, spirits and souls of so many, many people, who can know their fate; the fate of all those still here, still alive to see what is to become of the Supernatural Age.

-Chapter Fourteen-
GUESSING GAME

"Mom..., what is all this?" Nicki demanded. Like everyone else, she was dumbfounded. She was amazed and struck with an obvious lack of knowledge and understanding. "Is this God? Is God doing all this?" she asked.

As her and Leah nervously sat there on the couch and watched the countless, non-stop and unrelenting news footage, reports and testimonies revealing one horrific nightmare after another, what else was Nicki to think? What else was there for anyone to think? Everybody knew they were dealing with a higher power; a real live supernatural power beyond anything they've ever imagined outside of movies, and there was nothing pretty or nice about it.

Wrath..., judgment..., an invasion, a war on humanity, even the end of the world was on the tip of everybody's tongues. It was in everybody's minds. The 'End of Days' and apocalyptic scenarios were the only conclusions of which there'd be no escape. Love, peace, goodness, serenity and harmony were out the window and fury, violence and a world falling into darkness was in.

Topping everything off, everybody was helpless. They didn't know who or what they were dealing with, fighting with, or even pleading for mercy to. They didn't know where to turn, what to do, who to address or even how to address this higher power, this unseen force letting the world know just how puny, frail and powerless they really are and have always been.

God…? Crying out to God was the rampant and natural response, but as always and typical of a world blessed with the freewill and power to either invent the truth or adhere to the truth — who is God? Figments of imagination, wishful thinking, the karmic universe, an impersonal force, some sort of energy, gods of this and gods of that, home-made gods, customized gods, Brahman, Gaia, Allah, an advanced Celestial Civilization from another galaxy; calling out to God went right back into calling out to whatever was in the mind of the beholder.

It would go right back to guessing who God is in the same way many would guess as to what came first — the baby monkey or the adult monkey, or the male monkey or the female monkey, or how the baby monkeys somehow managed to grow into male monkeys and female monkeys to procreate baby monkeys which already existed without having to breed. Crying out to a million and one different versions of

God would once again prevail in most cases. Cries out to God would remain for the most part aimless and airy like their invented truths that magically become knowledge.

Of course, Jehovah — the God that gave this world the Bible, the God of Abraham, Isaac and Jacob; this God would of course be in the mix of people crying out to God. But this God, the God of all Creation, the God of Adam and Eve, the God of Noah's Ark, the God that parted the Red Sea, the God that ordained the Virgin Birth, the God that walked on water, raised the dead and washed the feet of men; this God had stepped aside.

The Resurrected Christ, the Sacrificial Lamb of God being God Himself, the God that promised a Second Coming, the God that foretold and fulfilled the prophecy of the Rapture, God the Father, God the Son and God the Holy Spirit, the...MOST HIGH...; this God, yes..., most definitely was in the mix of people crying out to God but by how many and for how long was up to the test.

The cries would not go unheard by the MOST HIGH. Though the cries were heard, most however would be given over to the "*god of this age*". They would be given over to the...*god*...that divvy's out gods. The cries would be given over to the *god* that opened the worldwide — Gods-R-Us — chain stores founded in the Garden of Eden by trickery. The cries would be given over to the devil—the god that has facilitated the people's freewill and power to fabricate the truth and worship *"what is falsely called knowledge"* as the Scriptures put it. Yes—the cries would be given over to Satan, the Dark Angel, the Fallen Angel…, but only for a season.

Leah would answer Nicki's frantic question. In a near trance, distant and staring at the television, at the moment gawking at a horrific slice of news footage of an old couple being mauled by a pack of domestic dogs, she slowly and somberly uttered, "No Nicki, this isn't God. God is gone."

It was a depressing answer, almost hopeless sounding. Even though she was seemingly numb and in a daze, Leah was quite aware. She was also frightened. She was frightened for Nicki. She was frightened for the whole world. How were they ever going to believe that God isn't behind all of these demonic attacks, UFO's in the sky, and the teasing, but precarious tremors of earthquakes, and the foreboding non-stop weather ravaging and antagonizing every corner of the world? Of course, it was only her faith and her trust in the Bible that moved her to suggest it wasn't God. She knew the scriptures, and there was one in particular that wouldn't stop pricking her brain and feeding her thoughts.

"God would send strong delusion, that they should believe the lie" was the scripture. And here it was, up front and center, she figured. The...*strong delusion*... was already playing on Nicki. As for God sending it..., it wasn't so much about Him sending it as it was Him allowing it. God was surely, but indirectly, behind all this madness Leah thought. It was only because God..., as He promised..., said the day will come; a day to which He'd remove Himself, His Spirit and His Church. The day has come and the gates of hell were now open—wide open.

With the thought bouncing around in Leah's mind, along with watching all the horrors going down, she quietly mumbled..., really just talking to herself. "The only thing God had to do was step aside." She groaned.

"What...?" Nicki asked, failing to hear, let alone understand what her distraught mother mumbled.

With a heavy sigh, "Ahh..., nothing...," Leah answered without breaking away from her near hypnotic gaze at the TV.

Leah realized nothing's changed. Taking Nicki's question a little further into account, she worried and wondered. How in the world will her precious daughter ever come to understand, but more importantly believe there are two higher powers in this world; the MOST HIGH and the Most Popular? How was she ever going to break down the walls in Nicki's mind and rip off the blinders from her eyes to see and really truly know that these two higher powers are the difference between Light and Darkness, Truth and Lies, Heaven and Hell, and Salvation and Damnation?

It's been a near impossible task thus far to get people of the world to understand that Satan, the "Most Popular" does indeed exist and has had only one goal to his being. And that is to steer people away from 'the truth, the whole truth, and nothing but the truth'. It is truth, the perfect, invincible, and unassailable truth that forever resides and encompasses the MOST HIGH GOD; the truth hand-delivered by Jesus Christ Himself, no less.

Be that as it may, the 'Most Popular' does a superb job getting people to flat out reject 'God's Truth'. He does a superb job getting people to ignore 'God's Truth', or better yet, getting people to alter and edit 'God' Truth' or add their two-cents to 'God's Truth', so as to shape HIM and mold HIM into a God that they'll be more than happy to worship and revere. As long as HE, the Almighty God, bows down and kisses the feet of their beliefs, their rules, guidelines, and lifestyles—God is great. Why wouldn't he be…? He was purchased like a brand new car at 'Gods R Us', sold to them by the greatest salesman, or 'con artist', of all time, by Satan—the 'Most Popular'.

Leah knows this. She knows because she's lived

the life of worshipping makeshift gods that would suit her beliefs, agree with her wishful thinking, and condone her lifestyle. Thankfully, she also now knows the other side of the coin. She now knows and has known for a while now the difference between the two. She's 'born again', her eyes are what is described as opened — it's as simple as that. It's a blessing, but the blessing doesn't and cannot save her precious daughter. Until Nicki comes to understand the difference between the two higher powers, the difference between God and the devil, there'd be no hope for her or anyone else for that matter.

Leah had a good idea as to what was coming. The world was ripe. It was ready to be primed and groomed for graduation. The darkness would move beyond getting people of the world merely conditioned to reject and ignore the MOST HIGH GOD of the Bible, or alter HIM and add to HIM by way of altering and adding to the Bible. From what she gathered out of the Bible, it was now time to get people of the world to stand with the darkness — raise their fist and openly curse the MOST HIGH GOD with passion.

It was time, and to be a time, to harvest the multitudes and persuade them to wittingly loath and denounce the Bible and its decree that Jesus is the Christ. It seemed an impossible task to even think it, extremely improbable and very unlikely knowing how the Bible and Jesus Christ is and has been so ingrained in world culture, but Leah also knows the powers of darkness are nothing to dismiss, or something by which to dare limit its skills and capabilities

From this day forward to the end of days, Leah knew that anyone who would dare to align themselves with the MOST HIGH GOD of the Bible would eventually be in grave danger in the world, even unto death and martyrdom. According to the scriptures; the Bible Believing Christians, the uncompromising followers of Jesus as the Christ and His Gospel would be first on the list to be attacked. After them, it would be the Zionists shortly thereafter finding themselves in grave danger. Devout Jews who'd never denounce Jehovah—the GOD of Abraham, Isaac and Jacob would once again find themselves running and hiding from the hostile horrors and atrocities that come with the evil face of genocide.

"Come on mom! How could God be gone in all of this?" Nicki argued. "These storms, and earthquakes and, and—well all of this stuff. You can't tell me this isn't God."

"I think its Satan, Nicki—it's Satan that's doing all of these horrible things right now. I think God is just letting him do it."

"Aahhh Jeez—mom, can we just get off the Satan crap? I mean look at what's happening. This is God!

There's something huge behind all this. This isn't some little red freak out of the Bible with a pitchfork and pointy tail. You can't be telling me he's the one behind all this — this judgment or whatever's happening to us. You can't be telling me that it's the devil hiding under the bed or the boogey man in the closet behind all of these kids vanishing and women no longer pregnant."

"NO..., NO..., NO...!" Leah stressed impatiently. "That was the Rapture, Nicki. Jesus took the Born Agains and the children, not Satan. Satan — well Satan's just capitalizing on God's miracle. He's using it to his advantage." Being frustrated and short, "Ahh, Nicki Dawn..., never mind...," Leah blurted as she threw her head down into her hands. She had a splitting headache; was emotionally drained and mentally exhausted to boot.

"It's too much right now Nicki. It's just too much to explain. Just know that it's not God. It's not God and it's not Jesus pulling the strings right now. God's not behind all these crazed demonic possessed people attacking and killing people. And it's not God that turned Sheefoo into a — well just know it's not God. That's all I can say right now."

Nicki, far from being even remotely convinced kept silent. Her body language however spoke volumes. She inconspicuously rolled her eyes and slightly shook her head in disbelief as she refocused her attention back on the TV.

It was an opportune time for Dmitri to jump in and feed the beast. "She's crazy…, crazy-stupid, Nicki. And you know it. Don't fall for her idiocy." He said very, very convincingly.

Nicki heard it loud and clear. So much so she had to look over her shoulder once again in an attempt to see who was speaking to her. She looked at her mom who clearly didn't hear anything of the sort. At any rate, Nicki agreed. Everything her mom said to her just didn't register, at least at the moment. What did she do? She went right back into trying to figure out God's role as the Higher Power in all of this malicious madness sweeping across the globe. 'Why is He doing this', continued to rage in her head, and Dmitri was right there to feed her — lie after lie.

Thinking about God's role in all that was going on was pretty much what everybody was doing. Very few considered the thought that God had stepped aside and Satan took over as Leah explained. Instead, questions and theories would continue to pour into the people's minds. News reporters, theorists and commentators would keep on speculating — suggesting this and suggesting that. People of all walks of life, from every culture on every nation under the sun would revamp and reanalyze everything they used to believe, everything they used to think, and everything they thought they knew and understood before the Mass Vanishing.

God…? Who is God? What is God? Where is God in all this? Why is this happening? Is it really the Rapture? Is it something else? Is God even involved? Is this an attack? Is this judgment? Is this punishment?

It went on and on. Questions and more questions on top of more questions went round and round. What's with the surge of apparitions and UFO sightings? What are they? Who are they? What's up with the cataclysmic weather patterns and earthquakes? What are we to do? Are we to pray? Are we to repent? Are we to fight? Are we to shape up? Is it the end of the world?

It was everything Satan wanted — mass confusion, mayhem, and carnage; but more importantly starvation. A world starving for answers would serve the Dark Angel well. It was everything he needed to advance his sinister agenda allotted to him by God Himself; the MOST HIGH. Time was short. Time was critical. And Satan knew it. He wasn't however impatient. He was instead measured and most methodical. His army of demon-angels was most vigilant, obedient and extremely careful to carry out everything they were told to do with sophistication and subtlety — even down to the slightest of whispers.

Leah went into the kitchen, mumbling to herself,

probably praying as she often does is what Nicki assumed. Jeering, "She is crazy!" she thought as she attempted to rationalize her mom's far-flung answer about Satan's role in all the madness. It was again, Nicki's thought at the moment, yet it wasn't Nicki's mind that drummed up the thought. Dmitri...; his celestial voice did it. He was relentless. He was not only back at it, but constantly at it. The devious Influencer assigned to her, and only her, was determined. It was time for another feeding. Like the timely nurturing of an infant; the demon was prompt, equipped and more than ready to do his thing. He's already had his vicious, even heartless, fun with the cat-attack fiasco; possessing Sheefoo, only to have the precious little thing brutally killed, by their own hand no less—but now it was back to business.

There he was..., Dmitri; the demonic celestial messenger hand-picked and trained by the high Prince of Influencers, Vy-Fonteé himself. Yes..., the demon was right there doing what he does best, what he's been trained and called to do—sway and persuade. He was cozied right up against Nicki's ear, making himself right at home; right there feeding her everything she needed to hear to oppose anything and anyone in league with the Most High God, Christ Jesus and the Holy Spirit. This of course would include Leah; her own mother.

Dmitri breathed his words into Nicki's ear like water pouring on a house plant. "She's not right in the head—she's lost it. But you've known that for quite some time now—her thinking hasn't been right for years." He whispered. "Her head's been spinning and it's still spinning. She's off her rocker, Nicki. I mean how stupid is that—that it's the devil doing all these things that only a 'jealous God' can do? You know better than that, Nicki—you're smarter than that. I mean really…! "He hissed. "She's gone, Nicki—your mother's gone off the deep end. Don't be fooled. She'll take you down with her—to the psychotic pits of stupidity and lunacy, if you're not careful."

Oh so soft and sweetly, did he plant the words. Being very cautious to leave no rock left unturned, like all the dark celestial messengers deployed, Dmitri was brief, to the point, but thorough, very thorough and methodical; for he'd done enough for now. He, in a sense, watered his houseplant, just enough to keep it alive and healthy until his next visit. Nicki was sure to flourish. The tireless demon was sure, comfortably sure at that. To Satan's good pleasure—and his for that matter…, yes…, Dmitri is sure to boast, Nicki Dawn is his to keep.

All the Influencers; they were all eager and faithful to obey their orders; to serve their lord and master. Ordered to feed the sheep; feed the sheep without ceasing; and that they'd do—as if they were created to do so. Uttering and whispering thoughts of doubt, planting seeds of scrutiny in regards to any mention of the MOST HIGH GOD—the Father, the Son, and the Holy Spirit was imperative. Distorting the truth, twisting the truth, concealing the truth; squashing any knowledge of the Bible, the Gospel and the Nazarene was a must.

The Influencers were good at it. They were in fact better than good; they worked to perfection and in most cases to completion—unto death of the manipulated soul. They've been relentlessly doing it for centuries and generations on in; why wouldn't they be good, if not perfect at what they do. Nicki Dawn unfortunately took in Dmitri's gentle, but diabolical seeds. She found herself quick to scoff and shrug off her mother's peculiar and off-putting Biblical assessment.

Going right back to the TV, Nicki continued to take in and digest all the horrific news footage, video feeds and reports. It didn't take but seconds for her to dismiss her mother and what she had said. Having been convinced that…'she knows better than that'…, that… 'she's smarter than that'…, as Dmitri suggested, she'd go right back to her original questions and own assessments in spite of Leah's explanation.

Once again, God—is this God? Is God doing all this? Why? The questions were still there. She also took a moment to ask herself as to whether or not she actually heard what she thought she heard; 'things that only a 'jealous God' could do'. What does that even mean; she wondered. She wondered how that popped into her head. Weird…, was about all she could say about it. She couldn't make heads or tails of it, and simply blotted the mystery out of her mind and moved on.

In light of all the supernatural activity and the undeniable fact that the world was dealing with a higher power, and being that GOD is, in most cases, always equated to the higher power; again what was Nicki and the rest of the world to think? All the things that were happening seem to fit and resemble nothing short of God-like power, as opposed to an intergalactic alien attack, yet UFO sightings were off the chart. It was hard, in fact, impossible to piece it all together, let alone any part of it. It was maddening.

Hour after hour, watching and listening to mother after mother and fathers in utter anguish, howling in tears and screaming as they'd testify and explain the loss of their children, grandchildren and great grandchildren. From the wealthiest Kings, Queens, Senators and the biggest movie stars in Hollywood to rural school teachers, Islamic Jihadists and the Zimbabwe tribes of Africa; the horrific testimonies, tales and stories were the same in every language and every religion from every culture in every country. The mothers devastatingly trying to describe how their babies were snatched out of their wombs; how they were unable to move as they watched the orbs move in and out of them leaving them empty and void of a due date.

People broken and shaking as they'd confess to being forced to kill their pets and loved ones due to whatever it was that turned their beloved kindred into crazed, murderous and vicious monsters. Watching the death toll rise across the world with each passing second would leave everybody in question as to who was next or if they were next. It was all a guessing game.

Suicides were skyrocketing. Billions were still separated from their families and loved ones. Not knowing where each other was at, wondering as to whether or not each other was safe, or dead or alive or taken in the Mass Vanishing would leave all of them swimming in the pools of unreserved fear and anxiety.

Yes—where's God in all of this? What, or who—just who is the higher power? And what does this higher power want? What is it doing? Why is this happening? Round and round Nicki went. She pondered quietly as she took on each and every one of these types of questions head on. When all of sudden, unexpectedly, her phone came to life just before midnight.

"Ringggg…, Ringggg…," came out of nowhere. It came from a phone that has been dead for the last forty some odd hours. Though it was dead and was proving to be of no use after countless attempts by Nicki trying to get through to someone, it would still be the phone that had never left her side. It would be the phone, like so many others that Vy-Apheélion's dominion and power managed to silence and disrupt until now.

The Dark Angels short and imperative season of conditioning the multitudes by starving them; depriving them from international chit-chat, was now over. It was time to shift gears and take the deception to another level. Playing on the frantic Earth Dwellers fears, shock and emotions was a must, but more importantly, playing without an end would be that much more serving.

Wisely, methodically, and by design—after nearly two days, it was now time to ignite the flickering flames of buzz to a full fledge fire. It was time to open the gates taking the trickles of conversation to a global flood. At the hands of the devil and his demons, the doors of communication, global communication would strategically be opened. Kitchen chit-chat, family huddles, street conversations and person to person feedback needed to expand—it was time.

People in France needed to converse with people in Mexico. People in New York needed to converse with people in San Diego. People on one side of town needed to converse with those on the other side of town. And like hungry piranhas frenzied for a piece of raw steak tossed in the water, people feverishly began to interact and correspond with each other via wire and waves. Nicki's phone ringing; it was only one of the uncountable drops in the flood of global communication instantly covering the planet, but it wasn't insignificant. The long awaited communication breakthrough, all the excitement it generated…, it was understandable. And Nicki Dawn was no exception.

Beaming with pure adrenaline, "Oh, my God!" Nicki shouted after her phone rang. She'd waste no time and answer it without even looking to see who was calling.

"Hello…, hello…!" she frantically answered.

"Hello? Nicki…? Nicki…, it's me—Carla." It was one of Nicki's better friends in their little hellion click.

"Carla! Jeez, Carla—man! Am I glad to hear from you? Oh, my God. I haven't been able to talk to anyone since, since—well since all of this stuff started happening. Are you ok? Are you getting all this stuff? Can you believe all this s…t?" she clamored.

Nicki was so fired up and ecstatic that she didn't realize how fast she was rambling, let alone how one-sided it quickly became with her barrage of personal questions. None of the conversation would be calm, cool and collect nor was it meant to be. Mild and pleasant it was not. Riled and wound up, both Carla and Nicki would fling their words back and forth rapidly and sharp.

"Yeah, yeah—I'm ok, Nicki. I'm ok, how 'bout you?"

"I'm goin' crazy, Carla. I just don't know."

"Sheesh—you got that right. I don't think anybody knows." Carla added with a sigh. "I'm glad you're ok though. Uhh…, hey—I heard about Chad. What the hell happened?"

"Oh, yeah I forgot—Chad. I don't know. He came over not long after that, that—whatever it was that happened. Were you held in place, Carla? Did you feel all that power or whatever it was?" Nicki asked without realizing she changed the subject.

"Yeah, yeah we all did—everybody did. Well? I guess everybody did except—I don't know? I guess there were some who were able to move during that freaky invasion, but they, you know—they disappeared."

Nicki stayed silent for second as she pondered her mom's ordeal through the Mass Vanishing. She saw it firsthand. She thought about how her mom was able to move when it all went down. "Christians—I think it was only the Christians who were able to move." Nicki said almost somberly.

"Yeah, that's what I heard too. At least that's what all the reports and people keep saying—that it was only Christians who were able to move into those—whatever they were—lights, doorways, stairs—who knows? That's the adults though. But oh my God—the kids, the children and babies, what's up with that? And did you hear they have yet to find a woman pregnant? They're saying that maybe there aren't any women pregnant which means no babies; no babies for what—another nine months? God knows—maybe never. This is insane!" Carla rambled off.

Nicki stayed quiet. Both she and Carla had to take a moment to sift through and absorb the verbal back-and-forth they've been flinging at each other. After taking in a breath and letting out another heavy sigh, Carla rekindled the conversation. Taking it down a notch, a little less excited she'd continue.

"So! What about Chad, Nicki? What happened to him?"

"Oh man, Chad—well like I said he came over not long after the Mass Vanishing. We were all freaked out and stuff, and Sheefoo—she came out of my room, peeking out and scared." Nicki explained as she began to tear up. She couldn't help it. She was hurt. Sheefoo was in a sense her baby.

Though distraught, Nicki went on. "I..., well I picked her up and she was trembling, and I started to pet her and stuff, and bam! She —, she just attacked Chad like a..., a frickin' mountain lion. It was crazy — freaky. She just went to ripping into Chad like no one's business. Me and my mom, right away we tried to stop her but wow — it was so fast and unexpected."

Nicki would break into a full-fledged cry as she reflected on Chad having to kill Sheefoo. "And then..., then Chad — he killed her. He broke her neck, but he had to — I guess. I don't know?" she cried. "I don't know if he had to. I think me and my mom could have caught her and...., and tossed her into the bathroom or something. But..., I don't know..., it was horrible Carla — just horrible."

Nicki felt bad for Chad. Hearing him scream for dear life was troubling. His wounds were nothing to minimize, but it was really Sheefoo, losing her little Sheefoo causing her eyes to well up with tears. Nicki went on to finish up with Chad's visit.

"After Sheefoo, well after Chad killed her — we started to bandage him up and calm him down. We were all still freaked out; not only with Sheefoo attacking Chad but everything — everything going on."

"Yeah — we all are." Carla gently butted in. "And then what?" she added.

"Well. It wasn't long before his dad — I guess making the rounds trying to find him came over here. He was worried about him being missing or not at home.

Man he was freaked out too. He was so relieved to find Chad though, but finding him all bloodied up and bandaged like some war casualty didn't help."

"Oh, man," Carla filled in, "Did you tell him what happened?"

"Yeah, we told him. We all told him what happened. He really didn't know what to say. He just walked Chad out the door into the car and who knows. Maybe he went home or to the hospital. I don't know. Now that the phones are working—I guess they're working," Nicki reasoned. "I'll try and get a hold of him to see how he's doing."

"Are you gonna stay home then?" Carla asked.

"Hell yeah…! Are you crazy?" Nicki blurted. "I'm not goin' out there. Not right now—not with all those demonic freaks and animal attacks. I think its contagion. Until we know its halfway safe to go outside, I'm stayin' right here. We have some food and water, but still, I hope this isn't going to be a long wait. It's a scary thought. Anyhow, my mom and I are just kickin' it right now. We're just gonna stay here and keep watching the news to see what happens next."

Carla perked up, "Your mom, oh yeah—your mom." She said. "I forgot. Isn't she, or wasn't she a Jef? Wasn't she like—like one of those Born Again Christians or something?"

"Yeah she is." Nicki confirmed, almost embarrassed.

"So she isn't missing or didn't vanish?"

"No. She's here." Nicki said. "She's still here."

"Huh! Oh well—I guess it wasn't all the Christians or Jesus Freaks that vanished." Carla surmised.

Once again, a bit somber, "No, I guess not." Nicki agreed. She couldn't help but hone in on the thought of her mom—how she lost her chance, how she could have vanished with the rest of her kind if she so decided. A sense of guilt would again creep into Nicki's conscience.

"Well—ok Nicki, I'll talk to you later. I'm gonna make some more calls. I still haven't got a hold of Lisa, or David—Chad either. Yvonne, Jase, Teri, and Ricky, and…, and Anna are all ok, but I guess Ricky's older sister lost her pregnancy and Teri's little brother, well…, I guess he vanished—it's what she said. She's pretty shaken up—her and her parents."

"Man…, what's up?" Nicki mumbled in frustration.

"I don't know…, Nicki. It's…, it's all just crazy. From the looks of things, I mean they haven't really confirmed it, but some of the newscasts are saying it seems to be children no older than eleven that vanished. Some say twelve, even thirteen and fourteen, but who knows? I mean geez—where are they? Are they here, are they gone, are they dead? Like…, did they go to heaven? Are they just invisible or coming back? Were they…, like taken by aliens? I mean what the hell—I don't know…, have you heard anything about any of this stuff?" Carla pried.

"Yeah…,"Nicki answered, "I heard the reports…, or at least some of them, that it was children twelve and younger. Thirteen, fourteen…? Like you said who knows at this point? It's still early. And like you, I don't know where they are or if they're coming back or if another round of taking more people is coming; I just don't know. I guess we'll just have to wait and see."

"What does your mom say, being a Jef and all?" Carla asked.

"Well…" Nicki murmured. "My mom say's they're in heaven—taken by God, by Jesus."

"Jesus? Oh brother," Carla scoffed, "I don't know about that."

"Yeah, well…, I don't either. But, it was in the Bible that this was going to happen one day. My mom talked about it every now and then and it sure looks like it happened. You know, maybe they are up in heaven. I don't know. Maybe the Bible is true. I don't know Carla? I guess—like I said we'll just have to wait and see what happens. Anyhow, I'm gonna make some calls too right now. I'll call Chad to see how he's doin'. Hopefully I'll get through. So I guess I'll talk to you later, huh. And hey—let me know if you hear anything else, ok."

"Yeah, ok. I'll talk to you later, Nicki. I'm glad you're ok…, love ya. And I'll tell the others."

After hanging up, Nicki was quick to share the news with her mom. Leah however was more interested in the fact that Nicki's phone was back up and running. Excited and eager, paying no attention to the hour, Nicki called Chad's house straight away, even while she was telling her mom everything that Carla had told her.

Paying close attention, Leah waited to see if Nicki would get through. Sure enough, low and behold, Chad's mom answered after a couple of rings. From there it was the standard back-and-forth conversation in regards to everything going on, and in less than a minute, she was talking to Chad.

-Chapter Fifteen-
NO WHEELCHAIR

Watching and listening to Nicki talk on her phone perked Leah up. She too got somewhat excited. A spark of life re-entered her otherwise deadened soul. Like her daughter, over the last day and half, she tried and tried again and again to get through to someone, anyone, even 911 on her own phone but failed miserably.

Joel was at the top of Leah's list. Speed-dial, voice-dial, manual-dial time after time, but getting through to him has been hopeless. She wondered about Joel. She thought about how she and Julie were to meet up with him when he got back from Lake Tahoe. She thought about a pleasant evening, talking to him and hearing all about his trip visiting his sister and brother. Now she just wanted to hear his voice, even his voicemail greeting.

She figured he was gone, taken in the Rapture. She wondered how it was for him, where he was at when all happened. In light of the thought of it though, she was finding herself somewhat torn. She was happy to think he was up with Jesus, but there was a part of her that wished he wasn't.

She knew it was wrong, that it was selfish but she was so broken and hurt about missing her chance. She felt so alone, so forsaken and scared. Still, she was perked up. She didn't waste any time. It was now just past midnight but like Nicki, the hour really didn't matter. Not really knowing what to expect; she immediately speed-dialed Joel once again.

Praying…, praying to hear his voice, his real voice, praying he was still here, praying he'd answer his phone, but it was all tied to first a hope and prayer to hear the phone just ring . And it did— the phone started ringing. Shaking, nervous, anticipating and full of anxiety, Leah listened and waited for an answer.

"Hello…," came from the other end.

"Joel…, Joel…! Is that you?" Leah promptly asked.

"Uhh, no…, no I'm sorry this isn't Joel. This is Randy, my name's Randy. I'm Joel's older brother." Having seen the Caller ID on Joel's phone, Randy continued. "Is this Leah?" he asked.

"Yes…yes it is." she said having already begun to sob. "Is Joel there? Is…, is he there with you? Can I please talk to him?"

Leah had an unpleasant feeling. She just knew he was gone, but she couldn't help but choose outright denial for the moment. She so much wanted to hear Randy say—just a minute or he's out back—anything, anything at all to suggest Joel was still here. The hope was however short-lived. Randy wouldn't have such comforting words for Leah.

"Umm, I'm sorry Leah but—well Joel's gone. He's not here." Randy explained as gently as he could.

It was immediately quiet after that, but only for a moment. Randy easily detected the news he had for Leah was heart wrenching. He wasn't surprised to hear her immediately break down. He'd hear muffled grunts, dead silence and a gasp for air, and again the same. He could tell she was crying uncontrollably. Leah doing all she could to keep her sorrowful cry silent didn't last long. Breaking and bursting into loud sobs and mumbling couldn't be helped.

Randy remained silent and politely let her weep. For a moment he thought about how and why she was here, still here on earth talking to him. Being that Joel mentioned everything about her, he knew that she, like Joel, was a Jesus Fundamentalist and shared the same beliefs. He wondered what the difference was between her still being here and Joel being whisked away.

"Oh, uhh—I'm sorry." Leah shakily uttered after gaining some composure. "I'm…, I'm sorry, I didn't—"

"Whoa, whoa—don't be sorry, Leah." Randy interrupted. "I'm…, well—I'm just sorry I had to tell you the news. I know you guys were close. Joel had a lot to say about you—all good I might add; all good. He was extremely fond of you and thought highly of you. He used to tell me that you were the little sister he never had — that he felt closer to you than any of us."

Randy was quick to console Leah's grieving, but at the same time he was actually glad to be talking to her. It didn't hit him right away, but now that he had her on the phone he instantly found himself wanting to ask her a ton of questions. He was longing for Joel just as much as Leah, but it was Joel's knowledge of the Bible that he seemed to be starving for.

Randy gathered enough to know that Leah was on the same page as Joel. He knew that he and she believed the same exact things. He knew they were both Jef's that wholeheartedly believed the Bible, the Gospel, the prophecies, the Rapture — the whole nine yards. He couldn't help but suspect Leah knew everything that Joel knew and here she was — someone within earshot to take up where Joel left off.

He didn't have any idea why she was still here and Joel was gone. It was sure to end up being just one more question he'd have for her. Randy was starving for answers like everyone else. He was however one who was setting his sites on knowing more of what was in the Bible. He wanted to know more about the Rapture. He wanted to know more about God and more about Jesus as she and Joel understood them, and knew them to be. He wanted details this time.

Unlike Rebecca and Jake, Randy wasn't ready to go right back into aimlessly wandering around chasing the winds of guesswork, wishful thinking, and entertaining overactive imaginations. He wanted substance, something real, and something with facts. He wanted the 'TRUTH'.

Randy, in a distant sort of way, seemingly knew the truth. He just wanted to know more about it. Leah would surely be a good start he thought, but not now. Now wasn't at all a good time. Right now, never once losing sight of Leah's brokenness, he did well to sympathize with Leah. They were both grieving their loss of Joel.

"Do you know what happened to him?" Leah asked with a sniffle.

"Yes. Yes I do. I was there. I saw him go. Well—at least from the corner of my eye I saw him go. It was—I don't know. It was scary—scary for me, but Joel? Joel was—I'd say calm. He was calm but excited at the same time. He wasn't scared. He looked like, I don't know—like an over excited kid on Christmas morning I guess you'd say.

After that blast, that lightning bolt across the sky, and the darkness, and being held in place and all—God that was weird. Shoot! I was freaking out. I mean—it wasn't only me but all the cars, the traffic—it all just stopped. Ah, Gees! I'm sure you already know about all of that." Randy uttered after catching himself going off subject.

"Yeah..., Joel..., he was with me." he said with a little quiver in his voice. "He wasn't stuck at all, though. I mean..., we were both in the cab of my truck, headin' to Reno — on our way to the airport and boom..., everything stopped. But it was the craziest thing — I couldn't move, but Joel..., he was..., he was able to move, no problem. In like seconds, wasn't more than 10..., 20 seconds or so that he, I don't know..., just seemed to know exactly what was goin' on. Then..., he like..., leaned over and put his hand on mine —" Randy said and abruptly stopped.

He choked up. He sighed and caught another breath. Clearly, he was still shaken up by the whole ordeal. Leah could hear it in his voice. She continued to listen with great interest as Randy moved to finish.

"I just couldn't move. I was clinching the steering wheel. I mean like really clinching it..., like white-knuckling it. I..., I couldn't let go. It was so weird. Anyhow, like I said he reached over and put his hand on mine to comfort me I guess. He told me a few things — good-bye and stuff, and he just got out of the truck and walked over to whatever he saw and just like that — he was gone. He disappeared." Randy explained, still in disbelief.

"What do you mean — he got out of the truck and

walked. He actually walked? The wheelchair," she excitedly pressed, "no wheelchair?"

"No! He didn't need his wheelchair. He was I guess healed or something. Joel actually got out and walked. I couldn't believe it, but then again, I couldn't believe anything that was going on at the time. Some lady—after everything that happened—some lady in another car said the same thing. She said she saw him get out of my truck and walk over to this—whatever the news is calling it— this vision, or doorway and he flat out disappeared. I have his stuff. I have all his stuff. His clothes, his fake legs and braces, I have the stuff just left there where he disappeared. I have his wheelchair and luggage that was in the back of the truck at the time and of course, as you know, I have his phone." Randy shared.

Randy was ready to tell her more, but would immediately pause. He again heard Leah weeping on the other end of the line. Politely and understanding, Randy would let her get it all out once again.

After a few moments, still sobbing, "He walked!" Leah exclaimed after catching her breath. It would however be tears of joy that would escort the question. Leah was overjoyed to hear of such news. Randy immediately rolled with it.

"Yeah he did. It was good. He actually walked." Randy happily shared as he switched modes. He wasn't acting so as to patronize Leah, he was actually happy to think about it as well. It was a joyful thought. He was able to relate with Leah's moment of being somewhat overjoyed. There wasn't really too much out there to be happy about. So much misery, death, carnage, and fear, you name it; it was out there. So, joy and happiness; it was welcomed anytime, anyway, in any form and any amount.

Just then, urgent and pressing, Nicki softly yelled, "Mom! Mom come look at this. Quick! Check this out. Hurry…!"

"What is it, Nicki? I'm talking to Joel's brother right now. I need this."

Still clamoring, "Mom— just look at this. It's beautiful. This is good news."

Capturing Leah's curiosity, she'd mosey over to the TV. "I guess there's an update or something." Leah said to Randy as she neared Nicki to see what she was raving about.

Randy knew exactly what the hubbub was. Sitting in the back of the living room, looking over Jake and Rebecca's shoulders while they sat on the couch, he too was catching a glimpse of the miraculous event transpiring on the world stage. Rebecca and Jake were clearly as excited as Nicki was. Curiosity would also capture Randy's attention.

"Hey Leah—I really need to talk to you. May I call

you up here in a while, maybe tomorrow morning—ten or so?"

"Yes, please do. I'd like that. I need to talk to you as well," Leah would say almost in a rush. She, like Randy, was eager to see what the ruckus was about. The phone call would end short and both Randy and Leah would sit down with their adjoining families and watch and absorb the newest miracle.

"In short—," Barry Bona excitedly clamored with his overtly thick English accent, "Some are saying she's the 'Queen of Heaven'. Others are calling her 'Our Lady' or the 'Lady of All Nations'. The 'Mother of God', the 'Virgin Mary' perhaps…, who knows?" He raged nearly uncontrollably and continued to rant.

"It is however reported that the looming weather conditions in the vicinity instantly and miraculously cleared in her presence. Peering out of doors, windows, even some daring to flock towards what seems to be a benevolent force, video cameras would capture the glimmering specter just outside of Lisbon, Portugal as it converted a dark and foreboding morning into what can perhaps now be called a beautiful day; weather-wise that is."

In minutes, the report would sweep across the entire world. It didn't take long before the latest supernatural event via satellite would be pasted on every TV, every monitor, screen and portal serving the watchful eyes and curious minds of people slowly, but surely adapting to the New Age...; the Supernatural Age.

"She's so..., so beautiful...," Rebecca remarked in utter amazement. Her sentiments were spoken barely above a whisper. Her voice was weak and shaky. She was weary, barely able to keep her eyes open for lack of sleep. The commotion going on over in Europe however was enough to momentarily lure Rebecca away from her emotional suffering. She really didn't know what this being, this Queen of Heaven was or what it had to do with her children and Joel's disappearance, but it had to be something.

"Yeah..., whatever it is, it's..., boy..., I don't know..., unreal," Randy mumbled without taking his eyes off the clips of video footage.

Some footage being better than others, the jittery home video feeds would roll, one after another. Different angles, different cameras going back and forth showing the apparition and the nervous gathering of people, some falling to their knees in reverence was enough to get the gist of the miraculous event. Lasting just over twelve minutes, hovering over the coast of Portugal at sunrise; the mysterious and alluring Queen of Heaven vanished in an array of lights dancing about the sky. She was there; she revealed herself and she was gone before any professional media outlets with their higher end cameras could catch her live.

From there it would weave in and out of different reporters eagerly interviewing different people. The adrenaline was high. Everyone was extremely excited, ecstatic, despite being inundated with grief and devastation. They were nervous and twitchy; some were leery, some were thrilled while others were near euphoric. It was all understandable? A vision like this, of this nature captured and recorded by so many people and televised worldwide…, it was unprecedented. To see it live only made it that much more sensational.

The interviews were the standard Q & A, some in English, others interpreted. The reporter's questions spoke for the entire world. Everybody was curious; everybody who had seen or heard about the apparition had the same questions.

Who is she? What is she? Is she an extraterrestrial? Is she an angel? Is she the Mother Mary of God? Is she a spirit, or even God? What does she want? Why here…, why Lisbon, Portugal? Was there any message? Did she speak? Is she here to help us…, here to save us? Does she know where the missing children and people are? Is she coming back? It went on and on. As for the answers, they too would speak for the entire world. Guesses, opinions and theories was all they'd amount to. As to any of them being correct had yet to be determined.

After a good fifteen, twenty minutes of undivided attention, quietly watching and listening to the wound up reports and interviews, Randy would break the star struck silence in the room.

"Queen of Heaven...huh?"

"Yeah..., I guess," Jake uttered. "That's what some of the people and locals are calling her."

"You know, I used to think these things were fake. I've heard of these types of visions and even seen some pictures here and there over the years of these..., these, whatever they are, supernatural sightings, holy visions, but I've never seen anything like this? Nothing like this..., this is too much. And the weather, the weather cleared up just like that...," Randy asserted as he snapped his fingers. "I don't know, Jake. This is crazy."

Jumping into the conversation and pondering, "Lisbon, Portugal...," Jake mentioned. "You know..., there was another sighting like this. Jeez..., I don't know, 19 something..., around World War I, but... uhh...it was in Fatima, Portugal. I wonder if there's something to that."

"Who knows," Randy stated keeping the conversation somewhat quiet and his eyes glued to the TV. "Who knows anything at this point? The only thing people seem to know about any of this craziness is in the Bible."

Randy was finding himself a little irritated despite being amazed over the vision in Portugal. He just couldn't get away from this feeling that everything he wanted to know about everything going on was in the Bible. He was sort of angry at himself for being so unfamiliar with it. And thinking about the long drawn out process and time consuming task of getting to know it at this point was driving him to the point of anxiety.

With everything going on and happening so fast, the thought of casually sitting down and sifting, and reading, and deciphering a thousand plus pages in the Bible just wasn't going to happen, and he knew it. It would take too long, he figured. Still, he was itching to know more about it. The thought of reading the whole thing was discouraging but not enough to pull him away from his desire to learn things. He just wanted to learn as much as he could and as fast as he could. He had his mind set on a crash-course, but where, how?

Joel's letter along with his list of scriptures instantly came to mind. It was already a good lead. Randy's thirst for knowledge, Biblical knowledge, however was bigger than a list of scriptures. He wanted more. He needed more. He really didn't know why, it's just what he was feeling inside. Puzzled, feeling inadequate and perturbed, he went on to share what he was thinking with Jake.

"The Bible…, man I don't know what to say about it. I can tell you this though—you know darn well everybody raced to find one when all of this…, this Rapture or whatever it is went down. And my guess is most of 'em like us only fumbled and thumbed their way through it. It's like where in the heck do you start, I mean look at this thing. It's as thick as a phone book," he said as he waved Joel's Bible around after picking it up off the table.

Discouraged, "Man…, the thought of reading this so as to understand what all this is about and what's really going on, it's overwhelming. Who has time for that?" Randy grumbled. "It's like…, like a two thousand piece jigsaw puzzle we have to painstakingly put together to see the big picture. Just the thought of it sucks." Assessing his thoughts he went on to finish.

"All's I know is Joel and the Christians kept saying this was going to happen one day. And here it is. Sheesh…, these animal attacks, and these demon possessed people on the rampage, this weather and these frickin' UFO light things and earthquakes…, are they in here? And what about this Queen of Heaven— this…, this Lady of All Nations or whatever the hell she is…," Randy barked pointing to the TV. "Is she in here somewhere? I mean yeah, we get it, the Virgin Mary, the Mother of God, or the Mother of Jesus. Yeah we know she's in here but what about all of this stuff.

What about this sighting in Lisbon?"

"Sshhh…!" Rebecca angrily ordered with what little energy she had left. "Please…, Randy. Can't it wait; I'm trying to hear this."

Both Randy and Jake turned to her and respectfully heeded her request, or demand if you will. Rebecca, even though she was mentally drained she was gripped by the news reports. And why wouldn't she be? Like so many others worldwide, she was a grieving mother. After having her children and unborn baby supernaturally disappear and out of the blue comes this angelic figure, this beautiful god-like vision appearing to the entire world, she had good reason to hush them up.

What she was watching was more therapeutic than anything else. She knew this glorious miracle floating in the sky was obviously connected to everything going on. She knew this Queen of Heaven had answers and she was anxious to get them.

In awe, as if sitting in the same living room Leah too gazed at the magnificent apparition as did Nicki Dawn. A shiver would slither in and out of Leah's body before she'd tense up like an over wound pocket watch. Unlike Rebecca, she didn't find the angelic vision therapeutic at all. Quite the opposite, sitting on the edge of her seat she was feeling uneasy and disturbed.

"Oh Lord..., what is this?" Leah whispered to herself in prayer. Unable to escape her knowledge of Biblical Prophecy, the End Times..., she couldn't help but cringe. Plucked right out of the Bible—'*signs and wonders, signs and wonders*' was once again the standout phrase stuck in Leah's head. As beautiful as the vision was, she thought it malevolent and dangerous. Contrary to Rebecca's and Nicki's excitement and praise, Leah found herself speechless; in awe, but speechless. She really didn't know what to say. She didn't know what to say but she knew how she felt.

Either way, regardless of what people thought of the image in the sky, good or bad, it was a sight to behold. Fleeting and sketchy it was not. It was there for all to see. Levitating, translucent, huge; as tall as a watchtower, maybe 200 feet high, like a Cathedral, a magnificent Temple—she glimmered and glowed with every color under the sun moving and meandering in and out of her like sparkling jewels. Even though the finer details were lost in the glow and brilliance, there was no question about it. The figure, the face, the features, the garb and the hair; the angelic visitor haloed with a dazzling crown was most definitely feminine. Queen was quite fitting.

Fascinated, even spellbound, all who'd set their

eyes upon the radiant, warm and welcoming apparition that lit up the sky marveled. People were easily taken in by her splendor and beauty. Seeing the wonder on television screens, VDT's (video display terminals), phones, monitors or what have you was amazing in itself but it paled to actually being there in person, in the vision's presence. It was just a given. People automatically knew that watching the video footage on televisions, electronic devices and digital media could never live up to seeing the enchanting manifestation live in all its glory.

Being there, being there to witness the instantaneous change in the weather by her mere appearance spoke volumes. It only made the miracle that much more glorious and magnificent. It instantly gave the apparition an aura of goodness, benevolence, even holiness. According to the news reports, apparently all the other horrors the world was dealing with had also miraculously came to a stop in the vicinity.

The peculiar, unpredictable and vicious animal attacks ceased. It was reported that the family pets were back to normal. There were even some reports of the demon-possessed people suddenly free from whatever it was that was ailing them or possessing them. The Queen of Heaven, this Lady of All Nations, her persona and appearance definitely made her mark on the entire world. And the world saw that it was good.

Barry Bona was right. In a lot of ways, it did indeed turn out to be a beautiful day, at least in Lisbon, Portugal. All things however weren't answered. Relief had come to the vicinity far and wide, but it was short of giving anyone any closure. People were still grieving and in despair over their lost loved ones, their missing children, vaporized pregnancies and hardships that came with the Mass Vanishing. The fear and shock—it was still over the top.

The powerful and mighty visitation, this Queen of Heaven didn't bring closure to Lisbon, but what she did bring was an open door not yet opened to the rest of the world. Lisbon, people in Lisbon were now able to, maybe not heal but at least lick their wounds. They were now able to somewhat pull themselves together, go outside and attend to things without being terrorized by bloodthirsty animals, precarious weather and homicidal maniacs. It was a huge relief.

As for the rest of the world on this day—they may not have gotten from the Queen of Heaven the open door to lick their wounds like the people in Lisbon, but what they did get from her was hope.

-Chapter Sixteen-
PIE IN THE SKY

After two days of living hell; dealing with the Mass Vanishing and the horrible, devastating and tragic aftermath, the people of the world now had a ray of light to set their sights on. They now had hope. And the blessing; the blessing was well received. Rebecca, dead tired and undone would be one of many to take hold of this new hope and grasp it for dear life. Being on the verge of shutting down, unable to keep her eyes open any longer, Rebecca would hold the hope close to her heart like that of a little girl clinging to a teddy bear for comfort as she'd slowly fall asleep.

Three or four times, getting softer and softer, "Sleep…, I need to go to sleep," Rebecca repeatedly mumbled until she went out like a flickering candle. Before you knew it, she was out for the count. Both Jake and Randy watched her shut down.

"Well, at least she didn't cry herself to sleep this time," Jake softly mentioned.

"Yeah, she's been through a lot. You too for that matter," Randy said. "God, I don't know what to say about Sean, and Skye…, or the baby for that matter. I mean, yeah I'm torn and miss them and I'm worried about them and all, but I know darn well, me missing them as their uncle can no way even come close to how you and Becky's gotta be feeling."

The simple comment hit Jake hard. He took a couple of seconds shaking his head as if he was contemplating on an answer but the words wouldn't come. Instead, unexpectedly he flat out broke down. He promptly planted his face in his hands and began to cry. Randy's words caught him off guard. He muffled his breakdown as much as could. He didn't want to wake Rebecca. That was part of it, but there was also the embarrassment factor.

Jake is what some would consider to be the man's man. Twelve years in the military, a war vet, a Marine; and now a hands-on Contractor unafraid of getting his hands dirty put him on the other end of the spectrum from America's prissy little, tantrum-throwing lily-soft Commander in Chief unable to throw a baseball twenty-five feet. Unlike Lowell Manning, the high-and-mighty liberal snowflake who would tremble at the sight of a BB gun; who loves to hear himself talk tough, like a bad-ass intercity gangsta despite the fact of hiding behind his mommies apron, a man-child sickeningly protected by an army of doting liberal sycophants and people addicted to living off of other people's money; Jake on the other hand truly was rugged, tough and fearless by nature.

He was stern, independent, proud, self-reliant and headstrong to boot. In other words, he just wasn't the type to be caught crying. It was a sorrowful sight, awkward, but quite understandable.

Randy kept quiet. He'd look down and away so as to give Jake a sort of makeshift sense of privacy. As he did with Leah during their phone conversation, he just went ahead and let him get it out. It was but a minute or so before Jake managed to snap out of it. Rapidly wiping his tears with his hands and on to his pants, he'd end with a hard sniffle and go right back into discussing the situation with Randy as if his out-burst never happened.

"It is hard, Randy. I just don't know what to say anymore. Man…, I feel…, I don't know…, I feel so f…n' numb. I don't even know what to think or…, or even how to think about all this stuff. My children…, gone! Just like that…, I just can't fathom it. Never in my life have I felt so…, so powerless, so helpless. It's humiliating. I feel useless." Jake grated.

"Well…, I don't know about all that Jake. Geez…, I don't know what Becky would do without you. I'd hardly say your useless, dude—not even." Randy praised.

"Yeah…, but it's the kids, Randy. I don't know where the kids are. I mean, I know there suppos-edly in heaven, with God or Jesus according to Joel, but then again, what about all of these other theories we've heard. Maybe the kids are still here. Maybe they're not even gone. Still, even if they are in heaven, it's not helping anyone down here trying to cope with this madness.

Too me, if God did take them…, it's just wrong. It's hateful as far as I'm concerned. I mean who would take children from their parents? That's not love. This is the God that Joel kept harping about? His Jesus…, this Jesus that is supposedly all about love…, you know what, I just don't see it. If God took 'em, I don't see love in that. What about his love for us? Doesn't he care about how we feel? Why did he take the children if he knew it would destroy us? I don't see any kind of love in any of this crap. I find myself getting angry at God for taking them; he has no right I say. Everything, all this thinking, all this not-knowing, it's numbing. You know, Randy — I'm just burned out. I'm so burned out."

"Well…," Randy intervened. "You've pretty much hit it on the head. I'm willing to bet its how a lot of people are feeling right now, probably most for that matter. With everything going on, the world doesn't know whether to curse at God or pray to God. My guess is most of 'em, like you is more apt to curse at God, but then again, there's a part of us that can't help but pray. It's weird."

He'd go on to finish. "I don't know Jake…, something tells me there's a lot more going on than what we're seeing. Yeah, we're seeing things but I'm not so sure that what we're seeing is where we're to stop looking. I guess it's…, it's like a veil. We're seeing all this stuff happening, almost like we're supposed to see it, like an audience watching a magician on stage. But something tells me there's something else, something behind the veil. I'd say that's where the truth lies…, behind the veil and I want to see it."

Jake didn't even respond. Somewhat distant and detached, he just looked at Randy. Randy however wasn't finished. He also knew that the conversation at this point was more like him thinking out loud than conveying a message to Jake. Still, despite Jake's blind stare, Randy continued.

"As for the kids…, I know they're not here. I know it's breaking your heart and Rebecca too, but I can't help but feel they're safe. The only reason the children were taken, and Joel, or the born again Christians is because, like Joel said…, they were supposedly to be spared from a literal hell on earth; the end of the world. If that's the case, if it is the end, if we're in for a hell on earth, then I guess God or Jesus taking the children would be love. As for us…, it isn't like we didn't know.

It's like.., like the sign was posted…–Danger, Thin

Ice–..., we could have believed it just like Joel, but we didn't. And posting the sign, posting it so people would know..., that's love. So it isn't like we can say God or Jesus isn't about love or doesn't or didn't care about us. The Bible told us this would happen. Right now, I'm just tryin' to figure out the difference between us and Joel. I can't help but wonder why he believed it and I didn't.

I mean I just don't get it. What is it exactly that makes one guy believe and the next guy not? What is it exactly that compelled Joel to trust the –Danger, Thin Ice– sign and compelled me to scoff and laugh at it?"

It was kickin' around thoughts like this that was really getting Randy flustered. On a role, he'd wind up his summary with a serious thought. It was one of the more serious and haunting thoughts he'd have over the last couple of days. It wasn't only until now that he'd share it.

"You know, Jake..., if they're safe, if the kids, your kids, all the children, toddlers and babies are safe along with all the Jef's, if all this is true about them being spared...; what does that say about us? It's not good..., it can't be good. I think we're in for a lot worse than what's happening now. That's why I'm skeptical about this..., this angelic vision in Portugal. It comes across as good but I can't help but wonder if it is? That's what's worrying me. I'm worried that the Bible is and has always been true. I'm worried that Joel and the Born Agains were right all along."

Unmoved and just short of sneering, Jake rebutted with a not-so-kind comment. "You sound like Joel."

Randy totally understood where Jake was coming from. On one hand he put himself in check, and realized Jake was right. But, on the other hand, he sort of liked the candid criticism. There was a part of him, deep down that was inclined to see Jakes remark as a compliment, even though Jake intended it to be quite the opposite; an insult. He'd role off the verbal punch and turn it into a halfhearted joke.

"Yeah…, pretty scary, huh…, I know…," Randy answered. "Actually, this is another thing that's got me worried," he added.

"Humph…," Jake uttered somewhere between an indifferent courtesy laugh and boredom.

Feeling a little uncomfortable, Randy would move to something else so as to get a rise out of Jake, to get him engaged if you will. Glancing back over to the TV, "So…, what do think about this…, this vision, this Queen of Heaven? She's definitely bringing something to the table. What do you make of it?"

"I feel good about her," Jake instantly answered without even thinking about it. But he was done, done with the conversation. After his direct answer he quickly changed the subject. Deep questions and heavy conversations was the last thing Jake really wanted at the moment, especially about God, the Bible and Jesus.

"You know..., I'm dead tired too, Randy. I think I'm just going to lay here with Becky and get some sleep as well. As for this Queen of Heaven thing..., well I guess we'll know more about her tomorrow. You might want to get some sleep as well."

"Yeah..., for sure," Randy agreed. It was just as well. Even though it was a new day, just past sunrise in Lisbon, Portugal..., in South Lake Tahoe and Tucson it was the wee-morning hours. It was going on 2:30 a.m. and going to sleep seemed only right. But Randy wasn't ready to dose off.

Like most, dabbling with short catnaps here and there has been the people's remedy for sleep with everything going on. Unlike Jake, he just wasn't ready for another short snooze. And he was a far cry from shutting down like Rebecca. He figured everybody would have to shut down for a long drawn out sleep sooner or later but for him, it was nowhere in sight, at least for the moment.

After grabbing another cup of coffee, leaving the TV on, leaving Jake and Rebecca to their sleep, Randy dimmed the lights and quietly slipped away. He moseyed out the back door onto the patio and planted himself on one of the tattered chairs. He lit a cigarette, took in a long hearty drag only to exhale a cloud of smoke to compliment a deep and heavy sigh. He was still rattled, but being off and alone was engaging.

As he sat there gazing out into the dark sky he'd take a moment and jeer at the howling wind kick up and down, rustling and whipping the pine trees back and forth. Still drizzling, the water would lightly cascade off the edge of the awning. He could hear sirens off in the distant.

It's been two days and still so much unrest he thought. He wondered what the sirens were for this time; where they were headed. Clearly—troubles, crimes, injuries, though the bulk of it was over, they were still going on. The sound that stood out the most though as his ears adjusted to his noisy little corner of the world was a shaky and unsettling voice. Not far off, out of the darkness from the thick of the woods, a lady somberly calling out for her children would paint a sorrowful picture in Randy's mind.

Worried, tearful and desperate, "Jessica…, Sara…, it's time to come home. Where are you? I know you're out here. Please come on home now," would echo off the hillsides and through the trees. A man's voice, and then another mans voice would follow suit. Listening to them calling out, considering their drive and urgency to brave the stormy weather, knowing their desperation, their denial and wishful thinking, saddened Randy. Maybe it was just the power of hope that these people were out calling for their departed children. Any case…, it was sad, just flat sad.

Taking it all in, it was hard for him to imagine that the entire world was in the same boat; desperate, broken and crazy. It was disturbing to say the least. As he listened to people in the distant crying out in search of their children—understanding and almost feeling the hope they had to think their missing children were merely lost in the woods; Randy hoped they at least had guns to ward off any crazed animal attacks or God forbid—one of the psychopathic demon-possessed maniacs.

Maybe they were lost, he thought. Then again, if their disappearance was anything like Joel's, chances are they were truly gone. As to where they were taken…, heaven seemed to be the best answer. It wasn't however the only answer.

As their search and voices faded off into the distance Randy would readjust his thinking. Halfway through his cigarette, his wheels of thought really started to turn, more rationally and methodical. He started to pick apart all the things that Rebecca and Jake were raving about, as well as the media coverage and newscasts. He'd try to piece it in with all the things that Joel had mentioned to him over the years.

There was so much. Joel had told him a lot of stuff, but bringing it all to mind all at once was impossible. Still, he was eager to rack his brain trying.

Randy has always had the ability to be a deep thinker. But Randy was Randy. By choice, being somewhat lazy in this department he'd more often than not opt out. He liked to keep it simple. Being that he was a well-brushed and seasoned electrical technician, spending twenty some odd years working at various casinos in Tahoe, at Harvey's for the last year and half; he's never really been short of using the analytical side of his mind. Even though he's always been quite capable, unless it directly affected him or happened to catch his interest, delving into the realm of deeper thinking just didn't appeal to him.

Over the years, the Bible and the Bible's Gospel of Jesus Christ did neither. He never saw the Bible as anything to be overly concerned about or mysterious enough to engage in a personal investigation. Nor did he seem to think it directly affected him, let alone catch his interest.

Like so many others, he never really gave the Bible or the Bible's Gospel of Jesus Christ the time of day, much less a second thought. Rebecca and Jake felt the same way. So did Joel for the longest time. It just didn't matter. To them, anything that espoused the Bible in an orderly fashion was religion or even worse, a cult. For whatever reasons they liked to think they were intellectually above the yarns of religion, like it was beneath them.

It didn't however squelch their belief in God. They believed in God. They also believed in most of the trimmings that come with God or a higher power. They just didn't care to make a big deal out of it. It was sort of a pompous way to flaunt being humble.

Religion..., he thought. Born Again Christians, Jesus Fundamentalist, Jef's—what's the deal? What was the difference? What was it that set the Born Agains apart? They believed the Bible; more importantly, the Gospel of Jesus Christ. But then again, a lot of people and religions do in one form or another.

"So..., I guess this idea of believing in God is pretty much worthless, huh...," he said out loud as if God himself was sitting next to him. He took another drag off his cigarette. Looking off into the distance, deep in thought, he'd add a little more to his thinking. "And..., I guess this idea of being a basically good and decent person, or a religious person, or a spiritual person doesn't amount to crap either..., huh! Well..., at least according to this..., this Rapture thing!" he argued.

He went on to think about all the evil people here on earth, people that he, and Rebecca, Jake and every other halfway decent person were left with. He wondered why good people, good and decent people, religious people and spiritual people were still here with the most evil of the evil and the Born Agains were gone. He wondered why the basically good people, the good and decent religious and spiritual people were still here with worst of dictators, people into genocide and infanticide, cold blooded murderers, deranged terrorists, rapists, molesters, con artists and the most vicious of thieves.

He wondered what it was that would thread him together with Satanist, Atheists, Skin-head Supremacists, and the heartless and violent souls that fortify the Drug Cartels and Islamic Jihadists. He knew the thread that stitched them together was there. He also knew that whatever it was, it couldn't be good.

Right away, he knew that he, as well as Rebecca and Jake were quick to think of themselves as true patrons who believed in God. But when it came to the Bible, in their minds, they didn't need a book as thick as a dictionary to tell them who God was any more than they needed a book to tell them what their favorite color was or what their favorite food was. More importantly, they didn't need a book full of campfire stories and fairytales to tell them how to believe in God or how to be close to God or at-one-with-God. From there, mild animosity and makeshift supremacy would only serve to protect them and their intellectual pride from anybody peddling Biblical scriptures to them. This would of course include Joel, their own flesh and blood, their own brother.

It was then, at that very moment, though distant and faint, that Randy began to feel a sense of rejuvenation. He snuffed his cigarette, straightened up in his chair, tightened up his jacket and restfully took it in. It was a reviving sensation; a spark igniting something real, something he's never felt before. Having nothing to lose and liking what he was feeling he decided to go with it.

The distractions, the thrashing wind, and the rain pitter-pattering on the metal awning would fade into a distant hum. Almost in a trance, going deeper, going into uncharted territory, Randy would go beyond the obvious. He went on to thinking about something that would have seemed to be unnatural in light of all the present conditions, circumstances, panic and chaos going on. Unnatural or not..., Randy would entertain his new visitor.

The analytical side of his brain began to percolate. What was happening sparked his interest. He was curious. Off and running, but running steadily and very carefully; his thoughts started to speak to him loud and clear.

"Truth is an amazing thing," he surmised. "It's eternal and forever. It's invincible. It's indestructible and unchangeable".

He logically deduced that there is no such thing as a new truth. Truth can be newly discovered, but it wouldn't be a new truth because the truth was already there; since the beginning of time. And if the truth has been there since the beginning of time, how could it be a new truth. Randy immediately drew his attention to the whole Bible thing. He deeply contemplated the logistics of it, both historical and spiritual. He started flipping through the pages of his memory recollecting some of the bigger than life Bible stories he had grown up with and a handful of scriptures he had come to know over the years.

Now, up front and center, right smack dab in the world's face is the Bible's Rapture proven to be true. As far as he was concerned it is no longer a thought or theory, or a matter of faith for that matter, because it's come and gone. It is no longer the wandering and aimless writings and babblings of some delusional servant of God lost in time. It is no longer a nuisance and a nauseating notion being endorsed, promoted and peddled by a batch of faith fanatics telling him it's the Word of God. The Rapture is and has always been the truth…; period. The Prophecy was true.

It isn't a new truth, Randy thought. It's actually an extremely old truth. It's a truth that had been declared centuries ago. He scratched his head and wondered about this. He knew something, something important was beginning to transpire but he couldn't quite put his finger on it. Piece by piece, layer by layer he continued to dissect his little lab rat—his thinking.

"Let's see!" he said aloud. "The truth about the Rapture was documented in the Bible. I get that," he said. "But…!" he declared. "This isn't, nor could it be the origin of it." In other words, the truth of the Rapture didn't come into existence at the time it was written. It had already been ordained long before it was written. Who knows how long for that matter? Only God knows he thought.

Randy instantly stopped in his tracks. Like he had caught something shining in the corner of his eye, he carefully stepped back and slowly scanned over that last thought. "Only God knows…," he slowly repeated. It was like a key that opened a long lost door; a door that has been locked since the day he was born. The truth of the Rapture was obviously already in order and established long before it was documented in the scriptures. It was already there. God already had the truth; he just had somebody write it down. This blew his mind. It amazed him.

Randy didn't quite know it yet, but in essence, he was finally being touched by the same spirit that touched his younger brother Joel. Though shaken and feeling vulnerable like the rest of the world, his senses were dialing into a new sensation of unknown origin.

He couldn't pinpoint the root of his newly enhanced deductive reasoning and thinking, he just knew it was there.

Still, in spite of his not knowing, that is to say where the feeling was coming from or what was leading him, it didn't hinder him from knowing how he was beginning to feel. He liked what he was feeling. He was beginning to feel a sense of comfort. It felt good and mildly reassuring, even exciting.

A vital, a precious and gentle seed had been planted in the heart of Randy. It was the Holy Spirit, the Spirit of Truth and it had indeed taken root. Like a newborn seedling barely poking its head out from the cold, dark and visionless ground and feeling the warm light of the sun caressing its face, Randy had sprouted.

Of the few Biblical scriptures he had come to know over the years, there was one that had instantly come to his attention. It was seemingly meant to be. It stood out and spoke to Randy loud and clear.

It was the one that had drawn him outside, away from the chaotic and disoriented conversations he had had with Rebecca and Jake. It was the one that pulled him away from the media whirlwind hurling his thoughts to and fro and up and down like a tossed salad. It had gently kidnapped his mind and took him away from the stark raving madness, and in-your-face devastation that had been combing the face of the earth over the last forty-some odd hours.

Yes…, Randy had a scripture in mind and with it came a sense of peace. He had something to start with. He closed his eyes and embellished the scripture that seemed to come from out of nowhere, yet he knew exactly where it came from. It came from the Bible, and how it comforted him. He unexpectedly found himself doing something he has never done in the course of his life; heeding the Word of God. His thought of the particular scripture was vivid and clear, he could see it as if it were written across the inside of his eyelids. Not only could he see it, he was beginning to hear it; speaking softly and true.

"Be still, and know that I am God…"

Was he finally getting a feel of what Joel was all about? Was he getting a feel of what had set his brother apart from him, Jake, Rebecca, and the rest of the world? He didn't know. The only thing he knew was something was stirring inside of him; something different, peculiar, even puzzling.

Still, in a strange sort of way, even though it was mysterious, it was joyful of all things. He smiled to himself. He didn't know where all these feelings were coming from. He didn't know where they were going either. It seemed strange because it was all so new to him—but it really wasn't anything new. It's been around for quite some time. It would be Jesus Christ who would put it so delicately and eloquently, so perfectly as to what was happening to him.

"The wind blows where it wishes, and you hear the sound of it, but cannot tell where it comes from or where it goes. So is everyone who is born of the Spirit."

Surely…, it wouldn't be until later that Randy would get the gist of these feelings coming over him. Surely…, he'd be formally introduced to this particular scripture plucked out of the Book of John soon enough. It was one of the many Scriptures on the list that Joel had left for them. Tomorrow, the next day, a week from now—only time would tell as to when Randy would actually take in the particular Scripture—pluck it out and take it to heart. Only then will he come to truly understand what happened to him.

Yes, the wind blows where it wishes. Like so many others, like Joel, like Leah—though touched, they knew not where it came from, or where it goes after it breezed through—breathing new life into them. Without even realizing it, Randy too has been touched and taken in by the Spirit of God. This night, Randy is what he thought he'd never be.

He is Born Again.

-*Chapter Seventeen*-
PSYCHICS IN SYNCH

"Hong Kong...! She said Hong Kong! That's the message I kept getting!" said Vera Smith-Copeland, a well-known psychic in mainstream America being interviewed. Thrilled, excited and adamant, "It's the message we're all getting!" she stressed in between her sobbing at the loss of her five year old daughter in the Mass Vanishing.

It was the very first thing that Leah heard as she woke up. Not wanting to miss anything, the TV was still on of course, even while she and Nicki Dawn slept. Falling asleep in front of TV's or some sort of media outlet, everything from phones to computers and waking up in front of them was pretty much the world standard over the last couple three days. It was totally understandable.

Catching the latest news involving mediums and psychics, Leah perked up right away. Finding herself uncomfortably sprawled out and twisted on the lounge chair underneath a wadded up blanket, she immediately sat up straight. She quickly snapped out of her sleepy stupor and sharply focused in on the update. Nicki was still asleep on the couch. Both of them had dozed off in the wee-hours like Rebecca and Jake did after getting their fill of the miraculous vision in Lisbon, Portugal and the barrage of interviews that directly followed. It was now mid-morning, just after ten and what had transpired, apparently over the last handful of hours while she slept was all over the news.

The media, social networks, blogs and twitter-feeds were going crazy—off the hook. Thanks to modern technology, hysteria once again had set the entire world on fire in a matter of minutes. Thanks to live-feed television, wireless video formats and social media readily available, anybody and everybody was able to see everything happening worldwide. With the exception of the Rapture's 2 minutes and 33 seconds mysteriously blotted out from being recorded, there's been nothing able to transpire on the globe without the whole world visually witnessing it.

The portals—oh how they served the devil well. To people; it was just the everyday televisions, LCD's, monitors, screens and live video feeds at everyone's fingertips. To Satan—they'd be the very ticket to his anticipated success. Eager to woo the world so as to win the world, the portals as the demons called it, were vital, much needed and most convenient. Harvesting everybody's attention, having every head turned and every eye peeled to see his power, verify his author-ity, and revere his glory was a must—and the portals would serve that necessity.

Having now free reign, being the Hand that re-strained Satan's full potential for generations removed off the face of the planet with the Rapture; stealing the hearts, minds and souls of people was going to be sim-ple for the devil having the all-mighty, all-powerful ground-breaking development of portals at his dis-posal. In order to win the world, Satan needed people, all people to see the magnitude of his power in real time. Yes, the portals—a television in every home, a monitor screen in every hand served him well indeed.

As for the people, they naturally wanted to see all that was going on. They were hungering for it, anx-ious and gripped by the worldwide events happening right before their very eyes. In essence, Satan had the world in the palm of his hand via Satellite, via technol-ogy, via live-streaming, via internet, via social media, via this and via that—etc., etc.

Only few however, having read the Book already knew how this movie playing out on every screen and monitor in the world would end though. And being in the last chapter of the Book wasn't comforting to say the least. Still, like Leah, even they were driven and compelled to keep their eyes glued to every portal available. Being familiar with scriptures, more impor-tantly scriptures that stood out, they also knew that they had to be careful—extremely careful not to be swayed. It was Jesus himself who warned them of the coming *"great signs and wonders to deceive, if possible, even the elect."* Only time would tell as to how many of the elect would turn to the Dark Angels trickery and how many would run from it.

The blatant, indisputable supernatural activity, now in the world's face is huge. Its presence and impact is beyond words. Words—mere words to say it was amazing, unbelievable or breathtaking—all of it seemed to fall short of how to describe it emotion wise. If it wasn't so tangible and real it would be unfathomable. It is a time like no other. Not since the miracles in the days of Jesus, and in the days of Moses or Noah dealing with the Nephilim, the highly advanced half angel/half man giants, has the world been so inundated with supernatural activity.

Leah contemplated on what she was watching—the vigor and fast paced interviews with the psychics and mediums. Leary and saddened, "...*choose you this day whom you will serve...,*" she whispered to herself. It was another one of those stand-out scriptures quick to jump onto center stage in her mind.

She feared for people. She feared for Nicki Dawn. She knew..., she just knew that people, like in the days of Noah were going to have a hard time figuring out the difference between the power of angels and the Power of God. Even worse, like in the days of Noah she also knew most would abandon God and willfully choose and serve the angels flaunting their heavenly knowledge and celestial skills and prowess.

It wasn't until now that Leah got the gist of what Jesus meant when he said that the last days would be like in the days of Noah. It was a frightening thought to say the least because she knew exactly why God wiped out the ancient civilizations in the days of Noah with the flood.

Leah, in spite of the unfortunate circumstances, was fortunate. She knew the Book of Genesis just as well as she knew the Book of Revelation. Contemplating and rehashing what the Bible reveals about the days of Noah—how demonic, wicked and advanced the civilization was, considering wayward angels interacting with man, even to the point of breeding a superior race; she wondered just how far things were going to go—and how fast. It sent a shiver up her spine. The sudden surge of mediums, clairvoyants and channelers uttering words and conveying messages from unseen forces, in her mind only affirmed the demons were already gearing up to openly and publicly interact with mankind once again.

She just sat there in awe and wonderment, but no less tense. Watching the newest rave consuming international news like a sweeping fire, Leah slowly shook her head as she was drawn to whisper again.

"Oh, Lord Jesus..., we're in so much trouble. Lord..., God help us...," she murmured in prayer. It was so upsetting. She took a moment and looked over at Nicki Dawn sound asleep on the couch and her stomach would again cramp and tie up in knots. She couldn't help but find herself worried sick over and over again. Although she was distressed to no end she was at least a head of the game as she watched the quote unquote movie play out via satellite with each passing minute.

Having read the entire Book, including Revelation—the last chapter, Leah was even more determined not to be caught off guard like she was when the Rapture came. Her senses were heightened. She was extremely vigilant and cautious of everything now, even her own daughter Nicki. Trust and faith meant more than anything now than ever before. The slightest miscalculation in trust or deviation from faith was sure to galvanize the fate of ones soul. It would mean the difference between life and death, and worse, heaven and hell. Leah knew this. In fact there were a lot of people who knew this...; millions. There were millions more, people like Randy beginning to figure it out as well. But, compared to those who didn't know, that is to say the billions; millions of people would sadly be only few.

Leah was disturbed to see the latest supernatural

event take form. To be honest, she was no more disturbed by this than all the other things going down. Perhaps it was the weight of adding one more suspicious phenomenon to an already heavy heart that was overwhelming her. Regardless, it worried her. It was yet another paranormal affair simply unheard of until now. It fit perfectly with everything else that's made its way into the…'never-in-history-has-this-ever-happened-before'…Hall of Fame; starting with the Rapture. And it hasn't even been a week. It wasn't only Vera Smith-Copeland, a lone, singled out medium who received the celestial message from another dimension; or two mediums, or three, or ten, or even a hundred mediums—it was hundreds of thousands of mediums who received the telepathic message.

Coming out of the woodwork, coming out in droves; mediums, clairvoyants, mystics, shamans, spiritualists, seers and channelers from every niche and corner of the world would receive and reveal the message. There were even a number of children, the youngest left after the Mass Vanishing; early teens from every country and every walk of life who could hear the voice and message from beyond. All of them were miraculously and amazingly in tune at the same exact time, as if they were antennas aligned to receive one message. For whatever reasons, they were selected, if anything handpicked to receive and spread the message. But whose message…?

It was a message that was one and the same; as was the voice itself. According to the mediums, it was feminine in nature; motherly, gentle and soft spoken. Simultaneously, the voice, the whispers fell only upon those who were open, gifted or sensitive to the Sixth Sense. Young and old, famous and world renowned mediums as well as those in the most remote of conditions, in every tongue, every language, in every country; as if of one mind, they all received the message. It was uncanny, unnatural, but most of all unexpected.

The voice and message came out of the blue, meaning there wasn't any séance type conditions or the mediums having to go into an altered state of consciousness; the voice just popped into their heads. Some were wide awake others were awoken from their sleep; midday for some, midnight for others depending on where they were at in the world. . According to them; all those who were able to hear, or receive the telepathic tidings; the message wasn't at all elaborate, or a riddle in need of deciphering. It was however fragmented…, in bits and piece, but no less plain and understandable.

All of them, the mediums, they likened the messaging to a radio; like dialing and tuning in on an elusive station in the midst of static and unstable frequencies. Still, the message was received rather quickly and it was very short and very simple. Despite its simplicity, the impact it had on the world was huge; nothing short of massive.

After piecing it together, it said, "The Glory..., the Holy Spirit..., the Comforter sent..., Hong Kong, China within the cycle of a day..., a promise — a message to the nations of the world."

Even though there was a roundabout reference to the identity of the higher power interacting with the mediums, and the world for that matter..., other names were still being bandied about. The Queen of Heaven, Our Lady, the Lady of All Nations, Mother Mary of God, Gaia amongst others, even God; they were all on the tip of people's tongues. The Queen of Heaven was however quickly finding its way to the top of the list; being the most popular of names strewn about. Still, it varied; depending on the religious or spiritual background of the individuals and groups. No matter the name variation; it was one and only one power the eyes and ears of the world had set its sights on.

A firestorm of interviews, blogs, tweets and press conferences pounded the portals. The revelation towered, even squashed the news of the scurrying world leaders scheduled to convene in Rome come tomorrow. The news of them getting together to discuss and implement a plan to deal with the crashed economies, mayhem and unrest paled to the news of the Queen of Heaven's second coming. Clearly, all hope to be had wasn't set on the world leaders or their summit addressing the global crisis. It was set on the supernatural revelation of the Holy Spirit; the Comforter. It was the Queen of Heaven seizing the world's attention. It was she who was gripping and capturing the hearts of people and harnessing their hope.

The mysterious announcement was planted with extremely short notice. Still it was inspiring and encouraging. Even though it was creeping well into the night in Hong Kong, even though the various modes of transportation were limited due to the global chaos; people and the media outlets if at all possible flocked to China's massive city as fast as they could. Getting positioned as soon as possible; if possible before sunrise was imperative.

It was windy and cloudy with an unusual thick mist of fog weaving and meandering its way over and through the city. Anticipating, vigilant and eager — the people gathered in the streets, different areas, different buildings and squares, on the outskirts of town, but mostly along the coast. Nobody knew exactly where the so-called Queen would appear of even if she'd appear at all, let alone the exact time. There was seemingly more of a sense of trust than a sense of hope amongst the people.

Despite the massive gathering, the rush and congested crowds, the people were remarkably polite and orderly. Many were of course wide-eyed and frenzied as they dashed about. Others however were feeble, slow and weak in the knees and having to be carefully assisted and escorted by loved ones. Most of them were broken like Rebecca, they were sobbing and weeping as they contemplated the connection between their missing children and this god-like manifestation expected to appear at any moment.

No matter the pace, all of them were no less fidgety. Nervous and antsy yes, but rude and pushy for the most part they were not. In fact, it was quite the opposite. Unruly behavior seemed to be nowhere in sight. If any riotous disturbances made its way into the crowds they were immediately snuffed out like stomping out little fires.

There was relief stations sprinkled about handing out food and water as well as people sharing their own rations. The unity, the sharing, the friendly and hospitable aura in and amongst the crowd was really quite amazing. The docile and respectful nature of the united masses wasn't at all due to Martial Law enforcing the city. It was more about the peace and holiness that seemed to resonate within the people's marvelous expectations. Clearly, their feelings, their sentiments, their emotions were mutual. Everybody understood each other. They understood why each and every one of them was there. They knew exactly what it was that was bringing them out of their homes and shelters to weather the weird stormy conditions and fight the wind; the miserable and relentless wind.

As for the tremors, UFO sightings, and crazed animals, on Satan's strategic command, they dwindled down; even came to a standstill in the Hong Kong vicinity; just like it did in Lisbon, Portugal prior to the Queens visitation. It was done on purpose to give the world the impression that peace and tranquility comes with the Queen of Heaven. It did indeed work. The world took notice to it, more especially in Hong Kong, as they anticipated the holy and glorious apparitions return.

The demon-possessed devil worshippers of old gone mad—Satan's expendable sycophants and followers scouring the streets; terrorizing the neighborhoods like the mindless and bloodthirsty zombies so commonly seen in horror movies...; they too came to a standstill. However, they and their carnage didn't stop on Satan's command. Satan had a different strategy when it came to them.

They were pretty much and rather quickly eradicated by Martial Law Militants, Global Police, and civilians protecting themselves and their families. After a certain point it was kill first, ask questions later when it came to these murderous maniacs. They were shot and killed in most cases when it came to the militants and police-soldiers. As for the civilians, it was all about killing the monsters anyway they possibly could. .

Whatever the means used to rid them from terrorizing the lands worldwide, the bottom line is their little zombie-like uprising and rampage…, although fierce, frightening and unnerving, it was short-lived. It didn't last very long. Satan had his fun with them, as did his demons. Giving these occult devotees the false impression that they'd be mightily rewarded in the afterlife for their allegiance and heartfelt devotion to Satan did nothing but give the powers of darkness a good laugh. There was no doubt about it; Satan loved their undying worship, but their reverence however did nothing to extinguish his hatred for them as humans. Having his devout followers purposely exterminated one by one fostered only smiles and delight—not the shedding of tears.

For those who know the truth, but more importantly 'believe it'; outside of Satan's love of self, his love to be worshipped, along with his love to…*steal, kill and destroy*…all things that God loves—if not for these facets of love there'd be no love at all.

Jesus told the world plainly, speaking of Satan:

"The thief does not come except to steal, and to kill, and to destroy."

Like cockroaches that reign in the darkness of a filthy kitchen — Jesus turned on the light and exposed the devil and his demons scurrying about in the sinful world. The entire world via the Bible has been officially enlightened, educated and warned as to who the devil is, what the devil does, why he does it, and how he manages

to do it. Jesus Christ knows the Fallen Angel and everything there is to know about him. Yes…, Satan is a thief and more as Jesus elaborates.

"He was a murderer from the beginning, and does not stand in the truth, because there is no truth in him. When he speaks a lie, he speaks from his own resources, for he is a liar and the father of it."

Unlike time and the times, being who he is since the beginning isn't subject to change. It is only a new day, a different day to treat and entertain the same ol' ageless evil. Satan had plans, new schemes and clever plots to implement his timeless endeavors. It was in fact already in motion. Wooing and charming the world with the Queen of Heaven's grandiose manifestation would easily captivate the vulnerable onlookers desperately searching for answers outside of the Bible.

Now that the doors were opened, given free reign, but more importantly permission by the Almighty God Himself—Satan did not hesitate. He'd waste no time.

The seeds of lies and deception he's carefully planted through the ages, on day one and for millennia thereafter; toxic seeds that would sprout only to be strategically nurtured, cleverly groomed, and cultivated, have come to fruition. The countless lies and deceit were always around, but now they would be allowed to blossom and bloom. The fruits of dishonesty have ripened and would be taken to new heights. The roses of trickery, now in full bloom, can finally be delicately pruned and manicured, embellished and refined to parade and demonstrate its full potential. When it came to Satan and his masterful tactics of deceit—it was out with the old subtle ways and in with the bold new sensational ways.

Via the mediums and channelers across the globe, all of them in perfect sync, all of them of one mind receiving one message at the same time; simultaneously announcing the Queen of Heaven was going to appear for a second time—the people made haste. They did not hesitate. They were all in the same boat; lost children, evaporated pregnancies, missing loved ones, scared, uneasy, and uncertain. They were all dealing with the same supernatural dilemma, the same dire circumstances, and terrifying conditions.

Religions, Gods and Beliefs; things that have no-toriously set people at odds against each other over the course of history were set aside as they savored and contemplated another vision of the Queen. Her first appearing and reappearing alone is and would be miraculous enough in its self, but it went further than that. For the entire world to gaze into the sky and see the one and only thing they've ever known to unite the world, to move them, and compel them to see and look past all their differences and disagreements, even past their hatred, racism, intolerance, and bigotry was an even bigger miracle.

Add that to the latest miracle; the hundreds of thousands of mediums worldwide receiving the same identical message from beyond, simultaneously no less, was the icing on the cake to which everyone would sink their teeth into. The gathering, whether it was on sight in Hong Kong, or privately surfing the portals; with the Queen of Heaven in mind, unity and togetherness was clearly the theme. On the surface, in view of all the devastation, grief and madness, it was a good and beautiful thing. It was however underneath the surface that some found to be very disturbing.

Leah would be one of them.

-Chapter Eighteen-
HONG KONG BOOM

At the moment, Leah wasn't gazing at the TV absorbing the updates regarding the newest sensation; the Mediums personal one-on-one contact with Queen of Heaven. Nor was she gazing out the window in hopes of seeing the 'pie in the sky'. She was gazing at Nicki Dawn peacefully sleeping on the couch.

As she did so, she debated as to whether or not to wake her up to watch the latest global development with her. Within thirty seconds she had her answer. She decided not to. There would be plenty more to come, she was sure of that.

Coverage of the world events was thorough, she figured, even to the point of monotonous at times. That was one reason. The other reason; sleep…, it was good Leah thought. It was good to see there was actually a short escape from the living nightmare terrorizing the entire world. It was temporary, far from a cure but no less an escape. Sleep was really the only thing one could count on to escape the madness.

Even though Leah knew Nicki's little nap would be short-lived, she thought it best to let her keep the gift while it was available. The both of them being so wound up, so edgy and full of anxiety over the last three days, seeing Nicki asleep was pleasant. It was nice, not only for her but for Nicki as well. Both of them she figured needed as much tranquility as they could possibly get.

Up and over in Lake Tahoe, Jake would not be so kind and considerate as Leah was to her daughter—at least not to Randy. Finding Randy slumped over the kitchen table, sitting on a chair with his head, shoulder and arms resting on top of Joel's Bible, Jake hurriedly walked over and gently nudge him. After Randy's, let us say...*born again*...experience out on the patio hours before, he eagerly came back in and delved deep into Joel's list of scriptures. Flipping through the pages of the Bible, looking the scriptures up, he eventually fell fast asleep. A bummer for him—at most it was only a couple hours of sleep before Jake moseyed over and abruptly woke him up.

"Randy..., hey Randy wake up—something's happening!" Jake said in haste.

Jake having been awake no more than twenty minutes already had a fresh pot of coffee brewed. Like Leah, he too woke up to see all the hubbub going on in regards to the mediums and clairvoyants interacting with the so called Queen of Heaven. It aroused his curiosity like everyone else. Jake was just as excited as the next guy. He couldn't sit on it. He felt compelled to tell someone and of the two nearest him, Rebecca and Randy, both asleep, Randy seemed to be his best option. When it came to Rebecca, Jake had the same compassionate sentiments for his resting wife as Leah had for her resting daughter. He didn't feel comfortable to blast Rebecca out of her sound sleep being that she was so worn out and undone.

"What is it, Jake? What's going on?" Randy asked half asleep.

"It's that…, that Queen of Heaven or Holy Spirit again. She's back. Well, sort of I guess. She's supposed to be reappearing in Hong Kong sometime today or…, or within a cycle of a day — I don't know…, something like that." Jake excitedly shared.

"Oh man…, I smell coffee," Randy muttered as he yawned and achingly picked himself up off the table.

"Yeah, there's a fresh pot, I just made it." Jake said as he poured a cup and brought it to Randy. He was quick to repeat what he had said when he woke Randy up.

"There's something brewing over in Hong Kong. I guess that…, that Queen of Heaven thing is supposed to appear in Hong Kong like she did in Lisbon. This time though…, I guess she's supposed to give us a message — some sort of a Holy Message." Jake rattled off.

With coffee in hand, "Whoa, whoa, whoa…!" Randy voiced as they both moseyed over into the living room to watch the TV. Jake's pace of explaining to Randy as to what was now happening was a tad fast. Keeping his voice down, not wanting to disturb Rebecca asleep on the couch, "Who…?" Randy asked. "Who's saying what…? You're losing me here. Slow down…, Jake. Who…?"

"Ok…, ok…," Jake said as he took in a breath to relax. "It's the psychics and mediums that are saying all this. It's not just a couple of them or one or two, it's all of them — all over the world. They're saying hundreds of thousands of them, everything from dog-whisperers to…, to shamans, priests, clairvoyants and even some children, older ones who didn't vanish with the rest, they're all like…, I guess, getting this message from the Queen of Heaven. She's telling them that she's the Holy Spirit — the Comforter, that…, that she was sent." Jake rambled off.

"What…? The Holy Spirit…?" Randy inquired while scrunching his face in bewilderment.

"Yeah, that's what all these mediums and channelers are saying. And I guess she's telling them that she's gonna appear in Hong Kong, China sometime today or…, or tomorrow."

Knowing his explanation was fuzzy and short of giving Randy a decent picture, Jake went ahead and finished off with a detour.

"Look man — just watch!" he said quietly as he

turned to the TV. "You'll see what I'm talking about. It's crazy…!"

It didn't take long before Randy got his fill as he attentively watched the latest news along with Jake. Leah too attentively watched in Tucson as did the whole world. The hours passed. Nicki eventually woke up. Rebecca eventually woke up. They too were briefed and filled in with the latest development. In a matter of hours, everybody in the entire world was clued in. Phone calls were made. Texts, instagrams, tweets and e-mails exchanged. Randy had another short chat with Leah. Nicki Dawn went back and forth with her friends. The buzz was thick and plentiful.

It went on and carried on for nine hours, from when Nicki and Rebecca first heard of it. It seemed to last forever, and it was now closer to grueling than a shot of adrenaline. The zeal and the rush began to wane. Many would lose heart. Others however remained hopeful. In Hong Kong, the crowds started to get restless. Some went home. The press conferences, interviews and reporters trying to keep the fervor alive lost its momentum and became somewhat boring. The overtly excited tweets and texting began to sour and flood the social media with doubts.

It didn't take but a minute though to turn things around. There was an abrupt change. It was blatant and sure. Within seconds, everything from attitudes to the weather flipped. Something was up. Like in Lisbon, Portugal, it was around sunrise. The wind, the miserable unrelenting wind scouring and haunting the lands for nearly three days had come to a still. It was eerie. It stopped, seemingly instantaneously.

The slumbering crowd was stirred and moved to wake each other up. They quickly rose to their feet. They shuffled and scurried about at first and froze; repositioned to catch whatever it is they were supposed to catch. They clearly felt the change in the air. It was intense. The voices and conversations softened to murmurs and whispers. Not wanting nor daring to miss anything, rigid and alert like perched hawks scouring the vicinity for movement, they waited, they watched and scanned the shifting clouds in the sky.

Within minutes…, six, seven, eight minutes at most, the fog began to dissipate. The blanket of clouds parted; a slit by which to allow and send a masterful ray of light would pierce through the opening. It wasn't but another handful of minutes before the clouds too began to dissolve. And behold, as promised by the Queen herself, just like the channelers and mediums by the hundreds of thousands emphatically insisted upon, conveyed and announced — the Glory, the Holy Spirit, the Comforter did indeed manifest right before the multitudes eyes just off the coastal outskirts of Hong Kong. And yes…, it was beautiful to the eye.

Like her first appearing in Lisbon, with hundreds or even thousands of media recording devices, the Queen of Heaven was once again plastered on every available screen and television worldwide. And once again, the world, the entire world would find itself on the edge of their seat. No matter where they were at or what they were doing, the portals revealed it all. Many people fell to their knees almost in unison — both those on the coast of Hong Kong and those witnessing the holy apparition via satellite. The world was sold.

The second coming of the Queen of Heaven was a huge, huge breakthrough for the world. It was also a huge success for the Dark Angel. The world, most of the world was now in the palm of his hands. Deception had sunk its talons deep into the souls of all those left to weather God's soon to come Tribulation. The White Horse and its rider in the Book of Revelation are now at the gate ready to be unleashed. For the time being, for most it is a wondrous thing — glorious, positive, encouraging, endearing and uplifting. But there were some who saw right through the beautiful angel of light hovering off the coast. They saw the darkness behind the 'Glory'; behind the so-called 'Comforter' — the 'Holy Spirit sent'.

The Queen of Heaven, the brilliant apparition basking in all its glory, wooing the crowds worldwide, relishing the reverence, the worship, and praise would savor the moment. Not more than five minutes would pass before a scream would puncture the euphoric bubble. It was a desperate and adamant scream out of the crowd of onlookers—a warning likened to the frantic and determined few on the Titanic yelling and screaming to the oblivious multitudes of the impending danger before its fateful decent into the eerie, cold and darkest depths of the Atlantic Ocean.

"THIS IS NOT OF GOD…!" came out of nowhere. Planted on top of a car, it was a man—an indigenous man, speaking in his native tongue, in Chinese. "This is not of God. This is not the Holy Spirit. This is not the Comforter!!!" he screamed as loud as he could. With everything he had, passionate and frantic he did his best to convey his sentiments to the mesmerized crowd.

"This is the devil!" he yelled. "This is Satan! Listen to me—we need to flee. We need to turn to Jesus…, to Jesus Christ. Leave this place!" he urgently pleaded.

Needless to say the crowd began to stir. Some ignored him, or tried to ignore him as they remained fixated on their newly arrived Comforter in the sky. Others perturbed began to grumble and jeer at the courageous man's rude and insensitive disruption but more importantly at what he was saying. Disgruntled, objecting—the grumbles began softly. The complaints were uttered under the peoples breathe at first, but soon shifted into a shouting match.

"Shut up...!" some yelled back. "Shhh...! Go away! Get outta here!" were being flung at the Jesus Fundamentalist like flurries of snow. The verbal retaliations were getting louder and louder as did the Jef's plea to rebuke to Queen. Curse words began to infiltrate the crowd's verbal assaults. The man warning the people of the evil at hand and the crowd defending their godly apparition clearly wasn't going to stop.

Irritable and pissed—hostility began to percolate within the crowd as the man of God ranted on. Like the street preachers who dared to speak out in Europe and modern America's iron-fisted liberal totalitarian culture—the crowd within earshot of the Jef started to take action. They aligned themselves and began to surround and close in on the noisy antagonist urging them to set their eyes on Jesus Christ instead of 'the Glory'. Cameras and phones nearest the confrontation were already turned from the Queen of Heaven—recording the unruly episode from every angle.

The newly manifested Holy Spirit—a counterfeit but no less very real remained steadfast during the commotion. Calm, unhurried and unshaken by the disruption, the apparition continued to hover and tower over the city outskirts, over the waters—up and over the coast in all its glitter, glamour and beauty. As the minutes passed, the Queen of Heaven would peacefully and lovingly deliver her holy message to the mediums, seers and clairvoyants across the globe. Things however were a little different a quarter mile away. Calm, unhurried and unshaken it was not. The ruckus continued.

The man atop the car pleading with anyone who would listen—telling the people that they needed to turn to Jesus Christ found himself in danger. Eventually surrounded and pushed off the car, a handful of men acting like the typical Labor Union thugs violently began to beat the brazen Jesus Fundamentalist down. Even though there was a small group of likeminded Bible believers and family members doing their best to protect the outspoken man, the efforts were quickly stifled.

It wasn't but seconds before the Jef found himself curled up on the ground. Tightly bundled, as tight as he could in the fetal position doing all he could to protect himself and deflect the kicks and belts beating him, he'd yell for them to please stop in between his pleading with them to turn to Jesus. The cameras kept rolling as the man being brutally beat to death started to black out. Just as he was ready to fall unconscious, something happened; something amazing. It was something that rivaled the glorious vision of the Queen wooing the people and psychics abroad.

BOOM!!! A powerful detonation, a discharge, an

invisible sonic burst if you will came out of nowhere and blasted the hostile thugs out in all directions— away from their bloodied and gasping victim. It was a supernatural explosion—like an invisible propulsion grenade. In a split second, the annoyed and pitiless brutes beating the Jesus Fundamentalist to death were blown out fifteen—twenty, twenty-five feet. They were literally blasted off their feet into the air like shards from a grenade.

The JF's friends and family wasted no time. They rushed into the clearing so as to aid their battered loved one. They picked him up to his feet. Holding him up; shoulder to shoulder they hobbled out of the arena of people. Seemingly by force, the people parted like the Red Sea as they made their way to safety. It was unbelievable—but why not? The Queen of Heaven levitating and towering over the coast a quarter mile away was unbelievable. Everything was unbelievable.

The unrelenting wind and unusual weather patterns plaguing the globe for three days was unbelievable. And to see the ominous weather conditions and wind miraculously and instantly come to a stop in the midst of the Queens appearance was unbelievable. The mediums, the psychics and channelers by the hundreds of thousands clearly receiving the same identical tiding and messages simultaneously were unbelievable. The UFO's and angelic orbs sporadically whisking in and out of view was unbelievable.

The hypnotic, unfeeling demon possessed people going crazy, fearless of being killed while killing and attempting to kill anyone and everyone in their path, yes…, it was unbelievable. The strange animal behavior; both domestic and wild animals driven to hunt, attack, and go on killing sprees…, yes – unbelievable. The missing children, and pregnancies instantly vaporized were unbelievable. And the Church, the Born Again Christians, the Jesus Fundamentalists, the Jef's, the true and devoted Bible Believers raptured, taken off the face of the planet was what else but unbelievable. Everything and everything happening was unbelievable. And this didn't even include the crashed economies, and the world shut down, and the chaos and mayhem, and people edging to the dire conditions of thirst and hunger.

People could only wonder and speculate as to what was next. The Queen of Heaven came and went as she did in Lisbon, Portugal. And like Lisbon, her second coming lasted exactly eleven minutes eleven seconds. This time however as promised, she dispersed a message to the nations via the Channelers and mediums. After she again danced off in an array of bouncing and colored lights, the world would buzz emphatically, hysterically and relentlessly once again.

The video footage of the Queen of Heaven's second

coming flooded the portals. It was plastered on every screen in every niche and corner of the world. But, to Satan's dismay, so was the miraculous rescue — the Jesus Fundamentalist being saved from his violent assailants. The entire world too would see the supernatural burst of invisible energy that blasted the hostile attackers in every which direction. Yes..., the entire world too would see what clearly looked to be the hand of God moving in to save the Jef from the vicious assault.

Enraged, "How dare you...!" cursed Vy-Deélia as he speedily flew into the vicinity of the crime to join a bunch of miffed and angry Influencers and lower-end demons of '*legion*'; all who were forced to stand down during the commotion.

Being Satan's High Commander over Legion, Vy-Deélia immediately caught wind as to what happened, as did the other Commanders. Vy-Deélia just happened to be first on the scene to confront Ay-Aerés; he who was sent to intervene in the violent attack on one of God's children. Needless to say, Vy-Deélia rebuked the act of one of God's Holy Angels stepping into the mix and obliterating the deployment of lower end demons swaying the men to beat down the passionate Jesus Fundamentalist daring to tell people to run and turn to Jesus Christ.

Unmoved by the indignant demon-angels dismay, "I was sent by the Most High," Ay-Aerés promptly declared.

"You have no right!" Vy-Deélia angrily proclaimed as he glared at Ay-Aerés standing by. The heated demon-angel was furious, but cautious. He took a step back, cocked his head and intensified his hateful glare at the Guardian Angel — an archangel at that, serving under the mighty Archangel Michael.

Irritated and bitter, Vy-Deélia shook his fist and yelled. "This is our time, Ay-Aerés. You have no place here."

Ay-Aerés just stared at the enraged demon. Firm, silent and unshaken by Vy-Deélia's unholy rebuke, Ay-Aerés didn't budge. This isn't to say the powerful archangel wasn't on guard and ready for battle. The confrontation, being no more than a mere standoff quickly ended as Vy-Deélia departed leaving Ay-Aerés firmly defending his post and holding his ground.

Vy-Apheélion and Vy-Fonteé, Vy-Gréthos, Vy-Pécula; all of them too were furious — as was Satan, more especially. With every evil ounce of hatred and power in them they resented the Most High stepping into the realm of the portals — raining on their parade if you will. The footage capturing the Jesus Fundamentalist being literally protected, supernaturally rescued and preserved, video footage dispersed and shared with the entire world was truly an act of God. His finger-prints were all over it. The seemingly insignificant miracle was purposely served up to rival and contend with Satan's grandiose appearance via the Queen of Heaven. And that it did—and that it did.

Using one of his own, a lowly Jesus Fundamentalist in Hong Kong, China who missed the Rapture—the Most High God of all creation made it known to the entire world that HE clearly wasn't absent. More importantly, HE made it known to the entire world that HE alone was in control. As the world was being rapidly primed and groomed to be conquered by the White Horse and its Rider, God via Jesus Christ made it known that HE was already poised and positioned to help HIS children through the coming judgment on the world, to save all those who'd choose to be saved and last but not least, fulfill his holy promises to HIS chosen people—the Zionists.

It was extremely comforting to those who were able to see the minor miracle for what it was. Leah would be one of them. She did indeed see the video footage of the Jef in Hong Kong being miraculously rescued by unseen forces. And yes, Leah wept for joy for she knew it was God Himself, His power and His glory that intervened. Truly, it spoke volumes as a heavenly reminder—as it was meant to be. Even though she was left, she now knew for sure she wasn't abandoned.

The beautiful promise and words of Jesus, "...*and lo, I am with you always, even to the end of the age*" would begin to find its way back into Leah's heart.

With soft, mild tears gently streaming down her face—partly ashamed and partly relieved—she'd leave the couch, leave the TV, leave Nicki and quietly head for her room. Making her way through the disarray, through the mess to the farthest corner of the room she kneeled down onto her knees and picked her Bible up off the floor. It was right where she left it after throwing it against the wall in anger three days ago. It was now however back where it belongs. It was back in her arms—the Word of God, the Love of Jesus, and the Truth of things and things to come.

-Chapter Nineteen-
MOTHER HEN

The Queen of Heaven, her visitations along with her kindred connection to humanity easily hijacked the traumatized world still in shock. With the Rapture and two days of living hell thereafter; two days of pure terror, panic, horrors and uncertainty worldwide, finally and thankfully there was light in the darkness.

Finally, a revelation, a sign, a visual of a higher power, a supreme being would harness the worlds undivided attention. People who had rushed to get their hands on the nearest Bible immediately after the Rapture, people who were moved to cling to the Word of God, and grip the Scriptures for dear life despite what they knew or didn't know about it were almost effortlessly lured away from it.

Desperate, lost and starving for answers, like Hansel and Gretel thinking themselves extremely fortunate, even blessed with a lovely little house of cookies and candy in the midst of the dark foreboding woods, the world would suddenly be given its own unfamiliar version of refuge offering sweet candy-coated messages to eat without even knowing the ulterior motive lurking under the cover of darkness and shadows.

Looking to the Queen of Heaven for answers instead of the Bible, to put it simply, was easy. One might say it's much easier to watch a movie than read a book; it was the same premise. It really wasn't so much about laziness as it was convenience in the darkest hours of desperation. Who could blame them, any of them? The Queen of Heaven was magnificent in its simplicity. Complete with visuals and simple, easy to understand words was much more gratifying than pulling words out of an elaborate book and have them marinate in the mind.

For most, it was too much trouble; which goes on to say things haven't changed when it came to anyone making a concerted effort to really get to know the entire Bible with any amount of intimacy.

Being tasked and intimidated with the heavy burden of having to sink their teeth into a book as thick as an encyclopedia at the spur of the moment, let alone over the course of one's lifetime was more than enough to discourage people, especially with a more suitable alternative to just sit there and absorb the Queen of Heaven and her Holy Messages.

Under the dire and horrific circumstances of being ravaged by unknown supernatural forces, it was actually a relief. Absorbing the Bible was more of a duty, a chore, an endeavor, a job, extensive. The Queen on the other hand was closer to a gift laid in the palm of the world's hands.

Likened to the drive-thru, fast food restaurants, or a hot meal ready in seconds via a microwave, compared to the long and grueling effort of getting familiar with the Bible, the Queen of Heaven was most appealing, and understandably so. It was liberating, if you will. Getting answers, insight and a sense of direction first hand from a very real, visible and tangible Higher Power clearly alive as opposed to sifting, and reading, and deciphering a thousand plus pages in the Bible was nothing short of a blessing. So it seemed.

Hence, the Bible's, for the most part, were closed. Thinking minds would turn to the Queen; the wondrous, breathtaking specter in the sky. Pleasing to the eyes, benevolent in nature, desirable for knowledge, perfect for healing and good for the soul; when it came to seeking the truth, as quick as Adam and Eve took their bite out of the proverbial apple, did the world follow suit. They would rush to their newfound house of cookies and candy readily available. Be that as it may, despite its veneer of goodness, there were some who refused to take part, let alone take a bite out of the fruit, you might say. There were some who weren't so quick to grab what was convenient, even sensible.

There were many who were indecisive, not sure,

hesitant and cautious, not so easily swayed to give themselves over to the Queens charms. Besides them, there were others still who flat out rebuked and cursed the Queen. Yes…, once again; the Born Again Christians — the JF's, the Jesus Fundamentalists holding fast to their Bibles; they refused to partake in the Queens glory. In short, just like the bold and brazen Jef in Hong Kong, likeminded, they too saw the Queen of Heaven for what she is; satanic in nature — demonic by all accounts. They want no part of her in spite of who she claims to be and what she's proving to do. Even though she comforts the multitudes; she's not the Comforter spoken of in the Bible, let alone the Comforter sent by Jesus Christ. She is a counterfeit.

"But when the Comforter comes, whom I shall send to you from the Father, the Spirit of truth who proceeds from the Father, He will testify of Me. He will teach you all things, and bring to your remembrance all things that I said to you…, that He may abide with you forever — the Spirit of truth, whom the world cannot receive, because it neither sees Him nor knows Him; but you know Him, for He dwells with you and will be in you."

This is the Comforter Jesus sent; the…*'Spirit of truth'* — the Holy Spirit. It wasn't that difficult for the Born Agains to know the Queen of Heaven impersonating the Comforter was anything but the truth. HE..., the Comforter..., is NOT a she. HE..., *the Spirit of truth, whom the world cannot receive, because it neither sees...Him...nor knows Him...'* was quite telling, being it is her, not Him, the world now sees, as well as she, not He..., the world now knows and receives.

By that, the schism was established — the divide. A rift was formed. A fence was built. The stage was set. And a choice was clear. Two sides, two beliefs, two Higher Powers, two fates would not only define the New Age, but crystallize it.

The days of billions of beliefs running wet, wild and free in the world, along with all their differences; they were now all gathered together like chicks to its mother hen. Every single religion, every tradition and every single belief handed down from generation to generation; though still alive and well..., they all now lay in the arms of the Queen of Heaven, like a billion little babies. Even the Christian based religions and traditions; they too lay in arms of the Queen. It truly was a new day; a new age.

The countless beliefs chained to countless versions of god — from every single customized version of god drummed up in the minds of people to every single homemade religion, from Atheists to Spiritualists and Agnostics to Nones, from every fabricated household religion without names that believe in a little bit of

DAVID ALAN SMITH

this and a bit of the Bible here, and a little bit of that and a bit of the Bible there, on up to the highly sophisticated organized world renowned religions; they were still plentiful and abroad, but each and every one them were collectively forced to retrofit their beliefs to correlate with the newest revelation—the Queen of Heaven. The only belief to oppose the Mother Hen, the only ones that adamantly refuse to gather with the other chicks in the world, or snuggle up into the arms of the Queen of Heaven was of course the Born Agains and the Zionists.

This was the New Age schism. In other words, everything from politics, religions, beliefs and traditions whittled down to one of two choices—not three, not four, not ten, not a hundred…, TWO, and only two choices. Everyone, sooner or later, would be forced to choose one or the other. Retrofit the things they believe and have believed into the ambiguous glamour of the Queen of Heaven…OR…, like Randy, wholeheartedly rebuke the Queen in the name of the Gospel of Jesus Christ and flush down the toilet every single belief and religious tie one had prior to the Rapture. To do that meant only one thing, and that would be to run as fast as you can to the Bible's open arms because you trust it to be 'the truth, the whole truth, and nothing but the truth.'

There would be no in-between. Indecision…;

yes—there was plenty of that, plenty of skepticism and suspicion, but the fact remained. From this day forward, there were only TWO sides by which to choose and devote to.

Needless to say; narrowing every single belief and religion in the entire world over the course of history down to two and only two visible sides by which to trust and choose was quite the feat. Whether by fate or by design..., the will of God perhaps; regardless of the unseen details, this is what it all came down to—embrace the Queen of Heaven or repel her. The incident in Hong Kong—the miraculous rescue of the passionate Jef made it obvious.

The second visitation of the Queen along with her first Holy Message and a few promises to all nations did many things. Most of it slithered in and out of the pages of the Bible only to mimic it. Like Jesus Christ, the Queen of Heaven brought hope to a lost world. Hailed as the Comforter—she brought comfort. As the Holy Spirit she brought a holy message. As the Lady of All Nations, she brought unity. She laid down hints at the feet of the people; suggesting Heaven on Earth, World Peace, Utopia, and Oneness. It was all there; ready to happen, meant to happen and sure to happen. The long awaited dream of a perfect world, a dream that's teased humanity for millennia was promised and near. It lay in wait just over the horizon.

Yes…, many things the Queen of Heaven did bring. But of all the things she brought, it would be the visual element of a 'Higher Power' that turned the heads of so many. And why wouldn't it. It mirrored what God did for His people in the days of Moses, and what Jesus did in the days of his first coming. The people would see and believe back then, why wouldn't they see and believe now. The bottom line is the Queen of Heaven brought proof; visual proof to the modern world by which to turn the element of faith on its head.

It was enough proof to buy humanity's attention, and lure the souls of the lost; especially in the darkest of days. Proof indeed; the Queen brought the element of god into the picture. She brought an element of god that people could actually see so as to believe. She brought an element of god that people could actually see so as to devote their faith, so as to drop to their knees and worship, to pray to, and pledge their allegiance. As for the Born Agains, the Queen of Heaven wielding the sword of 'seeing-is-believing' would not only test their faith, it would aggressively attack it.

With a few short words; a kind and gentle rebuke to a disciple who unreservedly gave himself over to 'seeing-is-believing'; the resurrected Jesus spoke to generations to come. The disciple Thomas, who did not, and would not believe Jesus raised from the dead unless his eyes sold him the goods, opened the door for Jesus to speak to the glory of faith.

"...because you have seen Me, you have believed. Blessed are those who have not seen, and yet have believed."

With the dawning of the Supernatural Age, the scripture would have to be taken to a whole new level. *'Blessed are those who have not seen, and yet have believed...,'* and continue to believe despite many signs and wonders that seem to prove otherwise was more like it. The Born Agains will be hard pressed to hold steadfast to what Jesus said to Thomas in view of the Queen of Heaven's glory and grandeur.

Taking sides was now up front and center and becoming more and more prevalent. On one side would be those who...because they have seen the Queen of Heaven...was sure to gravitate toward her and her holy messages. On the other side were, of course, the Born Agains, who wouldn't only refuse to gravitate toward the Queen of Heaven, but insist and declare she was pure evil despite her beauty and aura of comfort and peace. People would choose, immediately choose in most cases, but many remained undecided. It wasn't really so much about being neutral, as it was just being cautious. The undecided knew they'd eventually have to make a choice; which lends to what the Word of God made very clear in the

Book of Joshua.

'Now therefore, fear the Lord, serve Him in sincerity and in truth — Serve the Lord! And if it seems evil to you to serve the Lord, choose for yourselves this day whom you will serve...',

The New Age divide, choosing one side or the other was simple but powerful; powerful enough to separate the world masses like water mixed with oil. The separation was clear and definite. Splitting the multitudes, the nations, the communities, the neighborhoods, friends, and families quickly became the new norm. The signs, the miracles, visions, promises, and messages brought on by the Queen would persist as well as escalate, making the divide between the Born Agains and the rest of the world more abrasive and noticeable.

As it sits, the Holy Messages were most attractive, but it was the short list of promises the Queen was fulfilling with each and every visit that would draw the multitudes closer and closer. The Born Agains couldn't refute it, but it didn't mean they had to revere it, let alone glorify it. The promises made and the promises fulfilled didn't mean the promises came without a price. Its deception..., and deception is evil; that is where the Born Agains stood when it came to the Queen of Heaven. But it was a hard cookie to sell, being the Queen, the so-called 'Comforter' was clearly comforting the masses in distress. How dare anyone suggest something as beautiful as that to be evil?

In South Lake Tahoe, this particular mid-morning, it was yet another brittle battle being fought on the matter. Needless to say, there was no love to be found. There was only hostility, anger and venom.

"I'm telling you it was her, Randy. It was Skye," Rebecca angrily demanded. "Don't sit there and tell me my kids aren't here." Strong, sharp and firm; like that of a judge's gavel pounding down at the podium, "THEY — ARE — HERE…!" she fiercely asserted loud and clear. "They're here among us like this Queen of Heaven said they were. How could you even doubt it?"

Rebecca then started to cry after her burst of anger. Randy didn't mean to upset her — or Jake for that matter. Even though welling up with tears, she was far from finished and no less angry. She wasn't finished giving her brother a piece of her mind.

"And don't be telling me they're up in heaven, or that they were taken by Jesus either. That's a bunch of crap. They're here, I know they are. They've slept in their beds. Skye's Teddy Bear was on my dresser. She put it there—I know she did. She's letting me know she's still here." Rebecca belted as she managed to squeeze out a weak quivering smile at the thought of it. There was plenty of joy in the thought, but it was closer to entertaining a ray of hope more than anything else.

Being so distraught, forsaken and heartbroken, like so many other fractured and grieving parents, it was really impossible to smile at anything. Hope however was not only abundant, it was in demand and welcomed.

Jake didn't say a word. He really didn't have to say anything. Rebecca did just fine putting Randy in his place.

Already headed out the door, "I gotta get back to work...," Randy uttered after weathering his older sisters heated eruption and being told off, or reprimanded if you will.

"Yeah..., you do that Randy and while you're there, you better start thinking about which side of the fence you want to be on," shouted Rebecca out the window as he made his way across the yard. Randy jumped into his ol' pride-and-joy, started it up and sped off back to work. His ol' pride-and-joy— like the jerk from the Domestic Security and Surveillance said; the one that badgered Joel and himself at the checkpoint—better use them miles up before his truck is banned from the streets. But that, being as irritating as it is, it was the least of his worries.

"This is getting way outta hand...!" he murmured as he made his way back to Harvey's, the Casino where he worked. He was tensed up yet again. Unlike most of the world, unlike his sister and brother-in-law, this Queen of Heaven has and continues to make his life miserable, not better. Like many, he's just not comfortable with her or her weird Holy Messages; messages seemingly already starting to transpire right in front of his eyes.

It wasn't like everything was falling apart for him, he was just uneasy. For what it was worth, he knew he wasn't alone or the only one dealing with the tension. He'd find a little comfort in that. There was also Leah. She's been a wealth of information. Keeping in touch with her, talking to her, learning and getting to know more and more about the Bible, what's in the Bible, and the Gospel, about being Born Again and of course the End Times was helping considerably. Yes...the End Times—a time of great deception and great disaster according to the scriptures. It was definitely keeping Randy alert and on his toes.

'It's the end of the world as we know it...' popped into his head again. Humming along to himself, in his mind..., the catchy and fitting tune strangely enough seemed to ease the tension. Randy realized that his going back and forth with Rebecca and Jake as well as friends and co-workers was only a tiny part of what was making him tense. It was the End Times; hearing about these last days over the years was one thing, but actually seeing it and being in the middle of it is what really had him on edge.

It was so hard to tell as to what was good and what was evil. It was easy to believe in all the supernatural stuff going on because he was actually seeing it going down right in front of him. But, trying to figure out if it was good or evil; that was a different story. What happened to his sister, the poltergeist-like activity, beds slept in, Teddy Bears on the dresser; was it really good, a good sign—or something else? Was it really her kids, Sean and Skye? Are they really still here? Is God leading her to believe her kids were still here, still among us? Or is it the devil??? Thinking things through was now a dangerous game. The thought of losing one's soul if anyone got it wrong made it that much more extreme.

Heaven...? Hell...? Forever...? One way or the other when you die, no second chances, no safety nets, no purgatory, no reincarnation—thanks to Joel, Randy was warned many times over about eternal consequences. All the stuff that was never important enough to warrant much thought was now poking Randy's mind and imagination to no end; like pins in a pin-cushion. He was always pretty flippant about the whole idea of going to hell if he didn't get his beliefs in order. It was always laughable, but things have changed.

It was because of the Rapture; witnessing it first hand. The fact that it was true all along, a truth quietly sitting there in the pages of the Bible all these years only heightened his awareness, the wonderment, the seriousness, but more importantly the possibility that maybe, just maybe going to hell forever if one got their belief wrong was true as well. The thought was beginning to make him nervous. In other words, the days of snickering at the Bible's reputation of really truly being the...WORD OF GOD...were over and scoffing at the Gospel of Jesus Christ now seemed risky, if not downright dangerous.

As he sat there waiting at a stoplight, once again, something that Joel said every now and then began to float to the top of Randy's cup of recollections. It was another one of those one-liner scriptures that seemed to forever stick to the brain whether one liked it or not—sort of like unforgettable childhood lullabies. He'd say—

"The fear of the LORD is the beginning of wisdom".

Randy was beginning to understand the fear, and in turn more the wiser. The Rapture brought instant fear to the entire world. One could even say it put the fear of God in everybody, not some, not most, but EVERYBODY! All the same, it did almost nothing to concern people about going to an eternal hell if they'd die believing in the wrong things, in the wrong message, or in the wrong God. This is what was separating Randy from Becky and Jake. It's actually what separated Joel from the three of them before the Rapture.

The fear of the LORD…, the beginning of wisdom — maybe so, he thought to himself. He didn't know. What he did know was —

'Thou shall have no other god's before me' – has taken on a whole new meaning.

Randy didn't need Joel or anyone else to remind him of this particular scripture. It's always been stuck in his head; another one-liner. Only now — all of a sudden it's something to fear rather than something to ignore as he's done in the past. The fear of believing in the wrong things, in the wrong message, the fear of believing lies and putting his faith in the wrong higher power now has Randy thinking twice about everything going on. This is why he was having his doubts about whom or what was behind the poltergeist-like activity happening to Jake and Rebecca.

He was troubled by all of it — the in-your-face supernatural goings-on and paranormal surge happening to the world. It was because he himself was having his own personal encounters with something from another dimension. Was it demonic, again—he didn't know. Sometimes he hears what he thinks are voices, or a voice in particular speaking to him. Often just a word, sometimes two or three words spoken aloud with an occasional whisper here and there; all having to do with egging him on and encouraging him to abandon his eagerness to learn more about Jesus, the Gospel, the Bible, and its coverage of the End Times.

Dmitri, the demon-angel Influencer assigned to Nicki Dawn wasn't the only dark and dutiful messenger strategically deployed to separate teetering souls from well-versed family members and friends glued to the Gospel Truth. The demons were sent by the hundreds of billions; on a mission to snatch the truth away from the susceptible like snatching rattles away from babies. Randy was targeted, as was Nicki, simply because of their up-close and personal connection to Joel and Leah. The Influencers, and Vy-Gréthos' crossover demons were sent to lure them away from the light of the truth while they were still easy to fleece.

Randy was definitely feeling it—the tug-o-war—being pulled back and forth as to which way to go and what to believe. At times he wished he could just go back to being cool about it, to sit back, be neutral—tinker around with his own little homemade nameless religion formed around his own little version of God like he's done his entire life. Other times though he feels like he's supposed to just throw his hands up, give in and join the multitudes eager to pay homage to the Queen of Heaven and accept her as an essential element of God. Rebecca, Jake, amongst others he knew — in fact most of the world was already doing so.

As of now, he's done neither despite the peculiar persuasion of the ghostly voice he's been hearing and the sway of the world. Instead, he's sticking to the 'Jesus is Lord' crowd — the minority at odds with what was popular and easy to believe. There was a small part of him that didn't want to be a Jef — a Jesus Fundamentalist, but he just couldn't help it. He really had no rhyme or reason other than a feeling; a feeling that came with his cigarette on the patio that one early morning right after the Rapture. Still, even though he really didn't know why outside of this compelling feeling, it was enough to resist, question, and oppose the Queen of Heaven and her mysterious list of ambiguous messages — her Holy Messages.

There was of course the third group of people; the Zionists. Like the small handful of Born Again-Rapture Believing Christians who swam in the ocean of countless versions of Christianity, the Zionist too were in their own little boat. A small sect of hardcore Fundamentalist Jews loyal to the Old Testament; devout Jews, who were segregated, even set apart from the rest of the Jews tinkering around with their new-fangled versions of Judaism so as to snuggle in with the world.

Lukewarm Jews, liberal Jews, the 'in-name-only' Jews, the flippant and flimsy, non-practicing, watered down, whitewashed Jews and otherwise; the Zionists weren't anything like them — enough so that they'd often find themselves being ostracized and castigated by their Jewish counterparts. But that's neither here nor there. Obviously, the disdain and criticism, along with chastising and the mockery of fundamentalist's, both the Zionists and the Born Agains, even by their own, was nothing new; more especially over the last hundred years. It's been around. There's no doubt about that. It's only now though, that the scorn and contempt for them has been taken to new heights. It's now full of venom.

As it sits, like the Born Agains, the Zionists were adamant and extremely reluctant to revere the Queen of Heaven. They weren't budging, or even bending. It was only because they weren't quite yet sold on her. They were just as awestricken, astonished and amazed as everyone else, and like most, they were never going to go so far as to suggest the Queen was the works of Satan or evil. This is what made them different than the Born Agains.

Still, they were keeping their distance. They were

waiting. Holding steadfast to their core dogma straight out of the Old Testament—it isn't the Holy Spirit that the Jewish Nation, Israel or the Zionists have been waiting for. They're waiting for something else—the promised Messiah. This is why they're not completely giving themselves over to the Queen of Heaven—at least not yet, not until their coming Messiah emerges from it.

Unlike the Pagan religions, Eastern religions, and Islam, as well as New Age Practitioners, and the Christian religions, Catholics, Mormons, Jehovah Witnesses and every hodge-podge mongrel Christian belief in between, and the many brands and breeds of Jews…; the Zionist Jews were adamantly cautious, more prudent, skeptical and patient. They weren't so eager to rush in and hail the Queen of Heaven as one sent by the hand of their God—the God of Abraham, Isaac, and Jacob; I AM.

Be that as it may, the Zionists weren't the ones causing the rift in the world. They weren't the ones behind the divide, the global schism; the ones who were dividing the world into two groups. It was the Jef's—both the New Born Christians and the Born Agains who missed the Rapture. They were the culprits, or the champions depending on who was making the assessment.

Friend or foe…, the Jef's, who were extremely few

in numbers and even fewer who'd dare speak out against the Queen would do so very gently. Polite and respectful, they'd be—far from the loud and boisterous outspoken preacher in Hong Kong, but it didn't matter. Their mild conduct was, more often than not, met with hostility, resentment and fierce opposition, often violent at that.

The Mother Hen cradling all religions and beliefs in her arms was beyond reproach. When Randy said…, 'this is getting out of hand'—he was right. Jake and Rebecca's fiery backlash not ten minutes ago over a simple comment certified it.

-Chapter Twenty-
BABYLON PILLARS

The incident in Hong Kong most definitely staked its claim. BAM...!!! Like a bowling ball dropped to the floor, the episode hit the earth with a colossal thud, likened to super-hero landings seen in movies. It was solid and firm and it rattled the world's conscience to the core. It inspired others to follow suit. It sparked reluctance; even a resistance to the Queen of Heaven wooing the nations. With each and every visitation and message that followed, there'd be other Bible Believers and skeptics compelled to rise up, speak out and rebuke the Queen of Heaven's splendor and holy messages, but it was proving to be very unpopular.

The confrontations were very touchy. Some of the Jef's were able to speak freely without any violence or hostile repercussions simply because people, having seen the footage of the Hong Kong incident, would consider the thought. The Born Agains used it extensively. They referred to it and cited the example over and over to make their point that God did indeed step in; that He dropped a spiritual grenade into the situation — blasting the brutal mob of thugs out in every which direction to make His presence known.

Yes..., the entire world was quite aware of what happened to those who took it upon themselves to viciously attack the fiery Bible Thumper. It was a given. They knew something — something powerful stepped in to protect that bold and brazen preacher telling the people to flee from the Queen and turn to Jesus Christ. It was near impossible not to think that God, the God of the Gospel, or even Jesus Himself was behind the miraculous rescue.

Yet, as they did with the Rapture and for whatever reasons, the multitudes would resist the obvious. They'd ignore the evidence and censure the proof. Ignoring the proof and evidence, however, didn't eradicate it. It was there. Not only that — it was there forever; indestructible, impossible to destroy.

Even so, the Queen of Heaven, the bringer of good news and hope; being so beautiful, so encouraging, and inspiring, so gentle, kind, and motherly, entirely void of even the slightest hint of something bad, let alone evil and satanic — it was easy to understand why the majority would side with her majesty. This notion that it was the power of God that reached down and supernaturally rescued this deranged, Jesus-loving lunatic in Hong Kong from being beat to death was just a hard pill to swallow. Still, it wasn't anything to take lightly. It was that incident alone, that small, seemingly near insignificant street brawl that gave the entire world a reason to question the Queen of Heavens goodness, holiness, integrity, and motives whether they liked it or not.

It's why Satan and his minions were so furious, dismayed and annoyed. It wasn't only the incident itself, but God would not let Satan speak to the mediums so as to suggest it was the love and compassion of the Queen who had mercy on this belligerent Jesus-loving fanatic in Hong Kong; that it was she who reached out as any mother would to protect little children from being hurt.

The rumor got out, but it didn't get out by supernatural means, through the miracle of the mediums receiving the message and passing it on to the world. No…, the rumor that said it was the Queen's motherly love who rescued the man in Hong Kong was set a fire by the Influencers speaking to the minds of people. That's as far as Satan could go, the best he could do; and only what God allowed. Thus, the rumor sat as merely an opinion, a popular opinion, but still an opinion of which value wasn't worth much more than the bad breath that spewed out of the mouths of those who'd tout it.

I AM—the Most High God intervening at the height of the devils grand appearance to the world as the "Light Bearer" was no small matter. Rudely interrupting the splendor along with the little maneuver of plastering the video footage of the ghostly rescue for the entire world to see was carried out to perfection. The entire world was made aware of a rivalry; a supernatural rivalry It was more than enough to suggest two 'higher powers' at odds with each other along with the million-dollar-question. Which one is the 'good power', and which one is the 'bad power'. As strange as it seemed, it wasn't the Rapture but the small altercation in Hong Kong that narrowed every single belief in the world down to two sides; two Higher Powers — one choice.

In essence, if one looked hard enough, it was easy to determine nothing's really changed. The world really hadn't changed. It was right back to where it was before the Rapture; one choice — yes or no to Jesus Christ and the Gospel. The only difference was the stakes were raised; the heavenly realm with all of its supernatural traits and capabilities were now visibly evident.

Satan was given his chance to stake his claim to be like the Most High God without having to do it under the radar. Lucifer — the Light Bearer, God's once most glorious, most beautiful, and arrayed Angel of all angels that He created was allowed to manifest his glory to the children of God, of whom he hated with a passion — jealousy. And that he did — and that he'd do, indeed.

Randy, with all his heart totally understood why Rebecca and Jake, or most of the world's remaining population for that matter were so apt and anxious to devote themselves to the Queen of Heaven in all its grandeur. It was in fact hard not to; especially after she, through the clairvoyants reassured the grieving nations that the children, their children, every single child and unborn baby taken in the Mass Vanishing was safe, even among them to be communicated with as well as destined to return. It was so much better, healthier and far more encouraging to hear that instead of being told their precious children and babies were up in heaven with Jesus—taken by Jesus along with the Born Agains. It didn't sit well with most. Denial, if not hatred would still abound, and fester that much more.

When it came to the Queen of Heaven it wasn't so much about what the masses needed to hear as it was about what they wanted to hear. It didn't matter if it was a lie. Like the saying goes—people prefer to believe what they prefer to be true. Being told their children were near, amongst them, to communicate, destined to return—why wouldn't people gravitate to the hints and signs that it was really true in their hour of darkness?

The promise was just one of several mixed in with what's being called the Six Holy Messages given to all humanity. Three days after the Rapture, the Queen of Heaven set the world on fire when she revealed herself in Lisbon, Portugal. The next six days belonged to her as well—essentially renewing all creation if you will.

After Lisbon, it would be six consecutive days ushering six more glorious visitations delivering her six Holy Messages to the entire world. It would be six days of Satan's best. This time however it would not be just a young, child-like, naked and naïve woman in a garden—it would be the nations who'd take a bite of the apple.

In those six days the harsh and unusual weather patterns from continent to continent subsided as the Queen of Heaven promised. The rumbling earthquakes came to a standstill as promised. The abnormal animal behavior was neutralized as promised. And the demon-possessed maniacs along with their unpredictable carnage halted as promised. In essence, humanity was getting a taste of a very promising fresh new world in spite of economic havoc, grief and social anxiety. But that too was to be healed in time according to the six Holy Messages.

The Queen of Heaven in all her glory fulfilled her short-term promises—neutralizing the harsh weather conditions and animal attacks, etc. etc. In turn, she easily won over the worlds trust in her, which automatically gave credence to her Holy Messages. Through her and by her…, the scrambling lost and uncertain multitudes full of fear would find a ray of light, direction, hope, and a will to carry on, but most of all…, they would find comfort. After seven glorious visitations, the level of comfort was quite high, not perfect, but high and most assuring.

From Lisbon, Portugal to Hong Kong, China, then Alexandria, Egypt on down to Sydney, Australia — with the exception of Lisbon — the Queen of Heaven faithfully appeared as foretold by the multitudes of mediums, psychics and Channelers alike. From Australia, it was to the far north — to Russia's capital-of-old Leningrad; now St. Petersburg. Next, the Queens sixth visit moved over and down to Rio de Janeiro, Brazil. It was amazing, all of it — the visions, the miracles; it was beyond anything and everything the world abroad could have ever imagined. Yet here it was…, happening right before they're very eyes.

It also became very clear — the centuries-old ability of people actually being able to tap into a higher plane of consciousness, and interact with another dimension, into other worlds, and utilize the Sixth Sense was no longer a theory swimming around in the sea of suspicion and speculation. The abilities of psychics, mediums, channelers — the gifted if you will was now a confirmed reality. It was immediately accredited to 'the god-like authority of science'. It was proven. It was authenticated far beyond a shadow of a doubt and the world received it with open arms; others with caution and fear. Nevertheless, it was received to be as true as the sun and moon exist.

After revealing herself in Rio de Janeiro, being her fifth visitation after Lisbon, the Queen of Heaven would make known to the Channelers as to where the next and final appearing would be. Like the other revelations, the mediums wasted no time to inform the entire world as to what they were specifically told via telepathy. This time, however, the message given to the mediums as to where she would appear for the final visitation was a little different — intriguing, mysterious and compelling.

"The Babylon Pillars...!" said Vera Smith-Copeland. Always correct, getting it right every single time in regards to revealing the Queen of Heavens messages by her psychic abilities, Ms Vera as the public knew her sort of became America's main mediator; the mediums and channelers spokesperson..

Her countenance had changed though from her first television appearance a week earlier. She was no longer in utter despair and sobbing as she spoke to the reporters given that her five year old daughter was taken in the Mass Vanishing. She was instead a little more stabilized, even mildly elated. The Queen's holy message about the children and their whereabouts, that they were near, and here among us, to be communicated with did wonders for the grieving parents. Even though it was far from resolution, the message lifted their spirits considerably. It showed in Ms. Vera's demeanor as it did in Rebecca's.

Being referred to as the Comforter sat very well in the eyes and hearts of those who were comforted by her. Rebecca having lost, Sean, Skye and her unborn child Michael Ray was a perfect and prime example. Ms Vera; like Rebecca had definitely changed. She was still broken at the loss of her precious daughter. Even so, after the Queen's six visitations along with her fulfilled promises and Holy Messages; Vera Smith-Copeland was one of many finding relief and even joy in the enlightenment bestowed upon them.

Bewildered and confused, "The Babylon Pillars...," the reporting journalist inquired as she shook her head. "Hmmm..., perhaps I'm finding myself to be a little in the dark here Ms Vera, but—the Babylon Pillars? What does that even mean? I've never heard of it. Is it even a place, a city, a province, a..., a country?"

Catching her self rambling with question after question, the correspondent interviewing the esteemed Ms Vera had to abruptly stop and walk herself back with an apology. "I'm sorry Ms Vera," she said half embarrassed. "I guess what I'm asking is — what is the Babylon Pillars? More importantly, where is it or where are they?" she asked with a little more composure.

Ms Vera, with a kind smile answered, "First of all, Sara…, I just want to tell you how glad I am to see that it's just you alone hitting me with a barrage of questions. The press conferences, oh my god, they're just too hectic and nerve-racking to deal with. I'd be getting five times as many questions thrown at me from ten different people all at once. It makes my head spin — probably spin off my body if it weren't attached." she said in jest. After a cordial chuckle between the two, Ms Vera went on to answer Sara's questions.

"Well, Sara…, to tell you the truth — in all honesty — I'm not sure. The Babylon Pillars — I haven't a clue. But I am sure of what we've received." declared Ms Vera. "The Holy Spirit, the Comforter, the Glory returns with the cycle of the sun — a day, a night, Babylon Pillars, final visit — final message. Like all the others, the message we received, in every language known to humanity, I might add — it was really quite simple. The Queen of Heaven, the Immaculate Heart, Our Lady, the Comforter, the Holy Spirit, Gaia, the Glory — whatever one chooses to call this…, this element of God, perhaps God Herself — it's to manifest one last time. She's to bless us with the last and final Holy Message to humanity. Now, with that said—I really don't know what, let alone where the Babylon Pillars are though. I...or I should say we, my fellow mediums and I only know what we've been told."

Again, it wasn't just Vera Smith-Copeland sharing the revelation, it was all of them. It was all of the psychics, mediums and Channelers all over the world spreading the word in every language, both privately and publicly. It was uncanny, how they'd receive the messages simultaneously worldwide, but quite a reality, quite true. As if they were one, one people, one voice, one message—all of them, every single one of them was sure and adamant as was Ms Vera. The Queen of Heaven's last and final visit and holistic message would unfold at the Babylon Pillars. But what the Babylon Pillars are, or where it—or they are located was unknown. Nor were the Mediums told.

People didn't know where to go, where to flock, where to gather. Small handfuls of people would gather on different coasts here and there, holy places and the mountain tops across the globe, but the odds of being in the right spot at the right time were a zillion to one. Those who congregated on the random coasts and various sights all over the world did so more as a ritual. With their holy candles, incense, oils, prayer rugs, flowers, alcohol, drugs, rosaries, trinkets, shrines and statues from all the different religions; the people gathered in reverence to the world's Holy Spirit; the Heavenly Queen no matter where she'd appear. The fact that she was to appear was enough to worship and commemorate her and her mere existence. As long as they had their phones and media devices with them to watch her appearing no matter where it would be was suffice.

Some rushed to the ruins and partially restored streets of Babylon in Iraq, to the banks of the Euphrates River, but something really didn't seem right about that. Even though the Biblical Babylon was, in a sense, re-birthed with a handful of restoration projects, it was still extremely desolate and unpopulated. Still, it was Babylon—the only Babylon the world has ever known.

It was guesses and guesses only. The world waited. And within twenty-four hours, like every other visitation from the point of the mediums revelations, the world would see. The mystery, perhaps the mystery of 'Babylon the Great' was unveiled. The guessing was over. The Babylon Pillars was now a Kingdom, a new kingdom christened by the Queen of Heaven; instantaneously, in mere minutes…, Babylon was born…, or reborn.

A kingdom defined by borders; it was not—not this time. This Babylon was defined by its spirit. It was a

Kingdom defined by ideology, idolatry, affluence, indulgence and attitude. Babylon—meaning the…'Gate to God'… by the Akkadian ancients was back. Swollen with pride, zero fear of God, soaring over the heights of humanity, worshipping the rise of science and the accomplishments of man; proud, pompous, and powerful would build, erect and set the 'Babylon Pillars' in place, towering high above and apart from the rest of the world, figuratively speaking.

Four cities would receive the honor. Washington, D.C., New York City, Hollywood, and San Francisco would serve as the Babylon Pillars spoken of to the mediums. Within a day, they were deemed to be the mirror image of 'Babylon the Great' and all that it stood for. The four cities symbolized the four corners of the single, most greatest, world renowned metropolis and civilization known to the human race; surpassing even the Roman Empire. It is the 'head of gold' in the Scriptures, far more superior to all the lesser kingdoms that followed it in the history of mankind.

As one kingdom, the four esteemed cities can now brag and boast to owning its own separate corners of the world, its own identity, and lastly its own name. Four cities serving as one; they were together the center of trade, the hub of all religions, the symbol of wealth, prominence, pleasure, political power and military might. Babylon-America; deep in the arts, rich in culture, true to the godliness of liberalism, pushing the barriers of sexual liberation and uninhibited desires. A self-aggrandizing modern day kingdom, unabashed and shameless; redefining the moral high ground, idolizing science, technology, and literally worshipping Mother God Earth was the criteria that gave them the great honor from above. An honor bestowed upon them by no other than the Queen of Heaven was a great honor indeed.

The greed of Wall Street, the power of Capitol Hill, the idolatry of Tinsel Town and the decadence of the Sanctuary City swirling in and around the Silicone Valley, the four of them slithering in and out of each other like snakes in a den keeping each other warm, their incestuous relationship though miles apart from each other became Babylon, the Pillars of Babylon; Babylonia if you will, where *evil is good and good is evil*.

Seedy, yet sophisticated. Corrupt..., yet justified. Godly..., yet godless—an immoral yet sanctimonious kingdom of double-standards, where hypocrisy is embraced and depravity is celebrated, glamorized, glorified, honored, and respected. It was everything that moved an unsuspecting soul to unknowingly hail Satan the Most Popular in the face of Jehovah the Most High God.

As to why these four particular cities as opposed to every other city in the world, why America—nobody knew…, not even the Mediums. Some speculated it was due to the irrefutable position and reputation of greatness, liberal totalitarianism, and power unmatched by anywhere in the world. Still, nobody really knew, but it is what it is. Even though it was obviously symbolic; America, the New America, the part of America that conquered and obliterated the America-of-old was now nicknamed Babylon— New Babylon to be exact. Thus a kingdom by name was reborn; a kingdom in spirit defined by ideologies, philosophies and attitudes that exalt itself high enough to equate its mere existence to God status. Be all that it may be, Babylon's reemergence onto the world stage came as no surprise to the Born Agains of the day; for they knew all about it—foretold in the Book of Revelation.

As for the Queen of Heaven, it would not be herself that would appear high above the Babylon Pillars— the four cities. It would be four other apparitions, four beings, four angels, or four gods. Outside of the fact that they were all splendid in their own right, nobody knew what these apparitions were any more than what they knew what the Queen of Heaven is. Yes, they were beautiful, but not as beautiful, brilliant, or as radiant as the Queen herself. Nor were they as big. Still, striking and worthy, levitating over the outskirts of New York City, Washington, D.C., Hollywood and San Francisco, the prince of each city would beckon many to kneel on bended knee in their presence.

Even though it was the four magnificent angels that the people would see and record with their cameras, phones and what have you, it would be Satan's dark messengers they'd hear. It would be the demonic Influencers strategically deployed by the tens of millions who would speak directly to the Mediums and Channelers worldwide—who would in turn convey the last and final Holy Message. By them and through them, the sixth holistic message from beyond would be made known to all humanity. Again, the event would last just over eleven minutes only to end with another eye-popping finale. Like the Queen of Heaven, the apparitions, the Four Angels as it were, they too would dance and swirl out of view in an array of spectacular lights, simultaneously, altogether and on cue.

Like the previous six visitations, the video footage captured would once again flood the portals worldwide for all to see. Via satellite, international media, the internet and social networking—every monitor, every screen, every TV, every phone revealed all the splendor and glory that briefly hovered over the four chosen cities. The Holy Message as well; promised by the Queen, her sixth and final Holy Message, it too would find its way into every ear in a matter of minutes. Every medium, every clairvoyant, again perfectly in synch across the globe immediately publicized the message they received via telepathy during the holy visitation.

From there, after those seven consecutive and powerful days of godly visions and holy messages — the world would enter a new era, a new creation, and a new phase of evolution unlike anything that's ever been known to man. The visions and holy messages was for the most part enough to snap the world out of its stupor. It pulled people out of the mire and slump of just wanting to roll over and die. It gave the multitudes an incentive to carry on, stay alive and persevere. It was a wakeup call — a rallying call, a revival.

Global Affairs would act on the new visions and messages. The elitist sect of Ten Curators plucked out of the United Nations seven years ago — President Manning being one of them, managed to ignite a global plan using the visitations and Holy Messages as inspiration. By decree they launched the Term of Adjustment. It was more or less an intercontinental movement calling all nations and individuals alike to war against the chaos. Although decreed by law, it came across as a plea, a civil suggestion in the name of love and unity.

Set aside greed, and put away selfishness. Shelve extravagance; shun nonessentials and materialism — at least for a while until the world stabilizes. Apply to giving-not taking, be understanding, empathetic to each other, be lenient on debts, rents, etc. Share, comfort each other, and work with each other from neighbor to neighbor, community to community, class to class, country to country and nation to nation. Yes, it was an order, but it worked more as a voluntary commitment; a group effort. Marshall Law across the globe immediately implemented right after the Rapture was a given—natural and standard procedures if you will. The Term of Adjustment however was different. It wasn't calling on Law Enforcement and militaries into action, it was calling all citizens of the world into action.

For most, both officials and commoners, the feelings were mutual. It was understood. Citizens of the world were in total agreement. Law or no law, children or no children, pregnancies or no pregnancies—the bulk instinctively knew that concerted efforts had to be made in order to stabilize the trembling world dealing with the supernatural crisis.

Turning a world of broken, grieving, distraught, and frightened people fending for themselves into a world of taking care of each other became more and more common and plausible. Neighborly was a key word. International unity and oneness was making more and more sense.

The Global Media would waste no time to promote it. It took great strides to circulate the Term of

Adjustment. Infomercials, networking, public broadcasting, billboards, radio promotions, even on down to lawn signs and bumper stickers; it all served the communities well. It was declared a time of acceptance, a time of awareness, a time to admit, commit and readjust to the impact and reality of the New Age thrust upon them. Whether one liked it or not and as hard as it was—people had to comply with all efforts and initiatives taken to alleviate the mess. All obstacles that could possibly be removed so as to get the world moving again were to be removed as fast and efficient as possible. The New Age—the Supernatural Age didn't exempt anyone from having to rejuvenate, reengage and tend to their responsibilities.

Everybody knew that some things just couldn't be ignored let alone neglected. People had to eat. People had to drink. Even though a lot of it was make-do and at local levels it still had to be.

From parents to politicians, from farmers to merchants, from civil servants to truck drivers, students and soldiers abroad; people needed to move forward. They had to rise above their emotions, subdue the panic and conquer the confusion, but more importantly work together. Banks, militaries, merchants, and medical facilities worldwide had to bend, extend flexibility and foster understanding. Some would move faster than others. For some, it was harder than others.

Some were more compassionate while others more be-grudged. Some were forceful, some more gentle and patient.

Through it all, both the Born Agains clinging to Jesus Christ and the New Agers being drawn to the Queen of Heaven like moths to a flame were complic-it. The Term of Adjustment implemented by Global Affairs suited both sides of the isle. They were both on the same page. Their indifferences over the Higher Power didn't at all sever their sense of commonality — working together to smooth things over, helping each other, and consoling each other.

Still, even in the light of something good and positive in the making there was darkness in the mix. Ulterior motives were still lurking in the shadows. Deception would only sink its teeth and talons further and deeper into the neck of humanity.

-Chapter Twenty One-

SIX HOLY MESSAGES

A month would pass, rather quickly. Now into the first part of April; the world having no other choice would roll with the crisis and changes. The Term of Adjustment initiated by Global Affairs was good, but it was the Queen of Heaven that motivated every culture, creed, country and nation to uphold the humanitarian measures.

The Queens glorious manifestations along with the healing promises and six prophetic messages to the broken world is what gave the broken world hope. It was the Queen who would see them through. It was the Queen who set the world's sights on a whole new era—a whole new age..

Reminiscent of a kind and loving, compassionate mother gently taking the hand of a scared and nervous child, walking them to and through their first day at school—the Queen of Heaven being sold as the Comforter, the Holy Spirit, the Lady of All Nations, the Immaculate Heart, Gaia, and the Glory carried the world over and through their Term of Adjustment. The holy visions and promises were enough to give the frightened and uneasy citizens of the world an incentive to carry on. It gave them a will to admit, to accept, commit and readjust to their new lives, their new surroundings and awkward circumstances. It was enough to help them endure the difficulties and hardships, even receive it with open arms in some cases.

People, great and small, young and old, both powerful and subservient, both rich and poor, from nation to household; they may not have known exactly what to expect, but they sure knew where to look and what they're to look for. The Queen of Heaven is where they'll now look and her Six Holy Messages, now in stone like the Ten Commandments, is what they'll be looking for. Why…? It was because she is the one who turned a daunting, dark and foreboding future into a promising one.

It was promising for many — for most, but not for all. There were some who had their sights on a promising future, but it wasn't built on the Queen's promises. It was the promises of Jesus, His Second Coming and the life thereafter. The Born Agains, the Jesus Fundamentalists — although few, they were determined to hold steadfast to Jesus Christ, to the Gospel, to the Bible and all it had to offer.

It of course included all God had to say about the 'end times'; now happening right before their very eyes. Strange, they thought, how so few there were of them. Strange…, yes, but in all honesty, they weren't surprised.

It was just another thing Jesus told them to expect. Believing the Word of God has its perks; especially when it comes to knowing what to expect, more or less. The future is foretold…, even proven in many ways; but who in the world cares outside of the few who believe God.

This particular night, at Calvary of Tucson…, some of these 'believers' would meet yet again to address the latest bombshells.

"Listen, people…! Listen to me close. Please…, please listen!"

Standing at the podium, inside the disarrayed, dimly lit church, speaking to a handful of people scantily sprinkled about the pews was Robson Talgo. A standard, gritty, run-of-the-mill Born Again Jesus Fundamentalist would be the mild-mannered, quiet and reserved Postal Carrier addressing the small gathering. Like Leah, another believer who unfortunately made the same mistake as she when the Rapture came and went, Robson Talgo was doing his best to keep it together.

With no rhyme or reason, other than an unofficial count of hands from a small batch of lost and scared sheep, Robson led by the spirit stepped up to the plate. He would have to fill in where the primary Pastor left off—of whom was Raptured along with his whole family, his wife, kids, and his elderly parents. He was lost and scared himself, but something moved him to commit to being the makeshift Pastor.

He knew the roll, being that Pastor Lang explained many times over as to what the Pastors are called to do. He knew, but now he'd have to play the role, he'd have to deliver. He's the Sheppard now, there to 'lead, feed and protect the flock'. And that he'd do to the best of his ability.

So far..., he's been great; a great leader. Kind, ad- miral, empathetic, compassionate, strong, disciplined and firm; soldier-like at times, fatherly and brotherly at times as well, and yes..., friendly. The fact that he's also well-versed in Scriptures helps considerably. The man is proving to be the many things that make for an honorable leader. The congregation appreciates Robson tremendously and never cease to prayerful- ly thank God for him. Tonight, would be no differ- ent. Thanks were given and the gathering mindfully stopped and took heed to Robson calling them to lis- ten and listen close.

Leah would be there, in the second pew, atten- tively listening with the rest. She was there for many reasons, but she was mainly there because she knew it well—the church; Calvary of Tucson. It was her church as well as Joel's church before the Rapture.

She however never dreamed it would be her church after the Rapture. It still bothered her that she was here—still on earth. But she knew it was her decision, her mistake, her fault. She had come to grips with the fact that she just wasn't prepared. Ready..., yes by all accounts, she was ready, but prepared she was not.

Often, too often—'How could have I missed it'—she'd think. Yet, in the same breath she knew exactly why. She was misled—too assuming. The Rapture just didn't go down the way she was taught it would go down. She was ready for the 'zap-you're-outta-here-rapture', but far, far from being prepared for the 'free-will rapture'. It was a heavy price, but it's behind her now. She has a new problem to contend with. And she's here, here now listening to Robson dialing in on what is and is to come.

Up front and center, holding and waving a flyer around above his head, "This is it, people...!" Robson announced. "We already know this is what's coming. It's in fact already happening. I'm sure you've been listening to the news—to the latest developments. People are starting to hear welcoming voices. Friendly poltergeist-like activity is going through the roof. I know there's a few of you here now—Larry, Kim...,

Barbara—who's already dealt with these..., these paranormal visitations. I know I have!" Robson declared with an unsettled tone about his voice.

Soft sobs, whimpers and sighs would reverberate off the walls of the hollow, near empty church. Gatherings promoting Christ Jesus while railing against the Queen became unpopular. The crowds that flocked to the evangelical churches after the Rapture rapidly thinned with the Queen of Heaven's debut.

Now, a month later, it was the voices and the benevolent poltergeist-like activity leading people even further away from the Gospel of Jesus Christ—away from the truth. The sobs, the whimpers and sighs were coming from those who were wishing more than anything that these paranormal visitations were indeed from their departed loved ones and missing children. They however knew better. That's why they were there—fighting the temptation to believe the beautiful lies.

"Christian...! Please..., please believe me. I know it's hard! I know it's hard to believe it isn't our children and loved ones that everybody is hearing and dealing with—with all of these friendly visitations and voices. But we all know—we need to trust our Lord Jesus Christ, not..., not these demons. We need to trust the Word of God—not the Queen of Heaven or these Holy Messages given to us through the mediums. We know darn well what's true!" Robson beseeched.

"And we know they're not of God because of what they're saying!" said another sitting in the congregation—Amie, a real fireball, tough, geared up and ready for the battle to come. Leah loved her, Amie's her best friend. She's the sister Leah never had and the aunt-figure Nicki's come to adore over the years. Long before either of them gave their lives over to Christ, they've been close. In fact, Amie's fresh to the game. Like Randy, she's barely 'born again'; happened right after the Rapture as well.

Leah quietly looked down at her flyer as Robson kept speaking. It was a copy of the same flyer sweeping the streets like flurries of fallen leaves and plastered on every corner, post and billboard in every neighborhood, school, city and nation across the globe. The 'Six Holy Messages' was being touted as sort of the new Gospel.

As she gazed at the Queen's mysterious list of the Six Holy Messages, to her, just reading the list made her uneasy. Wondering on them, let alone seeing them take shape put a sense of fear in her. Only the first two on the list seemed to be already transpiring. Leah could argue with herself; she could be thankful that it's only two, or she could dread the thought of all of them coming to pass. She chose neither, feeling it best to just go numb at the moment.

Still, even though she's done it a hundred times over, she'd do it once again. She'd read off the list to herself one by one despite having them already memorized. Right off the page, they read:

1. The…Cleansing…is upon you.
2. The…Children…will assure you.
3. The…Prophet…will show you.
4. The…Power…is ahead of you.
5. The…Messiah…will deliver you.
6. The…Ancients…will teach you.

Leah's brief and silent evaluation of the list wasn't enough to distract her from listening to Robson address the congregation. She's heard every word. She took in a deep breath and sighed as she straightened her posture. Without missing a beat, she continued to listen as Robson continued to speak, trying to be as Pastor-like as possible.

"Ok, guys…, let's uhh…, I tell you what, let us please open our Bible's to Second Thessalonians 2:9-17 and pick this small handful of verses apart. In light of what's happened and now happening, these words penned by the Apostle Paul two thousand years ago are not only panning out to be true, but more importantly, starting to make more and more sense."

The particular scriptures spoke volumes. Robson

was quite right they were coming to life. Not only were they making more sense in regards to everything that was happening, but more and more sense in regards to what they as believers who 'believe God' needed to do in these last days.

As believers, both old and new, the Jef's would need to resist the powers of deception. They would need to combat and endure the Antichrist's coming persecution. Lastly, the scriptures reminded them of what they'd have to do to overcome God's soon to come wrath and judgment on a disbelieving world.

This was the hardest part—especially for Leah, Robson and every other Born Again who failed to trust God. In Sodom and Gomorrah, the scriptures depicting Lot's wife being told to leave and...'don't look back'...took on a whole new meaning to the Born Agains who missed out on the Rapture. Trusting God—that's what it was all about.

The Rapture, they knew what it was—that it was Jesus who had come to take them away as promised—to spare them from judgment to come. Yet..., for whatever reasons, like Lot's wife..., they stopped, looked back and stayed. It was enough to make them wonder if that particular incident recorded in the Word of God played a role in what happened to them; a forewarning perhaps, a cautionary tale.

Who knows? The only thing they knew is they may

not have been turned into pillars of salt like Lot's wife for looking back, but there was certainly a sense of regret that now haunts them. Regardless, they found a way to instead thank God they didn't share the same fate as Lot's wife; enough so to look at it as a blessing. Be that as it may, though it offered them some comfort, they still were prone to kick themselves in the butt.

Despite over two and half minutes of Jesus, the Holy Spirit and the Angels beckoning them, pleading with them to get on board the Rapture Train—they, like Lot's wife chose otherwise. They chose to look back and cling to their lives, to their world, their children, their loved ones, their pets and everything else in between. In essence, they didn't trust God to take care of the things they love and cherish had they'd gone.

They chose instead to trust in themselves to save and protect all that was dear to them. Yes..., it was regrettable because now, Leah, Robson and so many other Born Agains were grounded and plagued to endure the Tribulation even though it is not they as believers who are being judged.

Told many times over—they don't want to be here for the coming Judgments spoken of in the Book of Revelation, yet here they are. God's mercy on the youngest of the young and the mentally innocent, taking them with the Born Agains so as to spare them from the horrors to come was enough to make one wonder how terrible and how ugly it was going to be…, or get. As of now, only time would tell. And time was getting short.

Persecution has already started. The Antichrist, the phony messiah, was surely out there somewhere being groomed to woo the world. Satan was clearly rolling out the red carpet for him. And God's Judgments…, yikes—Leah thought, they were looming just over the horizon.

Tribulation and the Great Tribulation were sure to be the worst of the worst to come. It was all happening, already started, and it was dreadful to think about it. She couldn't help it. She wished there was something joyful to stick in the mix, but at the moment, she just couldn't find one to balance the equation. And gawking at the Six Holy Messages left by the Queen of Heaven via the Mediums and Channelers didn't help.

The Bible study came and went. As always, it was helpful, encouraging to say the least, and informative. But, it wasn't joyful. She did however think it good spending quality time with likeminded people. Her brothers and sisters in Christ were now, more than ever, closer to being family. They're relationships were getting tighter, more intimate and personal. It was a pleasant thought, but not really joyful. It's the circumstances behind these get-togethers and bonding that put a blot on joy; like ink on a white blouse.

Making her way home after the church gathering—wondering and worrying about all these things didn't put Leah in the best of moods. It wasn't a bad mood; it's just things weighed heavy on her heart. All of sudden, a spark of joy did manage to sneak in. As she drove up to park, she could see Nicki was home—the lights were on.

A gentle smile emerged, and it would take her home for the night.

-Chapter Twenty Two-

WHATS-HIS-FACE

"Hey, Mom," Nicki said as Leah shuffled through the door.

"Oh...! Hi honey," Leah answered with a quick glance at Nicki cozily planted on the couch under a blanket.

It was a rather distant hello though between the two. Leah, setting her purse down, tossing her keys on the nearby table and hanging up her coat was deep in thought. She was happy to see Nicki safe and sound, but some of the things brought up at the Bible study were still kicking around in her head. Nicki too was a little preoccupied catching the latest developments on TV.

Headed straight for the kitchen, "Do you want anything Nicki—juice..., water...?" Leah asked as she went to grab something for herself.

"No..., I'm ok mom. Thanks."

"Well now—don't you look cozy," Leah remarked as she sat down on the lounge chair, joining Nicki in the living room. Nicki politely grunted—lightly, just enough to acknowledge and respond to Leah's friendly remark. The small talk wasn't like it used to be.

Things have changed.

For Leah, Nicki Dawn, for everybody, worldwide at that— underneath the veneer of all the cordial exchanges was the haunting stark cold reality of having to adjust and contend with the New Age—their new world. Childless, no pregnancies, havoc, uncertainty, and fear on top of a new essence of God poised to straighten it all out—yes, small talk became rather hollow.

People were still in shock. It was impossible not to think about everything goin on, dwell on it, and pick it apart piece by piece. Still, even though small talk in a sense died when it came to a certain degree of sincerity—most would still at the very least go through the motions.

"So…! Anything new happening," Leah asked as she fixated her eyes on the TV with Nicki.

"Yeah…, I guess," Nicki mumbled. "I guess more and more people are getting signs—you know, of their missing children and loved ones. Some are even interacting with them. They're all sort of fleeting and faint though. They're calling 'em visitations."

"Yeah…, I've been hearing a little bit about it at work—some customers were talkin' about it. They were telling about their son and daughter-in-law having a visitation of their kid, or their grand kid, I guess. They were pretty excited about it."

"Shoot...! Watching TV..., man..., there are tons of people—they're like totally ecstatic and crying for joy and stuff. Even so, it's still pretty ugly out there. I mean things are moving—people are gradually getting back to work and stuff and they're sayin' the global economies are shifting a bit, stabilizing in some areas but a lot of it is still iffy. I guess the switch—you know—switching over to the Global Credits is working out pretty good, but its taking a lot longer than they thought for it to all kick in. Are you getting paid, mom, you know..., with the new system and all?" Nicki immediately asked while on the subject.

"Yeah..., but it's a little different than it was before. I mean I'm still getting credits, it's just that they're calling 'em Global Credits is all."

"I sure miss the days of cash." Nicki groaned. "It totally sucked when everyone had to turn in their cash for credits."

"Shoot..., Nicki—you were only nine or ten years old when that happened. Geez..., I have to laugh because..., I mean even the kids knew the Cash Relinquishment Exchange was a crappy deal." Leah asserted and added.

"Speaking of work and getting paid, I wish they'd give me more hours. It's getting tough. I just have to tell ya, I don't think we're gonna be getting a whole lot of the things we liked to have. You might want to get used to saying goodbye to sodas in the refrigerator, ice cream and frozen pizza's in the freezer…, and cookies and potato chips in the cupboards. It'll be mostly just stuff we need."

Nicki Dawn didn't want to believe it, let alone admit it but she had to. She knew the predicament they were in. It was the same with most of her friends as well. There were some who were more well off than others, but they too had to be prudent and frugal and watch their spending.

"So, what's the deal about these Global Credits? Are they like the ones you were getting before?"

"Sort of—I mean nothings really changed from how they transfer my wages into my account. It's still credits, but they're now documenting them as being Global Credits. From what I'm hearing, it's going to be set up to accommodate each Class of citizens. A-Class and B-Class citizens get A and B stuff, and the C-Class and D-Class gets C-Class and D-Class stuff.

We'll only be able to purchase certain things and a certain amount of things when it's all said and done. I'm pretty sure the A and B Class will get the goodies in life, and the rest of us will get the crumbs, but who knows. Maybe it's temporary—I don't know. They're supposed to be doing all kinds of new things. One world economy—humph! Why am I not surprised?" Leah said sarcastically, "Bible prophecy…, strikes again."

"What about the Debit Transfer Cards?" Nicki Dawn asked with a little anxiety in her voice.

"Well…, I don't really know. I don't how long it'll be before they issue Debit Transfer Cards or even if they will. It was nice to be able to transfer credits from my account to your card on the spot, but…, I don't know, honey. Who knows what they're gonna do."

"Crap…!" Nicki cursed in frustration.

"Well…," Leah paused, "I take that back. It's going to be the 'mark of the beast'. That's what they're gonna do."

"What…, you mean that thing that Joel was talkin' about that day—where you can't buy anything or sell anything without this mark on the hand?"

"On the hand or the head—the forehead," Leah corrected.

"Ssss….," Nicki hissed. "Well…, what the heck is it? What's it gonna be?"

"I don't know, dear. But we'll know soon enough. And we'll know when it happens. The only thing I can tell you is what Joel already told you. Whatever you do…, don't take the mark. It'll seal your fate—cost you your soul. That's the price of it. You can kiss any chance of salvation good-bye when you take it." Leah warned.

"Man…, it's weird—they were actually just talkin' about something along the lines of what you're sayin' on the news. You know…, getting all the banks and all this money crap back in order and fixing everything, the economy and stuff. I thought I heard them say something about every global citizen will need to be tied into the same system, or data base…, I don't know…, something like that. I think they said something about the Collective Bank, or wait—I think they said the Communal Bank. I think that's what it was."

"It sounds about right," Leah moaned, "Sounds like it's happening pretty quickly."

"Yeah…, I guess…, uh…, what's-his-face, umm…, that…, that Tony Giovanni guy over in Europe is stirring things up at Global Affairs—supposedly making things happen. I guess he's the one that came up with the Term of Adjustment; worked it all out with the other nations and stuff. Supposedly it's a big whoop-tee-do because he's never really been actively involved, or part of the GA's Ten Factions. He came out of nowhere."

Nicki went on, using her best fake English accent, "He's taken the bull by the horns, don't you know…! And it's a bloody good thing he is." She touted perkily. "Well—that's how Barry Bona puts it."

She's done it before. Jokingly mocking the famous, well-liked world correspondent from London wasn't anything new. It's always been in jest; and always off the cuff. She just happened to do it again; for no special reason other than to just do it—just being silly.

Leah wasn't amused. She immediately tensed up. She was far from even getting the slightest kick out of Nicki's joking around. It wasn't that Leah didn't find her daughters humor tasteless or inappropriate, because if the subject had been about anyone else—Leah would have chuckled right along with her phony, over-the-top English accent imitating Barry Bona. But it wasn't just anyone else that Barry Bona and Nicki were talking about.

Leah was already quite familiar with 'what's-his-face' as Nicki put it. The Jef's were already keeping a close eye on the world famous, celebrated and idolized 'Humanitarian Extraordinaire'; Tony Giovanni. A man whose face has been plastered on the cover of hundreds and hundreds of magazines over the last four or five years and covered by countless journalists and the subject of several documentaries, Giovanni is more than famous; he's worshipped and venerated like Mother Teresa.

Antonio Sean Giovanni was his full name. Robson even brought his name up at church this evening. Needless to say, he was already under suspicion. Leah immediately started to chew on Nicki Dawn's remark about Giovanni, but in seconds, before she even had a chance to digest it and discuss it any further—Nicki rolled right into some other disturbing updates.

"There was some other stuff too I heard — about an hour ago — and it was just horrible."

"Oh…, what's that?"

"The door-to-door census and the DSS clean-up ordered by Global Affairs is finding some more pets, cats, dogs, birds left alone inside some homes; a few already starved to death," she explained. "The rest they just killed on the spot."

"Oh…, Lord," Leah sighed in grief. Some of this stuff she just never thought of over the years, wondering what would happen to this world after the Rapture. Nicki was right — it was horrible.

"It's because the owners were missing, maybe taken in the Mass Vanishing, or just flat out missing, maybe lying dead in an alley somewhere." Nicki assessed. "In some cases, it wasn't because the owners were missing. DSS and the Census Workers were finding the owners dead in their own homes. Some were murdered, whole families in some cases, butchered, they think by those demon-possessed maniacs or robbers. Some were even found dead, killed by their own dogs.

It was sick, mom — and gross. It's like horror-movie stuff. They'd find some of these pets alive only by them eating the people and water in the toilets. They were interviewing some of the DSS officers, and Census Workers and people in the neighborhoods complaining about the awful and nasty stench of death coming from some of these homes."

Nicki's review was gruesome. It was tragic and disturbing, but she wasn't even half finished answering her mother's question as to anything new happening. There was more, much more.

Leah, a waitress at a local eatery, was at work all day and went straight to the church thereafter. Some of the stuff that Nicki was sharing was new to her. It was new and none of it was good.

As for Nicki Dawn, the more she'd share the more questions she'd have for her mom. No doubt, she was closer to her mom now more than ever in light of all that's happened. She'd find herself hanging out with her mom even more than her friends. She appreciated her, now more than ever. She trusted her more than ever. She would never admit it but Nicki was also finding Leah's Biblical knowledge quite comforting as well.

"Hey, mom, what's the deal with these people that went crazy? You know the ones that turned into like crazed zombies, possessed and attacking people like the animals—like Sheefoo—when she attacked Chad the way she did. I know on the news they're saying it was most likely a chemical reaction or radiation or whatever from the Mass Vanishing that made them go on their killing rampages, but I'm getting some crap on the internet that say they really and truly were demon-possessed."

"Well…, that's what I think Nicki. I'm pretty sure they were demon-possessed — just like some of those spoken of in the Bible." Leah casually answered. "Demon possession has been around a long time. It's not phony — it's very real. Jesus dealt with a bunch of it. It's all over the New Testament." she added.

Nicki pondered a moment as she contemplated on another matter. "You know there's something else that's really weird and floating around out there on the internet. They're sayin' all the people that went crazy, you know…, crazy like the animals — they're sayin they were all Satan worshippers."

Taken off guard, Leah had to pause and ponder a bit on the comment. "Wow…!" Leah said surprised. "I haven't heard about any of that."

"I know — weird huh," Nicki stressed. "They're not saying that on the news, but people have been checking up on all these famous rock stars like Dana Oz, M-Baal, Alester, and…, and that rapper Two-2-Go…, all of 'em turning psycho — going around killing and getting killed. Some of these movie stars too, and famous criminals and prisoners and stuff. There's a bunch of 'em — all over the world that turned into these bloodthirsty freaks." Nicki harped.

"Geez…," Leah gasped.

"Yeah…, I guess there was enough of 'em for people to take notice. People started doing web searches and checking to see what they all had in common. Sure enough — they were all into the Occult, and Witchcraft, and Satan Worshippers and stuff like that. It's in some of the reports too. Witnesses telling the authorities what they knew about some of the people that went on these killing sprees, butchering people, even murdering their own families — they said the same thing — that they were into witchcraft and Satan stuff."

"Wow…!" Leah said once again half-shocked. She was speechless, utterly speechless. 'Wow…' was about the only thing she could think of to say in regards to Nicki's shocking little news update. It was mind-boggling. She would eventually get a grasp though and manage to further her comment.

"Yeah…, that is weird. You're right about that. So! What do think?" Leah politely asked. "Do you think it's a coincidence that all these famous rock stars and famous people that suddenly flipped into mindless, murderous, zombies were all Satan Worshippers and into the occult, witchcraft? Do you think they were demon-possessed, and the animals too for that matter?"

"Umm…, you know what mom — I think they were. It's just too much to be a coincidence. But why — why would it be just the Satan Worshippers who get demon-possessed after the Mass Vanishing?" she asked in bewilderment.

Leah really didn't have an answer for her — at least not on the spot. She just looked at Nicki in silence, shook her head and shrugged. Her gesture made it quite clear. She didn't know why.

"I'm gonna ask Robson," Leah declared. "I'll call him tomorrow and maybe we can talk about it at our next meeting."

With Leah's remark, Nicki was reminded as to where her mother was tonight before she came home.

"So..., how was church?" she asked. "Was it good?"

Leah let out a heavy sigh. "Yeah..., yeah..., it was good. We had a lot to talk about and went over a bunch of stuff." Rehashing the evening in her mind she went on to give Nicki some details.

"You know, there's this guy..., Robson Talgo..., our makeshift Pastor —" she explained, or was going to explain before she switched gears in the middle of what she started. "You've met him Nicki," Leah said "You met him at that church barbeque last year, in November, American Indian, tall, long hair. He was the one that was talking to Joel and me by that fountain."

"Oh, yeah...," Nicki nodded. "I do remember him. He was nice, a nice guy — striking too. An Apache Indian, I think..., right?"

"Yeah…, that's right—good memory. Anyhow, he isn't Pastor Lang, but man—he's good. He would have made a great Pastor. It's too bad he became a postman. We needed more Born Agains like him to lead the flock, especially after the—*falling away*." Leah said.

"So! He's still here too…, huh mom—like you—missed out," Nicki remarked. By that, Nicki instantly knew—right when she said it that she put her foot in her mouth. It was the wrong thing to say. She didn't say it to rub it in Leah's face. It just slipped out. It was an innocent comment but it was cutting. Before Leah could even answer, Nicki quickly blurted out.

"I'm sorry mom! That was the wrong thing to say. I'm really…, really sorry." Thankfully, Nicki's snappy apology was quick enough to keep Leah's heart from falling all the way down to her stomach in pain. She was able to shrug off the thought of her missing out on the Rapture and went ahead and answered Nicki's question about Robson with a sigh, some calmness and composure.

"Well…, yes Nicki—he missed out in the same way I did. In fact several people in our little congregation missed out by making the wrong decision—Robson, Larry, and some others."

Unaware, Dmitri was right there pacing and hovering about the two—listening, waiting for a fitting moment to intervene. He'd cash in on Leah's remark.

"See...! Wrong decision to stay with you—she hates it that she's here with you," he cleverly whispered into Nicki Dawn's ear. "You saw how sad and angry she got, knowing how she's stuck here with you. Just the thought of it pisses her off. And you're sayin' sorry. Are you that stupid?"

Nicki immediately tensed up and did her best to pretend she didn't hear it. Leah caught Nicki's nervous shift—her jerky shake of the head like that of one snapping out of a stupor. Puzzled— Leah had to react.

"Nicki—are you alright?" She quickly asked.

"Yeah..., yeah I'm ok. I just got a crick in my neck."

Nicki's quick, but less-than-honest answer worked. Leah accepted it at face value. The hate-seed Dmitri so artfully planted worked as well. Doubt crept into Nicki's mind once again, but she kept it at bay as Leah went on to finish answering her.

"You know, we've already gone over us missing the Rapture..., several times over, but it is what it is." Leah reasoned. "Right now we're more focused on the here and now. Going to church means more now than ever before. It's gone to a whole new level and GOD in Heaven—does it ever help." She praised. "We go over so much—Scriptures, current events—like the surge of these voices and visitations, this Queen of Heaven, these six Holy Messages—stuff like that. We're keeping a close eye out for the Antichrist too."

"Oh man—the Queen of Heaven!" Nicki blurted out with a touch of enthusiasm. "All my friends are really into her, and her six Holy Messages, but I don't know Mom. Do you really think she's evil or the devil…, like you keep telling me? I mean—she's calmed this world down and given us so much hope. It's hard to imagine she's wicked? And her messages, they're…, I don't know…, they're not beautiful, but they're sure alluring. Do you think they're legitimate and real? Are they true—or will they come true?"

Leah was already sure of her answer; just like Joel going through the check point—she too was adamant and sure. "You can count on it Nicki. All six of those Holy Messages will come to pass. As to whether or not she's evil—you saw what happened to those people who attacked that guy in Hong Kong telling the crowds to turn away from her and turn to Jesus.

You can't look at that and say it was evil that stepped in to protect that Born Again from getting beat to death. There's no doubt about it. And I've already told you, honey. You're gonna have to understand that there's gonna be some wonderful things that happen, but it's all a snare.

There's gonna be some bad stuff too, real horrible stuff—none of it good. And in the midst of all the wild and terrible events…, well—you're gonna have to decide who to turn to—God, Jesus Christ…, or the world in rebellion. It's gonna come down to either turning to God or cursing God." Leah said to simplify it.

Continuing, "The good things promised by this Queen of Heaven, they look good on the surface but underneath the veneer, behind the veil—it's pure evil. It's Satan. I mean he's set the stage. He's rolled out the red carpet for the Antichrist—for Pete's sake. The Messiah will deliver us—the Prophet will show us…!" Leah said with negativity reciting two of the six Holy Messages. "If that's not enough to open people's eyes, or make them think twice about the Bible's validity…, well…, well maybe God's coming judgments will have to open their eyes. And they're coming Nicki. I hate to say it, but as sure as we're sittin' here, those judgments in the Book of Revelation are coming."

The thought of what she was saying steered Leah full circle, back to worrying about Nicki Dawn. Almost by habit, she couldn't help but go right back into pleading with her little girl.

"Ah, Nicki—I know I can't force you to believe any of this stuff anymore than I was able to make you believe in the Gospel and the Rapture. You're just gonna have to figure it out on your own. Pray, honey! Ask God—in the name of Jesus—to show you and He will. He will show you—I know it. Remember, I told you what God's phone number is—right." Leah said with a smile.

"Yeah, yeah, yeah...," Nicki mumbled as she rolled her eyes. "Jeremiah 33:3 — I remember." Thinking it silly — *"Call to ME, and I will answer you, and will show you great and mighty things, which you do not know."* Nicki recited word for word. Silly or not, it was enough to raise a friendly smile on Nicki's face as well.

For a brief and fleeting moment, they had actually tapped into one of those sweet, precious and few mother-daughter moments they had once knew so well when Nicki Dawn was younger; innocent and untainted. The moment was nice for the both of them. The smiles exchanged were well received. Leah would not waste the moment and immediately rolled with the pleasure.

"You remember...!" she cheered with glee while reaching over from the recliner to the couch — giving Nicki a gentle tap on her feet buried underneath the blanket. "I'm impressed!" she added.

After a couple of seconds of optimism, Leah would sigh and finish on a more sentimental note. "Oh Nicki — I'll keep on praying for you, dear. And the invitation to come with me to these church gatherings and Bible studies still stand. I wish you'd come with me." Leah pleaded.

Nicki kept silent. It was a silence that juggled contemplation and a bit of rebellion still lodged in Nicki's heart. She'd give it a good five seconds or so of thought before she'd respond to her mother's plea.

"I'll think about it mom. I've already been thinkin' about everything you've been telling me about God, and Jesus and the Bible and the Antichrist, Tribulation—all of it. I just want you to know that. Can we just leave it at that for now?" Nicki asked.

It was actually a wonderful answer as far as Leah was concerned. Nicki's interest in the things of God over the weeks have actually jumped in leaps and bounds compared to her hatred of it all before the Rapture. Pleased with the answer, even though Nicki's answer was indefinite, it was a good sign. It was also a good time to step back. Leah gently retreated from going any further with her Bible Thumping. From there, the two of them went back to watching TV.

The news was mostly repeating itself, but it didn't take away from the Media's readiness. It was quite awake, alert and extremely vigilant—ready to pounce like famished lions on any new developments. They had the entire world covered. With perked ears, and keeping a sharp eye out on any new signs or messages from the mediums, clairvoyants and Channelers, there'd be nothing likely to get by them anytime soon.

It wasn't but a few minutes before the phone rang; Leah's phone. By her side, sitting on the coffee table next to her she picked it up to see who was calling.

Quite pleased, "Oh…, good, it's Randy!" Leah said

as she gave Nicki Dawn a wide-eyed sheepish smile. It didn't take but a moment to scamper off to her room with a gentle hello.

Nicki smiled as well. She liked to see her mother's spirits lifted. It was rare these days. She herself felt good about Randy. She always liked Joel. Being he was always friendly and polite, she figured his brother couldn't be too far off. She really didn't know though. What she did know; even though he was hundreds of miles away, Randy was helping to mend Leah's broken heart. Either way — Joel, Randy — they were both a far sight better, even wonderful compared to the losers Leah associated with in her younger days. So, off to her room Leah skedaddled — to chat with Randy as Nicki continued to absorb the news.

Chapter Twenty Three

WHITE HORSE

"Hey, Leah..., I didn't wake you did I?"

"No..., no you didn't. In fact I just got home a few minutes ago from another Bible Study tonight."

"Oh yeah—how'd it go?"

"It was good—intense, sad, and edgy, but good—very good. So, how are things going with you? Have you found a church yet?" Leah eagerly asked.

Randy did find a church. Very pleased, he told her a little bit about it. Typical stuff—the location, the people, the experience, the pastors; two of them, one extremely young named Anthony and the other a woman, mid-fifties or so named Pearl. Randy thought highly of both of them. Leah was really glad to hear it. She was even more so glad he actually made the effort to find a church. It can be difficult; that she knew.

After that, they rolled into some more small talk—work, the weather, an off-colored joke about President Manning getting mauled by his dog after the Rapture; even shared a little guilt for exploiting the attack for a cheap chuckle. They inquired about each other's family members. Leah also told Randy that she did make it over to Joel's apartment to gather some things before

DSS and the Landlord ransacked it. Things got a little heavier though when it got into current events.

"So! What do you think about all these voices and visitations? I'm sure you've been hearin' about it." Randy confided.

"It's not good." Leah quickly answered.

"You know my sister had one—a little paranormal experience and she insists it's her children communicating with her. Man—did I ever catch hell from her when I mentioned otherwise."

"Ah, geez—I'm sorry Randy. You know we talked about this surge of visitations at Bible Study tonight. We think it's part of this Queen of Heaven's Holy Messages—the one about the children."

"The children will assure you." Randy quoted.

"Yep—that's the one. These visitations—they've barely begun. We think they're going to get a lot stronger and go a lot further than just sporadic hints here and there that keep people guessing. It's demonic—that's all there is to it." Leah declared.

"Yeah—that's going along the same lines as to what our Church Guy was sayin'. He said these voices and visitations were demons—that they're planting seeds to oppose the Gospel of Jesus. It's not what people want to believe though. They want it to be their children and deceased loved ones from the other side. I know I do." Randy added. "I hope it's…, it's—I don't know…, good — I guess. I hope it isn't demonic."

"One can only hope." Leah speedily shared. "We think it's the White Horse of the Apocalypse — all this stuff goin' on. I guess I've wondered how it was going to play out, but I never wanted to be here to see it."

"The White Horse…," Randy said half excited. "Man, weird…, I just read about that the other night; you're talkin' about the Four Horses…, right — in the last days? Yeah…, the White Horse; I remember — something about a bow, a crown and conquering the world. Well, shoot! It's right here in front of me. Let me read it!" He eagerly insisted. He grabbed his Bible and quickly flipped through the pages. Leah could clearly hear the rustling and the mumbling.

"Let's see…, Revelation…, Revelation…, right here! Revelation, uh…, Chapter six…, verse one — I actually highlighted it."

Leah kept silent. She was already quite familiar with the verse. She's read the verse often enough, but hearing a New Born Christian excited, eager and even mildly proud to read it aloud to her — not so often. She cherished the moment and let Randy follow through with his determination. She listened as he read to her like a proud elementary school child eager to show his teacher that he did his homework.

"Let's see…, '*Now I saw when the Lamb opened one of the seals; and I heard one of the four living creatures saying with a voice like thunder, "Come and see." And I looked, and behold, a white horse. He who sat on it had a bow; and a crown was given to him, and he went out conquering and to conquer.'* What is that about or…, or what does it mean?" he asked.

"Well…, the 'White Horse'…, we believe to be spiritual deception. Its rider…, *'He who sat on it'*…, is the Antichrist. He goes out and conquers the world in the last days. Conquering the world — I think goes along the lines of wooing and winning the world over. You know, God said he was going to send strong delusion these last days that people should believe *'the lie'*. People are —"

"Whoa, whoa — what's *the lie*?" Randy butted in. "We were reading something about that the night after the Rapture. It was one of the Scriptures in Joel's letter; one of the Scriptures he left for us to…, I don't know…, to have I guess to warn us of the last days — stuff to look out for. But, the Scripture said something about the lie…, believing the lie? So what is it? What's the lie?"

"Umm…, the lie…," Leah pondered. She had to think. "Well, *'the lie'* — some say it's the lie that explains away the Rapture. Others say *'the lie'* is the original lie; the lie that Satan planted in the beginning."

"The beginning…?"

"Yeah…, in the beginning; you know — Adam

and Eve in the Garden of Eden…, when Satan tricked them…, tricked them with '*the lie*'. And you wanna know what's weird about that?" Leah added. "It's the same lie he uses to this very day. It's the same lie…, over and over and over again. He's never stopped. He uses the same exact lie that he told Adam and Eve on all of us."

"Man…," Randy grunted, a little frustrated; not because of what Leah said though. He was frustrated at his lack of knowledge. "Ok…, let's see here—I remember the story. The serpent tricking Eve into eating the fruit, or whatever—but that's about it. That shows you how much I know." Randy said half embarrassed. "So, how does it go—what's it about?"

"Uhh…, let's see—in a nutshell—Satan pretty much told Adam and Eve that God lied to them. In doing so, he accused God of lying. It's why Satan is also called the…'*the accuser*'…in the Bible—or at least part of the reason why he's called the accuser. There are other things, but accusing God of being a liar certainly fits. So, you ask, what's the lie? I guess you can say it's the lie that tells you God's a liar. It's as simple as that. And the sin—well, besides the lie itself…, to believe the lie and…, and spread the lie, and teach people and even children the lie…, well, I'll leave that to your imagination as to how bad it is." Leah explained

"So…, that's the lie, huh." Randy affirmed.

"Well…, like I said…, it's subject to interpretation. Again…, some interpret 'the lie' as being the lie that explains away the Rapture. Personally, I think it's the original lie in the Garden, cuz it includes all the lies; sort of like an umbrella. The 'original lie' would include the lie that explains away the Rapture as well. It's just what some think. But, hey…! Since you got your Bible out, go to the beginning, to the first couple of pages — Genesis: Three. It's only a couple of verses." Leah said.

She had her Bible nearby as well. She grabbed it and the both of them shuffled to Genesis. For a moment there, Randy thought it interesting that he was going from the last book in the Bible; Revelation, to the first book, Genesis. It only made him wonder about everything there was to know in between. The thought was fleeting, but no less captivating.

Leah guided Randy to the particular Scriptures in Genesis and she read it allowed as Randy followed along.

"*Now the serpent was more cunning than any beast of the field which the* LORD *God had made. And he said to the woman, "Has God indeed said, 'You shall not eat of every tree of the garden'?" And the woman said to the serpent, "We may eat the fruit of the trees of the garden; but of the fruit of the tree which is in the midst of the garden, God has said, 'You shall not eat it, nor shall you touch it, lest you* die.'" *Then the serpent said to the woman, "You will not surely die. For God knows that in the day you eat of it your eyes will be opened and you will be like God, knowing good and evil."*

"Be like God...? Wow..., the hutzpah!" Randy lightly joked.

Leah chuckled. "Yep...! The hutzpah! Anyhow, if you look at it, there are some specifics, you know— specific lies in what he said, but it all boils down to Satan essentially telling them what God had told them wasn't true. He accused God of being a liar, and Eve..., and Adam—they chose to believe him. That's the 'original sin'; believing Satan instead of believing God. Of course, now it's all about believing Satan in-stead of believing Jesus."

"I see..., ok..., that makes sense." Randy shared. "And this part about...'*your eyes will be opened and you'll be like God, knowing good and evil*...,' what's that?"

"Yeah..., well—that's the specifics. '*You will not surely die*...' was and still is a lie..., obviously. And..., '*For God knows that in the day you eat of it your eyes will be opened and you will be like God, knowing good and evil*..., well just look at us...? We all like to think and believe we're '*like God*'..., goin' around thinking we know what is good and what is evil—when we're clueless." Leah asserted, but quickly corrected herself. "Well..., I take that back." She said. "It's more like people are blinded or duped — clueless is the wrong word. It's too harsh and insulting. We're talking about the power of Satan here, not naivety and the ignorance of people. We're like children…, like little toddlers when it comes to Satan's superiority and trickery."

"Geez…, that's comforting to know." Randy mocked. "Nice optics there, Leah. Sheesh…!"

"Yeah…, well — it's true. And God knows this. But you know what…? We may be born blind and…, shoot! I may as well say it…, who cares if it's insulting? We're born clueless, but we don't have to die clueless. We do have a book that tells us what is good and what is evil — the Bible. By that, I mean it's GOD who tells us what is good and what is evil — not man, and not Satan. Which goes full circle, right back to believing Him — believing God or believing Satan. So there…!" Leah proudly declared like she made the point of the century, but in jest.

"Wow, Leah — well said. You'd make a good pastor. In fact…, you're giving Joel a run his money." He praised.

"Oh, brother…, I don't think so, but thank you just the same."

"Ok…, ok, I think I'm getting this." Randy politely abridged. "So…, Satan's original lie continues to this day; telling us the things God says; which I take is everything in the Bible…, is nothing but lies and fibs."

"Not only lies…, but half-truths, and part-truths, or incorrect, or insufficient, or…, or unimportant — that's a good one — people ignoring the Word of God because it's just not that important. Satan loves to get that one over on people. Whatever…; again — fill in the blank! As long as the Bible, or the Word of God isn't received, or believed to be…'The Truth, the Whole Truth, and Nothing but the Truth — all is well with Satan."

"Humph…, it's pretty simple really, but man…, I don't know. And you're saying the sin in all this isn't only…*the lie*…by itself; its people believing the lie that condemns people."

"That's it! That's exactly right. In fact, you just hit on a certain scripture. Believing '*the lie*' wouldn't be a sin if people didn't know the truth. But we know the truth. That's why Jesus came; why God came, if you will. He came; He gave us the truth. So now, if you believe Satan, his lie, or if I believe the lie, it's no longer us being tricked into believing the lie. It's now us choosing to believe the lie. And this choice — to willfully and consciously believe the lie, or half-truths, instead of the truth; that's what condemns us."

"Yeah…, but we believe the truth right? So we're not condemned."

"Yep…, and feels good too, doesn't it."

"Well…, yeah…, yeah it does." Randy gladly

concurred. "So…, this Scripture you said I hit on— what is it?"

"Umm…, it's in the Gospel…, the Book of John, I think. It…, uhh…, well…, like I said…, if we didn't know the truth, then believing the lie wouldn't be a sin. Anyhow, some indignant Pharisees were giving Jesus a rash of crap after he shed some light on the truth. They were sayin' something along the lines of, "So…! What are you sayin'…? Are you saying we're blind?" they asked and jeered. And Jesus…, God—I just love how he puts things, and people in their place. He answered, sayin' *"If you were blind, you would have no sin; but now you say, 'We see.' Therefore your sin remains"*.

"The world's been given the truth, Randy." Leah continued. "The truth has been made readily available for everyone in one form or another. And because of it, there's no longer an excuse to justify one's decision to believe Satan over God; to believe the lie over the truth. I guess what I'm getting at is this truth is readily available; ignoring it or…, or being familiarized with it and simply choosing not to believe it, or people taking it upon themselves to customize it, or edit it, or add to it…, you know, turn it into a personalized belief system, or a religion, or a cult because they think they're eyes are opened, and think they're *'like God, knowing what is good and what is evil'*…, I don't know, Randy. I hate to say it, but I think this is the one and only sin that sends people to hell. It's because they choose to believe *'the lie'*. It's a sad thing, and I've been there, done that." Leah confessed.

"Yeah..., but geez, Leah—the entire Bible," Randy respectfully railed. "Who in the heck does that—believes every single thing in the Bible? Just knowing everything in the Bible isn't just some easy task. It isn't like taking an hour or so to read a couple of comic books. I mean, man..., I think it's asking someone an awful lot to take on the task of knowing everything in the Bible, let alone believing all of it." And you're sayin, if they don't..., they're goin' to hell. Wow..., I don't know about all that." Randy argued. "It just doesn't sound right."

"Well..., Joel did. I do. Every person that was eligible for the Rapture does, or did depending on whether they left or not. And you know what—Randy? I think you do as well." Leah charged.

"Humph...," Randy muttered, almost doubting it. But, he stopped and took a serious moment to think about it. Did he?

"Shoot..., I don't even know a fraction of what's in it." He reasoned. "How can I believe everything that's in it?"

"You don't have to know everything in it Randy to believe it—to believe its God who speaks in it. And you believe it—I know you do." Leah doubled down, pressing him.

Randy thought and thought hard. Shaking his head, he had to confess. He couldn't help it. And he couldn't believe he was so compelled to agree with her.

"You know..., Leah. It's weird, but I think you're right. I'm sittin' here lookin' at this thing, the Bible here in my lap, I don't hardly know anything in it, but..., but yeah..., I do believe it—all of it, without even knowing all that's in it. How can that be? How is it that I believe it's God who speaks from beginning to end." Randy asked perplexed.

"Hmmm," Leah hummed with a gentle smile. "It's what you call being 'born again', Randy. It's called 'faith'—the faith of a child. Welcome to the club. Welcome to the Kingdom of God. Jesus Christ..., our Lord and Savior, and the angels in heaven rejoice."

"Eh..., that's a nice thought there, Leah—beautiful..., really. But, man—I don't know." He uttered being still a bit uncertain and confused about things. "Geez..., believe, believe..., what do I believe—who do I believe? Well, like I said, I have to go with God—as of now I believe Jesus and..., and this here Bible. Why, I don't know, it's crazy—but I do. And I'm happy for it, I guess." He added. He felt good inside; comfortable, even.

"It's gonna be tough though, Randy," Leah stressed. "These last days, this New Age—just wait.

People are really going to think their days of being...
'like God, knowing good and evil'...are gonna go through
the roof. They're gonna think and believe they're eyes
have been opened more now than ever before. This
Queen of Heaven, these voices and visitations supposedly from the other side—it's all part of wooing and
winning the world over. As I said, it's the *'white horse'*
of the Apocalypse—spiritual deception."

"Oh yeah—the 'white horse'...," Randy recalled.
"Yeah..., so what about these other horses, you
know—what was it..., the red horse, and the black
horse, and..., and that other one, uhh..., gosh what
was it?" he mumbled as he quickly started to shuffle
back to the pages in the Book of Revelation.

"The pale horse...," Leah said to fill in the blank.

"Yeah..., the pale horse—that one is creepy." He
asserted. "And pale..., what is that—is that even a
color?"

"Uhh..., I guess. It's always been depicted as—I
don't know..., a sort of sickly, ugly-looking, swamp-
colored green."

"Yummy...!" Randy joked, "Pea soup, huh?"

"I'd say more like rancid and moldy pea soup."

"Wow..., even better."

With his finger now planted back on the Scripture
he had already highlighted in the Book of Revelation;
Chapter six—he proceeded to read it aloud to Leah.

"When He opened the fourth seal, I heard the voice of the fourth living creature saying, "Come and see." So I looked, and behold, a pale horse. And the name of him who sat on it was Death, and Hades followed with him. And power was given to them over a fourth of the earth, to kill with sword, with hunger, with death, and by the beasts of the earth."

Randy went on to comment, "Isn't Hades…, isn't that the word they use for Hell?"

"Yeah…, that's what it is. Hades following Death — nice huh," Leah said sarcastically.

"Sheesh…! And what about the 'red horse' and the 'black horse'…?"

"Well…, the red horse is war. I think it says the *'fiery red horse'*. And the black horse is pestilence and famine. The pale horse follows up with what they started."

"Man, I'll take the 'white horse' any day of the week over these guys…, the 'spiritual deception' stuff."

"Well…, we're already getting that right now, Randy. The 'spiritual deception' is rampant and getting worse by the hour. I mean, heck…, you see what's goin on."

With a sigh, "Yeah…, yeah I do." he concurred with a hint of discouragement.

Leah promptly jumped back in with pep, "The only thing we can do is stay strong, Randy. We gotta stay vigilant, and do our best to convince others, more especially our loved ones, to believe the truth instead of the lie.

"Humph..., it's pretty scary stuff—" Randy invoked.

"Yeah..., I know..., pretty scary. And it's just the beginning," Leah sighed with a heavy heart. "It's just the beginning."

To be continued:

THE SUPERNATURAL AGE

-A Cautionary Tale-

PART TWO

'...THE PROPHET...'

CPSIA information can be obtained
at www.ICGtesting.com
Printed in the USA
LVHW031000090121
675852LV00001B/73

9 781977 233417